Coming up Roses

RACHAEL LUCAS

PAN BOOKS

First published 2015 by Pan Books
an imprint of Pan Macmillan, a division of Macmillan Publishers Limited
Pan Macmillan, 20 New Wharf Road, London N1 9RR
Basingstoke and Oxford
Associated companies throughout the world
www.panmacmillan.com

ISBN 978-1-4472-6548-1

1 3 5 7 9 8 6 4 2

A CIP catalogue record for this book is available from
the British Library.

Typeset by Ellipsis Digital Limited, Glasgow
Printed and bound by CPI Group (UK) Ltd, Croydon, CR0 4YY

Coming Up Roses

Rachael juggles working as an author, coach and freelance writer – with the aid of quite a lot of tea. She and her partner (also a writer) live by the seaside in the North West of England with their six children.

For more from Rachael, visit her websites at rachaellucas.com and writeforjoy.net

You can find her on Twitter @Karamina and on Facebook at facebook.com/RachaelLucasWriter

For my lovely mum, Anne.
Thank you for everything.

Chapter One

Daisy could almost, just about reach to water the furthest edge of the rockery with the hose. If she just balanced on tiptoe and *pulled* . . .

She gave the hose another yank, stretching it out as far as she could, muttering to herself as she did so. It was proving impossible to get things done with the haphazard collection of equipment her parents had left behind.

She didn't hear the gate swing open. She wobbled. The slow dribble of water from the leaky hose made the old grey boulder she was perched on slippery and even more precarious. Crashing down into the newly weeded aubretia, she lost control of the hose. It spun round crazily, a rainbow arc of water sprinkling right across the path.

'Aaagh!'

Daisy looked up. Standing on the front path, half of her blonde hair beautifully blow dried and the other half now dripping wet, stood a furious-looking woman. She was probably only in her early thirties,

1

but her demeanour – and her dress – suggested she was definitely a Proper Grown Up. Her pale suede boots were darkened with water, and a string of droplets sparkled on the hem of her dress.

'I'm *so* sorry.' Daisy scrambled to her feet, embarrassed. She brushed away a couple of wet pieces of plant which were sticking to her jeans.

'The hose – I didn't mean to – it's my parents – they only have this stupid coiled thing like an old-fashioned telephone wire and it—' As she gabbled, the woman withdrew a cotton hanky from her bag (Daisy hadn't realized anyone actually used them any more, apart from her dad, who she lovingly thought of as a mad old fossil from another century). She dabbed at her forehead, her expression unreadable.

'It's absolutely fine,' said the woman, not altogether convincingly, taking a tiny mirror with a distinctive twin C design from her bag (even the not-exactly-fashion-conscious Daisy recognized *that* one) and frowning at her appearance. It didn't look very fine from where Daisy stood, covered in a layer of freshly dampened compost, a collection of painful rockery bruises just beginning to make themselves known.

The woman snapped the little mirror shut, having patted at her hair, which seemed to be magically springing back into shape. Presumably that's the effect of a posh blow dry, thought Daisy, catching a glimpse of her own reflection in the diamond panes of the front window. She'd knotted her long red hair back

2

with a piece of green gardening twine earlier, and a halo of orange fuzz had escaped, giving her the appearance of a mad gardening bag lady. That was, she thought, perilously close to the truth.

'I was *coming* to bring you this.' The woman pulled three brown envelopes out of her handbag. 'We had a stand-in postman this morning. He can't have been concentrating. This is Orchard Villa, isn't it?' She glanced at the front door, where an old metal sign, the enamel flaking away in places, confirmed her guess.

Wiping her hands down her jeans – noticing as she did so that the woman's perfectly plucked eyebrows flashed upwards for just a fraction of a second – Daisy took the letters, scanning them briefly.

'It is. These are for my parents – they're not here right now, but thanks. And I'm really sorry I soaked you.'

'Not at all.' First a handkerchief, now a very formal handshake, Daisy thought, as the woman reached out. Life in Steeple St John seemed like stepping back in time to the 1950s. She half-expected the grocer's boy to come cycling along the lane at any moment, his basket overflowing with today's delivery.

'Elaine Thornton-Green.'

'I'm Daisy. Daisy Price.'

Letting go of Daisy's muddy, still slightly damp hand, Elaine turned, taking in the front garden properly. Daisy watched as she scanned the overgrown cables of the rambling rose which hung, precariously

3

low and liable to take someone's eye out, over the archway at the front gate. The flower beds were choked with early spring weeds, determined to make their mark. The dead remains of last summer's valiant hollyhocks and foxgloves nodded, faded and limp, strangled by the relentless bindweed. There was so much to do, Daisy thought, but she relished the challenge. Here was a place she could hide away and escape from everything. A project like this was the only way she'd forget.

'Lovely to meet you, Daisy.' Elaine gave her a dazzling smile, as if they'd just been introduced at a garden party rather than in unfortunate, rather soggy circumstances. 'Hadn't realized this place had been sold. It's such a beautiful old Victorian house, isn't it? So awful watching these lovely gardens go to rack and ruin over the last few years. It used to be so pretty here.'

'Um.' Daisy looked at the front hedge, which she'd already hacked back to a more respectable height. The lawn had been cut, and she'd been feeling pleased with the work she'd done over the last few weeks, but looking at the garden with a neutral eye, she could see it still looked pretty chaotic. 'My parents own Orchard Villa. They've gone to India for a few months and I'm house-sitting – well, garden-sitting.' She pointed at her filthy jeans, by way of explanation. 'Hence the outfit.'

'Oh, you must excuse me.' A hint of pink rose in

Elaine's cheeks, and she looked slightly uncomfortable. 'I didn't mean—'

'No, you're absolutely right.' Daisy smiled at her. 'The gardens *are* a mess. I've been on at them for the last two years to get a gardener in and do something about it.'

'And lucky them – here you are, come along to save the day.' Looking relieved not to have caused offence, Elaine brightened.

'Something like that.' Daisy, thinking about the circumstances that had brought her to Steeple St John, closed her eyes for a brief moment.

'I'll look forward to seeing how you get on.' Elaine, smoothing her hair once again, took a step back. 'If you fancy it, I'm having a little gathering next Thursday evening at eight. We haven't been in the village that long ourselves. Thought it might be nice to reach out the hand of friendship to some women of our age. You know, it can be surprisingly tricky to make friends in a little place like this.'

Daisy gave a non-committal noise of agreement. She wasn't in Steeple St John to meet people, or to make friends. She was more than happy with her own company, and that of Polly, her parents' elderly golden retriever. She glanced down at the front porch where the dog lay flat out beside the stained glass of the porch, snoring on the terracotta tiles.

'Let me give you my card.' Elaine flipped open an engraved silver card holder, pulling out a chic, matt-grey business card. Daisy took it with mumbled thanks, popping it in her back pocket for safe keeping. She'd no intention of doing anything with it, but given she'd just soaked the woman, it was probably best she kept her sweet.

'Do try and come along.' Elaine gave her a bright smile. That 1950s manners thing again. She hooked her bag back over her shoulder and turned to leave.

'I'll try,' fibbed Daisy. 'I'm really sorry about the hose.' She made towards the front gate, holding it open.

Elaine slipped through, calling over her shoulder as she made her way down the path towards Main Street, 'Not at all. See you next Thursday!'

Daisy smiled back with a little wave, waiting until Elaine was out of sight before she stepped back onto the path, looking up at the solid Victorian villa before her, its faded red bricks glowing warmly in the morning sunlight. A quarter of a mile from the market square, Orchard Villa sat in around half an acre of gardens. The bricks of the house were laid in the traditional style, and high ornate chimneys twisted above a tiled roof. Decorative white-painted bargeboards sat under the eaves, giving the house the appearance of a Dickensian spinster in a lace-trimmed cap. It was safe here, closeted behind the overgrown hedge. She closed the gate safely behind her and turned back to the garden, locking out the world.

*

'You really ought to go, Daise.'

Daisy shuffled the phone under her ear, aware it was slipping. She carried on scrubbing at the filthy dog bowl. 'I'm not here to make friends, Miranda. Seriously, I just want a bit of peace.'

Her sister gave an exasperated snort which Daisy recognized all too well.

'You can't just hide yourself away like a hermit for the next six months until the parents get back.'

'I'm not being a hermit. I'm just – I'm not out in town every night like you, that's all.'

She tipped the soapy water out of the bowl, rinsing her hands, almost dropping the phone into the sink as she did so.

'I just think you need to get out and have a bit of a life. You're not going to bounce back if you spend all day gardening and all night swooning over Monty Whatshisname on *Gardening World*.'

'*Gardeners' World*. And it's Monty Don.' Daisy couldn't help smiling. They'd had this conversation so many times. 'And I don't want to bounce back.' She felt the familiar half-sick wave of pain and remembrance wash over her. It was a constant companion these days.

'Come on. You're twenty-nine, not ninety-two. I'm only saying this 'cause I'm your sister and I love you enough to be brutal . . .'

Rinsing a coffee cup, Daisy turned away from the

kitchen sink, opening the fridge as Miranda continued talking.

It was a constant source of surprise to Daisy and Miranda's friends just how different the two sisters were. Daisy's red hair was generally tied back with a scarf, her freckled face bare of make-up. Miranda, effortlessly glam, worked as an account manager for a multinational beauty company and was never knowingly under-tanned.

'Well, if you're going to be stuck in Steeple St John for the foreseeable, you'd better try and make some friends. You can't spend all day talking to plants. Hang on –'

Waiting obediently, Daisy peeled the lid from a four-pack of dips and tipped the contents of a bag of tortilla chips into a bowl.

She could hear Miranda instructing a taxi driver to take her to Bloomsbury. Her voice was confident and clear. For a second Daisy felt a pang of loneliness, realizing that she was settling in for another night alone – and that nobody was going to turn up with a takeaway and a bottle of wine. Not tonight, not ever. Not now.

She filled the dog bowl with water, setting it down by the back door. Polly, who was hoping for more food, raised one eyebrow at Daisy from her bed.

'I'm back – sorry.' Miranda's voice made Daisy jump. 'Seriously, Daise, you need to get out. You can't spend the rest of your life brooding and feeling sorry for yourself.'

'I'm not,' Daisy snapped, bristling slightly.

'You sure?' Miranda's tone was conciliatory, realizing she'd pushed a little too far.

Daisy sighed. It was always going to be hard for Miranda to understand how she felt. Surrounded by hordes of friends at school and then at college, Miranda was gregarious to a degree that made Daisy's head spin. She was always out, always on the phone, always had friends round staying the night or visiting. *She* didn't have any trouble finding people to share a coffee and a gossip. Thinking back, Daisy's friends had been harder won, but she'd always considered them a close-knit group. She gripped the kitchen worktop, remembering. The involuntary movement whitened her knuckles.

'I'll be fine.'

'Good. Just make sure you're not moping around for too long.' Miranda's tone was brisk. Probably arriving at the scene of her latest date. Daisy could picture her: a quick check of the lipstick and a smoothing down of the hair, pouting at her reflection in a window outside the restaurant.

With some hasty kisses blown down the phone, she was gone. 'Lots of love.'

Dismissed by her sister, Daisy looked through the kitchen window. Almost half an acre of land, most of which was choked with weeds. The twisted apple trees were just beginning to show the first signs of blossom, their roots hidden under a mat of thick couch grass. She was facing an enormous task. She groaned, realizing she hadn't taken the dog out that afternoon. She shoved the crisps and dips to one side and picked up the dog lead. Polly materialized at her side, sleep forgotten at the jingle of leather and metal, rheumy grey-ringed eyes suddenly bright. The clocks had changed at the weekend, leaving time for a last stroll before night fell.

Standing under an oak tree in the park, Daisy watched as Polly made her regular sniffing tour of tree trunks and lamp posts. Her elderly legs weren't up to much more than a quick walk these days, but the late evening sunshine had given her a burst of energy and she even managed a bit of stiff-legged cavorting across the grass. Daisy shivered, regretting her decision to come out without a coat. The evenings were still cold, and tonight's cloudless sky would make for a chilly night.

'Come on, Poll, let's get going.'

As she called, Polly veered off, disappearing through a hole in the hedge. As she was almost deaf and quite short-sighted, there wasn't any point in calling her. Daisy set off at a run across the park.

Squeezing through the gap, she saw Polly sitting obediently at the feet of an old man. He was leaning peacefully on the wooden gate of the churchyard, smoking a pipe.

'Polly! Sorry, she's a bit old. She gets a bit confused.' Daisy clipped on the lead and made to pull Polly away.

'Don't we all, my dear,' said the man, a smile curving underneath his moustache. He bent down and stroked Polly's ears. 'Lovely evening for it.'

'Beautiful. Getting cold now, though.' Having survived one encounter with an odd villager, Daisy wasn't keen on another. She took a step backwards and the dog lead tightened. Polly, smiling at the attention, was not budging.

'I always come down here, every evening, to say g'night to Violet.'

Daisy gritted her teeth, arranging her face into a suitably polite expression. It wasn't that she was rude, not as a rule. But she really wanted to get home, sink into a bath – she could feel herself aching where she'd fallen earlier – and curl up in her dressing gown with her comfort food and the television.

'Oh, really?' she said, politely.

'My wife. She died five years ago. She was a beautiful redhead, like you.'

'Oh! I'm sorry.' Now she just felt guilty.

'She was a lovely girl. We were married forty years.' He blew a kiss over the fence in the direction of a very simple headstone, where a single rose stood. 'Walking back into town?'

'I am.' Polly, taking her cue from the old man, stood up happily.

'Will you do me the honour?'

She couldn't help but be charmed by his old-fashioned manners. Feeling a little ashamed at her lack of grace, Daisy smiled back at him.

'Go on, then.'

'Thomas Broughton. Pleased to meet you.'

'Daisy Price.'

They strolled down the lane, Polly ambling by their side. Willow trees stretched their delicate fingers down to the bubbling water of the stream, the birds singing loudly in the last of the evening light. On the far side of the green Daisy could make out a dad and his son kicking a football back and forth.

'So what brings you to Steeple St John?'

'My parents moved here a couple of years ago, from Oxford – he was a professor of anthropology – and they fancied a quiet life with their retirement. I don't think they're cut out for English village life, though. Mum had a heart scare a year or so back and it's made them determined to get out and enjoy life while they can.'

'Good way of thinking,' said Thomas, with a nod of approval.

They walked together along the lane by the stream, the still-bare trees arching overhead.

'And where d'you fit in? You're a bit old to be living at home, aren't you?'

Daisy smiled at his forthrightness. 'I gave up working in an office a couple of years ago, and went back to agricultural college to study horticulture. I unexpectedly needed somewhere to live, which coincided with my parents deciding to go on a long trip abroad. They offered me the house – I get somewhere to stay, they get their garden sorted out.'

She thought back to her parents in their whirlwind of packing. She'd arrived at Orchard Villa as they were making preparations to leave on their version of a gap year trip to Asia – no hostels for them, though. They had rooms booked in luxurious hotels, and a detailed itinerary taking in some of her father's old haunts from his years of research. Polly, who would otherwise have been bundled off to stay with long-term dog-sitters, had been particularly pleased to see Daisy.

Daisy's father, quiet and thoughtful, had suggested that Daisy didn't overdo it but took some time to relax and look after herself.

'Nonsense, David,' her mother had said, kind but brisk as ever. 'Best thing you can do is throw yourself into a project, darling. Don't let the buggers get you down. You'll be fine.'

'There are some pretty gardens in this village.' Thomas interrupted her thoughts as they walked along. 'Not many I don't know.'

He stretched both hands out in explanation, showing gnarled, calloused fingers. 'Gardened the best part of sixty-five years. Badges of honour, these hands.'

Crossing the little lane, he motioned to the right. 'That's one of mine – or at least it was.'

A pebbled driveway led to a huge Georgian villa with gardens to the side and back. A bright estate-agent sign was nailed to the wooden fence.

'Evening.' Standing on the perfectly manicured lawn was a fluorescent-coated workman. He caught Daisy's eye and gave her a smile, clearly relieved to be heading home for the night.

'Evening.' Thomas nodded, curtly.

The man, straightening up the sign on the lawn with a shove of his boot, gave them a nod as he headed for the large pickup truck that was parked on the grass verge. Daisy looked up at the sign, taking it in. *Acquired by OHB Property Development*, it shouted, in bright red writing.

'Property development?' Daisy looked again at the house and garden. It was perfectly maintained, with not a single leaf out of place. She peered in through the window, where she could see the low lights of the kitchen casting a glow across spotless countertops. 'Doesn't look like it needs much done to it.'

'The house is perfect, you're right.' Thomas gave a sigh. 'And that garden – I worked that for years. Know it like the back of my hand. Bloody developers.'

He turned, and started walking at a surprisingly brisk march. Daisy tugged at Polly's lead, and she broke into a trot to catch up.

'You'll have seen it in the papers. It's happening all

over villages like Steeple St John. The gardens in lovely old houses like this one are too big for people nowadays, and the owners can make a fast buck by selling half of them off.'

Daisy turned back, looking at the houses that lined the lane. Each of them was set back from the road, closeted with a high wall or a thick hedge surrounding a huge garden dating from a time when people had the money to pay gardeners, or the time and leisure to spend their weekends working away at making them beautiful. Nowadays, she knew, everyone was keen on the easiest and quickest way of making the garden look good – and with mortgages going through the roof, selling off half the garden must be a tempting proposition.

'But aren't there rules about things like that?'

'There's rules – and there's rules.' Thomas rubbed his chin, shaking his head. 'Trouble is it's easy enough to get round 'em. Don't get me wrong – I don't have a problem with people needing somewhere to live, but there's enough disused houses sitting around this country. Why they don't do something with them, I'll never know.'

'Mmm.' Daisy had clearly hit a nerve. Much as she enjoyed chatting, she was quite relieved to see that they were almost at the end of the lane and in reach of home, and the sofa.

'Every time I look,' continued Thomas, who was on a roll, 'there's another developer knocking something down or putting something up round here. I can't keep up. Not to mention bunting and blooming cupcakes and all that Keep Calm and Carry On nonsense in the shops. Whatever happened to fairy cakes? I blame the Americans.'

Daisy couldn't help laughing. Thomas's irascibility reminded her of her dad.

Polly picked up speed as she reached the foot of Main Street, knowing dinner was imminent. She pulled on the lead impatiently, willing Daisy forward.

'That's me over there,' Daisy explained, pointing up the lane towards Orchard Villa in the distance. Knowing he was a gardener, she felt a bit ashamed of the shaggy mess of tangled foliage which hung around the gate, obscuring the archway that led into the Victorian house.

'Orchard Villa? That's another of mine. Looked after that for thirty years. Absolute shambles that garden is, nowadays.'

'Not for long. I'm going to bring it back to life,' promised Daisy. That's the second time someone's pointed out what a disaster it is, she thought. I must work on the front garden for now, just to get everyone off my back.

'I see you've made a start on the rockery at the front. I laid that, you know, back in '74. They were all the rage back then. And I planted that old wisteria round the door. I'm very fond of that one.'

Daisy felt herself smiling at him. Despite wanting

to get home, she found herself lingering as he asked about the health of the huge mulberry tree in the back garden, as if enquiring after an old friend. It really was lovely to hear someone else feeling the same enthusiasm for the garden that she had. During the last couple of weeks she'd been a virtual recluse, locked away in the house and garden, venturing out only to grab supplies of milk, chocolate and red wine. It was surprisingly nice to chat, even if it was to a kindly old stranger. Perhaps Miranda had a point. Thinking back to her first sight of Thomas, leaning over the gate of the churchyard, she felt a pang of sympathy.

'Would you mind – I'm sure you're probably busy.' Daisy knew already that he wasn't, and that she was asking as much to save him from loneliness as herself. 'I'd love it if you'd come round some time and give me some tips. I'd like to know what the garden used to look like before the weeds took over.'

Thomas looked utterly delighted, his pale eyes crinkling at the edges with happiness.

'I would be thrilled, my dear. I've got notebooks and records going back to the fifties in my study. I'll dig them out.'

Daisy watched from the street corner as Thomas made his way along the road and out of sight in the very last of the evening light. Across the road, the little Indian restaurant was filling up as too-tired-to-cook commuters made the detour from the railway station to pick up a takeaway. There was a constant stream of cars passing by, taking the rat run through Steeple St John to save the extra five minutes it'd take to go via the ring road. It was a peculiar mixture of town and village life – not quite rural, but definitely a far cry from Miranda's busy, whirling London life.

Daisy's phone flashed. Talk of the devil. It was Miranda, probably texting from the loo of whichever posh London restaurant she was in tonight.

Quite like this internet dating lark. This one's got a Maserati AND a house in Italy! Xxx

Daisy headed towards the house as she tapped her response.

Funny old evening. I met someone too. He's very sweet.

Miranda's reply shot back instantly.

Fast work. Impressive. Details?

Well, he's tall, fair, quite handsome.

Excellent . . . and?

Knowing her sister would be hanging on for the reply, Daisy counted to ten and hit send.

And about 85. Ha ha. x

Chapter Two

Daisy stared out of the kitchen window, willing it to stop raining. The wheelbarrow lay abandoned on the mossy patio. What she'd hoped was a spring shower was settling in for the duration. The skies were darkening. Time to curl up with some gardening books, a notepad and some toast. Daisy opened the bread bin, realizing as she did so that after last night's crisps-and-dips session, she'd ended up finishing off the loaf, absent-mindedly buttering and shoving in the toast in an attempt to blot out the late-night blues which had hit her, three-quarters of the way down a bottle of red and at the end of yet another viewing of *The Notebook*. She'd done a lot of comfort carb-eating of late. It was lucky, really, that gardening burnt off so much energy, or she'd be twice the size she was.

Polly raised one retriever eyebrow at her and thumped her tail apologetically. She was settled in her bed, and had no plans to go anywhere whilst the weather was determined to drag them back into winter.

Daisy closed the final kitchen cupboard with a sigh.

She'd searched, just in case there was a forgotten loaf lurking somewhere. There isn't anyone to buy it except you, she reminded herself.

Pulling on her dad's huge waxed raincoat, which covered her from neck to ankles, she grabbed Polly's lead from the dresser. The dog shrank down into her bed, trying to make herself invisible.

'Up. Come on, you, we're going to the shop.'

Saturday was market day in Steeple St John. Water from the tarpaulins covering the stalls was forming a river, which poured down the hill of Main Street, proving too much for the drains to cope with. Last week the little weekly market had been busy with harassed mothers and toddlers, women with granny-chic wicker shopping baskets, and old men watching the world go by. Today, however, Daisy was one of a handful of damp and grumpy shoppers, hunched under hoods or tucked under umbrellas.

'Nice weather for ducks,' said a voice from underneath the dripping hoarding of the fruit stall.

'Is it, though? I don't think I'd like this even if I was a duck.' Daisy handed him a handful of apples.

'I don't imagine it is, really. But it's what I'm supposed to say, isn't it?' He gave her a wry smile. 'You local? Haven't seen you at the market before – that's one-fifty, darling.'

She couldn't help laughing. 'Do they actually give you a script of appropriate things to say to customers?'

'Yep. Trade secret –' he leaned in, with a stage

whisper – 'We're like hairdressers. We don't get our pitch until we can recite them off by heart.' He handed Daisy her change.

'Well, I'm impressed. Ten out of ten – and in this weather, too. I'd be growling at everyone if I was stuck out in the cold.'

'I quite like it. And it's an opportunity to watch people. Every village has its own character, although they're all blending into one these days.' Raising an eyebrow, he motioned to a woman in a distinctive floral-print raincoat, complete with colourful wellies and artfully clashing umbrella. She looked like a walking advert for Boden.

'They think they're in an episode of the blooming Archers, half this lot. They've got an idea of what village life should be and we just see 'em coming. I sell more purple sprouting broccoli than I do potatoes these days.'

Daisy looked ruefully at her dad's too-big waxed coat and her filthy gardening boots. 'I don't really fit the mould.'

'Dunno, you look good to me,' he said, with a cheeky expression.

Startled by an unexpected compliment, Daisy stood frozen for a moment. He was, she realized, quite cute under the woolly hat. Curly dark hair, sharp blue eyes and an interesting-looking hooked nose, which gave him a slightly piratical air. Realizing she was staring, she felt her cheeks growing hot and stepped backwards. He held her gaze, unflustered. Flirting with customers might be part of the stallholder training, but she was most definitely *not* on the market.

'Oh. Right. Um, thanks.' Flustered, Daisy hurried off. She could feel his eyes on her as she bent over, trying to tie Polly's soaking wet lead around the post outside the little supermarket, water pouring off the back of her coat.

With no customers to be seen, the two women operating the supermarket checkouts were chatting comfortably, leaning across their tills, caught up in gossip as Daisy picked up a basket. They didn't acknowledge her presence, wrapped up as they were in a debate about something they'd seen on television the night before. Daisy scanned the magazine covers, basket hooked over her arm. *Comfort Food*, shouted a headline. Yes. That's what was needed on an afternoon like this – it felt more like midwinter than the beginning of spring. She grabbed a packet of chocolate biscuits, and threw a tin of Heinz tomato soup into her basket along with some cheese and a knobbly loaf of fresh bread. Standing at the till, she was just deciding whether a huge bar of chocolate was pushing it when she heard a voice behind her.

'Not such a good day for gardening, is it?'

She turned, recognizing the voice. It belonged to her new friend.

'Thomas! How are you?'

'Much better for seeing you, m'dear. Nasty weather, isn't it? More like January.'

'I'm only out for emergency supplies.' She waved the chocolate biscuits in explanation before putting them in her bag. 'I'm planning an afternoon by the fire working out what's going where in the garden.'

Daisy took her change, and paused a moment as Thomas bought his pint of milk.

'I don't suppose – I'm going for a cup of tea in the Bluebell, if you'd like to. No, I'm sure you've got to get on, haven't you?'

She couldn't resist. He sounded so hesitant and her soft heart melted at the thought of him sitting there alone in the rain.

'Not at all. I'd love to join you – what about Polly?'

'Oh, don't worry about her, we'll sneak her in. I've known Elizabeth, the owner, since she was a young lass. She wouldn't leave Polly sitting outside on a day like this.'

They made their way down the street. Thomas opened the door to a pretty cafe, with sprigged cotton curtains hanging over steamed-up windows, and charmingly mismatched old school chairs around wobbly-legged wooden tables. It smelt of vanilla, spice and fresh coffee.

Daisy hovered on the step with Polly. The last time she'd paid attention – on one of her infrequent visits in the last couple of years since her parents made the move from Oxford – the Bluebell had been a grotty greasy spoon which didn't appear particularly inviting. Now it looked lovely, but definitely not the sort of place that would welcome a soggy golden retriever.

'Bring her in.' The woman behind the counter gave Daisy a welcoming smile. 'Just don't tell anyone from Health and Safety. Come on, girl.' She beckoned Daisy in. Polly, grateful to be out of the rain, flopped down in the corner behind a table.

'Can we have a pot of tea and some of your lovely lemon drizzle, Lizzie?'

'Course you can, Thomas. You get yourselves warmed up, I'll bring it over.'

Daisy wiped the condensation away from the window, looking out at the rain pouring down. It was relentless, the grey sky seemingly holding an unlimited supply.

'This place has gone a bit posh since the last time I was in the village.'

Daisy fingered the Cath Kidston print curtains, taking in the colourful paintings on the wall, each with a discreet price tag neatly written on a dot of paper in the corner of the frame.

Thomas leaned in confidingly. 'Lizzie took over when her parents retired. She's a lovely lass, got two teenagers and she's on her own since her husband left. She's made a good job of it, hasn't she?'

Daisy looked around. A couple of other equally damp and grateful-looking shoppers were hugging warm mugs of tea. Radio 4 muttered away in the background, cosily. Colourful signs on the cork notice-board announced there was a book club that met once a month and a weekly knit-and-natter group, and new cake-making classes were imminent.

'She's made it the place to be, haven't you, my dear?' Thomas stopped talking for a moment as Elizabeth carefully set down a tray, handing them a pretty floral teapot, two mugs, and slices of cake big enough to satisfy even two hungry gardeners. He gave a nod of approval as she stepped back, smiling.

'And you make the best cup of tea in the county,' said Thomas approvingly, looking up at Elizabeth. Her eyes and nose crinkled prettily as she beamed her thanks.

'I've been looking through my notebooks,' said Thomas, after a pause while they both sipped their tea and appreciated the cake, 'and I've found my garden-ing notes from my years working at Orchard Villa. When this rain clears, perhaps we can arranage a time for me to come over and we can talk about your plans.'

'I'd like that.' Daisy, slightly begrudgingly, had admitted to herself there was a fine line between alone and lonely. She'd been there a few weeks, but the only visitor she'd had was her sister, who'd swooped down from London for a night bringing supplies from M&S, flowers, cake and a bottle of champagne which they'd shared while Daisy poured her heart out.

Watching the raindrops trickle down the window, she realized that she'd jumped at the chance of a cup of tea with Thomas, a relative stranger. She'd thought when she offered him the chance to help her out with the garden that she'd been doing him a favour – but, she realized with a half-smile, she was the one at sea.

'With your lovely red hair, when you smile like that, my dear, you bring me to mind of my Violet. Penny for your thoughts?'

'Just thinking it's strange the way things turn out.' She cupped the mug in both hands, not keen to talk about herself, but interested to know more about Thomas. 'Tell me about Violet. Was she from the village?'

'Violet?' Thomas laughed. 'Lord, no. Londoner born and bred, was Violet. She'd been married before – we both had, in fact. Back in those days, that wasn't the done thing. Her sister lived in the little mews cottages just down the back lane from the shop there, and she came out here to hide.'

'What was she hiding from?'

'Her husband. He was a big old boy, and a bit too fond of his ale.' Thomas shook his head, his lips tightening in a line as the memories came back to him. 'Nights when he'd had too much, he'd come home, and Violet would get the wrong end of his temper.'

'How awful. Poor Violet.'

'Yes, she'd nowhere else to go. In those days, people just stuck it out or hid when things were bad. But not my girl.' His eyes brightened, remembering. He sat up a little then, his chest puffing out with pride. 'She legged it. Took one overnight bag and left him to it. He came looking, one afternoon, but Edith just flat out lied. Told him she'd no idea where her sister was, that she'd brought disgrace on the family by leaving, and he was stupid enough to fall for it.' He gave a nod of defiance.

'Good for her. And then you two met?' Daisy, entranced, hugged her tea as she listened to his story.

'My first wife, Sarah, had died. She was only thirty, and I was a couple of years older. I'd been alone for a few years and I didn't expect to meet anyone again. I met my Violet at the village fête, and we were married within the year.'

'You must miss her terribly.' Daisy thought back to their previous meeting, and Thomas leaning over the gate of the churchyard wishing his wife goodnight. Her loneliness was nothing in comparison.

'I do.' Thomas closed his eyes, and Daisy felt suddenly awkward at intruding on his memories.

'Do you – did you have any children?'

Thomas shook his head. 'No, we were never blessed with a family. It's a shame. Violet would have made a lovely mum.'

'I'm sorry.' She reached out a hand, patting him on the arm.

'Oh, don't listen to me getting maudlin.' He grinned at her, perfect false teeth under his white moustache. 'I do all right. It's a funny old thing watching this little village – well, it's more of a town now, really, isn't it? – growing and changing. I've seen some real differences over the years. When you're a gardener, you notice things.'

'Well,' said Daisy, realizing as she did how much she looked forward to it, 'I'd really appreciate your help on the gardens at Orchard Villa. And they're not going anywhere.'

Thomas looked markedly brighter. 'That would be lovely, m'dear. Now, when shall we meet next? Shall I pop around in the week? Any time good for you?'

'Whenever suits you. I'm always in.'

Always in, no plans, thought Daisy. Safe in the garden. And that's just how I like it.

Daisy trudged down the hill, rain seeping in through the hem of her coat. It was funny that so far the only person in the village she'd met was sixty years her senior. This summer of house-sitting was going to be an odd one, if the only thing she had to look forward to was a cup of tea with an octogenarian and watching her plants grow.

Chapter Three

The next morning the rain had cleared. The sun hung in a bright blue sky, but there was still a late-spring nip in the air. After a sleepless night, Daisy had decided to make some more progress on the front borders before the village garden police had her rounded up and put in the stocks for bringing shame upon Steeple St John. She'd been bent double hoicking up some particularly stubborn thistles for ages, and her back was beginning to ache. She straightened, pulling off her fleece as she did so. She was roasting hot, probably beetroot-faced, and sweating. What she needed was a huge drink of Coke, and there was none in the house. Patting her back pocket to check she had the keys, she decided to reward herself with a quick trip to the corner shop.

Not that my life here's uneventful, she thought wryly, as she pulled the gate shut behind her.

'Ah, we meet again!'

Daisy, unable to resist a three-for-two offer when it came to chocolate, was just stuffing two bars into her

29

bag and preparing to stuff a third into her mouth as she opened the door of the little newsagent.

Standing right in front of her, immaculately dressed yet again – she probably gets out of bed and looks perfect, Daisy realized – was Elaine Thornton-Green.

'I was *just* thinking about you,' she said, brightly.

'You were?' Daisy plopped the chocolate bar back into the bag, slightly reluctantly.

'Yes. You haven't forgotten my little gathering on Thursday night, have you?'

Gathering on Thursday night. Daisy put her hand in the back pocket of her jeans, pulling out her keys, a crumpled tissue, a couple of dried-up leaves, and – Elaine's business card. Oh God, there was no getting out of this, was there?

'I'm not sure I can,' she said, automatically. 'I've got plans this Thursday.'

'Oh, that *is* a shame.' Elaine's face fell.

'Maybe another time?' Daisy felt a bit guilty. Not guilty enough, mind you, to change her mind.

'Yes, that would be lovely. Yes, let's do that. I'll give you a shout soon.' Elaine brightened at the thought, squaring her shoulders as she headed into the shop.

Elaine had seemed genuinely disappointed, Daisy realized, as she headed back to the garden with her bag of consolation prizes. She was probably just being polite. In any case, she wasn't ready to get out into the real world just yet, no matter what her sister might say about getting back out there.

She was quite happy with her little routine. It was safe. She got up, she gardened all day, watched TV box sets and ate chocolate, cried herself to sleep and then slept fitfully until morning. Her parents, who'd been planning to leave the house locked up for the duration of their trip, might have been surprised when she'd turned up, shell-shocked, on their doorstep a few weeks back, but they'd been more than happy to hand her the keys. Good old Daisy, her mother had said. Plenty more fish in the sea. This works out just perfectly for all of us, doesn't it?

Not really, Daisy had thought. But she'd bitten back her response with a smile, and waved her parents off as they headed for India. She was safe here, alone, in Steeple St John.

'Hey.'

'You okay?' Daisy, feet up on the sofa, was glad to hear Miranda's voice. The sisters had always been close, and with their parents on the other side of the world, it was comforting to know there was at least one person out there who'd notice if she fell off the face of the earth. Besides Thomas, of course. Oh, and there was always Elaine.

'You made it outside the garden walls yet?' Miranda's voice was teasing.

'Yeah, I had tea with my new friend Thomas.'

'I was thinking more people your own age, Daise.

31

Don't make me come up there again. I'll come, y'know. I'll force you to go to a barn dance, or whatever it is the yokels do for entertainment . . .'

'There's a Parish Council meeting next week. I could go to that?' Daisy had been reading the signs on the noticeboard outside the library when a woman beetled up, opened up the glass casing with an important air, and pinned her sign over the top of several others. 'Priorities, my dear,' she'd said. 'I hope we'll see you there?'

'Come on, Daise.' Her sister's tone softened. 'Look, I know you're feeling like shit, but seriously. I'm worried about you.'

Daisy adjusted the fleece blanket that was covering her knees, cradling her wine glass in her hand. It was easier when Miranda was bossing her about. When people started being kind she could feel the tears prickling, threatening to spill over.

'I'm fine.' It came out thickly, and she swallowed back the sob with a gulp of red.

'You don't sound it. I've got to finish up this project by the end of the week, but I'm going to come and see you as soon as it's done, 'kay?'

Daisy nodded, silently.

'Daise?'

Of course, she couldn't see down the phone. 'Okay.'

'Promise me you'll try and get out a bit?'

'I will. Speak to you tomorrow.'

'Love you.'

'You too.'

Daisy finished the last of the wine and headed upstairs. As she shoved her jeans off the side of the bed Elaine's card fell out of the pocket, landing at her feet. She picked it up and looked at it thoughtfully. Miranda would call that a sign from the universe. She turned it over, running a thumb across the expensive-looking card.

Elaine Thornton-Green
homevintagelife.com

Everything about it suggested luxury. Daisy rolled over, picking up her phone, and typed in the web address. Heading up the website was a picture of Elaine, smiling at a kitchen counter, a plate of gorgeous-looking scones in front of her. She scrolled downwards through the website. Elaine in a perfectly manicured garden, chic in a sunhat, a pair of secateurs in hand (which, she couldn't help noticing, looked like they'd never been used). How to make the perfect chicken soup. How to renovate a wooden dresser. Vintage styling for modern homes. It was a perfect lifestyle magazine, featuring Elaine as a sort of British version of Martha Stewart. No wonder she'd been a bit unimpressed with the chaos of Daisy's parents' garden. She didn't just *look* immaculate at all times. Her whole life was immaculate.

Sod it, thought Daisy. If I go to this thing, I'll get

Miranda off my back. There is *no way* that I'm going to have anything in common with this woman or any of her friends, and then I can just get on with being on my own. Leaving the card by the phone to remind herself to text in the morning, she rolled over and went to sleep.

It didn't occur to her until the following afternoon, as she felt her mobile buzzing in her pocket, that last night had been the first night she hadn't fallen asleep crying. Nor had she woken in the small hours with nightmares of familiar faces mocking her, laughing.

She checked her messages. Elaine had replied to the morning's apologetic response that she wasn't busy after all, and if it was still okay, she could make it.

SO glad to hear you can make it. Ours is The Old Rectory on Cavendish Lane. See you at 8. E. x

*

Cavendish Lane was the most sought-after street in the village. Each house was unique, set in huge gardens that backed onto the cricket pitch at one end and the allotments at the other. It was close enough to the train station that harried commuters could walk there in five minutes, meaning that houses on the street were often snapped up before the For Sale signs had even arrived on their perfectly manicured front lawns.

Daisy, feeling more than a little bit awkward, was edging her way slowly down the lane, trying to work out which was The Old Rectory. There were no numbers and half the houses appeared to have no names, either. But there it was – the name was painted on huge stone pillars which stood in front of a beautiful Georgian house. A precise row of five multi-paned windows stood above a panelled wooden front door at the end of a raked path of fine gravel. The path was lined with perfectly trimmed lavender bushes, not a single blue-grey leaf out of place. Daisy took a deep breath before pushing open the spiky metal gate.

As she drew closer she could see a hand-painted sign confirming she was in the right place. The front door was a pale, matt, expensive-looking grey-green. On either side of the tiled step sat two shiny bay trees, their slim trunks tied with bows of rough sacking material. Their painted wooden tubs were topped with a layer of blue-grey slate. It was perfect. Bracing herself, Daisy pressed the shiny brass doorbell.

'Ah, you must be one of Elaine's ladies.' A ruddy-cheeked, sandy-haired man opened the door. He wore a checked shirt beneath a ribbed woollen sweater, with standard posh-boy-issue thick brown cords. He reminded Daisy of an older Prince Harry. 'Come in.' He waved her into the hall, his voice well modulated and clear. 'Elaine?' He smiled at her, politely.

'Oh, lovely. Daisy!' Elaine appeared in the hall. She was slim and chic in a patterned wrap dress, with a pair of butter-soft leather boots which showed off slim calves. 'Excuse Leo, he's leaving us to it. Bye, darling.'

'Have fun, girls.' Leo stretched across, giving his wife a kiss which didn't quite connect with her cheek. Scooping up his car keys from the tall table by the door, he strode off down the path, pulling out his phone as he did so.

'Come through. Let me take your coat.'

Daisy allowed herself to be ushered into the house. The whole place was completely show-house spotless. The gleaming black and white tiles in the hall bore no wet dog footprints. There were no piles of unread post and junk mail on the dresser. There wasn't a teetering mound of coats on the bottom of the banister, either.

Elaine waved her into the kitchen with a gesture and slightly satisfied facial expression which suggested she was used to comments of admiration – not surprisingly. The kitchen was huge, immaculate and gleaming. Rows of smoothly painted wooden doors in a pale creamy white were tucked beneath acres of cool marble countertops. A double-fronted American fridge, bigger than anything Daisy had ever encountered, hummed quietly. There was an Aga here, too, but unlike the much-loved, slightly battered one back at Orchard Villa, this one was a buttermilk cream, and the metal fitments sparkled and shone.

Daisy took it all in with a little gasp of admiration. And – mmm, delicious. The most amazing array of sushi lay on huge white platters, the black and white contrasting against jewel-bright centres, stretched across the central island.

'This is gorgeous. And sushi, too. I love it.'

Elaine looked quite proud of herself. 'I made it myself. It's surprisingly easy, actually.'

'I didn't even know you could *do* that,' said Daisy, who until now had thought sushi mainly came from restaurants, or from those gorgeous takeaways at the train station.

'Oh yes,' said Elaine, airily. 'Doesn't take long. The secret's in a good knife. Much like gardening – I'm sure you'll agree, the tools are everything.'

Daisy nodded, looking around the kitchen as Elaine poured some soda water into a pitcher full of ice and mint. She was a bit dumbstruck by the gorgeous perfection of everything.

'Mojito?'

Daisy had to grudgingly acknowledge that her sister had a point. Faced with another evening with a bottle of red, a bag of Doritos and a rerun of *Friends*, this was rather nice. But where was everyone else?

'If you just pop through to the orangery, I'll be with you in a moment.' Elaine, who seemed a little distracted, looked over Daisy's shoulder towards the front door.

Daisy looked at the three doors that led out of the kitchen, and headed for the middle one.

Elaine laughed. 'That's the boot room. It's through there, on your left. Have a seat.'

Daisy stepped through into the biggest conservatory she'd ever seen. It was lush with plants, deliciously warm, and completely empty. Where was everyone? She picked up her phone, surreptitiously checking the date. No, it was definitely Thursday, and it was definitely eight o'clock. But the 'gathering' so far seemed to consist of two people.

She sat down on one of the sofas, sipping her drink, looking out at the patio, which stretched out beyond the glass. The garden looked amazing. Just as she stood up to investigate, she heard Elaine call out.

'Ah, doorbell!' She sounded relieved.

'Jo, this is Daisy. Daisy, Jo.'

Standing before her was a woman who looked a bit older than Daisy – early thirties, perhaps. She was dressed in a pretty sea-green patterned tunic, with long dark blue leggings, and a pair of sparkly green pumps. She tucked her pale blonde hair behind her ears, showing ornate beaded earrings.

'Just going to check if . . .' Elaine ducked back out of the room, not finishing her sentence, leaving a waft of expensive scent in her wake.

Jo caught Daisy's eye and raised her eyebrows almost imperceptibly, with a smile which made her feel slightly more at ease. She too had been given a glass. She sat down on the sofa opposite Daisy, who was swirling the ice of her drink, releasing delicious wafts of lime and mint into the air.

'Do you—'

'So are you—'

They both started to speak at the same time just as the doorbell rang again, making them laugh.

Daisy took another large mouthful of mojito, feeling the rum warming her throat. Everything was perfect on the surface, but the atmosphere was weird. Elaine was like a cat on hot bricks, much less assured than she'd seemed when they'd met. Daisy clutched her phone as a talisman. Miranda had been delighted to hear she was going out, but had been put on rescue alert. One quick text and her sister was primed to call, claiming an emergency, so that she could make her escape. It was a long-held pact which had saved both of them in the past.

'Here we are.' Elaine's smile was enormous now as she returned to the room followed by four women. 'So glad you girls could make it. This is such fun!'

'Steph, Jane, Sarah, Jacqui.' Elaine waved a hand to identify each woman, all of whom were dressed in almost identical outfits, like variations on a theme. 'This is Daisy' – Daisy stood up, feeling suddenly awkward – 'and this is Jo.'

They had the same expensively blow-dried hair as Elaine, but where she was willowy and chic in her wrap dress, they were dressed for an evening out with sparkly tops, skinny jeans and pin-sharp heels.

'The girls are all mums from Brockville Prep, where Leo is head.'

'Lovely to meet you, Daisy.' Steph appeared to speak for all of them. The other three held back slightly.

She felt herself being scanned, outfit-wise. She'd taken advantage of the early spring sunshine and had put on ankle-length trousers and a long fitted shirt, and twisted her unruly red hair back with two jewelled combs. Checking her reflection in the hall mirror as she'd left the house, she'd felt quite good. Under Steph's measured appraisal, she now felt distinctly gardener-ish and not at all glam.

Steph extended a hand, glancing in one of those micro-second looks that some women do so well from her own immaculately manicured hands to Daisy's short, scrubbed-to-within-an-inch-of-their-lives gardening fingernails. The handshake was brief and insincere. So much for Miranda's theory last night that Daisy might meet a brand new best friend. This lot were like the Mean Girls gang she remembered from school. While Steph was giving her the once-over the other three had spread out, helping themselves to the freshly made jugs of mojito, giggling in the corner like fifteen-year-olds.

'Oh yes, please do help yourselves,' said Elaine redundantly as she headed for the kitchen, bringing back another jug. Daisy caught Jane and Sarah – or Jacqui, she couldn't remember who was who – exchanging a glance, which suggested they intended to do just that.

'So, how do you know Elaine?' Jo, sensing an ally, leaned in closer to Daisy, her elbows on her knees.

'Oh – well, actually, I don't,' Daisy confided. 'We got

off to a bit of a dodgy start when I soaked her in the garden when my hose went haywire, and she invited me round. I wasn't going to come.'

Jo raised her eyebrows again.

'I mean,' Daisy realized that sounded a bit rude, and she was supposed to be making an effort to be sociable, 'I'm only in the village for the next six months. I'm staying in my parents' place while they're off travelling. Elaine asked if I'd like to come along. I didn't have any plans, and . . .' she trailed off, taking a sip of her drink, which had rapidly turned into a slush of melted ice and mint leaves.

'Let me top you up,' said Elaine, brightly. She handed Daisy a fresh glass. 'The girls are getting started on the sushi if you two would like to join us?'

Daisy and Jo both looked up. While they'd been chatting, Steph and her gang had headed through to the kitchen. They were cackling uproariously and somehow were already on their third drinks.

Jo leaned back against the kitchen counter, taking in the scene, not talking.

'Have you known Elaine a long time?' Daisy realized it was her turn to make conversation. This was ridiculous. She'd been stuck in Orchard Villa alone for weeks, and she'd forgotten how to talk to anyone who wasn't over eighty.

'Not at all, no. I do some counselling work at Brockville school once a week – we got talking the other day. My daughter's got some friends coming round tonight, so it seemed the ideal opportunity to get out and meet some new people. Working full time makes it hard to meet anyone around here.'

Daisy felt her shoulders relax slightly. Knowing Jo was in the same boat made her feel a bit less like the stand-out new girl in town. She definitely wasn't getting welcoming vibes from the other four, who had placed themselves on the opposite side of the kitchen island and were guzzling sushi in a manner most unbecoming of people wearing such skinny jeans.

'Well, this is lovely, isn't it?' Elaine, seemingly oblivious, smiled at them all. 'It's *so* tricky when we're all *so* busy to get people together, isn't it?'

'So what do *you* do, Daisy?' Jacqui (or was it Jane?) asked.

'I'm – well, I'm a gardener.'

There was a specific type of person who recoiled at the prospect, as if they thought that somehow just associating with a gardener would mean they'd suddenly be covered with greenfly and compost.

Jane-or-Jacqui was definitely in that bracket. 'Oh God, all that mud. I couldn't bear that. Leave it all to my other half. He loves it.'

'I think it sounds wonderful,' said Jo, kindly. 'Gardening is so peaceful, don't you think? Really gives you time to think. It's quite meditative, really.'

Daisy shot her a look of thanks. That was just how she felt about her time in the garden. Since childhood, when her dad had given her a plot in their little

Oxford garden, she'd escaped outside, hands filthy, never wearing gloves. She could lose hours in the garden, not really thinking about anything at all, and yet whenever she came back in to soak in a hot bath, bone-tired and filthy, she'd realize that her head was somehow clearer and life seemed much nicer. It was free therapy.

'Not my thing.' Steph sniffed, with a smile that didn't quite reach her eyes. 'Give me a day at a spa over grubbing around in the mud any day.' She stretched out her hands again, admiring her nails. 'I'm not paying thirty quid a go for shellacs for them to get ruined in a load of old compost.' She gave a tinkling laugh, and the others joined in.

Elaine looked at the two factions (that's exactly what it feels like, thought Daisy – they're on one side, and Jo and me are on the other) with a slightly alarmed expression.

'Gosh. Yes. Well, different strokes and all that, don't you agree?'

'Absolutely,' said Jo, reaching across and helping herself to another piece of sushi.

'These are delicious, Elaine. And you made them yourself?'

Jo seemed to have a knack for knowing how to put people at their ease. Daisy watched as Elaine relaxed, stopping her relentless hostessing for a few minutes whilst she explained how to make the sushi rolls, waving her elegant hands in demonstration. It was only Daisy who caught the hissed conversation between the other four as they knocked back yet another jug of mojitos.

'I told Michelle we'd be there by nine,' said Steph, turning her wrist to check the huge, clearly expensive watch. It glittered, catching the light.

Jane – or was it Sarah? Daisy still had no idea – popped a handful of sushi, quite openly, into a napkin, twisted it neatly, and popped it into her Mulberry handbag. She caught Daisy's eye, smirking. Daisy, feeling sorry for Elaine, looked down into her glass. These women were horrible, and Elaine seemed to be completely oblivious.

'Everyone had enough to eat? Gosh – I really ought to have made more sushi.' Elaine looked at the platters, which were now three-quarters empty, cleared by the four women. With their long skinny legs and arms, Daisy thought, they did look a bit like locusts. She hid a smile at the thought.

'Really sorry, Elaine, but we've got to get off.' Steph, clearly an expert at making a swift exit, picked up her bag.

'But – you've only just arrived!' Elaine's face fell.

'And you've been *such* an amazing hostess. So sorry we can't stay later. Michelle's having a little do in the Grey Mare for some of the PTA mums.'

'Oh, yes, yes.' As Daisy looked on, Elaine re-arranged her features. 'Yes, of course. Perhaps another time soon?' Her tone was almost pitch-perfect.

'Absolutely.'

Steph was two seconds from clicking her fingers to summon the others, thought Daisy, as they obediently followed her out of the kitchen. Elaine followed them, gathering coats and calling goodbye from the front step.

Meanwhile, Daisy leaned back against the kitchen worktop with relief, popping one of the leftover pieces of sushi into her mouth.

'Wow.'

Jo looked at her, shaking her head. 'I know.'

'I think we just met the school-gate mafia.' Daisy poured the remains of the cocktail into Jo's glass.

'Welcome to Stepford.' Jo clinked her glass against Daisy's.

Chapter Four

'What a shame they couldn't stay.'

Daisy avoided Jo's eye as Elaine walked back into the kitchen.

'Let me get you a drink, Elaine.' Jo made towards the ice machine on the huge American fridge.

'No, no, you stay where you are. If it's just us three, let's go through to the sitting room, shall we? I'll bring through another drink and some nibbles. It's just through the hall and second on the left.' Elaine waved her arm, pointing the way.

Daisy and Jo followed her direction.

'Here we are.'

They were now in a huge, yet cosy sitting room. Thick velvet curtains were drawn, and an elegant flower arrangement sat on the fireplace in front of the grate. The sofas were enormous, with neatly arranged throws and pillows scattered around artfully. Elaine came into the room, bottom first, bearing a tray with another jug of mojitos and some little bowls filled with savoury biscuits, which Daisy realized were home-made. After lighting some scented candles, Elaine finally sat down.

'Your house is so beautiful.' Jo looked around, admiringly.

'Oh, well,' said Elaine, looking pleased. 'It's my job, as well as my life. And Leo and I like the place to look good.'

'I had a look at your website,' Daisy said, slipping off her shoes and curling her feet up underneath her on the sofa. 'It's amazing.'

'The Americans love all that Old England stuff,' explained Elaine, motioning to the antique stoneware which filled the shelves on either side of the fireplace.

'So Daisy, d'you want to explain exactly how you soaked Elaine?'

It was Daisy and Elaine's turn to look at each other and laugh. With the other women gone, Elaine seemed to have loosened up a bit. She filled up her glass, echoed Daisy in slipping off her shoes, and sat back on the sofa.

'. . . and so I was going to say no and stay home for another night of red wine and chocolate,' Daisy continued, the rum having loosened her tongue, 'but I realized I really ought to get a bit of a life here in Steeple St John, seeing as I'm here for the next few months.'

'And what happens then?' Elaine asked the question that Daisy didn't want to answer.

'Honestly?' Daisy sat forward, propping her chin in

her hand, thoughtfully, 'I have no idea. I've got nowhere to go now that –'

Elaine cocked her head, waiting for the rest of the sentence. Jo, somehow sensing Daisy had said enough, reached forward for the little savouries, offering them to the others.

'Not easy meeting people when you're single in a town like this, is it?' Jo gave Daisy a comforting smile. 'Even harder when you've got a teenager who thinks you're the most embarrassing thing on the planet.'

'You have a teenager? You don't look old enough!' Daisy looked more closely at Jo's face. Surely she couldn't be more than thirty-five?

'Martha. She's fourteen. She was born nine months after graduation day. We've grown up together, really. She's lovely, when she's not awful. Depends on which side of bed she gets out of, at the moment.' Jo gave a half-frown, clearly visualizing some of her daughter's finer moments.

'I had no idea. You've done it all on your own? Her father's not around?' Elaine's tone was impressed.

'No, he's . . . we do fine on our own.'

Elaine reached out a hand in apology. 'Sorry, I didn't mean to pry.'

'It's fine,' said Jo, slightly guardedly. 'Anyway, when Martha went to nursery, I started doing voluntary work as a Samaritan. By the time she'd started full-time school I began training as a counsellor. I work full time now.'

'And you met Elaine through the school?' Daisy was piecing together a picture of Jo's life. It made sense, now, that she was such a peaceful, easy listener. It clearly came naturally. She could imagine her sitting in a therapy room, giving people the space to talk.

'Yes.' Elaine looked across at Jo. 'I don't tend to get involved with the school thing very often – nobody wants the headmaster's wife poking her nose in all over the place, do they?' She gave a little laugh. 'But I had to pop up to drop off Leo's phone last week, and I met Jo on the way out. We got chatting, and here we are.'

Jo nodded agreement as Elaine continued, 'Leo's very keen that the children and staff at Brockville should be given access to every support available.' Daisy noticed Elaine glance up at one of the many photos of her husband on the mantelpiece. The whole room was a shrine to their relationship – photographs of the handsome couple lined the shelves, all of which featured Elaine, Leo, or Elaine-and-Leo, in various glamorous locations, smiling out at the camera.

'Pretty impressive to have managed all that as a single mother, Jo.' Daisy couldn't help wondering where her own get up and go had disappeared to. Having switched careers and taken the plunge to retrain as a gardener, here she was living in her parents' house, unemployed and completely single. Jo and Elaine seemed pretty sorted in comparison.

Jo shrugged off the compliments, pulling back her

long blonde hair into a knot as she smiled. 'Not a big deal, honestly – I know people who have it far harder than I do.'

'I suppose, yes,' said Elaine, as if the idea had only just occurred to her. Living in this beautiful, huge house, with a doting husband and a successful career, Daisy imagined that it must be pretty hard to imagine how the other half lived. 'We're very lucky, really, aren't we?' continued Elaine.

Daisy bit back a pang of envy, taking a sip of her drink. She could feel a wave of self-pity washing over her, remembering how different life had been just a few months back. But things were different now. She really ought to try and make the best of them. She sat up in her chair, balling her hands into fists, telling herself to get a grip. It was always on the third glass of wine – or whatever – that her resolve failed her. Normally around this point she'd have to hide her phone in the bread bin to avoid the temptation to start stalking Facebook, or composing furious texts she wouldn't send. With company tonight, though, it seemed easier to just put those things to the back of her mind and chat.

It was another hour before Jo stood up, looking at the carved wooden clock on the wall, saying she really ought to get back to check on Martha.

'I left her at home with a friend watching DVDs and eating pizza. No doubt by now they'll have dyed the bathroom purple with hair dye and eaten every-thing in the cupboards.'

Putting down her glass, Daisy looked up at the time. It was almost eleven, and while she didn't have anyone waiting at home, Polly would be anxiously pac-ing the kitchen, ready for an evening stroll.

'It's been lovely.' Elaine offered her cheek for a kiss.

'It really has.' Daisy realized that she actually meant it. Once the mean girls had gone, they'd had a surprisingly nice evening.

'Perhaps we could do it again? A drink at the Grey Mare in a couple of weeks, maybe?' Jo pulled out her phone from her bag. 'I'll take your number, Daisy. Elaine, I've got yours.'

'Yes, please.'

Daisy strolled down Main Street, not noticing the chill in the air, feeling happier than she had in weeks. She popped her head in through the front door, whis-tling to Polly. 'Come on, girl, I'll take you for a quick scoot round the park.'

Daisy had been heading up to the supermarket, keys in hand, when the doorbell rang the next morning.

'Oh, I've caught you on your way out.' Thomas was standing on the step, a pile of faded notebooks under one arm.

'Just heading up to grab something to eat.'

'Let me give you these, and I'll walk up to town

with you. Just thought I'd give you a head start by passing them on.'

Thomas handed over the notebooks.

'Have a look through these when you get a moment. It'll give you some idea of what's hidden underneath the bindweed and sticky willow.'

'Oh, these are perfect, Thomas, thank you.' Daisy flipped one open.

The books, beautifully illustrated with sketches, were inscribed with Thomas's copperplate writing, alongside copious planting notes.

He leaned over, tracing a gnarled finger across the page, smiling to himself.

'"September 1955 – Wisteria Sinensis" – that's the wisteria that covers the front door. I remember the day I planted that. I'd been out the night before playing cards in the Grey Mare and I'd had one too many ales. Got a right telling off from Mrs Smith-Beddoes, the old owner, when I turned up half an hour late to do the garden. She docked five bob off my wages.'

'These are gorgeous, Thomas. They're going to make my job a lot easier. Thank you.'

Popping them carefully on the dresser in the hall, Daisy pulled the door behind her and they set off towards the centre of the village.

'I don't suppose –' He paused for a moment, looking at her sideways. 'You wouldn't fancy keeping me company at the Parish Council meeting, Daisy?'

Daisy, who could definitely feel the after-effects of

last night's mojitos, wasn't quite sure she was up to a gathering of village worthies. But Thomas had been so kind, and he looked so sincere . . .

'Oh, okay then.' Just once. One meeting to tick the box, and she'd wangle her way out of anything more.

Thomas beamed at her, his tone one of relief. 'I am glad. I've been trying to keep a low profile and not get caught up in village affairs, but when they decided to make a bid for Britain in Bloom, I knew there wasn't much chance of hiding from Flora.'

'Flora?'

Thomas shook his head with a smile. 'Chair of the Parish Council. Head of this, chief organizer of that. She's – well, you'll find out. Reminds me in a funny way of my Violet. She doesn't take any nonsense.'

They'd arrived at the lane that led down to the village hall. A battered Volvo estate turned the corner and pulled up. Hanging out of the window was the head of a hugely excited brown and white spaniel, barking with excitement.

'Afternoon, Ned.'

'Thomas.' The driver opened the car door, which creaked alarmingly. Unshaven, with a scruffy jumper on, he climbed out and whistled to the dog, which jumped out and stood to heel, panting.

'Daisy, you'll not have met Ned. He's our new vet.'

'Nice to meet you, Daisy.'

Daisy shook his hand. Ned was in his early thirties. He looked like he'd been dragged out of bed, and had thrown on the first things he'd found on the floor.

Clearly aware of his outfit, Ned looked down at his jumper, which was inside out and covered in pieces of straw. 'Sorry. Been with a mare who was foaling this morning. Haven't had a chance to get back.'

'Oh, how lovely. I'd have loved to be a vet.' Daisy smiled at him. 'I was hopeless at science though.'

'Ah, yes. Bit of a tricky one, that.' Ned pulled a hand through his sandy blond hair, which left it standing on end.

'Ned's another one who's been roped in to take part in the committee meeting, haven't you?' Thomas explained, kindly.

Ned rolled his eyes, pulling a face that made Daisy laugh. 'God, yes. I came up with the idea it'd be good to get a bit more involved in the community, show we're really part of the village. So the next thing you know, here we are.'

'Try and sound a bit keener, Ned,' said Thomas, laughing. 'I've just persuaded Daisy to join us. She's a bit of a gardening expert, y'see. And if there's three of us who're new to the committee, there's safety in numbers . . .'

'Excellent idea. Come and join us, Daisy. We can sit at the back of the class.'

Ned's green eyes sparkled at the prospect, making him look more like a teenager up to tricks than a fully fledged vet.

Somehow the idea of sitting through a boring

meeting with Ned and Thomas making her laugh didn't seem quite so bad. Rumpled and chaotic, Ned had the air of a mischievous overgrown schoolboy. And she couldn't spend *every* moment of the next however-many months she was here watching TV and talking to plants.

Thomas took Daisy's arm, and the three of them headed in to the village hall.

An hour later, with a bacon roll wrapped in a paper bag and a takeaway coffee in her hand, Daisy headed back to read the notebooks Thomas had left. The meeting had gone past surprisingly quickly and with Ned and Thomas for company, it had even been quite – well, she wouldn't go so far as to say fun, but she'd promised she'd go along to the next one.

Hands full, she was struggling with the keys. She could hear her mobile phone ringing where she'd left it on the dresser in the hall, but the front-door key was sticking again. By the time she got in there was a new voicemail message flashing on the screen.

Daisy, it's Elaine. I really hope you don't mind me calling like this – I know we said we'd get together next week, but I could really do with some help and I've got a proposition to put to you. Can you give me a shout when you get this message?

*

'This is *so* kind of you.' Twisting her long hair up in a knot, Elaine turned, tipping the water into the pot. Loose leaves, of course, Daisy noticed. Elaine didn't seem the type to shove a teabag in a mug under any circumstances.

'No trouble,' said Daisy, kindly. It was only a ten-minute walk up to Cavendish Lane, and having flopped down in the sitting room with a bacon roll and a coffee for half an hour, she felt rather less delicate.

She'd strolled along the lane, peering into the gardens, sizing them up. There wasn't one that wasn't impeccably maintained. Not a leaf was out of place. Clearly either the street had some very dedicated weekend gardeners, or someone was making a fortune keeping them up for the well-off owners.

'Milk? Sugar? I've made some shortbread, it's just cooling over here, look.'

Elaine pointed to the tiled windowsill. Laid out beautifully on an Emma Bridgewater platter were the most gorgeous hand-made petticoat tail biscuits that Daisy had ever seen.

'Just milk, please. And I couldn't say no to those, they look divine.'

'Come and sit down, then,' said Elaine, picking up the teapot and placing it on a floral tray, 'and I'll explain.'

Daisy followed her through to the orangery where a fat ginger cat lay basking in the sunlight. He looked up sleepily, chirruping acknowledgement.

'That's Hector. Beautiful, isn't he?' Elaine patted the sofa, and Daisy sat down beside her, pulling down her shirt to cover a hole where a rose bush had snagged at her leggings. Elaine, as usual, was perfectly turned out in a navy and white polka-dot shirt, red scarf and slim-fitting navy trousers. Daisy ran a hand through her red curls. She couldn't actually remember brushing her hair that morning after she'd climbed out of the shower.

'I've got a proposition for you.' Elaine waved a hand in the direction of the window, indicating the gardens outside. 'I've had a call from the Parish Council. Someone's pulled out of the village Open Gardens in six weeks' time, and the committee have offered me the slot.'

'Wow, congratulations!' Daisy, who'd been visiting her parents the year before last on the weekend of the Steeple St John Open Gardens, knew what a huge deal this was. The annual one-day event raised huge amounts for charity, but only a limited number of village gardens were featured and spaces were very highly sought after.

'I need this place to look *perfect*,' Elaine continued. 'Obviously, I'll be doing several features on my website, and with most of the village passing through the garden, I want it to be at its very best.'

Daisy stood up, holding her cup of tea, and looked out onto the garden. The flagstone patio, flanked with mossy pots full of ferns, and the vibrant green of hostas in shoot, was picture-perfect. Leading on to the grass was the most beautiful curved stone staircase

57

set into an immaculate lawn, edged with weed-free borders which were just bursting with old English cottage garden perennials – foxgloves, frothing yellow achillea just coming into bloom, delicate Alchemilla mollis, each leaf filled with a sparkling circle of dew, bright-leaved early geraniums – all at a stage of growth which Daisy's expert eye could tell would mean the most breathtaking display in a month or so's time.

'It's perfect.' Daisy turned back, reluctantly. 'You've done an amazing job. I can't see what you need me to do.'

'Me?' Elaine laughed, drily. 'I haven't a clue about gardening.'

'But – I've seen your website. All those gorgeous photos of the plants and the greenhouse and you working in the garden?'

'Oh, they're *my* photos, yes. But I don't do the work – I wouldn't have a blooming clue.' Elaine arched an eyebrow in amusement, clearly surprised at Daisy's naivety.

'I've had a chap from Beaconsborough come in twice a week, but he has just broken his leg in a motor-bike accident.'

Daisy, trying to repress her glee at getting her hands on such a beautifully kept garden, turned back to the huge window of the orangery, looking out at the wide sweep of lawn.

Elaine gave her a dazzling smile. It was, Daisy

couldn't help noticing, the kind that suggested she was used to people saying yes.

'Can we take a look outside?'

'Of course.' Gathering the tea things and placing them on the tray, Elaine stood up. 'We can take the drinks outside. I'll show you around.'

The garden was beautiful. Its manicured splendour was such a contrast to the chaotic, overgrown wilderness of Orchard Villa's garden. Daisy felt herself relaxing as she strolled around, taking in the carefully planned border plantings, where she could see thought had been put into making sure that there was colour and interest throughout the seasons. The vegetable garden was a work of art, a perfect *potager* with raised beds edged with woven wicker and rows of vegetable seedlings standing to attention. But she'd committed to getting the garden sorted out for her parents.

'It's amazing, Elaine, but I—'

'Oh, *please* say you'll help. It would be such fun to have you popping round.'

Daisy knelt, pulling out a stray weed seedling which had sneakily taken root in the fine gravel of the path. She imagined pottering around, listening to the radio in the huge, wooden-framed greenhouse as she planted up hanging baskets and took cuttings. Everything here was in perfect condition, with no expense spared. And living rent free at her parents' place was still making a dent in her savings, no matter how frugally she lived. And most importantly, she'd graduated from her course, and needed something on her gardening CV to prove she knew her stuff . . .

'Well, I could maybe manage a couple of mornings a week . . .'

'I'd pay you, of course,' said Elaine, with the casual air of one who doesn't have to think about money. She named a sum which would more than cover Daisy's weekly expenses. That was the clincher – she'd need every penny of those savings when her parents got back, to pay a deposit on somewhere to live.

'Sounds perfect.' Daisy cast another glance around the garden, this time with a proprietorial air. It was breathtakingly gorgeous, like something you'd see on a *Gardeners' World* feature. The house was *huge*, too. Running a website or being a head teacher must pay an awful lot more than she'd realized. This place must be worth a small fortune.

Chapter Five

Daisy spent the morning getting to know the Old Rectory garden. She arrived at eight-thirty, just as Leo, Elaine's husband, was heading out the door. He slammed it hard behind him, his mouth a tight-set line. Looking up, his expression changed instantly on seeing her.

'Oh hello, Daisy.' His voice was slightly too bright. 'You're visiting early.'

'I'm here for the garden?' She looked at him with a questioning frown, indicating her fleece sweater, sturdy work boots, and grass-stained jeans.

'Right. Of course.' He looked at her as if he had no idea what she was talking about. 'Must get on, I've got a meeting before assembly.'

He strode past, leaving a trail of surprisingly strong aftershave behind him. It caught the back of Daisy's throat, making her pull a face as she rang the door-bell.

'Daisy! I wasn't expecting you quite yet.' Elaine pulled the door open. She looked a little pale, her eyes red-rimmed with tiredness. It was the first time Daisy had seen her looking anything other than perfect: her hair was twisted up in a loose bun, feet bare.

'I'm really sorry – I thought we said half-eight.' Daisy peered over Elaine's shoulder at the clock in the hall, checking the time.

'No, you're right.' Elaine reached up, patting her hair in an unconscious gesture. 'It's just been a bit of a morning, that's all. Come through.'

'I'm in muddy boots.' Daisy made to bend down and untie the laces.

'It's fine.' Pulling the door closed behind her, Elaine appeared to take a deep breath to steady herself.

'Is everything okay?' There was definitely something up. Leo had looked distinctly unhappy as he'd headed out.

'No, no. No, everything's fine. Fine.' The tone was clipped, the words final.

'Shall I just let you get on? I don't want to hold you up this morning.' And, thought Daisy, she'd be far happier out there with the plants than in here with the weird, frosty, stilted atmosphere. You knew where you were with plants. She'd realized, pottering around the gardens during her time at college, that the comfortable certainty was what she loved about gardening. It had started when she was a child, finding solace in getting her hands dirty first of all, then watching the magic as the seeds she planted grew up – up – up into sunflowers, and huge runner bean plants, before drying out, dying off, and producing more seeds so the cycle could begin again the next spring. Her dad, recognizing his daughter's need for time alone to process her thoughts, had been happy to foster her love of gardening, despite having no interest in it himself.

Daisy made her way up to the garden shed, where she dumped her bag and phone, and lost herself for a few hours amongst the plants.

Pausing in the sunshine for a moment, she trailed her fingers through the low hedge, filling the air with the familiar, soporific scent of lavender. In an unguarded moment, she closed her eyes, an unwanted memory stirring.

Sun was pouring in through the big Georgian windows, music on low coming from the radio. Flour-covered worktops, lavender-scented shortbread, Jamie's hands around her waist, grabbing still-cooling biscuits from the rack. Daisy slapping him away, laughingly. Their best friend and flatmate, Sylvia, blonde ponytail curling over her shoulder, looking up from her end-of-term study notes, a frown on her face . . .

Daisy shuddered, blanking out the picture.

'Daisy?' Elaine's voice brought her back to the present.

'It's nothing.' Daisy grimaced, giving her head a shake. Elaine was looking around the vegetable garden with a pleased expression.

She patted the flowers. 'Smells are so important in a garden, aren't they?' Daisy spoke brightly, changing the subject. She didn't want to think about it. Brush it under the carpet. Put it to one side. 'I wrote a lot about that in my final-year project during my course. So we want to make sure we involve all the senses here.'

Safer ground, literally. Daisy felt herself relaxing as with a practised eye she scanned the garden, assessing the levels of foliage growth, checking the structure of the planting.

'I don't mind what it costs. I just need you to make this place look perfect. I've planned a week-long series of articles on gardening for the website to co-incide with the Open Gardens. A sort of record of the preparations.'

Elaine's eyes lit up with an idea.

'D'you know what? It takes me an *age* to get all the plant names right. You know this –' she motioned to the plants, vaguely – 'stuff by heart, don't you?'

'It sticks in my head, yes.' Daisy had been teased all the way through college by the younger students for her encyclopaedic knowledge of Latin plant names. She'd no idea how, but for some reason while her course-mates would be struggling to memorize the complicated patterns of archaic language, she found it simple. Having spent a few years drudging away in an office job, Daisy had eventually decided to follow her heart and retrain as a gardener. It had given her a passion and commitment for the course, which a lot of the younger students hadn't seemed to feel. That was something she, Sylvia and Jamie had all had in common, as mature students. She shook her head a second time, irritated that she'd let her mind wander back there again.

'Sorry. What were you saying?'

'How would you fancy writing a series on my website? I bet you'd be fantastic.'

'Seriously?' She'd written a bit for the university magazine, and writing about gardening was pure pleasure for her. The chance to share her thoughts with Elaine's thousands of readers would be amazing. 'I'd love to!'

'Shall we start with a trip up to the garden centre next week then? Monday or Tuesday? You choose what we need, and I'll buy you lunch.'

Shopping for plants with someone else buying? It sounded like heaven. Much as she loved the back-to-basics of clearing through the wilderness at Orchard Villa, the idea of popping out and buying whatever she needed would be bliss. And lunch into the bargain.

Right on cue, Daisy's stomach growled. She'd had nothing but a couple of slices of toast at breakfast, and she was ravenous. If she left now, she'd have time to grab something from the bakery on the way back – and Polly had been home alone for long enough. She was getting a bit leaky in her old age, if she was left in the house too long.

'Tuesday works for me. That sounds perfect.'

*

'Two beef and blue cheese pasties and a jam dough-nut, thanks.'

Daisy ducked into the baker's shop just as the sign on the door was being flipped over to 'Closed'. The other customer, a tall, dark-haired man, was wearing a reflective vest and muddy, dark tan work boots.

'Oh – and a bottle of Evian.' The accent was Irish – soft and lilting.

'You on a health kick, George?' The woman behind the counter gave a laugh, handing over his food.

'Something like that. Cutting out the Coke – that's a start, right?' Dark eyebrows raised in collusion, he turned to Daisy.

She gave a vague smile in response. She looked sideways at his reflection in the window as he passed over a jingling handful of loose change. She was trying not to stare, but she'd *definitely* seen him somewhere.

'I'll have that last pasty, please.' She looked up from her bag, pulling out her purse.

'Girl after my own heart.' He gave her a wink, blue eyes sparkling, and strode out of the shop. Daisy watched as he made his way across the market square, unwrapping his lunch from the paper bag, not waiting to sit down. She paid for her food and wandered down the road, happily tired after a good morning's work.

The local paper, the *Argus*, was waiting for her on the doormat, along with a disapproving Polly. Too old to bounce with excitement at the prospect of a walk, she instead made her intentions quite clear by sloping off towards the back door, glowering. 'Go on then, off you pop,' Daisy said as she let her out, one hand rifling in the paper bag for the still-warm pasty. Perching on the kitchen counter, she balanced the paper on the worktop, crumbs spilling down her shirt.

GARDEN-GRABBING PROTEST

The front cover of the paper showed a huge group of people, waving beautifully designed and – Daisy noticed – very well-punctuated placards. It was a very Middle England, 'Up With This We Will Not Put' sort of protest. The kind, she suspected, that probably came with folding chairs, wicker picnic baskets and a selection of nibbles from the little Waitrose in town.

'"If this village is taken over with horrible red brick modern monstrosities, it will lose all the character that's been preserved here for 500 years," a spokeswoman for the Village Preservation Society informed our reporter,' Daisy read on.

'"I've lived in this village all my life and I'm 84 now."' She looked more closely at the photograph that accompanied the article, realizing as she did that Thomas was quoted as a village stalwart. She smiled, thinking he'd probably be amused by that title. *'"Young folk have to have somewhere to settle, and God knows, this place is out of their financial reach. We need a solution to that, but it*

shouldn't necessarily lie in ripping up the fabric of the village. Some of these gardens are part of history."'

'Too right!' agreed Daisy through a mouthful of food, turning the page to read the final paragraphs.

'Property developer Stephen O'Hara, joint owner of OHB Developments, spoke exclusively to us this week: "Unfortunately whilst many residents of the village have the foresight to see that, with a national housing shortage, we are actually providing a much-needed service in the community, there is a minority who would rather preserve the village, and their memories of life here, in aspic.'"

Logic told Daisy he had a point, but thinking of the beautiful garden along the lane which was destined to be torn up, she felt a bit sick. She turned the page, deciding to put it out of her head.

'These are *gorgeous*,' Miranda said thickly, through a mouthful of chips. 'You sure you don't want anything to eat?'

Daisy pinched a chip, blowing on it before biting it in half. They weren't just any old chips, her sister was right. Still not worth almost a fiver, mind you.

'I'd just eaten when you rang to say you were on the train.'

Miranda pulled a mock-guilty face. 'Sorry for springing on you with no notice.'

'God, no.' It had been such a relief when her sister had called, saying she was on the way through for a surprise visit.

Walking down from the station together, arm in arm, they'd grabbed the last window seat in the Grey Mare pub, just getting there before the swarm of London commuters made their way down Main Street, loosening their ties, nipping in for a quick one on the way home from the office.

'It was funny. I was on Marylebone High Street seeing a client and I just suddenly got the urge to get on a train. I realized as soon as I did that you might have been out, or something.'

Daisy took a last mouthful of her drink, and looked across at her sister, raising her eyebrows self-mockingly.

'Hardly. My social life in the last month has consisted of one night out and a Parish Council meeting.'

Miranda gave a snort of laughter. 'Well, you did say you were planning to hole up here for the summer and lick your wounds.'

'That's not *exactly* what I said.'

'Yeah, well, under the circumstances it's not surprising. You heard anything from *him* since you've been here?'

Daisy shut her eyes.

'I've blocked his number.'

There was a note of finality in her voice, which stopped Miranda from pushing any further. Daisy reached across, inspecting the little aluminium bucket that held her sister's chips. She recognized it as the sort of detail Elaine would love. Everything was just so, perfectly quaint and designed for people with a hankering for vintage style. Not vintage prices, mind you, thought Daisy, looking at the menu again. It was a blessing, really, that she didn't have much of a life here in the village, or her savings would have disappeared in no time. Thank God she was going to be getting a regular income from the work on Elaine's garden.

'Are you staying over? It'd be lovely to have some company – we can maybe watch a film and have hot chocolate by the fire?' It sounded a bit desperate even to Daisy's ears. Night after night alone in Orchard Villa was sending her a bit crazy, though. Independence and isolation weren't all they were cracked up to be and a familiar, comfortable face made her long for a cosy night in, chatting and laughing.

'I can't, Daise. Got an eight-thirty appointment with the UK sales manager. I'll get the last train tonight, though, if you'll walk me up to the station?'

'Deal.' She swallowed the desire to beg her sister to stay over and get the early train. She didn't have any overnight things with her, for one thing – and there was no way that there was anything in Daisy's hotchpotch wardrobe of gardening clothes, floaty tops and jeans that would cut it in a high-powered sales meeting.

'So tell me more about this night out you had with the village girls?'

Daisy pulled her chair in closer. Miranda placed

her chin on steepled fingers, ready for gossip. With her customary confidence, somehow Miranda managed to catch the eye of the young barman, motion with her two fingers, and have a further two drinks materialize at the table in seconds. Daisy thought of the times she'd spent standing at the crowded bar back in Winchester, money in hand, raising her hand and eyebrows hopefully for about ten minutes before anyone would serve her. Somehow her sister had been blessed with a double helping of entitlement when it was handed out.

'Right. Well, there's Elaine. She's a lifestyle blogger – hang on,' Daisy scrolled down on her phone, finding the site and handing it over.

Miranda scanned a couple of pages of the website with a knowledgeable nod. 'Very nice. She knows her stuff – 25,000 Facebook fans. Our digital marketing department would snap her up if she was looking for a job.'

'I don't think that's on her radar. There's obviously a lot of money in blogging if you know what you're doing. She's got this gorgeous Georgian house on Cavendish Lane, an immaculate garden, the interiors look like something from a Martha Stewart magazine, and she cooks like a dream. Oh, *and* a handsome Prince Harry lookalike husband who's head of the local prep school. They moved here a couple of years ago.'

Daisy took the phone back, slipping it back into her jeans pocket.

'Mmm,' said Miranda. 'All sounds a bit *too* perfect, if you ask me. Martha Stewart ended up in prison, remember.'

Daisy gave a snort of laughter. 'I hardly think Elaine's the prison type. She's super-posh.'

'It's never the ones you'd think,' said Miranda, with a knowing look. 'There's no way they could afford a place on Cavendish Lane on a head teacher's salary.' She popped a final chip into her mouth with a slightly smug expression, indicating she'd made her final point. Sisters, Daisy thought, could be seriously infuriating.

'I honestly don't think she's got a secret career as an arms trader.'

'Whatever,' said Miranda.

Daisy pursed her lips and kept quiet.

'What about the others?' Miranda pushed the wooden board which had held her food to one side and sat back, crossing her legs. She flicked a crumb off her lap.

'Well, there was a group of four women – can't remember all their names, but to be honest they were pretty unmemorable. As far as I could see they were only in it for the booze and Elaine's amazing cooking. It was a bit embarrassing.'

'Awkward.' Miranda pulled a face.

'She didn't seem to notice,' Daisy continued. 'She's nice, but a bit – unobservant?'

'Just as well, by the sound of it.'

Daisy thought for a moment. She'd been musing on it earlier whilst working in the garden, and actually there'd been a split second when she'd felt Elaine knew *exactly* what they were up to, but then the perfect hostess mask had slid back into place.

'And the other one?'

'Jo. She's actually really nice.'

'As opposed to Elaine, who isn't?'

Daisy gave a huff of mock-irritation.

'No, I mean she's a bit more – well, normal. D'you know what I mean? I can sort of see how she doesn't know anyone here if they're all like those skinny locust women. She's got a teenager, works as a counsellor. She's got that sort of air about her.'

'What, you mean all Guardian-reader, knit your own yoghurt?'

'No.' Daisy rolled her eyes at Miranda, wondering if she was being deliberately obtuse. Jo was really lovely – the more Daisy thought about her, the more she felt she was someone she'd really like to get to know. She'd found herself looking forward to their planned drink. Elaine was lovely, but there was a carapace of perfection which was hard to get through. It meant conversations with her never seemed to get beyond a level of polite small talk. 'She's more that sort of person who you start talking to and realize half an hour later you've told them your life story?'

'Oh, God.' Miranda actually reared back at that. 'I know the sort of person you mean. Very nice, but I

73

don't want someone winkling my secrets out of me by accident.'

'You have secrets?'

Miranda, who was an open book, laughed at the idea. They sat chatting for a while longer before deciding to get another drink.

Daisy looked across at the bar. Maybe she could try Miranda's method. She pointed at the two glasses, raising her eyebrows and smiling, just as a tall, dark-haired man in a suit looked across and caught her eye.

Shit.

He gave her a half-nod in greeting, leaning forward to speak with the barman. Daisy could feel herself going scarlet in the face, and there was nothing she could do.

'Daise? You okay?'

'Fine. Fine.' She reached for her glass to take a nonchalant sip. It was almost empty, with only a sliver of ice melting in the bottom. Flustered, she missed her mouth and the liquid dribbled down her chin and onto her T-shirt.

'You sure you need another?'

Daisy looked up into a pair of piercing blue eyes. Oh, for God's sake. It was George, the pasty-eating man from the bakery. His immaculate grey suit was a far cry from the workmanlike jeans and safety waist-coat he'd been wearing the last time she saw him.

'I'm SO sorry. I was trying to order a drink and somehow—'

'Well, you got one. Two gin and tonics, was I right?' He put down two glasses on the table. Miranda had perked up considerably. Daisy could feel her sister's Potentially Available Man radar sweeping across the table.

'Daisy, you're a dark horse.' Miranda moved her chair sideways, making space. 'Will you join us? It's the least you can do as my sister has conned you into getting us a drink.'

'Daisy.' Ignoring Miranda, he looked straight into Daisy's eyes, extending a hand in greeting. He didn't sit down. 'Very nice to meet you, Daisy.' He repeated her name gently, holding her gaze. His eyes were pretty impossible to ignore.

She gave herself a sort of inward shake, remembering the drink slopped down her top. She put a protective hand to her chest, straightening up.

'I'm so sorry,' she repeated, hearing herself becoming clipped and formal. 'Let me give you the money for the drinks, at least.' She reached down into her handbag.

'Not at all.' He shook his head, stepping back. 'Consider it a welcome to Steeple St John drink. You can get me one back sometime.'

He headed back towards the bar. Relieved, Daisy watched him walking away. She'd managed not to make a *complete* idiot of herself.

'I'll do that,' she called, slightly too late.

'I'm sure you will.' The confident reply, with an

expression which caused a sensation in her stomach she'd long forgotten, reached her loud and clear.

Miranda leaned across the table, clapping her hands together in a teacher-like gesture.

'So, Mrs No Men Ever Again, what happened to the vow of chastity? D'you want to explain yourself?' She took a mouthful of gin and looked at Daisy.

'I – well, I was trying to sort us out with a drink. You need to give me some tips.'

'Tips? Downright gorgeous Irishmen are bringing you gin and tonics when you catch their eyes across a crowded bar, and you want me to give you tips?'

Objectively speaking, he *was* quite handsome, thought Daisy, taking a surreptitious look across the bar towards him.

'We haven't met as such. It's just this place – I keep bumping into people when I'm out and about.'

Miranda looked out of the window at Main Street, where a stream of traffic was passing by. Daisy followed her gaze.

'That's not surprising in a place this size. The odds of finding a good-looking bloke out here in the sticks are pretty slim – everyone here's either married or past it. I reckon you're onto something there. Grab it.'

'I'm *not* interested.' Daisy stood up to go to the loo, banging her head on an artfully placed metal milk churn as she did so.

Washing her hands with the expensive soap, then staring vaguely into the mirror as she applied the equally luxurious hand cream, she let herself think for a moment about the mysterious Irishman. He was definitely handsome. Miranda thought he was a catch – maybe she had a point.

Chapter Six

'Pass us those secateurs, Daisy.'

Thomas was balancing slightly precariously on a stepladder, head and shoulders inside the skeletal framework of a clematis. Holding on with one hand, Daisy reached down into the long grass where the secateurs lay.

Armed with the pages of his old planting notes, Thomas and Daisy had set about the garden together. She'd woken to a surprisingly cold April morning, the long grass around the trees of the orchard flopping over as if weighed down with the burden of dew. The sun was shining now, and the overgrown lawn was slippery. She put a foot on the bottom rung of the ladder, holding it steady as Thomas chopped away. He'd refused to have any part of Daisy climbing up and doing it herself.

'Reckon once we clear off the worst of that dead sticky willow, you'll find these borders aren't as bad as you think.' From his vantage point, Thomas was scanning the garden.

'Hope so,' said Daisy, anxiously. She was more concerned with getting her elderly friend down to ground
level. The next stage of their plans could be organized
much more comfortably whilst sitting on the old wood-
en bench on the little terrace. Even with her couple of
days a week working on Elaine's garden, and the writing she was doing by night, gathering together information for a series on her website, they were making
good progress, but Thomas was surprisingly stubborn
and prone to forgetting his age.

'There we are.' Thomas threw down a couple of dry,
twiggy armfuls. 'That'll be much better come July
when it flowers. Little and often, that's what these
gardens need.'

He clambered down from the top of the ladder,
pausing for a moment to look up at his handiwork.
Daisy took tremendous pleasure in seeing the garden
beginning to take shape. She could never be happy in
an office, shoving pieces of paper around and never
seeing an end result. The few years she'd spent pushing paper had been utterly depressing. Thank God
she'd taken a risk and thrown herself into retraining.
Even with everything that'd brought, she thought –
realizing as she did that the memories were becoming
less vivid and painful.

The garden at Orchard Villa had been ignored by
her parents, and by the previous owners. But having
been carefully planted by Thomas all those years ago,
a lot of the borders had taken care of themselves, and

the job was proving less terrifying than Daisy had anticipated. She was cataloguing all the plants, taking photographs of their progress, and had managed to carefully scan Thomas's beautiful notes and save the images on her laptop. It had the makings of an interesting article – maybe she ought to be keeping a record of it on a blog, like Elaine?

'You pop the kettle on, dear, and I'll have a go at clearing this long border here.' Thomas handed back the mug he'd emptied earlier, easing out the stiffness in his back with an alarming crack. 'Not much fun, this ageing lark, Daisy. I don't recommend it.'

Daisy watched Thomas out of the kitchen window as she waited for the kettle to boil. His long years of experience showed in the methodical way his hands wove through the winter-dried foliage, quickly gathering a wheelbarrow-load of leafy detritus for the compost bin. He'd known and loved that garden – and so many others in Steeple St John – all his adult life. He was part of the fabric of the village.

'Tea break.' She passed him a steaming mug. Thomas wrapped his hands around it gratefully.

'I haven't felt so useful in years, Daisy. We're making a real difference today.'

'I couldn't have done this without you. I really appreciate it.' She felt a wave of affection for her new friend. If someone had told her that the first new friendship she'd make in her new life would be with an OAP, she'd have laughed her head off.

'So what's your future plan, young lady? You can't stay round these parts forever – you should be off adventuring with folks your own age.'

Daisy gave a sigh.

'I was supposed to be working alongside my boyfriend when I finished college. We had a place lined up in France, working on a historic garden renovation project in a little village in La Charente Maritime.'

Thomas put his cup down. He looked at her steadily.

'Supposed to be?'

She took a deep breath. Since she'd arrived in the village she'd been closing it out, refusing to talk about what had happened in any detail, first with her parents, and then when Miranda tried gently to ask why she'd arrived, late at night, her little car stuffed full of boxes, clothes hanging out of hastily packed suitcases.

She began carefully. 'We had our bags all packed. Me, my best friend Sylvia, and Jamie. We were the only mature students on our college course and we got on straight away. We shared a house with a couple of other students. It was lovely.'

She thought back, remembering the nights they'd sat up, filthy and exhausted after long days doing practical work, watching television, drinking wine, and chatting. 'We were all set.' She took a moment to sip her tea, shuddering as she continued. 'And then I walked in on the two of them. They were –'

'Say no more.' Thomas put a hand on Daisy's arm. 'I'm sorry, my dear. You deserve better.'

His hands were dusty, the knuckles ingrained with dirt from a morning in the garden. She felt another wave of affection for him.

'I'm an idiot.' She felt her voice waver for a second, and swallowed hard. 'I trusted him, and Sylvia was my friend. *Good old Daisy* . . . too bloody thick to see what was going on right under my nose.'

'You can't blame yourself for the way they behaved, Daisy.' Thomas shook his head.

'Anyway.' Her voice was a little bit too sharp, but it felt surprisingly good to have finally got it out in the open. *Maybe* this was the start of getting over it. She'd been so tired the last few nights, she'd been falling asleep without lying staring at the ceiling, the picture of those last moments running over and over like a film reel.

'So that was that. As my stuff was packed, I just threw it all in the car and drove until I hit Steeple St John. Dad and Mum were going travelling, but they said I could stay in the house.'

They'd been alarmed, of course.

Daisy remembered her mum's surprised expression. This sort of drama was Miranda's forte – she'd always been the one allowed free rein on her behavior, and she'd had plenty of scrapes before she settled down to city life. Daisy had always been pigeonholed as the easy-going sister – she'd had to be. Left to her own devices in childhood whilst Miranda spent a couple of years in and out of hospital being treated for leukaemia, she'd found her solace in the garden. She was too young, really, to understand what was going on – all she picked up on was the atmosphere of anxiety, and hushed voices, though she'd try to eavesdrop in the upstairs hall, lying on her stomach with her ear to the floor, carpet dust in her nostrils. Growing up, Miranda had been fussed over – Daisy had understood why, and loved her sister so much that she didn't resent it – but she'd always been the easy one, until now.

But there she was, reliable old Daisy, tear-streaked and humiliated, everything she owned in the back of a beaten-up old Vauxhall, homeless, jobless, and utterly distraught.

'I said to you I thought that Jamie was a bit cocky,' she overheard her mother muttering as she poured a hefty measure of brandy into a glass.

'She needs a bit of time to lick her wounds, that's all,' her dad's voice rumbled through from the kitchen. 'She can stay here while we're in India. You know I think Polly's too old to be staying with a strange sitter, in any case.'

As if hearing her name, Polly looked up at Daisy, her eyebrows furrowed. Daisy reached down and stroked the soft fur of her ears. Enjoying the attention, the dog laid her head in Daisy's lap.

Her mother had never been much good at

whispering quietly. Her voice carried from the hall. 'I'm not sure about leaving Daisy here looking after the house and heading off on our trip.'

'Maria, honestly. She'll hear you.'

'Oh David – I don't mean to be unkind. I just want everything settled – and that includes Daisy.'

Daisy hid her face in her hands, feeling a wave of nausea passing over her. The rejection, the humiliation – she felt like she was going to throw up.

They sat down on either side of her, her mum passing over the glass.

'Drink this. You'll feel better, I promise.'

Brisk and not cosily maternal, her mother's expression suggested she was just as concerned as her dad, but in her own way. She reached out, patting Daisy on the knee.

'You're welcome to stay here, darling, while we're away. You can have a go at getting this garden back into shape, if you like.' She brightened at this as she spoke. 'It's always good to get your teeth into something when you're feeling a bit blue. A project will do you good.'

Numbly, she'd agreed, allowing herself to be shipped up to bed like a child, obediently taking a towel and some overnight things. Her dad had brought her up a mug of cocoa.

'Just like I used to do when we were back home in Oxford,' he smiled.

She'd lain there all night, face aching with all the

tears she'd shed. Jamie had been so funny, and vibrant, and charming, and such a lying *snake*. What was she going to do without him?

Having shared the tale, Daisy sat back, chin in her hand, with a sigh.

"We might think we're looking after our garden, but of course it's the garden that is looking after us', said Thomas, with a kind look. 'I'm not going to say any such nonsense about being young, or there being plenty more fish in the sea, or any of that. But time – and a spot of gardening – heal most things, I've found.' He placed his mug down on the table.

'Now let's get back to it.'

Chapter Seven

Daisy heard Elaine's laughter as she headed through the stone archway of the Grey Mare. After a long day in the garden, she was really looking forward to a drink and some food – and despite her previous misgivings, to a chat with Elaine and Jo. It was fun working alongside Thomas, but she was beginning to crave company in the evenings. It was a good sign, she recognized – she must be getting back to some kind of normality.

'There you are. We've ordered some Pimm's.' Looking up with a smile, Jo reached across the table, taking the waiting glass from the enamelled metal tray. She tipped in the jewel-red mixture with a splash of ice and fruit, handing it to Daisy as she collapsed into the wooden chair.

'I needed this.' Daisy took a mouthful, closing her eyes blissfully.

'Long day?'

'I got up at six. I'm trying to get as much done as I can before the Open Gardens.'

The cottage two doors along from Orchard Villa was one of the stars of the show, it turned out, and Daisy realized that in its current state, her house was going to be seriously letting the side down. With Thomas's help and a lot of long days, they'd made a real difference. The hedges were neatly trimmed, the rose arch over the gate showing the first signs of flower buds.

'And she's done wonders in my place,' said Elaine. 'She's a bit of a hit with my readers, too.' She gave Daisy a smile. It had been a real thrill to see her first blog article go live on Elaine's site, and she'd found herself hooked on refreshing the page, watching as readers from all over the world commented on her words and Elaine's beautiful, artistic photography.

'I could do with someone to come round to mine to have a go at the back garden,' Jo said, thoughtfully. 'I've been trying to bribe Martha to cut the grass, but it's pretty fruitless trying to get a fourteen-year-old to do anything she doesn't want to.'

Remembering their own teenage years, they all laughed.

'I'll nip in and get a menu, shall I?' Daisy scanned the tables nearby, but there were none to be seen. She was ravenous, and the smells wafting out from the pub kitchen window were making her stomach growl.

'The burgers here are to die for – have you tried them?' Jo gave a groan of anticipation.

Daisy, who'd already sampled the magic that was a

simple bucket of chips, could well believe it. Her stomach gave another warning rumble. 'Back in a sec.'

As ever, there was a group of commuters propped up against the bar, suits on, having a quick drink on the way home. Daisy slipped in amongst them, reaching for one of the hand-written menus, which stood on the counter. As she turned, she felt a hand on her shoulder.

'Daisy, hi.' It was Thomas's vet friend from the other day. He was standing waiting to be served. The woman behind the bar passed him over a velvet-black pint of Guinness, condensation streaming down the side of the glass.

He raised it towards her with a look of relief, and took a long drink.

'Ned.' She smiled in recognition.

'Sorry.' He indicated the glass, wiping a moustache of foam from his upper lip. 'Been a long day. Well, to be honest, they're all long days. I'm bloody knackered.'

Daisy returned his smile.

'Can I get you a drink? Are you—'

'Oh – no, I'm here with friends. Just outside.' She waved in the direction of the beer garden.

'Of course.' He shook his head slightly, a baffled expression on his face. 'Village life. I forget everyone knows everyone around here.'

'Not me,' said Daisy, simply. 'I hardly know a soul.

This is the second night out I've had since I've been here.'

Ned rubbed his stubbled chin, absent-mindedly. Unlike their first meeting, he wasn't covered in straw, but Daisy noticed there was a hole in the sleeve of his jumper, and the cuff had a piece of yarn hanging loose. He looked like he needed a long sleep, and a good meal. His green eyes were underset with dark shadows. Daisy was half-tempted to invite him round for lunch one day, look after him a bit.

'That makes me feel a bit better. It's been nothing but work for me. By the time I get to bed I'm asleep in seconds. Whoever thought being a vet was glamorous?'

'Well, that's what happens when you've got to keep the boss happy, I guess.' Daisy pulled a sympathetic face. 'I'd better get this menu back, the girls will wonder where I've got to.'

'Course, yes. Sorry. Sorry. Off you go.' Ned took another mouthful of his beer. 'Maybe see you at the next meeting? Doesn't look like we've got much chance of getting out of it, even if we did beat a hasty retreat last time.'

Daisy nodded, turning away with a smile. Much as she didn't want to get caught up in Parish Council business, she didn't want to let Thomas down. At least with Ned there, there'd be at least two of them below retirement age.

'I'll see you there.'

'Look forward to it. Well, that's not strictly true,' said Ned with a rueful smile. 'But – oh, you know what I mean.' He raised his eyebrows over his pint glass.

Daisy laughed. 'I do. See you soon, Ned.'

'Did you get lost?' Elaine and Jo were both looking perplexed as she returned, menu in hand.

'I got chatting, sorry.' She spread the menu out on the table.

Jo leaned forward, tucking her long blonde hair behind her ears thoughtfully.

'I don't know why I bother looking,' she said, sitting back again. 'I have the same thing every time.'

Daisy, who was ravenous, would have happily ordered and eaten one of everything, but settled on a chilli burger with a side serving of fries. Elaine chose a salad.

Waiting for the food to arrive, relaxing in the last of the sunshine, they sat chatting, getting to know each other a little better.

'So what made you decide to train as a counsellor, Jo?' Elaine sat back in her chair, flipping a beermat back and forth.

'I sort of fell into it, really. When Martha went to preschool, I wanted to do something – I was going mad stuck at home, and having come straight out of university into antenatal classes, I hadn't had much of a chance to make friends. We were living in Slough, near my parents.' Jo gazed skywards, remembering.

'Oh, so you haven't always been in the village?'

Daisy held her glass up to the light, absent-mindedly swirling the ice back and forth. Impatient for dinner, she'd already picked out the strawberry and cucumber and eaten it.

Jo shook her head. 'No, we moved here a few years back before Martha started secondary school. Our catchment school was enormous and pretty terrifying, and we'd spent summers here in the village when I was a child. My great-uncle had a cottage on the other side of the railway.'

Elaine put down her glass, looking pleased. 'Oh, how funny – I did just the same. We spent every summer here with my grandparents. Our paths probably crossed as children.'

'So go on,' said Daisy, who wanted to hear the rest.

'Oh yes.' Jo slid the jug across the table towards Elaine, who tipped the remains into their glasses. 'So I ended up volunteering as a Samaritan, and it snowballed from there. I took a couple of part-time courses, and one thing led to another. I qualified a few years back.'

'And you work at Elaine's husband's school?'

'Brockville are very hot on pastoral care.' Elaine repeated her comment from their previous meeting, as if she'd read the prospectus. 'When Leo took over as head eighteen months ago, they'd just taken Jo on.'

'I do a couple of mornings there a month. Mainly group work with some of the kids.'

Daisy had discovered Brockville while out walking

Polly. A huge, rambling Victorian building, it had been a private school for many years. Parents from all over the county trundled down the little lane and through its wrought-iron gates every morning, children bundled into the back of glossy Range Rovers and expensive convertibles. It was a far cry from Daisy's colourful concrete primary school back home in Oxford.

The food arrived just then, the young waitress setting down the plates with a cheerful smile.

'So you must be pretty sorted, then, being a counsellor?'

Jo gave a snort of laughter. 'You'd think, wouldn't you. Unfortunately self-development's a bit of an ongoing process.'

Elaine shook her head, swallowing a mouthful of salad before she spoke. 'It's absolutely not for me,' she said with a shudder. 'I like my skeletons well and truly locked up in their cupboards.'

'Funny you should say that.' Jo put down her fork, resting her chin in her hands.

'Go on,' said Daisy, leaning forward with interest.

'I've been doing some reflective work recently – we go over our practice with supervisors, talk about how we could have done better, things like that . . . and there's a pretty big thing standing in my way.' She cast her eyes down, taking a breath, and helping herself to the drink that had just appeared on the table.

Jo's voice was low. Daisy and Elaine leaned in,

listening intently. Jo took another sip of her drink and continued.

'All the way through university I had a really close-knit group of friends. One of them, though, was my best friend – Tom Fox. We did all the same courses, spent all our time together.' She sighed. 'We had a massive falling-out the day after graduation, and we haven't spoken since then.'

'What's to stop you getting in touch? He's probably on Facebook, isn't he? Have you looked him up?' Elaine reached for her handbag, ready to pull out her phone.

'I don't – no, don't look.' Jo's pale face looked panicked suddenly. 'Martha was born not long after I graduated from university. Nine months, to be precise.'

Daisy looked at Jo, frowning. 'So she's –'

'Yes.'

'And you've never told him?' Daisy realized she'd blurted it out, but – 'What on earth did you fall out about?'

'Oh, God.' Jo shook her head again. 'Graduation night. We all got drunk, crashed at a friend's place. After four years of being just good friends we ended up in bed together. Next morning I woke up and told him it was a mistake.'

'And don't tell me,' said Daisy sagely, feeling like an expert on men. 'His pride was wounded.'

'Completely. He and I had always fought like brother and sister because we were so similar. And I was as stubborn as he was. So we headed back home – me to Slough, him to Manchester, and we just didn't speak again.'

'And Martha?' Daisy speared a tomato.

'I didn't realize I was pregnant. Thought my periods were just a bit erratic and by the time I twigged, I was almost five months gone. Picking up the phone to Tom seemed impossibly hard then, so I just . . . left it.' Jo twisted her hair up in a knot, her brow furrowed at the memory. 'Life got in the way. Next thing I know, I've got a fourteen-year-old who wants to know why she doesn't have a dad named on her birth certificate, and I'm wondering how to reconcile myself with being a counsellor who's living a lie.'

Daisy reached across, squeezing Jo's hand. She wasn't the only one who needed this friendship, it seemed. Jo caught her eye in thanks.

'You poor thing. What a burden,' said Elaine.

'Talking about it's only the first step.' Jo picked at her burger, which had lain untouched while she'd spoken. 'I really need to bite the bullet at some point and get in touch.'

'Well, that bit's easily remedied. That's what Google's for,' said Elaine, reaching again for her phone.

'Oh, I know where he is – or at least I've half an idea. He's quite a well-known poet. I saw one of his poems in a newspaper review recently – it was all about lost friendship and half-forgotten memories . . .' Jo looked away, flushing slightly.

'Oh.' Daisy felt a wave of empathy for Jo.

'Yes. And I – this might sound a bit silly, but I thought for a moment it might have been about me.' She took another large mouthful of her drink, looking into space, lost in thought.

Elaine was tapping rapidly on the screen of her phone, brow furrowed in concentration. 'Tom – Fox, you said?'

'Yes.' Jo looked half terrified, half relieved that Elaine had taken it out of her hands. She sat back, releasing the twist of hair from her hand so it fell down over her shoulders in a curtain of pale white-gold.

'Nothing on Facebook – but then he's a poet, that's not really his market,' said Elaine, expertly. 'Hang on, I'll check Twitter, all the writers waste time on there . . . aha. What d'you think?' Elaine slid the phone across the table.

Jo didn't move for a second. Daisy leaned in to look at the tiny square profile photograph. He appeared to be crouching in the picture, one dark curl flopping forward over his eyes, battered jeans and a grey shirt on – she peered more closely – and stroking a cat. It all looked very artistic.

'Amsterdam,' read Daisy. 'Very poet-ish sort of place to live.'

Jo plucked up courage and reached across, picking up the phone cautiously.

'Oh!'

Daisy gave her knee a little squeeze of reassurance. 'What d'you think?'

'He hasn't changed a bit. Oh God.' Unconsciously she ran a hand through her hair, wrinkling her forehead. 'And somehow I look every day of thirty-five. I bet he's got a glamorous Dutch girlfriend called Mariette or something.'

'You do not look anywhere *near* thirty-five,' said Elaine, firmly, taking the phone back and tapping something in the search bar. She frowned at the screen for a moment, lips pursed in concentration, scrolling downwards.

'Nope,' she concluded, putting the phone down on the table so they could see another photo with a paragraph of text underneath. 'Single, according to an interview he's done on this poetry blog. And –' she looked at Jo with a reassuring smile, 'no children.'

'Well, none that he knows of.' Jo exhaled, closing her eyes. 'That's something, I guess. Because God knows what's going to happen when I open up this whole can of worms.'

She'd almost finished her drink and reached for the jug, absent-mindedly, an expression of surprise flitting across her face as she registered it was completely empty.

'It's not going to be easy,' said Elaine. She looked across, seeing the waitress bringing out a tray of food to the table nearby. Pointing at the jug, she mouthed a request for another before turning her attention back to Jo, who sat clutching her empty glass.

'That's an understatement.' Jo gave a wry smile.

'But you're doing the right thing. Martha's old enough now to deal with it, and hopefully to understand a bit about why you didn't tell her before.'

Daisy had been trying to imagine how it'd feel to deal with something that size at fourteen. She'd been convinced that she was old enough to be treated as an adult back then. Now she was twice that age, she still didn't have a clue how to behave.

'I think I've got a good idea how she'll react,' said Jo, with a grim expression. 'Explosions, huge teenage angst, and no doubt it'll all be my fault.' She raised an eyebrow.

'But you have to hold onto the fact that you did the best you could at the time,' said Elaine, reaching across to squeeze Jo's knee in comfort. 'That's all we can ever do.'

Jo bit her lip thoughtfully, looking at Elaine with a curious expression.

'You sound like you know what you're talking about.'

Elaine shook her head, a half-smile playing on her lips. 'Skeletons in cupboards, darling, remember. I keep mine locked away neatly. Ah, lovely.'

The waitress reappeared, bearing a full jug of Pimm's, breaking into their conversation. Just at the right moment, Daisy thought. Whatever mysteries lay behind Elaine's perfect facade were staying well and truly hidden, and that was clearly just how she liked it.

'Cheers,' said Jo, topping up their glasses. 'I really appreciate you two being here for me.'

'That's what friends are for.' Daisy smiled back at her, realizing as she said it that there was real feeling behind the clichéd phrase.

'And when Martha hits meltdown point, you can come and let off steam to us. I remember being pretty hideous as a teenager – but my sister Miranda was a million times worse.'

Jo looked thoughtful. 'I'm not sure Martha's really going to explode. I'm more worried she's going to be really hurt – we've been so close, always. And this feels like – no, it is – a massive betrayal of her trust.'

'Well, we'll hold your hand.' Daisy looked at her steadily.

'We will,' agreed Elaine, pushing her plate away, her meal half-eaten. 'You know, sometimes it's easier to share things with people who don't know anything about your past.'

Daisy nodded with feeling. She'd only been in the village what felt like five minutes and somehow, already, she felt more rooted here than she had in her time at agricultural college. No point thinking about the fact it wasn't going to last.

'I'm very grateful for you two girls,' Elaine continued. 'It's not easy making friends in a place like this, and it's not easy to stand up and admit you're lonely and you don't know a soul.'

'I think,' Jo put down her fork again for a moment, 'it's a lot more common than we realize. Places like Steeple St John – people move in thinking they're going to have the perfect village life. It doesn't always work out quite like that, does it?'

Elaine shook her head with feeling as Daisy began to speak.

'The only person I've spoken to other than you two is Thomas, my gardening friend, who's eighty-four. My social life isn't exactly sparkling.' Oh, and Ned, the scruffy vet – she'd forgotten him.

Jo nodded agreement. 'It's hard when your children are older and you're working. If I'm honest, Elaine, I wasn't sure I wanted to come the other week, but I'm glad I did.'

'Thanks for that,' said Elaine, joking. 'I'm awfully glad you did. Leo's never around. And he doesn't seem that keen on having me around at school functions, either.' She gave a small sigh.

'So how about you, Daisy? Any skeletons in the cupboard you want to share with us to make me feel better for hogging the conversation?' Jo's eyes sparkled with laughter, her tongue loosened by the Pimm's.

'No skeletons,' said Daisy. 'Just one shitty ex and a very much ex-best friend. But they're in the past.' As she spoke she realized it was true. Thomas's theory about gardening being therapy really worked –

somewhere along the way the searing pain of the wound had stopped aching, and now all she was left with was a scar. One she'd always carry, and definitely one which would leave her a bit cautious in the future. But it felt good to realize Jamie didn't have any hold over her heart any more.

'That sounds pretty healthy,' said Jo. She stood up. 'All that Pimm's. Must run to the loo.'

Daisy grabbed her moment to ask Elaine's advice. 'I've been thinking – d'you think I should start keeping a diary of my progress on the garden? Maybe some kind of blog?'

It would be something else to put on her gardening résumé, too – with her parents gone for six months, she could follow the garden through the season. It might even make an article for a magazine, if she did a decent job of it.

'Oh yes, wonderful idea!' Elaine pulled out her phone again. 'Yes, definitely. People love that sort of thing. And it'd be so lovely for you to keep, too, as a record.'

Daisy had been keeping notes and taking photos as she went along. Leafing through Thomas's old notebooks the other day, she'd realized it'd make the sort of thing she'd love to read.

'I might need a bit of help.' She was feeling inspired now, realizing that the garden was once again giving her something to look forward to and a purpose. And she had friends, too. A whole life was beginning to unfurl.

'Not a problem at all. Once you've done your bit in the garden at mine tomorrow, let's have a coffee and I'll show you how to get started. It's *so* simple. I just *love* the idea.'

Locking the big wooden door, Daisy kicked the battered snake draught excluder back into place. She'd made it back in her first year of secondary school in sewing class, and it was still in one piece, almost. The only thing she'd ever sewn, she was inordinately proud of it and it reminded her of home.

Polly glanced up from her bed, half-opening an eye. She didn't seem to want to raise her aged bones out of sleep and parade into the garden for a late-night pee, clambering to all fours with a groan as Daisy watched, waiting patiently. Daisy was in a good mood. The evening had been lots of fun in the end. She could feel the friendships growing, tiny little shoots reaching out. It was just like bringing on spring seedlings – it took time and nurturing, she thought, but it was worth taking it slowly and carefully.

Opening the kitchen door, Daisy heard Polly growling, an almost unheard-of event.

'You all right, darling?' Polly was standing quite still, her hackles raised, old teeth bared in warning.

At the top of the garden, frozen in the moonlight, stood a fox. One paw was raised in the air and for a second the three of them stood there, caught in time, sizing each other up. With a sigh, Polly seemed to recall she was no match for a young vixen, and at the same moment the fox skipped gracefully out of sight.

The walk home from the pub down Main Street had been chilly, the clear sky providing no warming cloud cover. There could still be a late frost, and if there was it was going to play havoc with the magnolia, which had been warmed into early flowering by the unexpected sunshine of the last couple of weeks. Crossing her fingers that it wouldn't get any colder, Daisy grabbed her book. Maybe a couple of chapters before she fell asleep . . .

The phone was ringing for ages before Daisy realized it wasn't in her dream. She reached out, finding her mobile first, throwing it to one side as she realized the sound was coming from the home phone on the other side of the big bedroom. It was still pitch dark outside.

'Hello?'

'Darling! Did we wake you? David, what time is it at home now?'

'Mum.' Daisy, prising her eyes fully open, looked at the alarm clock on the bedside table. 'It's half past three in the morning.'

'Oh.' There was another pause, and the muffled sounds of her mother clearly explaining, hand over the mouthpiece, 'David, it's the middle of the night, not breakfast time at all. It's half past three.'

'Mum? I'd quite like to get back to sleep.'

'Sorry, darling. Oh well, you're up now.'

Daisy gritted her teeth. This was pretty typical of her parents. Both academics, they were that curious mixture of frighteningly bright and incredibly scatter-brained. Well meaning, but a bit unthinking.

'I am, yes.'

'Right. Well. The thing is, darling, that we're having a wonderful time.'

'I'm really happy for you, Mum,' said Daisy, hopping from foot to foot in the chill air. Across the floor, a cosy bed with a duvet and a warm patchwork quilt was calling her name.

'We've fallen in love with the East. Absolutely besotted. It's heaven here.'

'Great.' Daisy muffled a huge yawn.

'We're thinking we might extend our visit by a few months.'

Oh, now *this* was good news. With her parents off travelling for a bit longer, she'd have time to really make a difference to the garden. She'd probably be even more excited about it if it wasn't the middle of the blooming night.

'That's great. I'm really pleased. Amazing news!' Her voice was hearty. Please, please let me go back to sleep, she thought.

'Really?' Her mother's voice echoed down the line. 'Are you sure you're all right with that, darling?'

'Yes, yes, definitely. Really more than all right.'
'Well, that *is* a pleasant surprise.'
'G'night, Mum. Love to Dad.'

Chapter Eight

The Steeple St John village hall had been built with a millennium grant in 2000, and so was far from the usual dilapidated brick building with wonky loos and freezing cold linoleum floors. When government cuts had seen the town's library closed in favour of one central library an unhelpful seven miles away, the people of the town had gathered together to create their own community-based library, run by volunteers and headed up by Flora Douglas – retired head teacher and, as Thomas had explained previously, stalwart of every committee in the village. Her library was open three days a week, and the hall was packed from morning until night with Pilates groups, meditation classes, baby yoga, and countless educational after-school classes for the over-scheduled children of the village.

Flora was at the helm of the Parish Council meeting today, hair an immovable, immaculate helmet of ash grey, a pink silk scarf tied around her neck, setting off her pale skin and blue eyes beautifully. She stood up from her central position at the front table. Daisy had slipped into the back row of seats, running late. There was a moment of chatter before Flora clapped her hands together. She swept the room with an expert glance and the room fell silent. There was no mistaking her history as a head teacher. Daisy felt herself sitting up straight and putting her knees together, primly.

'Ladies and gentlemen: I'm going to make this a quick one, because I don't want to overrun when we've got Mindfulness for the Absent-Minded at half past, and we need to get the mats out. But I thought I'd update.'

Daisy rummaged in her bag, realizing she'd better turn her phone off. Looking up, she saw Ned sitting at the opposite side of the room, arms folded across his chest, legs sprawling out into the aisle. He turned, sensing her, and gave her a broad wink.

'And that's the trouble, you see.' Flora was finishing up. Her brief update had taken twenty-five minutes so far. 'If you don't have any village connections, you aren't going to feel a sense of responsibility for what happens if you sell up and bugger off.'

There was a murmur of agreement. Daisy, who'd drifted off and had been thinking about the detective thriller she'd been watching last night, shook herself back to the present moment.

'And unless anyone has any further questions, that will be all.' Flora's voice carried across the sound of people who were already preparing to head out of the room.

There was a scuffle of feet and a screeching of chairs on the wooden floor as everyone headed for the exit.

'You're for it now,' said a low voice in her ear. Daisy looked up.

Ned stood beside her, an amused expression on his face.

'What d'you mean? Oh God, let me guess. She can tell when you're not paying attention, right? I had a teacher like that. Used to spend every lunchtime in detention when I was in fourth form.'

'You weren't paying attention? I'm shocked,' teased Ned. 'You missed the really exciting bit about the painting of the new double yellow lines. They've waited seven years for them, y'know.'

'I heard that bit.' He did make her laugh.

'I was meaning . . . watch out at six o'clock.' He nodded very discreetly towards the front of the room. Flora was approaching at speed, followed by Thomas.

'Ah, Thomas said we were getting some more young blood. Daisy, isn't it? And you're new to the village?'

'I am, yes.' Daisy felt slightly uneasy. Flora was wielding a clipboard and a purposeful expression.

'Daisy's living at Orchard Villa,' Thomas explained. 'We've been doing a spot of work on the garden.'

'Not before time,' said Flora, in a slightly school-marmish tone. She pursed her lips.

Daisy shuffled her feet, awkwardly. Every time someone passed comment on the previous state of the garden, she felt a bit guilty, as if *she*, and not her scatty parents, had been the one to ignore it until it reached a level of overgrowth reminiscent of Sleeping Beauty's castle.

'It's very good to see you here, in any case. And you're a gardener?'

'She's a very good one,' said Thomas, with a hint of pride. 'Not often I've seen one who has the practical skills *and* the theoretical knowledge. She's like an encyclopaedia when it comes to Latin names, is Daisy.'

Ned gave a low whistle of admiration, laughing. 'I know who to pick for my team if I'm entering the pub quiz, then.'

'You'll be an asset to our horticultural committee, then. Next meeting's Friday week. Do say you'll come along and give us a hand?'

Daisy's vague protestations that she didn't know how long she'd be in the village carried no weight with Flora.

'Many hands make light work, my dear.'

And so, somehow (wondering afterwards quite how it had happened, and deciding that Britain was probably held together by people who'd fallen into things, too polite to say no) she found herself obediently writing down her mobile number and email address.

Walking back towards Main Street, where Ned had

left his beaten-up old Volvo, Daisy couldn't work out quite how she'd been bounced into it. 'It was a bit like school. She might as well have said "See me after class, young lady" – she reminded me of my old head-mistress.'

'Well, you've signed your life away now.' Ned gave her a sideways look. 'All I did was pop in too, remember. "Tick the box," we said. "Get involved in the community," we said. And now look what's happened. We've been assimilated by the Flora-Borg.'

'It's a hard life,' Daisy teased.

'You have no idea, Daise. No idea at all.' Swinging into the front seat of his mud-splashed car, he raised a hand in a farewell salute. 'See ya.'

She watched him pull away, laughing.

'Daisy!'

She was heading back towards Orchard Villa for something to eat when she heard Elaine calling and crossed the road, meeting her outside the gift shop.

'I'm going for a coffee at the Bluebell. Are you busy? Fancy joining me?'

Daisy realized she'd kill for some of that lemon drizzle cake right now. 'Yes, please.'

They passed the little market square, where a woman in jodhpurs and long brown leather boots was dragging a sack of carrots towards the open door of her Land Rover, which was parked half on, half off the pavement.

'Hang on, darlin'. Let me give you a hand with that.'

The fruit and veg stallholder appeared from behind the canvas hoarding. He wiped down his hands on his apron, grabbed the heavy sack and tossed it onto his shoulder as if it was weightless. 'How many d'you want?' He looked up, catching Daisy's eye with a nod of recognition. 'Nicer weather today, hey?'

He slid the sack into the boot of the woman's car, closing the boot for her, before turning back to focus his full attention on them both.

'No photos today?' He raised an eyebrow at Elaine, flashing her a cheeky smile as he slipped back behind the stall. 'I've got the place looking perfect for you, polished my plums and everything.' He indicated the beautifully laid-out display, selected a scarlet apple and tossed it across to Elaine, who caught it neatly, one eyebrow flashing upwards in triumph.

'I'll inspect them later, if you're lucky.' Elaine turned on her heel in a swirl of hair and expensive perfume. Daisy stood for a second, half laughing, half amazed.

'I'll look forward to it.'

They headed down towards the Bluebell Cafe.

'You've got a bit of an admirer there, haven't you?' Daisy looked at Elaine.

'Oh God, no,' said Elaine, shaking her head. A blush stained her cheeks, contradicting her words. 'Mark's just a bit of a flirt, that's all.'

Daisy raised an eyebrow, laughing. 'First-name terms?'

'I quite often take photos for my website on market day. American readers love that whole quaint English village thing. Mark's very sweet really, chats away while I take photographs, that's all.' They stepped into the cafe, breathing in the vanilla-bean and coffee scent.

'Mmm, heaven.' Elaine changed the subject. 'What d'you fancy?'

She sat down, loosening the belt on her navy mac. Today's outfit had a French influence – her hair knotted in a loose chignon, a few artful strands escaping. At her neck she wore a jauntily knotted red and white silk scarf. Her long legs were encased in cream cigarette pants which showed off her slender ankles. Daisy glanced from Elaine's perfect outfit to her own. She'd pulled on her favourite jeans and battered cowboy boots, aware she'd better make an effort for the Parish Council meeting. She still looked scruffy in comparison.

Daisy had sat absorbed in Elaine's online world for a good while the other night. The website depicted a beautifully drawn picture of English village life – and of her picturesque house, her delicious food, her carefully photographed craft projects, and her dry, archly funny tales of her eccentric headmaster husband (never referred to by name, only as My Dear Husband; but it wouldn't take a genius to work out where Elaine lived, nor where he worked – there wasn't much privacy these days). It all looked – and sounded – utterly blissful. Each article was followed by a string of enthusiastic comments, asking where she'd bought her furniture, rhapsodizing over Elaine's lovely home. Daisy had been shaken back to the real world by a call from Jo.

'Daisy, have you got a moment?'

'Course. What's up?'

Jo had explained in an anxious, quiet voice that she just needed a moment to run something past her. Daisy, glad of the chance to get out of the house, had grabbed her bag and headed up towards Jo's little cottage, taking a bottle of red just in case Jo's dilemma needed something stronger than a coffee.

It was a pale-faced Jo who opened the cottage door. Taking one look at her, Daisy raised the bottle with a sympathetic smile.

'Oh, yes, please.'

Jo fished a couple of wine glasses out of the dish-washer, motioning to Daisy to sit down on the battered, dusty green sofa which took up the back wall of the kitchen.

'Muuuuum,' came a voice from the hall, 'can I go round to Jessica's house to do my science project?'

Martha appeared in the kitchen, giving Daisy a sweet smile at odds with her frankly terrifying appearance. She was crammed into a too-small black T-shirt printed with closely written song lyrics which – Daisy squinted, making out several choice expletives – were fortunately pretty indecipherable.

She slid across the kitchen tiles, crashing into her mother's arms with a giggle.

'If I promise to be back by nine and I empty the dishwasher when I get back?'

'Make me a coffee tomorrow morning and you've got a deal, sweetheart,' said Jo, smiling over the top of her daughter's head. They hugged for a brief moment before Martha pulled back, giving her mum a kiss on the cheek and skipping off.

'Fourteen going on four, sometimes,' explained Jo, smiling after her fondly. 'She goes from ranting about feminism to snuggling up on the sofa with me watching old Disney movies.'

'Back at nine – promise!' The voice echoed through the hall, accompanied by the banging of the front door.

Jo sat down on the arm of the sofa, holding out the two glasses whilst Daisy tipped a generous slug of red into each one.

'So what's up?'

Jo closed her eyes, taking a mouthful of wine. She took a deep breath.

'It's Martha. She's been lovely all week.'

Daisy frowned. In her limited experience of teen-agers, parents were more often seen hitting the Merlot after a long week of fights over GCSE choices and unsuitable boyfriends. Jo was in a state of angst about her daughter being lovely?

'Thing is, I've been thinking a lot about what I was telling you and Elaine the other night.' Jo took another sip of her wine. 'Martha's my life. I adore her.'

'And she loves you to bits, too – you could see that tonight.' Daisy reached over, touching Jo's arm gently.

'But I've got no choice but to blow her life apart.' Jo slid down from the arm of the sofa, curling up beside Daisy. 'I can't keep this from her any longer, but when I do – what if she hates me, Daisy?'

A tear slid down her cheek. She rubbed it away before continuing. 'What if she wants to go and live with Tom in Amsterdam? What if she runs away? God, the stories I've heard of teenagers on the streets . . .'

'This is on your terms, remember,' said Daisy, hoping it sounded comforting. Jo was on a roll now, though. The scenarios she'd been imagining were tumbling out one by one.

'What if he's a complete shit to her? What if he tries to *steal* her?'

Daisy looked at Jo steadily. 'I can't see anyone doing anything to Martha that she doesn't agree to, can you?'

Jo gave a slightly damp smile. 'True. If she's one thing, it's bloody-minded.'

'And that's not a bad thing.' Daisy tipped another measure of wine into Jo's already empty glass. The reality was that it *was* a huge thing Jo was facing, but at least she wasn't alone.

Jo sighed before knocking back the contents of her glass. 'I have no idea what to do next,' she said. 'But the only thing certain is that I can't ignore the situation any longer. It's not good for Martha. Or me. Something has to change.'

Daisy had walked home late that evening under a bright moon, through the quiet streets of Steeple St John. Letting herself into Orchard Villa, she'd decided that if she had a choice, she'd choose Jo's cluttered, untidy little cottage – complete with dusty window-sills and flowers drooping, long past their sell-by date, in a vase of murky-looking water – over the brittle perfection of the Old Rectory.

'Afternoon tea for two?'

There was a tiered cake stand, the top layer piled with tiny, delicate cream-filled choux pastry buns, the next with still-warm scones, and the bottom with per-fectly presented sandwich triangles, each with its crusts cut off. A huge pot of tea and two china cups filled the remaining space on the tiny round table. The Bluebell was famous for its afternoon teas, and Daisy could see why. A sign on the wall announced proudly that the ham in the sandwiches was from local pigs, and the jam home-made from raspberries from their own allotment.

'Hang on a sec.' Elaine reached into her bag again, pulling out her camera just as Daisy, her mouth watering, was reaching for a ham sandwich. 'Would you mind? The light is perfect and this is gorgeous. It'll make a great shot.'

'I don't know how you have the patience. D'you take photos of your dinner every night?' Daisy snapped her hand back out of reach.

Frowning into the camera, Elaine took a moment to reply, her tone slightly arch. 'Would you like the honest answer, or would you like me to pretend that I don't?'

'If it's any consolation, it makes some sense to me,' Daisy said, consolingly. 'I've set my alarm for five in the morning to get the perfect set of photos of the garden. When I was writing up my dissertation, I spent a whole week getting up early to take a whole series of them with Jam—' She stopped herself, mid-sentence.

'The ex-boyfriend?'

Daisy poured in the milk slowly, stalling for time, gazing at the whirlpool that formed with intense interest. She really didn't want to go into a whole conversation about Jamie, but she sensed Elaine was interested.

At least every time she said it out loud, it took a bit of the sting out. It was a moment before she spoke, twirling her spoon as she thought.

'Jamie and I met in the first week of our horticulture degree. Like me, he'd come into gardening later. There was a gang of older students who'd all been working or off travelling and we got on really well, ended up sharing a house in the centre of Winchester.' She picked at the fabric of the tablecloth, pulling at a loose thread until it snapped in her hand. 'Anyway. We'd our future all mapped out until I walked in on him with my best friend – well, very much ex-best friend – in our kitchen.' She took another sip of tea.

'You poor thing. What an absolute shit.' Elaine shook her head in disgust.

'I know.' Daisy agreed. And her so-called best friend hadn't been any better.

Jamie had been so matter-of-fact about it. The image, vivid as a film reel in her mind, was running again. She could see her boyfriend, one hand in his back pocket, kissing her best friend. Sylvia sitting on the kitchen worktop, her long legs wrapped around his waist. Her hands snaking up his shirt, his free hand curled in her hair. The casual way he'd turned on hearing the door open as Daisy walked in to retrieve her forgotten phone.

'Anyway.' She shook herself, freeing herself of the memory. 'I'm well shot of him.'

'Yes, you are. I wish –'

For the briefest moment, Elaine looked as if she was about to unburden herself of something. She raised a manicured hand, covering her mouth. Daisy leaned forward, inviting her to go on, but she shook her head with a smile.

'Oh, it's nothing.' And in an instant, Elaine's poise

returned. She straightened her back, selecting a scone and slicing it very precisely.

'Anyone else on the horizon?' She was buttering the scone now, with an intense focus. Daisy, who'd wolfed down the ham sandwich already, took a drink.

'For me?' The thought hadn't really crossed Daisy's mind. Remembering their night in the pub, she heard Miranda's voice in her ears: *'the chances of meeting anyone in a place this size . . .'*

'Not much chance of meeting anyone in a place like Steeple St John. Everyone's married, as far as I can see. You're lucky to be out of all that.' Daisy cocked her head, looking at Elaine thoughtfully. 'Leo seems lovely.'

In truth, he was a bit *too* charming for Daisy's liking. He'd taken to appearing when she was in the garden, complimenting her on her outfit (which was almost always the same battered pair of jeans and a T-shirt), or her earrings, or the colour of her hair. Jo would probably say Daisy's discomfort suggested something terrible about the state of her self-esteem – she'd never been much good at taking compliments.

'Leo?' Elaine brought her cup to her lips. 'Oh yes, my husband is the epitome of charm and considera-tion.'

With a little laugh, Elaine placed her cup back onto the saucer, twisting it round until the patterns matched up perfectly.

There was a note there that jarred, just for a second.

Daisy remembered that morning she'd arrived as Leo stormed out of the house, leaving Elaine red-eyed in the hall. Maybe living the perfect existence was more stressful than it looked.

They headed back into the market square. Daisy left Elaine with her starry-eyed stallholder, who somehow managed to juggle flirting with serving customers *and* starring in a set of photographs. She headed down the hill towards Orchard Villa. Steeple St John was looking particularly beautiful in the spring sunshine. She dodged a gathering of mothers, chatting as their toddlers clambered on the War Memorial, their push-chairs parked in a neat, expensive row. The owner of the little gift shop looked up as Daisy passed, smiling a greeting. The pale brick of the clock tower glowed softly in the sunshine, and beyond the houses the Chiltern Hills curved away into the distance. She nipped into the newspaper shop, humming to herself happily, to see if this month's *Gardening News* was out.

Daisy had been working every hour she could on the garden of Orchard Villa, taking photographs of her progress as she went, and still fitting in as much work as she could in the beautiful surroundings of the Old Rectory. Not only was Elaine happy to pay a decent hourly rate, which was making a real impact on Daisy's savings, she'd also handed Daisy a platinum credit card.

'I want the gardens *completely perfect* on the day.'

Daisy, who'd been working with plants for long enough to know that the vagaries of weather combined with the unpredictability of gardening meant nothing was ever guaranteed, had wisely said nothing.

'Ow.' Daisy winced as a rose branch whipped back from its ties, hitting her in the face. She was tying down the long stems, laying them horizontally to encourage flower growth. She pushed her hair back from her face with her forearm, seeing a smear of blood on her shirt. The thorns must have caught her scalp.

'Daisy, are you all right?' Elaine appeared from the kitchen, hair tied back in a neat ponytail, a perfectly pressed floral apron around her waist.

'Fine. It's just a scratch. I'm just finishing up for today, anyway.' She batted at the strand of hair, which was flapping in her eyes again.

'You're bleeding.' Elaine's brow puckered in concern. 'Come in for a moment and I'll make some tea. I've got some macarons I've just finished photographing for a how-to piece.'

Elaine's baking was more than enough of a lure to tear Daisy away from the disobedient rose bush. Clipping back the recalcitrant stem, she climbed down from the stepladder and made her way down the flagstone path.

'You've scratches all over your arms, too.' Tutting, Elaine handed Daisy a medicated wipe from a newly opened pack. Looking up into the long mirror that stretched along the kitchen wall, Daisy caught a glimpse of Elaine's anxious expression and her own mud-streaked, blood-spattered forehead. She rubbed at the scratches dutifully. 'It's fine. I'll have a shower when I get back.'

Elaine placed a plate of beautiful, pastel-shaded macarons on the table and turned to fetch the teapot. Classical music was coming from the radio in the background, and the only sign of baking was an opened bag of flour, the collar folded down neatly, set against the marble worktop. Elaine's camera sat to one side. She'd clearly just finished the last of her photographs for the website.

'Mmm.' Daisy popped one of the delicious morsels in her mouth, whole. It was nicer than anything she'd tasted from a bakery.

'Oh, they're quite simple. I'll have the how-to up on my website later on; you can give it a try at home.'

'Okay. I'll do that if you pop out and tie back the rest of that Rambling Rector before he takes over the trelliswork.'

'No thanks.' Elaine laughed as she poured out the tea. Over the last few weeks, Daisy had watched how Elaine threw herself into the creation of her website. Photographing the food, writing instruction guides, and taking pictures of the garden took up huge amounts of her day. She was always happy to stop for a tea break when Daisy finished in the garden, bringing out her latest baking, always beautifully presented on a tray. Leo seemed to work remarkably long hours – he was very rarely around.

The delicate scent of Earl Grey filled the air. 'You stick to the gardening and I'll do the cakes. Deal?'

Daisy clinked her teacup gently against Elaine's. 'Deal.'

They shared a smile.

Daisy left an hour later, armed with some home-made essential-oil-scented bath salts which Elaine guaranteed would soak away any aches and pains from a day beating the roses into submission. Their fragrance filled the top floor of Orchard Villa as the big claw-footed bath filled with water. Daisy sank in gratefully. It had been a long week – she'd spent all day putting the final touches to Elaine's garden, ready for the big event. It was amazing how quickly she'd been absorbed into the day-to-day of village life – the Parish Council meetings, the funny little signs on the village noticeboard . . . the other morning there had been a photograph of a runaway hen pinned up there with the words 'Do You Know This Chicken?' Underneath, someone had scrawled 'Answers to the name of Korma'.

Smiling at the thought, she lay back in the deliciously scented water and closed her eyes. It was bliss.

Chapter Nine

Daisy took a last look around Elaine's garden, picking up a couple of fallen petals from the late tulips. The garden was spotless, the grass trimmed and manicured. Not a blade of grass dared move out of place. Even the Rambling Rector rose was now tied down and stretched out across the trellis, its leaves vibrant green in the early-morning sunshine. Iridescent drops of dew nestled in the leaves of the rows of lettuce. The gravel paths were raked to perfection. She was scared to leave it in case anything fell off in her absence, but today was the big day. Time to hand the garden over to Elaine, and let her take the glory.

'This is my only day off this week, y'know.' Ned yawned hugely, stretching his arms above his head. His pale blue shirt came untucked, loosing itself from a pair of battered chinos.

'As gatekeepers,' said Flora, with a disapproving look at Ned's attire, 'you're the first point of contact for visitors to the Steeple St John Open Gardens.'

Daisy hid a smile, pretending to scratch her nose, as Ned, pulling a face, tucked his shirt into his trousers and stood to attention. She'd left Elaine's garden, ready as it would ever be, and headed up in her car to the white gates on the edge of the village, boot loaded with several boxes of colourful fabric bunting. In an operation reminiscent of a wartime mission, Daisy had received a text: *The boxes have been delivered – please confirm receipt.* Given that they'd been dropped off by the husband of one of the committee members, she'd thought it was a bit over the top – but the Open Gardens were serious business.

'That's better.' Flora clicked her pen, scanning her ever-present clipboard. As president of the committee, she was dressed for the occasion in a navy skirt suit and pale pink flower-patterned blouse, her ash-blonde hair sitting obediently beneath a light blue sunhat despite the early hour.

It was only half past seven on the morning of the late May Bank Holiday Monday. The village of Steeple St John had come to a complete standstill. Only the occasional car pottered down the main street, the usual rat-run of commuters still in bed. Making the most of their day off, thought Daisy, who'd been up since five and was already in desperate need of an infusion of coffee. The sweet smell of freshly cut grass was everywhere, the sound of last-minute hedge trimming echoing through the winding streets. Walking up to Elaine's house as the sun rose, wanting to be sure that none of the plants had fallen over or died in her absence, Daisy had seen someone from the committee actually *sweeping* the market square. Everything was expected to be perfect.

Thomas, who was on gatekeeper detail alongside Ned, gave Daisy an approving smile through his moustache. 'You've done an excellent job, my dear. I'm looking forward to toasting you with a glass of Pimm's later on.' He adjusted his shirt collar, releasing it from beneath his beige cardigan. Even in the midst of the early summer heat he looked dapper, and today looked likely to be a dream day. Elaine, who'd been stressing out about the forecast, had panic-ordered several gazebos, planning to erect them across the terrace and most of the borders if needed. Daisy had realized it was probably wise just to let her get on with it, and had carried on putting the finishing touches to the garden.

'No drinking until we check everything's running smoothly, Thomas,' said Flora, warningly. 'Now we really must get on. Thanks for bringing me that bunting, Daisy. Now, Thomas, we've really got to get this lot hung up before half past eight. Come along.'

Thomas pulled a mischievous how-I-suffer face at Daisy as he allowed himself to be shepherded out of Elaine's garden to complete the final, final, 'very-much-last-minute, my dear' checks of the other gardens which would feature in the display.

'You don't fancy nipping up to the station cafe and

picking up a couple of takeaway coffees, do you, Daise? I'd kill for some caffeine . . .' muttered Ned, who had been left to set up the folding table where each visitor would receive their guidebook, a map, and the all-important pink sticker ('You don't let anyone in without one – not even friends or family,' Flora had warned Daisy, darkly).

'Go on then.' Picking up her keys, Daisy slid into the car and headed up to the station. She was lucky that she'd managed to sidle out of an official role in today's proceedings, explaining to Flora that she really wanted to be on hand ('Just in an advisory capacity, you understand?') in Elaine's garden. Flora, who was increasingly aware that Elaine's influence could be of huge benefit to the fundraising side of the Open Gardens, had backed down without comment. The church roof was in a state of some disrepair, and the Parish Council had already raised it as a topic for the next meeting.

'Here you are.' Daisy put down the paper cups she'd bought at the station cafe.

'I've got you an espresso, to get you going, and a double-sized latte, extra hot. That'll keep you topped up for the next hour or so.'

Ned, his arms overloaded with a pile of printed guidebooks, gave her a grateful smile.

'You are a star, Daisy.' He dumped the books on the table and fell on the coffee, mock-panting with relief. Downing the espresso like a shot of tequila, he opened his eyes wide. 'That's better. I've had a bugger of a week – ended up covering on call for one of the others, and last night when I finally could get some sleep, I lay awake half the bloody night.'

With a groan, he slumped down in the folding chair Flora had provided.

'I'd better get a move on,' said Daisy, checking the time. 'I need to get changed into something respectable before the visitors start arriving.'

Ned looked at her with curiosity. 'You sure? You look great as you are.'

She looked down at the sawn-off jean shorts, flip-flops and T-shirt she was wearing. 'Something tells me Flora wouldn't agree.'

The sun was beating down on Steeple St John. A steady stream of visitors had been making their way through the side gate of the Old Rectory since the doors opened to the Open Gardens at 9.30. Leo had flitted back and forth, in full charm mode, welcoming people graciously and praising the efforts of 'my lovely wife'. Thomas and Ned were now sitting under one of Elaine's many spare gazebos at the white village gates. They'd be there all day, handing out the badges that allowed visitors free access to the village gardens, taking notes on planting schemes and soaking up the festival atmosphere. The rare Bank Holiday sunshine had brought visitors from miles around, and the local shops were doing a roaring trade in ice creams and sunhats. Apparently, according to a delighted Flora, the pop-up W.I. cafe had sold out of every type of cake and had to make an emergency run to restock the tea supplies.

'Pimm's?' Jo, who'd installed herself in the garden (complete with requisite badge, having taken a wander around the village with Martha earlier), didn't wait for an answer. She was wielding a huge jug, and tipped a hefty measure into Daisy's empty glass.

Daisy groaned. 'I'm going to have a hangover by about seven this evening at this rate. I'm getting too old for drinking in the afternoon.'

Elaine emerged from the kitchen, hair held back by a pair of enormous sunglasses. She was in a cerise pink linen shift dress, an ecru cardigan draped over her shoulders.

And that, thought Daisy, is the difference between someone like Elaine, and someone like me. She looked at her own flower-sprigged sundress. She'd found it in a vintage shop in Winchester, and she'd paired it with her favourite, battered denim pair of Converse sneakers and a denim jacket she'd found in her mum's wardrobe which had probably been on the go longer than Daisy had been alive. It was lucky that Elaine had proved to be sweet-natured and thoughtful, or her perfection would be quite unbearable.

'I'll give you a hand in the kitchen, shall I?' Jo scooped up her glass and headed inside.

'It's been a very mild spring, hasn't it?' An elderly

lady interrupted Daisy's thoughts. 'Good for us gardeners.'

She was holding a wicker basket over her arm, stacked full of tiny pots. Clearly she'd been one of the early risers who had cleared out the plant sale – when Thomas rang from his lunch break at the Grey Mare, he'd told her gleefully that the stall had completely sold out before noon.

'Oh, this isn't my garden.' Daisy felt she had to explain. She'd spent the whole day helping out when Elaine was asked awkward questions about cuttings, or the best runner beans to grow in their heavy clay soil. Elaine had been keen to let people know that Daisy had taken over almost all the garden work, but Daisy, equally keen for her friend to maintain her image of perfection, kept shushing her. She'd managed to pop in and out of conversations with helpful suggestions, whilst maintaining the facade of being just another Open Gardens volunteer, checking people in and out as they arrived in the garden.

The woman looked down at Daisy's arms, giving a smile of recognition.

'You've got the bug, though, haven't you?'

Like most gardeners in the village after long weeks of preparation, Daisy's arms were covered in tiny scratches, her fingernails short.

The woman smiled. 'I'm Charlotte. I'm a friend of Thomas's. Well, I was his wife Violet's best friend, actually.'

Daisy felt herself smiling. She stood up, holding out her scratched, still slightly grubby hand in greeting.

'And you must be Daisy. Thomas has been telling me all about you.'

'Oh, he's so sweet. Thomas has been so lovely.'

Daisy, who was feeling the effects of her mid-afternoon Pimm's, was unusually effusive.

'You've been good for him, my dear. I think Violet would be pleased to know he's found some purpose. He's been a bit of a lost soul until you came along.'

This was lovely to hear, thought Daisy. She'd become very fond of Thomas, chatting away to him about everything under the sun while they worked. Over their tea breaks, and as they hacked away at the overgrown garden and tidied the orchard, she'd told him all about her childhood, her parents, Miranda's illness, and so much more. Other times, they worked together in an agreeable silence.

'Oh, hello.' Elaine, who had returned carrying a jug of her freshly made elderflower cordial, placed it down on the table. 'I've made a cool drink – but maybe you would rather have a cup of tea?'

'Lovely. Oh, yes please.' The woman sat down gratefully, setting the basket full of plants at her feet. 'It's been a long day.'

'Daisy, do me a favour?' Jo called out through the stable door, with a pair of soap-covered Marigold gloves on. 'D'you see those three teapots up on the little table by the gazebo? Grab them for me and I'll wash them up before any more visitors appear. There's a group of women I recognize from Martha's school on their way over – I just saw them hovering outside the front. They're going to be after some of Elaine's scones, I reckon.'

'Excuse me a moment.' Daisy climbed out of her chair. 'If anyone comes in whilst I'm up there, can you do me a favour and just check they're wearing their pink stickers?'

'I think that's a fair swap for a comfortable chair and a cup of tea, my love. Of course.'

The edges of the lawn had been trampled on, and were sagging into the border in places. Daisy could see the tips of several of the delphiniums had been nipped off and bagged by canny gardeners, who would have them dipped in hormone powder and sealed off in little bags by now, safe on their way home. It was a common enough gardening trick, but the plants were now looking a bit tattered around the edges. A couple of weeks, though, and there'd be no sign anything had happened – at this time of year the garden changed daily, the unstoppable wave of verdant green taking over, filling every gap in the pots and borders. Daisy picked up Elaine's Emma Bridgewater teapots, realizing as she did that she may as well pour the remains over the compost.

She tipped the contents of the three teapots onto the leaf-filled compost bins. Fishing out a couple of ice-cream wrappers thrown in by well-meaning garden visitors, she hooked the empty teapots onto her fingers and headed back down to the terrace.

'Yes, I know, my angel. I wish you were here, too.'

Daisy frowned as she overheard a voice drifting across the garden. She'd thought the place was deserted, having checked in and checked out the last group of garden visitors herself a moment ago. Perhaps it was coming from next door?

'I can't wait. I'm imagining it right now.'

The voice was definitely coming from somewhere in the garden.

Daisy, having located the sound, stepped cautiously towards the back of the grey-painted potting shed.

There was a groan.

'Soon. God, yes. I want you. *So* much.'

Oh my good God, thought Daisy. That's *Leo* I can hear. Knowing every inch of the garden, she was able to keep herself hidden whilst tiptoeing carefully towards the back of the shed where she could see him, his back half-turned, talking urgently but quietly into his mobile phone.

She scuttled down the garden at speed. Elaine, as she'd suspected, was pouring their elderly visitor a cup of Earl Grey.

'Tea, Daisy?' Elaine looked up, oblivious.

'Let me just – I'll –' she stuttered, 'I'll just pop these in to be washed.' Oh dear God, thought Daisy. Poor

Elaine. She clattered in through the back door of the kitchen.

Jo, happily washing up, was slightly merry from an afternoon of Pimm's, humming to herself. She looked up as Daisy crashed the teapots down onto the marble counter.

'You okay? You look like you've seen a ghost.'

'Worse than that. That *bastard*.'

'Jamie?' Jo grabbed a tea towel, drying her hands and rushing across the kitchen to stand in front of Daisy, pushing her hair out of her face, frowning in concern.

'God, no. Way worse than that. I've just heard Leo on the phone, talking about – ugh –' Daisy shuddered. 'Taking about what he'd like to do to someone. And given that Elaine's standing out there serving tea, we can be bloody sure it's not her he's got plans for.'

'Jesus.' The normally unruffled Jo recoiled.

'Are you girls going to be much longer?'

They both jumped as Elaine popped her head in through the kitchen door.

'Just coming. I was just getting a—'

'Paracetamol,' finished Jo. 'She's been out in that sunshine all day.'

'Yes.' Daisy fished around in her handbag, which was lying on the kitchen table. 'Terrible headache.'

'I'll leave you to it, then. Thomas's lady friend Charlotte is absolutely charming.' Elaine smiled at them beatifically, and pulled the door closed.

Daisy slumped down on a chair.

'So how do you propose we tell Elaine that her upper-class twit of a husband – who, incidentally, I've never liked – is having it off with some filly from the village?'

'I think,' said Jo, one finger on her cheek, thoughtfully, 'not today. This is *her* day. Leo's still going to be an adulterous shit tomorrow. I'm home in the afternoon – why don't we pop round here then – would that work?'

'Yeah,' said Daisy, shaking her head. 'I was going to be here tomorrow anyway.' She gave a hollow laugh. 'Believe it or not, I was coming round to clear up the damage from this afternoon.'

Daisy was dazzled by the late afternoon sun as she stepped back into the garden, and it took her a moment to focus. She could see Elaine half-sitting against the terrace wall, flipping back her hair as she laughed. Beside her, coming into focus as Daisy's eyes adjusted, she could see Thomas's elderly friend, who was beaming with happiness, smiling up into the bright blue eyes of –

Oh, for God's sake. This was supposed to be a peaceful afternoon in the garden, and now *everything* was going haywire. She tried to step backwards into the kitchen, but the door had swung shut behind her so she banged her heel instead, giving out an involuntary yelp of pain.

'Daisy, there you are.' Elaine reached out a beckoning hand of welcome. 'This is Charlotte's nephew –' she looked at him for confirmation.

'George,' confirmed Daisy. Elaine raised a quizzical eyebrow.

'We meet again.' George looked pleased to see her. His bright eyes twinkled blue in the summer light.

'Yes. We've met.' Realizing she was being rude, Daisy gave herself a mental kick up the backside, pulling herself together. She stepped across the patio and took his extended hand. He shook it with an amused expression.

Daisy fiddled with a strand of purple aubretia that was hanging down between the stones of the terrace wall.

'This place looks gorgeous.' George scanned the now-empty garden. Fortunately the promised gaggle of village mothers hadn't materialized. Leo, Daisy presumed, had made himself scarce.

'Yes, you've done a wonderful job, both of you.' Charlotte looked from Daisy to Elaine, her dark eyes squinting into the sun.

'Oh, I haven't done a *thing*,' laughed Elaine. 'I'm sure Thomas has told you all about it.'

'You've done so much today. And this place has your heart in it,' said Daisy, passionately. She felt a wave of protectiveness for her new friend, oblivious as she stood there that her house of cards was about to fall down around her ears.

'Would you show me around, Daisy?' George looked to Elaine politely, seeking her permission. 'I'd love to have a proper tour. I've been enjoying the chance to get an inside look at some of the gardens here in the village.'

'. . . And this is the vegetable garden. It's designed in the style of a traditional French *potager*, with everything easy to reach, and a mixture of produce and flowers.'

'Very impressive,' murmured George. 'Haven't a clue about gardening myself, but it looks great. You've got a real talent for this.'

'Oh, I didn't actually design it,' Daisy began to explain.

George turned to her as they reached the top of the garden. They'd stood for a moment, looking across the low stone wall that dropped away steeply, dividing Elaine's garden from the Steeple St John allotments. With the unexpectedly warm spring everyone was ahead of themselves, and the patchwork of plots was dotted with early salad crops, the first shoots of courgettes spreading out across carefully prepared, sun-warmed earth. Gardeners were hoeing their patches, wheeling barrow-loads of topsoil from one spot to another. Several could be seen standing by a colourfully painted shed, chatting over tin mugs of coffee.

'The thing is,' George began, turning to her and fixing her with his mesmerizing blue eyes, 'I think the garden's gorgeous . . .' His Dublin accent was low and persuasive. 'But here's the thing, Daisy. I'm a great believer in signs. When I saw you in the baker's, I thought to myself, if I see that beautiful red-haired girl again I'm going to ask her out for a drink. And then there you were, in the pub, clicking your fingers at me.'

Daisy laughed, protesting. 'That's not exactly how it happened.'

'Well, anyway, I didn't feel I could ask you out with your sister sitting there, so I thought maybe it'd be third time lucky.'

He moved a fraction closer to Daisy again. She caught a faint scent of aftershave, something woody and fresh.

'So here we are.' He reached across, lifting a stray rose leaf from Daisy's shoulder. 'And I'm wondering – would you come out with me sometime, Daisy?'

He looked directly at her. He looked younger up close, the laughter lines not so evident today.

Daisy thought for a moment, testing out how she felt. Leo might be a lying shit, but that doesn't mean George is, she reminded herself firmly. And he's only asking you out on a date, not for your hand in marriage. She could hear Miranda telling her to *just bloody well get out there.*

'Yes.' She smiled at him. 'Yes, that'd be lovely. I'd like that.'

'Great.' His accent was stronger suddenly as he

grinned back at her, pleased with himself. 'Shall we say Friday night? There's a little place in Great Thorndon which does lovely meals. If the weather stays nice we can sit outside in the gardens. You'll love them.'

'That sounds wonderful.' He did have a nice smile, thought Daisy. Her ex, Jamie, had been incredibly intense – all dark, flashing eyes and brooding silences. She'd spent a lot of time recently, whilst gardening, musing on whether the meaningful silences that had characterized their relationship had been more a sign that they'd run out of things to say to each other than anything romantic. Perhaps it had really been nothing more than a student romance – albeit one between mid-twenties students, not first-time-away-from-home, innocent eighteen-year-olds.

She jumped slightly as George traced a finger down her forearm, barely touching her skin. She looked down, watching the hairs on her arm stand on end.

'You've scratched yourself.'

His voice was gentle. His eyes didn't stray from hers for a second but held her in a steady, confident gaze.

'Rose bushes.'

His fingertip lingered on her arm a moment. The physical contact was a shock to her system after months of being single. She stepped back suddenly, surprised at the intensity of the feeling.

'So. Friday night, then?' Her voice was clear and

slightly too loud. It broke the spell of the moment. He cleared his throat, pulling his phone out of his pocket to check the time.

'Grand. I'll call for you at eight.'

He frowned slightly, glancing down again at his phone.

'I'm sorry, I'm going to have to dash off. Something's come up with work.' With an apologetic shrug, he stuffed his phone back in his pocket.

'I should be giving Elaine a hand, in any case.' Daisy looked down beyond the vegetable garden, through the trellis that divided the garden. In the distance she could see a group of women heading up towards them, a gaggle of toddlers swaying their way across the lawn, tottering precariously close to her newly repaired box hedge.

'I might just hover here for a second and guard my planting.' She motioned discreetly towards the approaching visitors.

'I'll see you Friday, Daisy.' Surprising her, he reached across and kissed her on the cheek, faint stubble scratching her skin, the scent of his aftershave lingering for a moment after he pulled away.

'Friday,' she agreed, and he was gone. She spun round, looking back for a moment across the allotments. A colourful windmill whirled round in a sudden breeze. She stood for a second, holding on to the stone wall. It had been a long, confusing day.

A sudden last rush of visitors made their way in.

Daisy watched as a young family from London tried to herd their three children up the garden and back down again. The mother, her short hair ruffling in the wind, laughed aloud as she chased a toddler across the grass.

'It's like herding cats,' smiled the father, scooping up the smallest, a crawling, round-faced little boy of about one, into his arms. The baby grabbed a fistful of his hair and shouted with delight.

By the time Daisy made it back down to the terrace she'd been subjected to yet more cross-questioning on the best type of runner beans and on the Native American 'three sisters' planting method from one of the women, who had just taken on a plot at the allotments. Daisy had then been heading back, having gathered an armful of weeds that had sneaked up behind the shed, when a different woman approached wielding a notepad and pen. She'd taken pages of notes during the Open Gardens, and wanted to ask Daisy all about the planting schemes in Elaine's garden. She was, she announced bravely, intent on having her brand new garden featured next year. She explained to Daisy that hers was a newly built house, built in the old garden of a house along the street. Daisy, recalling the incongruous new red-brick houses she'd recently seen, swallowed her surprise. She hadn't expected someone who'd been party to the dreaded garden-grabbing, the cause of so much conflict in the village, to be a keen gardener herself.

When everyone had finally left, Elaine looked at her watch. 'Four-thirty. And that –' she slid the garden gate bolt shut with a decisive click – 'is that.' Turning back, Elaine gave Daisy a slightly arch look. 'Charlotte's nephew seems very nice.'

Remembering the sensation of his finger brushing against her skin, Daisy gave a shiver. 'He is.' She felt a smile curving at the corners of her lips.

Somehow, though, she didn't feel comfortable chatting about her plans, knowing what she and Jo had to do to Elaine the next day. As they prepared to leave, Daisy could see Leo outlined in the window of the orangery. He was sitting, completely unconcerned, feet up on the table, reading the weekend newspapers with a pot of coffee by his side. No doubt lovingly prepared by Elaine, she thought, glaring at him pointlessly. What an absolute shit.

Chapter Ten

Daisy woke up the next morning sick with anticipation at the thought of facing Elaine. She couldn't leave it, could she? She had proof that her friend's husband was up to something. She'd lain awake for hours in the middle of the night, remembering how it had felt to be confronted with Jamie's infidelity.

What was worse, though? Walking in and discovering him in the act? Or having a brand new friend point out that they'd pretty good evidence your husband was a total pig? It had been an unsettled night, and she'd woken at six as the first warm rays of sunlight hit her face, feeling the dull ache of dread in the pit of her stomach.

Shuffling downstairs, pulling her dressing gown around her more tightly, she flipped the switch on the kettle and turned on the radio, humming along to the music in an attempt to fill the silence. Poor Elaine. She'd built her whole existence on having a perfect life, a perfect home. And meanwhile . . . Daisy shuddered.

She couldn't just blurt it out to Elaine over coffee. Maybe Jo would know the answer. She picked up her phone, sending a brief message.

You got five minutes? I need to ask you something.

She jumped as the mobile started ringing in her hand immediately.

'Jo. Thanks for calling. I'm sorry, it's really early.'

'It's fine.' Jo sounded bright. 'I've been up since six. I've got a client at eight.'

Jo did a lot of her counselling work from the tiny converted garage which was tucked into the side of her little mews cottage. Clients, who often couldn't take time out of their working days, would visit before they headed up the hill to the station and into the whirling rush of London trains and offices and traffic. Jo was such a calming presence that her little practice was thriving, a constant stream of clients keeping her busy all week long. Daisy, soothed by Jo's calming voice, found herself pouring out her worries.

'It's about Elaine. Well, it's not, it's Leo. Oh God . . .' and all the words tumbled out in a rush. 'Do you think I'd be doing the right thing, telling her?'

'I've been wondering the same thing.' Jo's tone was quiet, her words thoughtful. 'I'm not doubting what you heard, but . . .'

Elaine's lifestyle *was* her life. Her entire existence was based on her beautiful house, her perfect husband, her lovely gardens. If I stamp in there and accuse Leo of being unfaithful, thought Daisy, it's possible it might backfire. Not to mention the fact that – well, is that the sort of thing you can do with a new friend? She sighed.

'I think maybe we should just . . . keep an eye on him?' It sounded a bit pathetic, but stamping in and setting off World War Three didn't seem like the best option, either. Not until they had some kind of concrete evidence that Leo really *was* a shit.

'Mmm,' agreed Jo. 'I think our focus has to be on Elaine. We need to be there for her. There's no harm in keeping an ear out for signs of Leo being up to something.'

With that agreed, Daisy hung up, sagging down onto the sofa with a groan of relief. She'd never been a great fan of confrontation. She couldn't help thinking back to the night she'd slunk away from Winchester, filling the car with bags and boxes, not staying around to face up to the aftermath of Jamie cheating on her with their supposed best friend. She shuddered at the thought. Thank God that was all in the past.

She peered out at the early-morning sunshine, resolving to think about the good things the day held. She had been rather vigorously encouraged onto the allotment committee at the previous Parish Council meeting, with Flora clearly very keen to see her get to work straight away. She'd been instructed to meet Thomas, who'd been a bit vague about their mission, saying he'd explain more on the day. Whatever it was, a bit of gentle pottering around in the peace of the allotment plots had to be better than the alternative. Presenting Elaine with evidence that her husband appeared to be a total shit could – and would have to – wait.

Swallowing the hint of a feeling that she was being a bit disloyal, she headed upstairs to get changed into her gardening clothes.

'I'm terribly sorry, Daisy my dear, but I'm going to have to love you and leave you,' explained Thomas as they met at the foot of the lane that led up to the Steeple St John allotments. 'I've been having a bit of trouble with this leg.'

He pointed downwards, indicating his left leg with a gnarled finger. He was leaning lightly on a walking stick, a black ring-binder under his free arm.

'Oh, Thomas – have I been working you too hard in the gardens?'

He straightened up, shaking his head vigorously. 'Gosh, no. No, not at all. Just an old injury. It plays up from time to time. Don't worry about me one bit.'

He hitched his beige cardigan back up his shoulder and started walking, one leg dragging with a pronounced limp. Polly strolled alongside them, tongue lolling, enjoying the sunshine.

They made their way up through the path towards the allotments, Daisy matching her stride to Thomas's careful one. As instructed, she had brought along an A4 notepad and had a couple of pens tucked away in her bag, as well as a flask of coffee, a couple of sticky Bath buns from the bakery, and a couple of bars of chocolate – just in case. The allotments were reached via a muddy, rutted track, overhung with hawthorn trees, sunlight dappling through the branches. The early summer scent of elderflower and cow parsley blew on the breeze, birds singing overhead.

'Monty, get back here!'

Daisy watched as, with paws thudding and ears flying, Ned's unruly spaniel galloped down the path towards them. Polly, still on her lead, perked up, pricking up her ears, wagging her tail in welcome. Monty overshot the mark, bouncing past them in a whirl of lolling tongue and excitement, then springing back to greet the more sedate retriever with enthusiasm.

'Ned, there you are.' Thomas, pausing for a second, leaned on his stick.

'All right, Daise?' Ned was strolling down the narrow path that led between the plots. He was shading his eyes against the sun, the sleeves of his pale blue shirt rolled up, the tails coming untucked from a pair of battered brown cords.

There was a small wood beyond the allotments that had been planted in the year 2000, a regular haunt for village dog-walkers, who appreciated the chance to let their canine friends hurtle around freely without fear of crashing into children playing, which was a concern (mentioned with regularity, Daisy had noticed) in the village park. As a consequence, the path that led up to the woods, flanked on either side by manicured, beautifully maintained plots, was lined with hand-painted 'Keep your Dog on a Lead' signs. Monty couldn't read, and Ned, in his perpetual state of post-on-call exhaustion, clearly wasn't paying attention. Scenting something exciting on the far side of the allotments, Monty hurtled off across neatly raked earth, tiny cabbage seedlings flying in the air in his wake. Daisy, knowing how much effort went into maintaining a plot, winced. Polly stood by her side, obediently.

'You'd better watch out. That dog's going to get you in a lot of trouble,' she pointed out, realizing as she did that she sounded just like Flora. Thomas chortled with amusement beneath his white moustache.

'I told you, Ned, this one will have you – and the dog – under control in no time.'

Ned glanced at Thomas before the two men turned to her, laughing. Thomas had made a similar remark the other day, when she'd organized him into hoeing the long border whilst she repotted a batch of young plants.

She wasn't sure what was so funny. Mind you, maybe if she just nipped across and popped the young plants in when Ned had gone, the gardeners would be none the wiser.

'Monty. HEEL.' Ned whistled loudly. Monty's head popped up from where he'd been nosing around. He was underneath some carefully placed netting, which had been draped across a section of plot to protect the vegetable crop from birds and butterflies.

But not dogs, thought Daisy ruefully, as Monty, suddenly obedient, lolloped across towards his owner, the blue netting having caught in his collar. It sailed in the air behind him like a superhero cape.

'Monty, you are a Very Bad Dog.' Ned, crouching down to untangle him from his decoration, looked up at Daisy with a sheepish grin.

'Do you *have* a lead for him?' Daisy could hear the slight hint of asperity in her tone. She sounded like her mother. Honestly, though. Ned was a *vet*, for goodness' sake. He should be an expert on animal behaviour. Instead he had a lunatic spaniel rampaging around destroying other people's hard work. She could feel herself frowning in disapproval and worked hard to arrange her face into a polite, neutral expression. Ned and the dog were as bad as each other.

Ned bent down, clipping a long rope lead onto Monty's collar, ruffling his ears in sympathy as he did so. 'Sorry, mate. We've got to be on our best behaviour here.'

He was infuriating. Lips pursed with mild disapproval, Daisy turned, taking a moment to look around the wide sweep of the allotments. Luckily there was nobody else there, which was unusual. Whenever she'd taken Polly for a stroll up there (always on a lead, she thought, reprovingly) the place had always been a hive of activity, gardeners standing around leaning on forks, discussing their plans, comparing notes and swapping seeds. Today, though, the place was deserted.

'Lucky this place is empty, you two, under the circumstances,' said Thomas, jolting her from her thoughts. 'Flora'd have your guts for garters. She doesn't take any nonsense.'

Thomas opened the folder and removed a crisp piece of paper from a plastic insert. Ned peered over his shoulder, interested.

'Looks like a map of the allotments. We searching for gold?' Ned looked up, smiling at Daisy. The disobedient Monty stood at his feet, eyes bright, panting happily. It struck Daisy that the two of them were surprisingly similar in looks as well as nature. Monty, his long pale hair ruffling in the light wind, gave a bark of surprise as Daisy laughed aloud at the thought.

'What is it?' Ned put a hand to his head. 'Have I got straw stuck in my hair again? Tell me it's nothing worse.' He patted his shirt, checking his appearance. 'D'you know, I walked into the surgery after being out at a difficult calving the other day. Can't have fastened the overalls as well as I thought, because . . . well, I'll spare you the details.' He pulled a wry face.

'Right, you two. You're here on Parish Council business. If Flora thought you were standing around chatting, you'd be in trouble.' Thomas's voice was mock-stern, and his blue eyes were twinkling. He shook the piece of paper.

'I'm not going to be able to help out, I'm afraid. This leg's a bit of a nuisance.' Thomas lifted his right leg in the air, waving it back and forth to demonstrate. 'So I'm afraid you two are going to have to get on with it.'

'You're not just passing through?' Daisy looked across at Ned, realization dawning.

'No, no. I'm here on official Parish Council business. I thought it was just us two, though, Thomas.'

'That makes two of us. I thought you and I were doing the allotment thing together.' Ned and Daisy both looked at the old man, expectantly.

'Sorry, folks.' A smile appeared underneath his moustache. 'You two must have had your wires crossed. Anyway, I need your young legs. The committee wants a report on these here allotments.' He waggled the piece of paper at them. 'Daisy, did you bring the notepad and pen?'

She patted her bag, nodding.

'Great stuff. Right, what I need from you two is a note of which allotments aren't up to scratch. There's a waiting list a mile long with everyone getting into this whole vintage lark.'

Thomas handed the allotment plan to Ned. It was a beautifully drawn map.

'Now, Flora's wanting this back for the meeting later this week, so don't go losing it or dropping it in the compost heap.' Thomas looked at Ned with a mock-accusing expression before glancing down at his watch. 'Is that the time already? I've got a game of dominoes with the chaps from the Legion at twelve.'

And with that, he turned and started making his way briskly down the little path that led to Main Street, and therefore to the pint of bitter that had his name on it.

'He's made a bit of a fast recovery, hasn't he?' Ned nodded after Thomas as they watched him make surprising speed down the hill, his walking stick barely touching the ground.

'Mmm.' Daisy looked on, her forehead puckered in thought. Hadn't Thomas said it was his *left* leg that was causing the problem? She shook her head in confusion.

'Right, then. Shall we get to work?'

'I feel like a poacher turned gamekeeper,' grumbled Daisy as they headed up to the top of the allotment field, having agreed to work their way through methodically, marking off each plot on the Parish Council map, and noting down any comments as they did so. They'd looped the dogs' leads around a handy gatepost, leaving them in the shade where they flopped together, comfortably.

Daisy stepped over a low dividing fence and onto the first plot.

'This one looks like it hasn't been done in centuries.' Ned poked at the desiccated remains of a sunflower. A handful of dried-out seeds fell to the ground, getting lost in a tangle of chickweed and couch grass.

'Oh, but look, they've started digging over the

potato bed there,' said Daisy, her heart softening. There was a narrow strip of freshly turned earth, and a battered old spade was balanced alongside the rickety shed.

Ned looked up at her through his untidy thatch of sandy hair, and raised an eyebrow. 'So that's a no, then?'

He gave her a conspiratorial smile and ticked the corresponding part of the plot map.

'Next.'

Daisy shot him a look of gratitude and they stepped back across into what was clearly a no-brainer. This plot must have been measured out with a set square. Neat rows of broad beans stood to attention against evenly spaced bamboo supports, precisely tied together with green gardening twine. The edges of each bed were closely strimmed and the dark earth was hoed smoothly, with not a stone or a weed to be seen. Daisy bent down, seeing an intricately painted stone, decorated with flowers, nestling in the soil. Leaning in closer, she traced the words with a finger.

In Loving Memory: William Douglas. Your beloved wife, Flora.

Oh, poor Flora. Daisy felt a sudden pang of guilt, thinking of the times she'd silently sniggered at Flora's obsessive control-freakery about everything to do with the Parish Council. She could imagine Flora up here, keeping up the allotment they'd lovingly tended together, filling her days with committee meetings and protests about the village redevelopment . . .

'Ned, look at this.' She beckoned him over.

Dropping down to his knees, Ned read the inscription on the stone and recoiled backwards.

'Jesus, Daise. I didn't have Flora down as the DIY-funeral type.'

Ned stood up, brushing pieces of grass from the knees of his trousers. His expression was a picture – eyes wide in shock, eyebrows shooting up into the tangle of sandy hair. He shook his head.

'He's not *in* the plot, you idiot,' said Daisy, laughing.

'I did wonder.' He held out a hand, pulling her up from the ground. The muscles in his arms stood out under the already dark farmer's tan he'd gained from days spent working outside.

Daisy took a step back, bemused by her reaction. That she was even noticing the muscles on Ned's arms was a definite sign she needed to get out a bit more. It was just as well she had a date with George on Friday night.

'Come on, you.' Ned tapped at the allotment plan with a biro in mock-impatience. 'This is my only half-day off this week, y'know.'

Halfway through, they stopped for a drink from Daisy's flask, sitting companionably with their backs to the wall of the disused shed where they'd tied up the dogs. The allotments were still empty, save for an elderly couple who'd made their way up the hill with a wheelbarrow, nodding and smiling hello as they passed.

'God, I hope they weren't on the condemned list,' said Daisy, looking at the list in Ned's hand. She leaned across him, trying to see.

'Gerroff,' he said, laughing. 'I'm in charge of the paperwork. You're just the hired help.' He pulled it just out of her reach, waving it in the air.

'Me?' Daisy snorted. 'Without me, you'd be clueless up here. You can't tell a weed from a wheelbarrow.'

'She's got a point,' said Ned to his dog, who wagged his tail approvingly.

Daisy peered up the hill, trying to work out which of the plots belonged to the couple.

'We didn't say no to any of the ones up there, look.' Ned spread the sheet over his knees, indicating a sea of ticks. 'In fact,' – he looked at her sideways, a slow smile spreading across his face – 'we haven't said no to very much, yet. We're going to have to up our game for the last quarter.'

They both turned, then, looking down at the neatly manicured vegetable plots which stretched down towards the low walls of the gardens beyond. There weren't any which looked like they were ready for the chop. Daisy pulled at face at Ned.

'We'll need to go back up and have another look.'

He groaned, sensing the lunchtime beer he'd mentioned was slipping ever further away. 'Come on, then, let's give it a go. And no making up sob stories about people breaking their arms and having no way of feeding their families if they lose their plot this time . . .'

'But what if it's true?' Daisy laughed, brushing damp grass from the bottom of her jeans as she stood up. Looking across, she could see the old stone wall that edged Elaine's house and beyond that, the curve of the apple trees that marked the beginning of the perfectly maintained *potager*. Imagining her friend inside, oblivious, Daisy turned away, shutting down the feelings of guilt she could feel rising inside her. Until she had concrete evidence, she couldn't go marching round there demanding that Elaine confront her husband with the truth. She hid a sigh.

'Let's get these ones ticked off, then we can head up top and work out which ones are for the chop.' Ned, striding across the grass paths which divided the allotment, was moving at speed now and she found herself scuttling to catch up.

'Right. All these are perfect. Agreed?' Pen poised, Ned looked at Daisy for confirmation.

'Yep. Okay, so let's go back up and see if we can suggest a couple that might need a bit of a reminder to tidy their plots up a bit . . .' Daisy looked dubious.

'Lovely day, isn't it?'

The old man who'd passed them earlier was sitting on a folding deckchair with a flask by his side. His wife was kneeling close by, pulling out weeds from between young broccoli plants. Daisy and Ned exchanged a look of relief. They weren't for the condemned list, luckily.

'I feel even worse now,' whispered Daisy as they stood at the far side of a lumpen, half-dug plot which seemed to be a haven for weeds. 'What if these people are their friends?'

'You're worse than me, honestly.' Ned shook his head, laughing. 'We get all sorts in the surgery, claiming they can't afford the treatment their pets need.'

'But how on earth d'you turn them away? That's so hard.' Daisy thought of Polly's recent vet's bill – she'd developed some kind of doggy eczema and it had cost a fortune, but fortunately her parents had paid online. She couldn't imagine kind-hearted Ned refusing to treat an animal.

'It's not easy. We've got an emergency fund at the surgery, but making the call's not an easy one.' He looked across the field, rubbing a stubbled cheek, thoughtfully.

Being a vet was definitely a vocation. Every time she'd seen Ned, his eyes were dark with shadows, hair standing up on end, exhausted from a night of working. 'You don't mind all the stress?'

'Goes with the territory. I knew all this when I took on the job.' He folded up the piece of paper, absently, until it was a tiny square. 'My parents were vets, y'see, so I grew up with all this.'

'But you didn't want to join the family practice?'

Daisy reached across, taking the minuscule folded scrap from his hands, gently unfolding it and smoothing it out. Flora was going to go mad. Perhaps she could photocopy it later on, or get a new copy from the library, and redo all the necessary ticks and things.

'God, no.' Ned shook his head vehemently. 'I'd never have been taken seriously. So when I graduated, I applied for a handful of large animal posts across the South East – far enough from my family back in Cornwall that nobody could accuse me of using family ties, close enough to visit.'

'And do you?' It was interesting to hear more about Ned's life.

He laughed, raising his eyes skywards. 'Every time I get a bloody day off, I seem to end up stuck in a field with you. If it's not the allotments, it's the Open Gardens.'

'Not my fault,' protested Daisy, amused. 'I'm supposed to be here for a quiet life.'

'There are worse ways of spending a day off,' said Ned. 'Come on, we'd better get this lot done or we'll have Flora on our back. I've got a load of paperwork to get done tonight, as well. Nightmare.' He shook his head.

'We're nearly done here,' said Daisy, feeling sorry for him. 'You get off, and I'll finish this lot. Looks like these are a matter of just ticking the boxes in any case – they're all perfectly kept.'

'I was going to suggest a pint as a reward.' Ned looked torn, checking his watch.

Not thinking, he unclipped the lead which secured the two dogs. With lightning reflexes, Monty hurtled off down through the allotments, Polly following him at a rather more sedate canter.

'Bloody hell, Daise.' Ned pointed down the path where, in the distance, a figure could be seen gesticulating wildly in the direction of the two runaway dogs, who were now hurtling across a patch of cabbages. 'It's Flora.'

'Monty! Polly!' They yelled in unison, laughing helplessly as Flora approached.

'For goodness' sake, you two.' Flora's voice carried across the allotments, crisp and disapproving. 'Can you not read a sign?' She waved her hands in the direction of the numerous 'Keep Control of Your Dog' signs, shaking her head, lips pursed in disapproval.

Monty and Polly, sensing her ire, slunk back to their owners and sat down by their feet, panting.

'We'll have that drink another time. I'd get out of here fast if I were you,' said Daisy in an undertone. 'I'll deal with the fallout.'

'I owe you one.' Ned shot her a relieved smile, clipping the rope lead back onto his dog's collar. He stood up, pushing his hair out of his eyes.

'You definitely do.' Flora was almost upon them now. 'Now go. And take that lunatic dog with you.'

Ned headed down the hill, Monty orbiting around

him like a brown and white satellite, ears and tail flying.

'Daisy, dear.' Flora, dressed in a pair of neatly pressed jeans and a pale pink polka-dot blouse, had a woven basket in each hand. Daisy braced herself for the explosion.

'I'm really sorry – the dogs got loose and—'

'Oh, never mind,' said Flora. 'No harm done.'

Daisy took a step back in surprise. She'd been braced for impact, but none was forthcoming.

'Have you done the deed?' Flora looked at her, her sharp eyes narrowing as she looked across at one of the scruffier plots. It was pretty clear that she was behind the decision to kick the negligent gardeners off the allotment gardens.

'We've had a look around, yes,' Daisy began.

'Splendid. Kind of Ned to get involved. He's a hard-working young man, isn't he?' Flora's voice was approving. 'Are you rushing off? I'd love to ask your advice about these redcurrants I've planted – the leaves are curling *most* alarmingly.'

'I'd love to have a look,' said Daisy, relieved. She pulled her hand out of her pocket. The crumpled map was safe for now. She followed Flora up the little hill to the neatly planted rows of potatoes which marked the beginning of her plot.

'It's an aphid attack. Won't do any major damage, but you can spray the leaves with a solution of washing-up liquid to get rid of them if you like.' Daisy straightened up. 'Your plot is beautiful.'

'Do you think so?' Flora beamed, her eyes crinkling in pleasure.

'Absolutely.' Daisy's eye fell again on the hand-painted memorial stone lying on the earth. 'Have you been on the allotments for a long time?'

'Well, we've had the plot for twenty years,' said Flora with a gentle nod of her head, indicating the stone. She opened the door to the little green shed, pulling out two folding deckchairs. 'Have a cup of tea with me before you go?'

Daisy, surprised to be invited, gave her a smile as she replied. 'That'd be lovely.'

'My late husband, William, spent most of his spare time up here,' explained Flora, passing Daisy an en-amelled mug. 'I realized, as I've taken over the plot since he passed away, that it was rather a nice escape for him.' She gave a wry smile. 'I can be a bit – bossy, sometimes.'

Daisy opened her mouth to protest, but Flora continued.

'No need. You know, the only man I've met in life besides William who was any match for me was Thomas.' And with that, the slightest pink rose on her papery cheek.

Daisy hid a smile as she spoke. She'd noticed Thomas seemed to have a soft spot for Flora, too –

whenever he mentioned her it was with a fond, teasing tone. 'He's a lovely man, isn't he?'

'Very much so. And you've brought him out of his shell, rather, which is lovely. I gather it's you and Ned I have to thank for finally getting Thomas along to the Parish Council meetings?'

Daisy remembered the three of them heading into that first meeting together, her arm linked through Thomas's, Ned joking that there was safety in numbers.

'He seems to be enjoying it now,' she acknowledged.

'Well, I'm very grateful to you two young ones for doing this today,' said Flora, waving across the stretch of allotments that spread out below them. 'I've become very fond of the people up here – it's a real community. The Parish Council were coming under pressure to provide new plots, but I couldn't very well come along and start telling people they weren't pulling their weight.'

Daisy cringed, thinking of the allotment plan in her pocket. She and Ned had been too soft-hearted to mark any of the plots down as completely neglected, putting a question mark next to only the most unkempt and chaotic. Even as a temporary incomer to the village, she didn't want to get a reputation as the person who'd chucked people off their much-loved plots. There had to be a solution, somehow.

'I read an article in a gardening magazine recently

about people in London taking half shares in plots if they don't have time to manage a whole one. Could that work?'

She looked across at the tired, weed-choked plot across the path, where the earth had been half-turned and then abandoned.

'I think it's a wonderful idea.' Flora waved across as a man wheeled a barrow up the path towards his plot. 'Hello, Dave. Daisy here tells me my redcurrants aren't for the chop after all.'

The man put down the wheelbarrow and made his way across to them. Ruddy-cheeked, with his checked shirtsleeves rolled up against the sunshine, he stopped at Flora's shed and pulled out a handkerchief to wipe sweat from his forehead.

'Bloody hard work in this heat, eh, girls?'

Flora laughed. 'Dave, this is Daisy.' Flora looked disapproving, but her tone was amused. 'I'm still working on getting Dave along to one of the Parish Council meetings.'

'I'm helping out at the fundraising barbecue for the church roof, though,' Dave protested.

'Yes, and we're very grateful for that,' smiled Flora. 'Our Daisy's a bit of a gardening expert. We were just discussing clubbing together up here, and helping each other out a bit.'

Dave gave a thoughtful nod. 'Sounds like a plan. Jack over there –' he indicated the half-dug plot she and Ned had stood looking over earlier – 'his wife's been in hospital for a bit. Hasn't had a chance to get up here.'

Thank God all they'd done was put a question mark next to that plot on the map they'd been given. It would make far more sense to get the allotment workers – who seemed, from what she could see, to have a pretty good sense of community in any case – working together to help each other out.

'I'd love to give people a hand if they need it,' she found herself saying.

'Daisy, dear,' beamed Flora, 'that would be wonderful. I've been considering setting up an allotment group up here.'

'Another bloody committee,' Dave groaned, rolling his eyes at Daisy with a laugh. 'I'm only teasing, Flora. It's not a bad idea. My brother's got a plot over in Beaconsborough – they have a meeting once a month, do seed swaps, that sort of thing.'

'Wonderful.' Flora turned to Daisy. 'If you could help us out, dear, we'd be very grateful.'

With another commitment in her diary, and the roots of village life growing ever stronger within her, Daisy headed for home, leaving Flora hoeing between her courgette plants, smiling contentedly. Now, if she could only work out what exactly Thomas had been playing at, when he'd suddenly lost his limp and hurtled down towards his pint with a redundant walking stick . . .

Chapter Eleven

It was Friday night. Daisy stood in the hall of Orchard Villa, trying to convince herself she was completely calm. Five to eight, and she'd been ready for half an hour. She looked at herself again in the mirror. A gallon of her sister's expensive hair serum had smoothed down the fuzz of red curls which normally haloed her face, and tamed her long red hair into gentle waves. Had Miranda been there, she'd have insisted that her elder sister wasn't wearing anything like enough make-up, and Daisy would have been dodging helpful applications of bronzer and eyeliner. Instead, Daisy's green eyes were shaded with just a hint of hazelnut-brown eyeshadow, and a slick of mascara emphasized the length of her lashes. She rubbed a rose pink onto her cheeks, and applied a similar shade of lipstick. Looking in the mirror, she wondered if it was a bit too understated after all and she just looked pale and uninteresting . . . oh God, maybe Miranda's approach was right?

She turned to run upstairs, deciding to add a bit

more make-up, just in case she looked less under-stated and more can't-be-bothered. The home phone started ringing – sod it, whoever it was would have to wait. Walking into the bedroom, she sat down on the bed for a moment, suddenly breathless with nerves. It'd been three years since she'd been on a date with anyone, and she'd never been much good at it before then.

She swallowed. It was only a date, not a lifetime commitment, she reminded herself. She heard the familiar buzz of her mobile ringing from within her bag. Whoever it was was persistent, if nothing else. She pulled it out, checking.

Mum and Dad mobile, flashed the screen. Oh God, not now. She tapped the silence button, deciding that whatever they wanted could wait. Or not, as the case may be: a text flashed up moments later.

Can you ring us when you're free? Got something to discuss.
Mum x

Knowing her mother, it was probably 'can you measure the cushions, I've seen the perfect covers in a market in Mumbai', or something along those lines. Daisy wasn't in the mood to deal with an in-depth conversation. They could hold on, at least until she'd got rid of these first-date nerves. She shoved the phone back into her bag, turning the volume off.

She'd popped round briefly earlier to check on

Elaine – or rather, ostensibly at least, to check on Elaine's garden. Her friend had been pottering around the kitchen, quite unconcerned, putting the final touches to a collection of photographs of her favourite salads.

'Fingers out,' Elaine laughed, slapping her away as she tried to pinch a tomato. 'You look like you need a seriously long bath to get those hands properly clean.'

Daisy looked down at her still-faintly-grubby hands. 'I can't help it! I can't garden properly unless I—'

'. . . feel the earth. We know.' Elaine, laughing, completed her sentence. With an unconscious gesture she smoothed down her linen shirt, which remained impeccable as always. She turned away, looking out of the window and across the neatly trimmed lawn, where the allotments stretched away out of sight. 'I'm glad you do, anyway. My garden looks perfect thanks to you, Daisy.'

'Promise you'll let Jo and me know how tonight goes?' Elaine wiped her hands dry on a paper towel, popping it neatly into the bin as she spoke. 'You can always text from the bedroom,' she continued, with a wry arch of her brow. She knew as well as Daisy that wasn't going to happen.

'Definitely not the bedroom.' Daisy felt a swoop of panic at the thought. She could cope with a date, but there was no way she was ending up in bed with George, no matter how beautiful his cornflower-blue eyes or enticing his Dublin accent. She'd been lured into bed by Jamie's charms despite her misgivings. This time around she wasn't rushing into anything.

The sound of the doorbell brought her back to the present. Too late to put on any more make-up now – she stole a peek out of the bedroom window and saw George standing below, running a confident hand through his newly cropped hair before glancing behind him to check his car was still there. Daisy echoed his gesture, putting a reassuring hand to her hair too, running a hand through the unfamiliar smooth waves before heading downstairs.

She pulled open the door just as George was about to knock. He dropped his raised hand with an expression of surprise.

'Wow.'

Daisy straightened the shoulder of her jade-green cardigan, lost for words. All the matter-of-fact confidence she'd convinced herself she was feeling had evaporated, leaving her feeling exposed and dumbstruck.

'Hello.' It's just dinner, Daisy, she reminded herself. He's not Jamie. It's a casual date.

'Daisy. You look beautiful.' George grinned at her, stepping back to let her out through the door. 'Shall we?'

George's car was an immaculate Audi convertible. Daisy sank back into the leather upholstery and inhaled the scent of luxury. It was so far removed from her own tiny, rusting scrap that it felt like climbing into the first-class section of a jumbo jet.

'This is nice,' she sighed. Some people might take this sort of thing for granted, but it was rather lovely to be whisked out on a date – with no strings attached, she reminded herself, recalling Elaine's entreaty that she just relax and enjoy herself without thinking about anything other than the present moment. Jo's Zen approach had clearly begun to rub off.

'Isn't it?' He gave the leather armrest beside him an appreciative pat, and turned on the engine. It thrummed expensively. 'It's only ten minutes up to Great Thorndon.'

Circling the little roundabout at the foot of Main Street, a casual hand on the wheel, George drove up the hill and out of Steeple St John. They wove through the narrow countryside roads, the evening sunshine dappling light on their faces through ancient trees that arched overhead, their leaves vibrant green. Daisy, realizing the wind was creating havoc, grabbed her hair into a ponytail and twisted it round her hand to keep it from tangling.

'I'm sorry, I didn't think.' He cast a quick sideways glance at her, slowing their speed slightly. It made an instant difference to the amount of air whizzing past.

'It's fine.' Daisy held onto her hair, laughing into the wind. She'd never ridden in a convertible before, and it was exhilarating. 'You must love this car at this time of year?'

George kept his eyes on the road ahead, but she could see his expression was amused. 'I do that, but I have to admit it's not mine, unfortunately.'

Had he hired a car just for this evening? Daisy took a look at him, sideways.

After a moment, he glanced across at her, a mischievous expression on his face. 'It's my brother's car. I thought you'd be more comfortable in this than in my beaten-up old van.'

Daisy laughed. 'That's a relief.' She settled back in her seat, feeling more at ease. 'I inherited my dad's old Vauxhall years ago. It's usually covered in compost – as am I.'

She adjusted the hem of her linen sundress slightly. The floral patterned fabric had ridden up, showing a slip of pale thigh. Maybe Miranda was right about the benefits of fake tan – she did look a bit ghostly. But George didn't seem to mind. She saw him sneaking a glance when he thought she wasn't looking, and ducked her head, hoping he wouldn't pick up on the blush staining her cheeks as he did so. She took a surreptitious glance at his shoes and smiled to herself. Her sister would approve – she was a stickler for decent footwear on a man, and these were dark brown leather, just worn enough to look comfortable, and most definitely well made. He might not be able to afford a super-posh convertible Audi, but he wasn't on his uppers like Jamie had been, either.

During their time at college, she'd worked part time to keep some money coming in, but Jamie had claimed he preferred to focus on his studies. In reality, that had meant she shared her income, and he was more than willing to help spend her wages. She hadn't realized until afterwards just how unbalanced things had been, but the last few months of working on the garden at Orchard Villa had given her time to think. Good old Daisy, Jamie had repeated, over and over. Well, not any more.

The wheels of the car crackled on fine gravel, shaking Daisy from her thoughts, as they pulled into the car park of the pub. The Sentinel, by the looks of it, was an Audi sort of place. She'd been imagining a cosy little local pub serving poshed-up ploughman's lunches, but this place suggested money: the car park was full of Jaguars, Range Rovers (without a hint of mud, she noticed, thinking again of her own filthy Vauxhall) and, right in the corner, carefully placed to avoid any accidental bumps, an Aston Martin. She looked down at her sundress – she'd found it in the Steeple St John charity shop earlier that week – and felt a clutch of panic in her stomach. It might be an expensive label, but it was still pretty casual. This place looked far dressier than she'd expected.

It was too late to have a clothes crisis now. George hopped out of the car, slamming his door shut. Before she could get her bag from the footwell in front of her, he was opening the passenger door for her.

'I didn't say it before, but you look beautiful.' He flashed a smile, raising an eyebrow in admiration.

You did, actually, thought Daisy. But I'm not going to point that out.

'I'm sorry – there seems to have been a bit of a mix-up.'

The woman at the front desk of the Sentinel looked down at her grey clipboard. The booking sheet in front of her was filled in neatly, a thin line scored through each name as each table had arrived. From inside Daisy could hear a hum of conversation, just that little bit louder than midweek. There was a definite Friday-night feeling to the place, and it was, like George's car – not his car, she reminded herself – expensively upholstered. The village pub, all oak-beamed ceilings and thick stone walls, had been given a designer up-grade. The walls were a smooth pale grey, the beams and the ceilings whitewashed. On the floor were dark slate tiles, and in the corner stood a sleek, black log-burning stove.

They were standing looking in on all this from a little greeting area, where the woman was tapping the clipboard with her pen thoughtfully. George leaned across, trying to read the woman's booking sheet.

'I booked it myself the other day. O'Hara. There can't be many of us around here, surely?' He gave her the smile that had worked wonders on Daisy earlier in the week.

She spun round the clipboard, offering it to him.

George ran a long finger down the list of bookings for Friday night. 'The only booking you've got for eight-thirty is—'

'Little brother. I can't get you out of my hair at the moment, can I?'

Daisy did a double take. The accent was identical, and when she looked up, so were the bright blue eyes. George's brother traced a finger down the booking list with a nod of approval.

'Eight-thirty p.m. That's us. Evening, Sarah.' He winked at the receptionist, who blushed prettily.

George took the clipboard again, looking down at the booking sheet. 'Stephen.'

'That's m'name.' Stephen winked again, this time at Daisy.

'I booked a table the other day – I called and booked in the name of O'Hara, for eight-thirty.' George was frowning in confusion. Daisy, aware that the other diners were beginning to look up from their conversations, sensing something was going on, shuffled backwards slightly.

The receptionist looked at George, and back at his brother. They gave her identical, crinkly-eyed smiles.

'Twins,' said George, in case it wasn't clear. Daisy and the receptionist exchanged a glance which said that yes, it was perfectly clear to anyone. The two men were identical – the only difference, as far as Daisy could see, was that George was slightly taller.

'You rang the other day.' The receptionist had the expression of someone who'd just realized her own mistake. 'I scribbled it down on a Post-It note in the office, and meant to transfer it onto the booking sheet. When I got another call from an O'Hara with an Irish accent, I just assumed you were confirming the booking.'

Stephen threw his arm around George's shoulders. 'Sure, that's no problem. We can just budge up a bit, can't we, bro?'

George looked at Daisy, eyebrows raised in a silent query. He gave an impression, though, thought Daisy, that he was unruffled by this turn of events. She resolved to do the same, squaring her shoulders.

'I'm sure it'll be fine, George. Hello, I'm Daisy.' She held out her hand to Stephen. He shook it vigorously.

'Grand to meet you, Daisy. Michelle will be glad of the company, I'm sure. She tells me all I do is talk business over dinner when we have a night away from the kids.'

From behind Stephen's shoulder, George gave Daisy a slightly rueful smile which she returned brightly, having resolved to make the best of things. A lot of women would say that sitting opposite not one but *two* handsome, blue-eyed Dubliners wasn't the worst thing that could happen on a Friday night. And it definitely took the first-date pressure off.

'Stephen?'

Daisy felt eyes burning into the back of her head and turned round slowly, discovering the owner of the sharp voice she'd heard. Standing in the porch, her long blonde hair immaculate, was a woman who had to be Michelle. She was impossibly thin, pipe-cleaner legs clad in skin-tight black trousers despite the June heat. She was taller than Daisy, thanks to a pair of stiletto sandals which wrapped in a criss-cross of tiny strands across perfectly pedicured feet. Daisy gave an involuntary glance down at the cute, summery linen wedges she'd put on an hour before. They suddenly looked clumpy and graceless.

'What's going on? George, what are you doing here?'

'Michelle, darling, this is George's new girlfriend he's been keeping hidden.' Stephen, clearly used to his wife's peremptory tone, caught her by the waist and pulled her gently forward.

'Not girlfr –' began Daisy, awkwardly. George gave a wide smile and said nothing.

'We're just out for dinner,' Daisy continued, aware that she was being scanned up and down by Michelle's all-seeing eye as she spoke. 'Only there was a bit of a mix-up with the booking, and—'

'And there's room for all of us. You'll be glad of a bit of girl talk, Michelle, I'm sure?' Stephen, apparently oblivious to the atmosphere, gave a huge smile and propelled his clearly unwilling wife forward just as the waitress beckoned them to a table.

Once they'd settled and been served starters, the woman from the front desk came towards them. 'Everything all right?' she asked, her voice discreetly lowered.

'Grand.' Stephen, swallowing a mouthful of delicious-looking terrine, nodded, looking around for agreement.

Daisy shot George a quick glance. He raised an eyebrow so quickly she wasn't sure she'd imagined it.

'Lovely, thanks,' said Daisy, politely. She'd already devoured the delicate puff of trout mousse which had rested, looking as beautiful as it tasted, on her bone china plate. The starters were delicious, but tiny. She hoped nobody else had heard the growl her stomach had just made, but she was holding out for the main course being a bit bigger.

So far, they'd managed some typically polite conversation about the weather (surprisingly warm, they all agreed, even for June in the south-east of England) and Stephen had deferred to George on the wine choice, saying he knew more about that sort of thing.

'So,' said Michelle, dabbing at her still-perfect lipstick with a napkin. 'How did you and George meet?'

'She conned me into buying her a drink after work one night. I'd just got off the train from a meeting in London, and there she was.'

Daisy laughed. 'I didn't exactly con you. You just accidentally got in the way of me trying to get another gin and tonic.'

George's eyes caught hers, sending an unexpected fizz of electricity up her spine. 'Well, I'm glad I did.'

Michelle gave a tiny snort, breaking the spell. 'The joys of young love.' Her cynical tone didn't match her words. She turned to Daisy. 'So what is it that you do?'

'I'm a gardener.'

'Really?' Michelle cast a quick look down at Daisy's fingernails, as if to confirm it. Daisy curled her hand around the glass. She'd scrubbed them clean and filed them into shape, but they were short and stubby compared to Michelle's perfect talons, brightly painted and filed to sharp points. Everyone in Steeple St John but Daisy seemed to have immaculate nails.

'Stephen's a bit of a garden fan, too, aren't you?' Michelle's tone was arch. 'You two should talk shop.'

Daisy noticed George giving Michelle a quieting frown. Michelle took a sip of wine, hiding a cat-like smile behind her full glass of red. The waitress whipped away the plates from their starters as they spoke.

'Hush now, Michelle.' George turned to Daisy, smiling at her reassuringly. 'I'm sure Daisy's got no interest in that sort of thing.'

Daisy found herself prickling slightly at the patronizing implication that she wasn't up to anything more than polite small talk. She took a sip of wine, avoiding George's eye.

As the main courses started to arrive, conversation turned to Ireland. Daisy noticed that when George and Stephen spoke about their homeland their accents thickened. It took a moment to tune in and understand every word they said.

'Have you ever been to Ireland, Daisy?' George reached across, topping up her glass.

'Not since I was a little girl, no. My dad worked for a while as visiting fellow at Queen's University, so we went over there a few times when I was small. But I've never been to the South.'

'You'd love it.' Stephen picked up a piece of bread, breaking it into pieces before eating it in rapid bites. Michelle looked on, lips pursed in an expression of mild distaste. Daisy, who suspected the addition of herself and George to their table hadn't been as warmly accepted by Michelle as her husband might have thought, felt a wave of discomfort. There was no chance of this evening getting too intimate, after all – the atmosphere was veering between vaguely polite and positively frosty.

'The sea bass?' Their waitress returned, her arms stacked with more plates. The service was more in keeping with a posh London restaurant than a little village pub; but this place wasn't like any pub Daisy had ever visited. She'd noted the prices with a silent gulp of horror, before deciding that she'd just have to put her half on the credit card. The Grey Mare seemed ridiculously cheap in comparison. The waitress quietly and efficiently served the food and backed off, invisible once again.

'So have you been in the village long, Daisy? I

haven't seen you around.' Michelle speared a slender stem of asparagus, cutting it into tiny, precise pieces before popping one into her mouth. Daisy felt a pang of empathy with the asparagus. Michelle was reminiscent of the women who'd turned up at Elaine's house that first night – brittle, unsmiling, and without an ounce of warmth. She shuddered at the memory.

'I've been here a few months. I'm just staying in my parents' house while they're off travelling.'

'Another thing you've got in common with George, then.' Stephen gave her a smile. He, at least, was trying to make her feel at ease. 'He's staying with our Aunty Char.'

Daisy remembered Charlotte's basket full of plants, and her eyes bright with laughter as she explained how she'd cleared the shelves at the plant stalls. Somehow, Daisy hadn't thought to mention to Thomas that she was going out with George. Thinking back, she couldn't put her finger on why.

She fiddled with her fish, trying to make sure she didn't accidentally take a mouthful of bones. She'd no idea what had possessed her to choose the most awkward food possible. It had been a panicked decision made at the last moment – fish, that'll do, she'd thought, as the waitress and the other three looked at her expectantly.

Michelle leaned forward, her long fake-tanned arm stretching gracefully across the table to steal an olive from Stephen's salad.

'We've been over here a couple of years now. There's a lovely school for our little ones – Brockville Prep – have you heard of it?'

'Oh, yes.' Daisy was grateful to latch onto something, anything that was familiar. 'My friend Elaine's husb— er, I know someone who works there.'

'You know Leo Thornton-Green?' Michelle turned, sharply. She sat forward, her pointed chin balanced on a slender, bright-tipped finger.

'Not really.'

Michelle's eyes were on her, her gaze intent. This must be how it feels to be trapped by a cobra, thought Daisy. Michelle sat back slightly, her chin angling upwards almost imperceptibly.

'It's his wife I'm friends with. Leo's not –' She stopped herself for a moment. Not my cup of tea, she thought. Not the sort of man I'd want my friend to be married to, if I had the choice? 'Not really around much. I tend to pop round to do the garden while he's out at work.'

'Oh, so you're their *gardener*,' said Michelle, dismissively. She settled fully back in her chair, disinterested again, picked up her slender phone with its sparkling case and started scrolling down the screen.

Daisy looked at George, who was also sitting back against his chair, fingers steepled in interest. She took a too-big gulp of wine, stalling for time, feeling it hit the back of her throat with a wallop. She leaned forward, taking a sudden interest in her complicated fish once again.

Another awkward half-hour passed before the plates were cleared away. Stephen was perusing the pudding menu, Michelle still glued to her phone. George seemed oblivious to Daisy's discomfort.

'D'you fancy a coffee, Daisy?'

Thank goodness the end was in sight. George might be handsome, with twinkly blue eyes and an accent that could make anything sound appealing, but the meal had been torturous.

'That would be – lovely.' She tried to keep the relief out of her voice. Thank goodness it was almost over. 'I'll just – excuse me for a moment.'

Escaping to the loos, she closed the door and pulled out her phone.

> Okay, you win: text report. NOT, I should add, from the bedroom.

She hit send on a group text to Jo and Elaine, watching as the message status flicked to 'delivered'. She couldn't be ages, or the other three would wonder where she'd gone. She tapped another message onto the screen.

> Cornered into dinner with his brother and super-frosty wife. I'm STILL bloody starving. Think I'm definitely destined for single life.

Jo's response flashed back.

Interesting choice for a first date. You surviving, though?

Daisy texted quickly in reply.

Definitely not. But better run, they'll think I've got stuck in
the loo.

'So.' Stephen's voice was casual as he leaned forward, passing Daisy the sugar. 'You're living in the big
villa on the lane? Orchard Villa, you said, George?'

'Yes – well, temporarily. My parents have gone
travelling. To be honest, though, I'm far keener on the
place than they seem to be.'

'Really?' He cocked his head slightly, eyes bright.

'Stephen.' She looked up, catching George flashing
his brother what looked like a warning look.

'I was telling Stephen the other day how much
work you've been doing on the garden,' said George,
smoothly. 'That'll be why he's asking all the questions.
You've got it looking grand out front now,' he waved a
hand, describing an arc, 'with the rose thing and the
flowers and all that.'

'Thanks.' She was flattered someone had noticed the
work she and Thomas had put in. With the summer
establishing itself, the garden was beginning to take
shape beautifully, and their work was revealing the
structure of the planting. It was kind of George, who

definitely wasn't a gardener, to notice. She caught his eye and gave him a genuine smile of gratitude.

Stephen, who'd busied himself with stirring the coffee, seemed to have lost interest in the conversation. Daisy, more than ready to make her escape, was quite glad to absorb herself in sipping her espresso and gazing surreptitiously at the other diners. She was almost certain that the couple she'd caught sight of beyond the pillar were a high-ranking politician and – wasn't that Sylvia Diamond, the actress? She tried not to make it obvious she was scrutinizing them from afar.

Michelle, animated for the first time that evening, followed her gaze. 'It's him,' she confirmed with a knowing nod, lips pursed in disapproval. 'Dirty *bugger*. This place is perfect for people like him – nobody round here would breathe a word because they're all at it.'

Stephen, whom Daisy had thought wasn't paying attention, leaned forward, looking sideways at Michelle. 'Not all of us, eh, sweetheart?'

Michelle responded with another of her tiny, self-satisfied, cat-like smiles. 'Absolutely not, darling.'

Daisy hid a shudder. She couldn't put her finger on what it was about the couple that made her feel so uncomfortable, but behind the expensive clothes and the perfectly done hair, there didn't seem to be much – *anything* – there. Certainly no warmth or affection.

Stephen gave his wife a proprietorial pat before

turning his attention back to the little dish of chocolates that had arrived with the coffee. As he did so Daisy watched Michelle covertly. Her nostrils curled, almost invisibly, and she gave her husband a fleeting look of such disdain that Daisy, startled, looked away.

'God, I'm truly sorry, Daisy.' George opened the car door at the end of the evening.

She shook her head, laughing. 'It's not your fault. How were we to know your brother had double-booked the same place?'

'Serves me right for trying to be cool.' He climbed into the convertible and switched on the engine, rumpling his hair with a genuinely rueful expression. 'And the food wasn't even all that.'

'My fish was lovely, in between the bones.'

'And you're sure you didn't want to stay for another coffee and liqueurs with Michelle and my brother?' George paused a moment before reversing the car out of the parking space. The car park was quite a bit emptier now, only a scattering of expensive vehicles dotted around on the gravel.

'Quite sure, thanks. I didn't realize that place had rooms as well.'

'Luxury ones, at that. Well, it's lucky for us they were spending the night, or no doubt they'd be following us back into Steeple St John for a nightcap.'

Daisy looked down at her knees. Thank goodness it was dark and he couldn't see her flushing scarlet. It had been a few years since she'd been on the scene, but after a disastrous attempt at a date, surely he wasn't suggesting –

'I'm not sure I'm –' she stopped, not quite sure how to put it. God, it had been a while since she'd done all this, but surely he wasn't proposing they head straight home to bed?

George slid the car to a halt, checking for traffic before he pulled out onto the narrow country lane. 'I wasn't angling for an invite.' He laughed, putting her slightly more at ease.

'Tell you what. D'you fancy another coffee?' He took a left turn, steering the car down another narrow, tree-lined lane, then turning onto the dual carriage-way to London. It was ten o'clock and the evening light was fading quickly.

Despite the after-dinner espresso, Daisy's head was reeling slightly from a large glass of white and a pre-dinner gin and tonic. The food had been so deli-cately proportioned that she was utterly ravenous. Michelle and Stephen had put away the rest of the wine, clearly glad of a night away from their two daughters, who were tucked up in bed at home with Great-Aunt Charlotte.

'Daisy?' George pulled the car into a service station.

'Are we out of petrol?'

'No. But if you fancy that coffee?' George indicated the sign in the window.

Daisy gave him a grateful smile. 'I'd love one.'

Five minutes later Daisy was installed on the sofa of the service-station cafe, waiting for George.

'Vanilla latte, no sugar.' He put the tray, which held another coffee and a couple of huge chocolate-chip muffins, down on the table.

'I know we've just been to the best little gastropub in the area, but these are my secret vice.' He gave an apologetic smile, and handed one to Daisy. 'I couldn't help noticing you didn't eat much of the fish.'

'It was a bit tricky, between the bones and the Spanish Inquisition from your sister-in-law.'

George rubbed his jaw thoughtfully. 'She's a bit of a one, Michelle. Hard as nails. Hangs around with a gang of other mothers from that posh school of theirs. You wouldn't want to cross them.'

'I think I already have,' said Daisy, remembering the huddle of identical women at Elaine's house that night, who'd headed off to meet up with a Michelle. It couldn't be coincidence – they were like peas in a pod.

'It's not quite how I imagined this evening, either, if that's any consolation.' George's eyes caught hers. 'So let's start again, shall we?'

'Hello, George. I'm Daisy.' Feeling slightly bolder now she was in a brightly lit cafe, Daisy held out her hand. It says something about me, she thought to herself, that my comfort zone is a Starbucks in a service station and not a posh restaurant populated by errant MPs. She smiled broadly at the thought.

'George O'Hara.' He reached out, shaking her hand

with a laugh. 'So come on then, Daisy. Tell me something about yourself. What brought you to Steeple St John?'

'Well, I was running away from my boyfriend and my ex-best friend, who I'd found having sex up against the kitchen worktop on the final day of term of my horticulture course.' She took a sip of her coffee. 'What's a nice Dublin boy like you doing in a village like this?'

'Me? Oh, well, my ex-wife decided she wasn't that keen on being married after all. She went off to find herself on a yoga retreat in Thailand, leaving me up to my eyes in debt and deep in the shit. We owned a chain of restaurants back home. We'd never quite recovered from the whole Celtic Tiger thing when she up and left.'

Daisy looked at George for a moment. So he'd been married already – he was probably only a few years older than her, and already divorced – or separated, at least. Perhaps the slightly cocky air was a mask for his apprehension about starting over again. He was looking at her as she considered this, his eyes twinkling with amusement.

'Come on, now. You were joking?'

'Were you?' Daisy parried straight back. If he wasn't, it was a hell of a story. Mind you, she still had trouble getting her head round exactly *how* stupid she must've been herself, not to see what was going on with her best friend and her boyfriend right under her nose.

'No, I'm deadly serious.' George tipped his paper cup towards Daisy's in a toast. 'And I'm glad I am, because it means I got to have dinner with you. Even if it was with the unexpected pleasure of my brother's company – not to mention his lovely wife.' He rolled his eyes and continued casually, 'So, this sleazy ex of yours. Is he off the scene now?'

'Well and truly.' As she spoke, a frown flitted across Daisy's face. She scanned her thoughts over the last few weeks, realizing with certainty that no, she wasn't harbouring a secret longing that Jamie would re-appear and sweep her off her feet. She'd even laughed about the whole saga the other day with Ned. They'd sat, laughing and chatting, as they took a break from their mission at the allotments. She smiled at the memory of their morning.

'I'm glad to hear it.' George half-raised his mug in a gesture of acknowledgement.

'So how about you?' Daisy sipped her latte, curling her feet underneath her on the boxy leather sofa. The service station was neon-bright, noisy and chaotic, but they were wrapped up in their own little corner, oblivious to it all.

'I've got a restaurant in Dublin, which needs invest-ment more than it needs me there running it – I've got my cousin Nuala in there running it for me – and I've got responsibilities. I need to make money, fast. Up 'til recently I was a sleeping partner in the family business. So while Stephen's driving around with his two flash cars –' George indicated outside to the convertible – 'I'm driving round in my beat-up old van and putting everything I can into the restaurant business.'

There was something in that Irish accent that Daisy couldn't resist. She leaned forward as he spoke, soaking up his voice. He could charm the birds out of the trees . . .

'I'm sorry, I'm going on. So what are your plans, Daisy?'

She gave herself a little shake. Where to start?

'I don't know. In an ideal world, a successful gardening business, I suppose.' She swirled her coffee, thoughtfully. 'I'm not cut out for office life – I know that much.'

George reached across. 'You've got foam on your nose.' He brushed it away gently, smiling. His eyes were almost indigo now, Daisy noticed.

George took her hand, lacing his fingers through hers, confidently. He seemed so sure of himself, and she found herself swept along.

'I like you a lot, Daisy. And I'm not all that sorry our fancy night out ended up in a roadside cafe with terrible coffee.'

He leaned forward once again, but this time – taking her by surprise – it was to kiss her.

Anyone up for an end-of-night report?

Daisy, sitting up in bed, completely wide awake and zinging from head to toe, sent out an exploratory text. Within seconds, her phone was bleeping with texts from Jo and Elaine, both demanding details.

It might have started like a nightmare but – well . . . we had coffee in the services on the A41 and he kissed me in Starbucks. I feel about fifteen.

Smiling to herself as she replied, then curling herself up in the blanket, Daisy sat back against the pillows. There'd been, she realized as she plugged her phone into the charger by the bed, another missed call from her mum. God, it was far too late to start having a parental conversation – besides, she'd no idea what time it was in wherever-they-were now. It'll wait for the morning, she promised herself, setting the phone to silent mode.

She relived the evening in her head over and over again until she finally fell asleep, not long before the midsummer sun was rising and the birds were beginning their morning chorus outside her window.

Chapter Twelve

Flattened by the heavy-limbed exhaustion that follows a sleepless night, Daisy was woken by the doorbell. It was ages before she realized the persistent ringing was coming from outside, and wasn't part of her weirdly complicated dream – which had also involved the sound of heavy thumping, as if someone was chopping wood. Pulling on a dressing gown, she hurried downstairs and opened the door.

'Morning, love. That's your sign up.'

Daisy rubbed her eyes, looking at him blearily. 'What sign?'

The man brandished a clipboard at her, waving towards the rose arch over the front gate. What the – ?

A For Sale sign, eight feet high and brightly coloured, had been hammered into the lawn. She looked down at the list on the clipboard. Orchard Villa – Mistlethrush & Goodwin, said the printout, with a large blue tick next to it.

'You all right, my love? You look like you've seen a ghost.'

'No,' Daisy stormed. 'I am definitely *not* all right.' Absolutely furious, she slammed the door in his face. She could still see him, standing nonplussed, head shaking, through the glass of the door.

What the *hell* was going on? She spun round, trying to remember where her phone was. Hurtling upstairs, she picked up her mobile and hit return call, not caring what time it was in India. There must be a logical explanation.

'Darling! At last.' Her mum's voice sounded tinny and distant. Daisy pressed the volume button impatiently, holding the phone away from her ear as she did so.

'. . . and so we didn't have a chance to speak to you about it. There'll be someone in touch shortly about putting up a sign.'

Daisy raised her eyebrows, taking a breath to try and calm herself before she spoke. She sat down on the edge of the bed with a heavy sigh.

'Darling? This isn't a very good line at all.'

'I'm here.' Her voice was icy cool. 'So let me get this straight. You've put Orchard Villa on the market without even *talking* to me?'

'Well, dear, we've been trying to get hold of you for a few days, in fairness.' Daisy recognized that tone. The soothing, slightly cajoling voice her mother had used over the years when strong-willed Miranda threatened to go off the rails. Easy-going Daisy, though, had always been the straightforward one. Was that a hint of surprise travelling down the line from India?

Daisy gritted her teeth. Admittedly they *had* tried to ring, but even so. 'You said you were staying on for a few months' more travelling.'

'I know, dear, but as I would have explained earlier this week – *if* you'd returned my calls or picked up the phone –' Daisy could imagine the precise expression on her mother's face as she said these words – 'we've decided to stay on a bit longer. We've met a marvellous couple – Pru and Gordon, they're writers.'

Sod bloody Pru and Gordon, who sounded like sitcom characters. Why on earth they had to appear and start complicating Daisy's life, just when things were going well, was beyond her.

'I'm very glad to hear that,' lied Daisy. 'But I don't understand why that means you're selling Orchard Villa. I've been working on the garden for ages, and I've been creating a series of articles for a friend, and . . .' she trailed off, realizing she sounded about five.

'We're going SKI-ing, darling.' Her mother laughed, sounding rather pleased with herself. Daisy repressed murderous thoughts.

'Do they even *have* snow in India?' She ought to know that sort of thing, really. Also, what on earth were her aged parents doing taking up high-risk sports in their dotage?

'Not that kind of skiing, silly. Spending the Kids' Inheritance. S – K – I. You see?'

Oh, brilliant, thought Daisy. Even better. 'I do see, yes. So you're becoming eternal students and turfing me out. It's fine.' Passive aggression had never worked on her mother in the past. Not surprisingly, it had no effect this time, either.

'For goodness' sake, darling. We're hardly slinging you out on your ear. It'll take a while to sell, and you're welcome to stay there in the meanwhile. You're bound to sort something out, you always do. Good old—'

'*Do – not – even – start,*' said Daisy, furiously. If she heard that particular phrase one more time, she wouldn't be responsible for what she'd do. 'It's fine. I'll manage. I have to go, Mum, there's someone at the door.'

'We need to talk about the details,' her mother began, trying to keep Daisy talking.

'Later. I'll call you tonight.' And with that, Daisy ended the call, throwing the phone onto the pillows in disgust.

'Are you sure there's not some kind of mix-up? I can't quite believe they'd sell the place from underneath you,' said Elaine, shaking her head. They'd driven together to the nearby town of Wellbury to meet Jo for lunch and were sitting outside in the sunshiny garden of a lovely little cafe, waiting for her to turn up from her previous client meeting. Daisy, still fuming at her mother's blithe assumption that her reliable elder daughter would just 'sort something out, darling', was relieved to discover the cafe had an alcohol licence, because coffee was definitely not going to cut it. Elaine, wisely, had offered to drive. Daisy was half-way down a large glass of white already, one moment saying she didn't want to talk, the next ranting furiously between swigs.

'Every bloody time. *Good old Daisy*, she'll sort herself out. Not a thought for where I'm supposed to go, or for the fact they told me to make myself at home. And all the time I've spent renovating the garden! And what about Thomas?'

Jo, who'd slipped into her chair unnoticed by Daisy in full flight, took the opportunity to kiss Elaine hello.

'God, I'm sorry.' Daisy leaned across, accepting a kiss on the cheek from her friend, stemming the flow for a moment.

'You got the text?'

'I did, yes. I know you're probably feeling pretty let down right now, but—'

'It's fine,' said Daisy, with a sigh of resignation. 'Believe it or not, I'm used to this sort of stuff. I'm realizing at last that the trouble with being the easy-going, reliable one is people tend to just walk all over you.'

Jo nodded, letting Daisy fill the space in the conversation, allowing her to work things out for herself. She was a good listener, and Daisy could easily have filled the afternoon with her grumblings – but she buttoned her lip, remembering this was Jo's only hour off work.

'There's got to be a way around this, surely?' Elaine, ever practical, pulled out her omnipresent Moleskine notepad and held her pen poised. 'Let's have a brainstorm.'

'Seriously, Elaine, I'd rather not. Let me wallow for a day or so. Then we can start sewing prawns in the curtains, or inventing a rumour about ghosts living in the attic for the village newsletter.' She scooped up a mouthful of delicious aubergine dip. This place was, as was always the case with Elaine's choices, out of the ordinary. From the outside it gave the impression of being nothing more than your average quaint, pretty little cafe, complete with hanging baskets on the white-rendered walls either side of a tar-black door. But the food was absolutely heavenly, and Daisy, who'd been too busy to eat breakfast, having spent the morning fuming whilst gardening at lightning speed to relieve her tension, was ravenous.

'Anyway, enough about me,' she said, turning to Jo. 'What's happening with you this week? Any exciting news?'

Jo looked up from her salad, pausing with her fork in mid-air. She'd been quiet since she arrived. Daisy realized suddenly that Jo, too, had something on her mind. But where she'd rambled on and on, Jo had just sat peacefully, waiting for a chance to talk. She watched as Jo ran a hand through her blonde hair, gathering it up in a clip before letting it all fall free again so it hung over her face.

'Yes. No. I don't know.' Jo's face twisted anxiously. She fiddled again with her hair.

'What's up?'

'It's Tom.' She mouthed his name, as if someone might overhear.

Daisy and Elaine exchanged glances and pulled their chairs closer to the table simultaneously, leaning in towards their friend.

'He's won a major poetry prize. I read about it in the books section of the Sunday paper.'

'And?' Elaine had leaned forward, chin in her hand, eager for more information.

'He's coming over from Amsterdam to collect it in person. To Southbeach. There's a big literary festival, and a prize-giving. It's a big deal.'

'Oh God,' said Daisy, feeling a wave of apprehension on her friend's behalf. 'Are you going to go?'

Jo pulled a face. 'I've been mulling it over since the weekend. All I've got to lose is sixty quid in petrol, my self-respect, possibly my child . . . oh, and the contents of my house. If I leave Martha unattended she'll have half of year ten round for one of those Facebook parties you hear about, and I'll be run out of Steeple St John.'

'She could stay with me.' Daisy realized as she opened her mouth that she'd have no chance of keeping Jo's strong-willed teenager under control if she decided to rebel. She had enough trouble looking after an aged golden retriever.

'Cope with Martha for a weekend? She's bloody hard work.' Jo closed her eyes, remembering. 'Last weekend she sneaked off to the Red Lion with a ton of eyeliner on and came home plastered on cider. I managed to sober her up with pints of water and black coffee, but then she insisted on staying up watching her favourite bands on the Kerrang channel until four in the morning. She's so bloody obstinate.'

Elaine raised the bottle of wine in Jo's direction, a questioning look on her face. Jo shook her head, and Elaine tipped the last of the drink into Daisy's glass.

'It's fine. Martha is very welcome to spend the weekend with us,' said Elaine, firmly. 'These things happen for a reason, Jo. Tom turning up a few hours from here not long after you decided you need to get in touch is a sign. Leave her with me – I mean, Leo's a headmaster, for goodness' sake. I promise she'll be safe.'

Daisy darted a look at Jo, remembering her friend's panic that night they'd talked in the cottage. Accepting the theory of facing up to Tom was one thing – but the reality must be terrifying.

'We'll see,' said Jo, politely. 'There's a lot to discuss before then. I need to think.' She ran her hands through her hair, her pale face pinched with concern.

Daisy looked at her, an idea forming. 'I'll come with you.'

Jo put down the spoon she'd been tapping anxiously on the edge of the table. 'Would you really do that for me?' A degree of colour returned to Jo's cheeks at the thought of not facing it alone.

'Course I would.' Daisy desperately needed an escape, and Jo needed moral support. A weekend away in Southbeach, where she could concentrate on something other than gardening and the life she was about to lose in Steeple St John, was just what she needed. She reached out a hand to Jo with a warm and genuine smile. It would be good to give something back, even if it was just a bit of moral support in gorgeous seaside surroundings.

'That's what friends are for, remember?'

Daisy collapsed through the door, her head throbbing slightly from drinking in the afternoon. Her plans for the rest of the day consisted of coffee, a corner of the sofa, a heap of magazines and something trashy on television. Grabbing a bottle of full-fat Coke, a six-pack of Penguin biscuits and the remote control, she flopped down on the sofa. Everything else – the house, which she supposed would need to be tidied up if it was now for sale, and the garden, which she couldn't think about right now without feeling a twist of sadness welling up in her stomach – it could all wait until tomorrow. She flicked on the television, finding an episode of *Friends* and snuggling down. She had enough chocolate on hand to obliterate any feelings, and a tub of ice cream in the freezer. That'd do for now.

She stood up an hour or so later, realizing she'd better let Polly out into the garden for a quick leg-stretch. She whistled, opening the front door. Polly meandered past, stiff-legged from her afternoon snooze. Daisy stood in the doorway, looking out at the huge For Sale sign, cursing its existence.

It was only habit that made Daisy pick up the phone when it rang beside her on the dresser. If she'd only been thinking straight, she'd have ignored it and headed back to the sofa.

'Miss Price?'

'Daisy, please.'

'Matthew Goodwin, Mistlethrush and Goodwin. Can I just say it's an absolute honour to be taking responsibility for Orchard Villa.'

Daisy rolled her eyes at her reflection in the mirror of the dresser. She noticed as she did so that she had chocolate smudges all over her chin. She rubbed them away thoughtfully. She realized he was still talking, but she'd no idea what he'd said.

'Mmm,' she said, vaguely, hoping it would fill in the gaps.

'It's a real treat to have the opportunity to market a property like this. These big Victorian villas don't come up for sale very often. I'm sure it'll be off your hands in no time.'

A bit more salt for your wound, there, Miss Price, thought Daisy. It might be a jewel in your agency's crown, but I happen to be quite attached to that garden, never mind the house. She could imagine this Matthew Goodwin with pound signs in his eyes. No doubt her parents would make a fortune from the place, which was lovely for them but was going to leave her distinctly lacking in somewhere to live. If only they'd given her some indication . . .

'So we'll be round ASAP to take the measurements, just as soon as your parents have got the contracts back to us. There's always going to be a bit of a delay with the time difference, but it shouldn't take too long.'

There's no rush, Daisy mouthed silently. In fact, she thought, wondering if the old sewing-prawns-in-the-curtains trick actually worked, the longer the house takes to sell, the better.

'Well, in that case, I'll wait to hear from you – thanks for calling.' Daisy hung up, realizing as she did so that he was still talking. Never mind, she decided. He'll ring back if it's important.

Retreating to her hideaway on the sofa, she heard the bleep of her phone. Oh God, had her parents given the estate agents her mobile number, too? She groaned, picking it up from the table.

Sorry last night was a bit of a disaster. Fancy dinner tomorrow to make up for it? G x

She curled her feet up beneath her on the sofa, smiling to herself. Now in theory, according to Miranda's incredibly complicated Rules of Dating, she was supposed to ignore this text for at least three hours before casually replying with the suggestion that she was out somewhere doing Something Very Interesting.

I'd love that.

Sod it, thought Daisy, who was tired of playing by the rules.

Great. How about I swing by and pick you up at 8?

Clearly George hadn't read the rules either.

Chapter Thirteen

It was almost eight in the evening, and Daisy's hair looked like she'd stuck her finger into a plug socket. Having decided to have a pampering day and ignore the million things she could be doing in the garden (somehow there didn't seem much point at the moment, with the house up for sale and everything up in the air), she'd followed a recipe she'd seen on Elaine's website for a natural hair conditioner. It had looked, and smelt, seriously dodgy when she put it on, wondering as she smeared the paste of olive oil and avocado onto her long hair whether she'd misread the instructions. An hour and seven washes later, she'd managed to stop smelling like a salad, but her hair was now rebelling.

Bugger, bugger, she thought, trying to find a hairband or some grips to pin it back. There had to be some in – ah, thank goodness, there they were. With a prayer of thanks to the hair gods, she twisted the front section into loose plaits, weaving them together at the crown of her head.

'Look at you.'

Daisy was taken by surprise by George, who leaned down, kissing her gently on the cheek.

'Hello,' he said, his mouth still close to her skin. The combination of the deep Irish accent and his breath on her skin made the hairs on the back of her neck stand on end. She inhaled sharply, looking up into his eyes. They were really quite dizzying in their intensity. She took a step back, surprised at her reaction.

'Hi.' She chewed on her lip, looking at him standing in the doorway. He was in a faded pair of jeans and a white linen shirt, the sleeves rolled up to reveal tanned arms. A thick leather belt with a heavy, battered silver buckle sat on his hips.

'Do I pass?' He grinned at her, raising two bags in his hands, indicating their weight. 'I hope you don't mind, but I had an idea.'

She looked at the bags, realizing they were full of shopping, the clinking suggesting wine.

'I don't get a chance to get in the kitchen much at the moment – Aunt Charlotte's not much of a fan of my cooking, and we didn't have that much luck with dinner the other night. So I thought maybe I could cook for you here?'

Her first thought was – *thank God* I cleaned up the kitchen earlier. Her second, which followed the briefest moment later, she pushed to one side. There was something in that slightly cocky, I'm-not-even-going-to-run-this-by-you attitude that made her slightly uncomfortable. Was she being a bit control-freaky? It was, after all, a nice idea. She stepped back to allow him in, narrowly missing Polly, who'd clambered out of her spot in the evening sunshine of the kitchen to investigate what all the fuss was about.

'Hello, my darlin'.' George put down a bag and rubbed the dog's ears affectionately. She gave a gruff little noise of approval and turned back to her bed.

He's nice to dogs, Daisy reminded herself. That's a good sign.

'Come through.' She motioned him into the kitchen, where he put the bags down on the long, scrubbed pine table. 'I've never had a real live chef cook for me before. I'm a bit worried I don't have the right equipment.'

George, a bottle of wine in hand, looked up from the bag he was unpacking with a laugh. 'Sure, you look like you've got the right equipment from where I'm standing.'

Daisy burst out laughing. 'I thought you Irish boys were supposed to have a way with words.'

He pulled a mock-dismayed face. 'I'll have to try a bit harder. That was a bit corny, wasn't it?'

She hitched herself up onto the kitchen table, legs swinging. 'I don't think we've got a corkscrew. Is this the wrong time to admit I always cheat and buy screw-tops?'

'Don't worry yourself. I've come prepared.' George

reached into the bag that had been slung over his shoulder, pulling out a fabric bundle. He untied the fastening, revealing a couple of chefs' knives and a professional-looking stainless-steel corkscrew.

'I can't cook without my own knives.' He passed her the wine bottle. 'Now if you open this, it can breathe while I prepare the starter.'

'Can I do anything to help?' Daisy peeled off the foil, watching as George laid out the ingredients on the table in front of her. Slipping down from the table, she fetched couple of wine glasses from the cupboard and placed them beside him. He looked across his shoulder at her, not pausing from his work.

'Do you like scallops?'

'God, yes.'

'Glad to hear it. I love a girl who likes her food.'

'I'm always starving at the end of the day – gardening leaves me ravenous.'

'Then,' said George, reaching across and opening a second bottle of wine – this one white, the condensation trickling down the sides of the glass, 'you and I are going to get on just fine, Daisy.' With an irresistible smile he poured her a glass, and another for himself.

'I always like to have a glass while I cook. *Sláinte.*'

'Cheers.'

He clinked her glass gently, looking directly at her with those mesmerizing blue eyes. There was no escaping the fact that he was ridiculously handsome, and the attention was extremely flattering.

She perched on the table again as George slid the sizzling scallops onto a bed of jade-green leaves. In the past, Daisy had lost her appetite when she'd met someone she liked, but there was no chance of that happening tonight. She reached across, pinching a dark red disk of chorizo which had fallen from the frying pan onto the table.

'Oi, you,' said George, catching her eye with a smile. Defying him, she popped it into her mouth, laughing. 'Take the wine outside, I'll be there in a second.'

Daisy placed the glasses on the table in the garden. She'd already set a little jug of flowers there, gathered that evening from the borders, which were now vibrant with colour. Night-scented stocks perfumed the air, and in the evening light the starry flowers of the nicotiana glowed bright white in the pots behind her, laced with an underplanting of lacy green ferns. It was lovely to relax in the last of the sunshine, a glass of wine in hand, listening to the sounds of George clattering around in the kitchen, humming to himself as he cooked her dinner. She sat back, head against the back of the chair, and closed her eyes. This all seemed very civilized. After Jamie, she'd been pretty convinced that she wasn't going to get involved with anyone in a hurry, but George was charming, and easy company. It didn't do any harm that he was gorgeous. And – her stomach growled again, anticipating the feast – he could cook.

'Here we are.' She looked up at him. He was balancing two plates on his arm, and had a bowl of bread in his other hand.

Daisy was presented with a warm salad of scallops, chorizo and watercress. She leaned across, pouring some wine into his glass. They sat chatting about nothing much – the weather, life in the village, the upcoming fundraising barbecue for the church roof which his aunt was helping with – for a good half an hour. She could feel the wine going to her head a little, but the sensation of being fed, and admired, was intoxicating in itself.

'I'm a bit surprised by the size of this place.' Sitting back, his wine glass almost empty, George motioned vaguely to the gardens that stretched beyond them. Out of the shade of the house, the apple trees of the orchard were lit up by a last blaze of evening sunlight, their leaves glowing. The garden looked beautiful at this time of night, when the light was low enough that the borders Daisy hadn't quite tidied up blurred into an impressionistic haze of washed-out pastel shades.

He stood up, peering towards the back of the garden. 'What is it, half an acre? Three quarters?'

'I don't know. Half, maybe?' Daisy, who was trying to avoid thinking about the garden, was vague.

'Would you show me around before I cook the main course? I'd love to see it.'

She couldn't resist an opportunity to show off what she and Thomas had achieved. Slipping out of her seat, she stretched across the table and hooked the wine bottle with one hand, pulling it towards her.

'Shall we have another glass?'

'Sounds good to me.' George took the bottle from her gently, filling each glass with the floral-scented white wine, which suited the fragrant evening garden so well.

'So what're your plans, with this place on the market? Are your parents looking for a quick sale?'

They'd made their way to the far end of the garden, beyond the apple trees with their tiny young fruit bunched on the branches. The last of the sunlight warmed the earth of the vegetable garden, long shadows of the fruit cages cast across the grass.

'I haven't a clue. My sister's got a place in North London – I can stay with her for a while, I suppose . . .' Daisy trailed off, looking down the garden towards the back of Orchard Villa. She loved her days pottering here with Thomas, and the time she'd spent working on Elaine's garden had made her feel she was really getting somewhere, honing her skills. Just the other day, Elaine had commented that a neighbour had been asking quite a few questions about her new gardener. If she'd been staying, there was definitely the potential here in the village to create a good life and put down roots.

All that was going to come to nothing, though, with the house on the market. She gave a sigh. She'd arrived in Steeple St John determined to keep her head down and avoid taking any part in village life, but somehow she'd found herself being woven into the regular meetings of the Parish Council – and Ned's company made the allotment committee, which had started out as a polite obligation, into one of her favourite parts of the week. She smiled to herself, thinking of their last escapade at the Parish Council. Ned had insisted they play a game incorporating lines from *Star Wars* into their conversation with Flora and the other members of the committee. By the end of the night Daisy had been bent double, helpless with laughter, her sleeve stuffed in her mouth to keep herself quiet. Ned, who'd been the one making her laugh until she cried, had sat, innocent and injured, when Flora looked across at him disapprovingly.

She rubbed her hands on her arms, absently. A light wind was ruffling her hair and she shivered unexpectedly, realizing as she did that she'd been daydreaming for ages.

'Shall we go back down? You look like you're getting chilly.' George's words broke through her thoughts. This was why she'd wanted to avoid getting into a conversation about the garden, and the house being sold. Her previously buoyant mood had deflated, despite George's attentive and charming company. She shook herself, trying to put it out of mind.

'Shall I clear these away?' They reached the terrace, which was still warm, sheltered as it was by the stone walls of the house. Daisy made to pick up the plates they'd used for their starter.

'No, don't worry, I'll do it. Honestly, it's no trouble.' George stood up, looking down at Daisy's empty plate with a smile. 'I love cooking for people who appreciate it.'

It was lucky, thought Daisy. The food was delicious, and she'd never mastered the art of a dainty appetite.

'It was gorgeous. If you're sure?'

With a quick movement, George scooped up the plates, stacking them neatly. 'Just give me a few minutes. How'd you like your steak?'

'Umm.' Daisy stalled for a moment. The truth was pinkish but definitely not gruesomely bloody, but was that a terrible admission of failure to a chef? 'Medium, if that's not the greatest sin known to man.'

'Not at all.'

With a smile – which sent a prickle of warmth right down to her toes – he leaned across, his arm brushing against hers as he caught her wine glass with a finger to pick it up.

'You sure you can manage all that?' Daisy half-stood, as if to offer her help, but with a shake of the head he motioned for her to sit down.

'You enjoy the last of the sunshine. I'll only be a sec.'

She pulled her cardigan close around her shoulders. It might be June, but the evening heat soon faded away.

Occupying herself whilst George cooked, Daisy

found the box of matches she'd left by the clay chiminea on the patio. She watched the paper lining she'd placed in there flare up, catching light quickly, and then the firelighters which ignited the kindling underneath the logs. She searched in the little wooden cabinet on the terrace wall for some outdoor candles, which she lit and placed on the table. George popped out carrying a glass bowl full of salad leaves, dotted with herbs.

'Once the sun goes down behind the thatch in the evening,' Daisy explained, 'it gets cool in the shade here pretty quickly.'

George reached across, warming his hands against the now-bright flames.

'I love sitting outside. A fire's a grand idea.'

He disappeared into the kitchen again, returning a while later with delicately peppered steaks served with sweetly charred vegetables, and some sort of delicious summer-vegetable puree. He brought out another two wine glasses and replaced the half-drunk bottle of white with the expensively labelled red, which had been allowed to breathe for an hour.

'How did you do all this in that time?' The steak was delicious, melting in her mouth. Daisy gave a sigh of contentment. She put her fork down for a moment, savouring the food, looking across at him.

'I prepared it in advance. There's not much else to do on the weekends at the moment whilst I'm over here.'

'Do you get back to Dublin often?' Daisy hadn't been to Ireland in years. She tried to picture him strolling across the Liffey at dusk, surrounded by huge historic buildings illuminated by the setting sun. It must be a beautiful place to live.

'Not so much at the moment. I'm trying to focus on putting in the hours to get money to bail out the restaurants. I could do with a miracle, really – or a lotto win.' Lost in thought, he gazed up the garden towards the orchard.

'It's getting late. D'you want to go inside, or . . . ?' Daisy looked across at the chiminea. Often in the evenings she'd sit out here for hours, wrapped in a blanket, watching the flames.

'No, it's beautiful out here. Come sit by the fire.'

They pulled their chairs round so they were facing the crackling flames, side by side. Daisy could feel George's thigh warm against hers. He turned for the wine on the table behind, his shirt riding up for a second so that Daisy saw a flash of tanned, muscled back. Full of wine and delicious food, she felt the warmth of desire rushing inside her, and had a most un-Daisy-like urge to reach out and slip a hand underneath his white shirt.

He turned back, bottle in hand. Reaching across, he took the hand that was holding her wine glass and cupped it in his own, holding it steady, pouring in the red wine. Her heart was thudding in her chest now. He was close enough that she could reach out and –

His eyes met hers, and she heard a catch in his breath.

'I don't think we need this, d'you?' he said softly, taking the glass from Daisy's unprotesting hand. He turned to her, a gentle hand brushing back a long strand of hair which had fallen across her cheek, tucking it behind her ear, his hand curling around the nape of her neck. With a practised gesture, his thumb caressed her jaw for a second. She looked into his blue eyes, heard a voice in her head saying *live dangerously*, and fell into a kiss.

Chapter Fourteen

'Do you want me in gardening clothes, or something more respectable?' Daisy called downstairs to a waiting Elaine. She pulled her battered jeans off the end of the bed, scooping up her favourite Head Gardener T-shirt as she did so, and ran downstairs, hair flying.

'No, you look gorgeous like that. Cut-off jeans and flip-flops and a vest – you look super-cute. Very relatable.' Elaine tucked a strand of hair behind Daisy's ear. 'Have you got anything to make you a bit less . . . fuzzy around the edges?'

Running upstairs again, she found the trusty hair serum and smoothed a handful through her hair, looking at herself in the mirror. Sitting in the sun had brought out more freckles, but she was definitely glowing, in any case. She swiped on a bit of brown eyeshadow and some mascara and lip gloss. She didn't want to look like she was trying too hard, but the informative articles she'd written for Elaine's website had proved surprisingly popular, and now Elaine had decided to take some photos and add her in as a gar-

dening expert, writing a weekly column. It was exciting and a bit scary – but, thank God, it was something
positive. It'd keep her mind off the house stuff for the
morning. The thought of explaining to Thomas that
afternoon that Orchard Villa was on the market made
her feel faintly sick. The fundraising barbecue at the
pub had turned from something she was looking forward to into a grim prospect. Maybe it'd pour with
rain and the whole thing would be cancelled . . .

It didn't look like there was much chance of that
happening. They headed up through the village
towards Elaine's house in gentle early-morning sunshine. Elaine, who'd wanted to catch the best light for
her photos, had texted her cautiously at seven a.m.

Don't like to intrude, but – you still okay for this morning?

You're not intruding. I'm walking the dog (and no, ha ha,
that's not some weird euphemism). See you in half an hour?

Daisy, who'd been up ridiculously early, tapped a
reply. She'd been surprised, but slightly relieved, that
George had been keen to get off reasonably early the
night before. He hadn't suggested staying, and she
hadn't offered. Afterwards she'd wondered, vaguely,
why he had been content to kiss her but then disap-
pear into the night. He'd charmingly explained that he
must love her and leave her, as he had some work to
take care of before the morning. Maybe, she'd thought,

remembering the long hours she often worked in the garden before anyone else was up, restaurant owners ended up working hard at the other end of the day.

'This won't take long,' explained Elaine, clicking her camera into place on a tripod. 'I just want a few photos of you to accompany the features, and then I thought it might be fun to do an interview on camera, if we have time?'

Yikes. Daisy had imagined a couple of quick snaps and a headshot to go alongside the features she was writing. *On camera* sounded awfully professional, and a bit nerve-racking.

'If you can just –' Daisy stepped sideways obediently as Elaine posed her into a supposedly natural-looking position. It felt anything but. 'Hold that for a second, then we can get you with the sun at the perfect angle.' She leaned down, adjusting the focus. 'Perfect. Now if you can just take this.'

Elaine handed her a spade, holding it carefully to avoid getting dirt on her trousers. 'Just do a bit of digging in this bed, and I'll take some photos.'

'I'm in flip-flops, though. I'd be shot by the health and safety police if they saw me.'

'Doesn't matter. You look good . . . And now come over here, and if you can just kneel down and just look like you're tending to this bed – the colours here are beautiful.'

The long, elaborately planted border was looking gorgeous now. Delphiniums reached upwards, their flowers cerulean blue. The scents of sage and of tiny catmint flowers mingled in the air as bees worked their magic, buzzing back and forth on the flowery spikes. The last dots of dew sat cushioned in the fat leaves of the sedum plants. It was, Daisy acknowledged, the image of perfection.

It was quite fun allowing herself to be directed into position by Elaine, who predictably wanted everything just so for the photographs. Fortunately, Leo was out of the way. He seemed to be increasingly absent – working very long hours, Elaine explained, on some kind of grant application. They seemed to exist on a ships-that-pass-in-the-night basis, Daisy thought. It wasn't the sort of relationship she'd like – but it clearly worked on some level. The longer they left it without saying anything about what she'd overheard, the more she began to doubt herself. She'd gone over it time and time again, wondering if she'd misconstrued what had been said. Without any concrete proof, there was no way they could say anything, really. Daisy looked down across the terrace to where the golden stone of the Old Rectory glowed in the morning sunlight. It was an idyllic setting.

She leaned forward briefly from her careful pose, spotting a piece of bindweed. It had sneaked, disguising itself, through the leaves of a rose bush. She eased it out carefully. Unchecked, it could strangle the life out of almost any plant, stealthily using the plant as a support before cutting off the light and smothering it.

No wonder gardeners loathed it. One tiny half-inch piece of root was all it took to create a whole monster. She unwound it carefully, scooping the soil out of the way to find the root – it would have to be disposed of carefully or the weed would be back, stronger than ever. She stood up again, brushing dusty fingers clean against her cut-off jeans.

'I've never asked – you said you used to spend summers here in Steeple St John.'

Elaine, hands on the small of her back, stretched thoughtfully, arching gracefully.

'I did, yes. This was my grandparents' house. My parents worked abroad and I spent term times at boarding school, so my summers were always spent here. When my grandfather died a few years ago, he left it to me. We'd been working abroad. Leo was head of a school in Dubai, but he –' There was the briefest pause. 'We decided to come home to the UK. They were looking for a new head at Brockville, and it all just seemed perfect timing. We moved in over that summer.'

'It's beautiful.'

'We're very fortunate,' said Elaine, in a tone that didn't quite match her words.

Daisy sensed the subject was closed, and turned her attention back to the garden.

'I've got my own secateurs in the greenhouse, Elaine, it's fine, I'll just –'

Elaine, shaking her head, was brandishing an

immaculate, brand new pair, the handles printed with a pretty floral design. They didn't bear much relation to the beaten-up old favourites that Daisy normally toted round the garden, a piece of frayed twine acting as a hanging loop.

'You're selling a lifestyle, my darling.' Her tone was brisk, with a note of amusement. 'You need to look the part. These have been supplied by a company who sponsor my gardening section. Just snip away and look pretty.'

'But these are hopeless,' Daisy, ever practical when it came to gardening, protested weakly.

'That doesn't matter. Now, can we have that pretty face you make when you're concentrating, please?'

She wasn't aware she made any particular face when she was concentrating. She snipped away at the climbing roses, collecting the dead heads into a woven wicker trug. Normally she'd just sling them in a plastic tub, but there was a world of difference between her muddy-knees-and-hair-tied-back-in-a-ponytail style of gardening, and the perfect English postcard image portrayed on Elaine's website. She had grown to love Elaine, who had a sweet heart and a dry humour beneath the brittle, not-a-hair-out-of-place exterior. But the whole concept of lifestyle gardening was miles away from anything Daisy would want to do with her own life. Gardening – like real life – was hard work, muddy, and often pretty thankless. She carried on working as Elaine snapped away, trying hard not to think about the For Sale sign that loomed outside the pretty rose arch of Orchard Villa.

'See you this afternoon?'

Photographs done, Daisy was ready to head home.

'Yes, I'm looking forward to it. Leo's promised to be back by twelve, so we'll see you later. I think he's hoping to charm a few potential parents, with the Brockville open day coming up.'

Daisy made her way back to Orchard Villa, studiously averting her eyes to avoid looking in the direction of the sign. Showered and changed into a summer dress, she scanned the sky. Hopefully a stray thundercloud was waiting to empty its contents over the village, and the fundraiser would be cancelled. No such luck – she'd have to face Thomas, and tell him their beloved garden was on the market. With a heavy heart, she picked up Polly's lead.

'Come on, lovely. Loads of dropped sausages for you, I suspect.'

She felt a bit better with Polly by her side for moral support. They strolled up Main Street together.

'Hello, gorgeous.'

Daisy half-turned, recognizing the voice straight away.

'I wasn't talking to *you*,' said Ned, with a snort of laughter. He bent down, ruffling Polly's ears. He looked up at Daisy, then, his face flushing pink. 'Not that you're not gorgeous, Daise.'

She raised an eyebrow, amused at his embarrassment.

'Yes. Well.' He grimaced, changing the subject. 'Anyway.' He looked back at Polly. 'No Monty to annoy you today, my darling.'

Polly had enjoyed a few walks round the park with Monty, but she had no trouble letting him know when she'd had enough of his youthful antics. One sharp look and a warning growl and he'd back off, deferring to her age and wisdom. It was unusual for Ned to come out without his bouncing, exuberant companion, but today he was alone, carrying a bag full of –

'Polly, get out!' Realizing he was distracted, Polly had reached under his arm and worked her nose into his bag, which was full of sausages.

'Oops. Contribution from the surgery for the barbecue,' explained Ned, standing up quickly and holding the bag out of reach. 'If that was Polly's response, you can imagine what Monty would've been like. I've left him back in the flat. He's probably eaten about fifteen pairs of shoes by now.'

'You're supposed to be a pillar of the community, y'know,' said Daisy, as they headed up towards the pub, falling into stride naturally.

'I like to think of myself as an accessible sort of vet.' He looked at her sideways, his green eyes narrowed in amusement.

'That's one way of putting it,' teased Daisy as they

headed through the stone archway and into the beer garden of the Grey Mare.

Flora's bunting was out once again, anchored to the huge oak tree at the foot of the beer garden and reaching out across the car park. In a corner the local brass band were warming up, a discordant cacophony of honking and parping which made Daisy smile. Scarlet faces matched their uniforms. One of the men looked up, giving Daisy a grin and raising a pint in welcome.

'Morning, Daisy, love.'

It took a moment of squinting at him in the sunlight before she realized who it was.

'Dave! Sorry, didn't recognize you all dressed up like that.' It was Flora's friend, the ruddy-cheeked allotment gardener. Without his customary battered cords, faded chambray shirt and flat cap, he looked quite different.

'You're looking very posh.'

Dave's scarlet suit had a black collar, the edges trimmed in gold. Ornate embroidery decorated the cuffs of his sleeves. He tugged at the collar of his shirt, adjusting his bow tie. 'Posh and hot,' he agreed, with a grin. 'I'll be needing another drink after this.'

'I'm looking forward to hearing you in action,' said Daisy.

He gave her a cheery nod and picked up his baritone horn, polishing it briefly with a chamois leather cloth before putting it to his lips.

Pulling on Polly's lead, Daisy turned around, realizing as she did that she'd made a fatal mistake.

'Daisy, Ned. Wonderful.' Flora, for once without a clipboard, looked up from the table where she was folding raffle tickets. 'You two at a loose end?'

'I'm not sure,' said Daisy, stalling, turning to Ned quickly. The first rule of village life, she'd discovered, was always to look purposeful when you turned up to an event like this, otherwise you'd be instantly pressganged into helping.

'We're supposed to be doing, the, er – the thing.' Ned scrabbled around, hopelessly, for an excuse. It was futile, and they both knew it.

Flora looked at them both over her reading glasses, eyebrows raised skywards, lips pursed. She was an old hand at spotting shirkers.

'Well, we could really do with a hand here on the raffle stall for an hour or so. Have a seat.' She stood up, stepping out from her position by the entrance to the beer garden, and indicated the two folding chairs. 'If you could just fold these tickets and pop them in the tub, I'll get Thomas to bring you both a drink. Oh splendid, Ned, are those for me?' She took the bag of sausages out of Ned's hand and scuttled off.

'An hour or so, my arse,' snorted Ned. 'We're stuck here, sausageless, for the duration.' He pulled his chair in, sinking his chin into his hands with a theatrical sigh.

'Don't tell me – this is your only day off this week,

right?' Daisy laughed at his crestfallen expression. She scooped up a handful of raffle tickets and shoved them sideways towards him.

'It's fine. It's absolutely fine. Look at that –' Ned, ticket in hand, pointed towards the opposite side of the beer garden. They could see Flora talking to Thomas, gesticulating in their direction. 'At least we've got a pint of cider on the way.'

'You're easily pleased, Ned, aren't you?' Teasing, Daisy gave him a shove.

'Not at all.' He attempted a smouldering pout, his long eyelashes fluttering on his cheeks. 'I have hidden depths, actually. Like Greta Garbo.'

'Right,' scoffed Daisy.

'Mind you, I don't *vant to be alone* . . . In fact, now you mention it . . .' Ned began, but Thomas interrupted.

'What's that about Greta Garbo?' He'd made his way across to them while they'd been chatting and laughing, and placed two drinks carefully down on the table. 'One of my favourites, she was.'

'Ned's just been explaining how similar they are,' said Daisy, giggling. 'You were going to say something, Ned?'

'It's –' Ned shook his head. 'It was nothing. Just a – just a joke.'

Thomas looked amused. 'You two are as bad as each other. I always had you down as a sensible girl, Daisy. I'll be back in a moment. Just going to check what time the band is playing.'

She had, too, Daisy thought, in moments between the silly banter with Ned that kept them both amused. There was something about his company that brought her out of herself, made life funny. And she'd needed that this afternoon – she still had no idea how to tell Thomas about the house being up for sale, meaning their time together working on the garden could soon be coming to an end. The thought of leaving Orchard Villa – and Thomas, and the girls, and the village – washed over her with a sudden feeling of desolation.

'Right, then,' said Thomas, returning. He pulled up another chair, and picked up some of the tickets they were still folding. 'How many of these is Flora wanting you to do?'

'About eight million, it feels like,' grumbled Ned. He stood up, stretching unconsciously, T-shirt riding up over a tanned, surprisingly toned stomach. 'Just nipping to the loo. Back in a sec.'

'You'd better be,' said Daisy, darkly. 'I don't want you missing out on any of the fun here at raffle central.'

'I wouldn't miss it for the world,' said Ned, flashing her a dazzling smile before disappearing through the fundraising information tent and in towards the pub.

'No Elaine today?' Thomas scanned the gardens.

'She's coming along later,' explained Daisy. Thomas had a soft spot for Elaine, having known her grandparents for many years.

Thomas put down the pint of bitter he'd been

holding, looking at her directly with his pale blue eyes. 'And your parents have put the house up for sale?'

'How did you know?' It had been no time since the sign was hammered in, and the estate agent hadn't even taken any details, let alone put any information in their window on Main Street.

Thomas shook his head, smiling through his white moustache. 'Daisy, I've lived in this village all my life. There's not much gets past me.'

'You saw the sign?' She cringed. She really ought to have sought him out yesterday, but she'd been so wrapped up in getting ready for her date with George – and, she realized, thinking about it, in hoping that if she didn't say it aloud, it wouldn't actually be real.

Thomas explained. 'I was talking to Elizabeth in the Bluebell Cafe this morning. The chap with the van who puts up the signs popped in yesterday afternoon.'

There were some things you couldn't keep quiet in a village like Steeple St John. You simply had to sneeze, and a day later everyone would be convinced you had pneumonia. And yet . . . Daisy frowned, thinking again about Leo's phone call.

'He was complaining to Elizabeth that he'd met some rude clients in his life, but the red-haired woman from that big villa up on the Lane had taken the biscuit. Apparently,' said Thomas, looking at her with amusement, 'she slammed the door in his face.'

Oops. Daisy cringed. That poor bloke had only been doing his job, and she'd been horrible to him.

'So it didn't take much for me to put two and two together, my dear. And from the look on your face, I suspect it wasn't expected?'

She shook her head.

'I'm sorry to hear that. That must have come as a bit of a shock. And after all your hard work, a particularly difficult one.' Thomas reached across, covering her freckled hand with his gnarled, weather-beaten one.

'*Our* hard work,' exclaimed Daisy emphatically, the words tumbling out in a rush. She was so relieved not to have had to tell Thomas herself. She hadn't quite realized just how tense with anticipation she had been at the thought until she was off the hook. 'I can't help feeling they just wanted me to come and act as the hired help before they put the place on the market.' She'd been thinking about this earlier, wondering if she was being cynical. Even as she said it, it sounded a bit unlikely to her ears.

'I don't think that's the case, Daisy.' Thomas shook his head, his words gentle and wise. 'Our gardens give us more than we could ever offer them.'

Daisy looked up at him thoughtfully. 'I suppose they do.'

'We go out there and tend them from the bare earth of spring, through the full flush of the summer, all the fruit and flowers, and then it all dies off again.

Gardeners are born optimists. Every year we start afresh.'

'That's a good way of thinking of it.'

He gave her a kind smile, squeezing her hand again before he stood up, readying himself to make his way over to the table where Daisy recognized his domino-playing friends from the Legion. Flora looked across at them from the other side of the gardens, giving a smile which Daisy couldn't help noticing was aimed rather more at Thomas than at her.

'If there's one thing I've learned in this life, my love, it's that you never quite know what's around the corner. Easier to just enjoy life day to day. I can assure you, Daisy, whatever happens with Orchard Villa will be the right thing for the time.'

'That sounds very Zen,' said Daisy.

'You don't get to be my age without learning a bit along the way. Life just keeps on happening, though. You might as well appreciate it.'

With that, Thomas left Daisy sitting absent-mindedly folding the last of the raffle tickets, watching as the village came together for the fundraiser. Flora stood near the big gas barbecue that had been hired for the occasion. Clipboard in hand, directing people to their stations, she was organizing a group of slightly dejected-looking fathers who'd been put on barbecue duty. The wives, a group of laughing mothers who'd clearly worked out that the secret to dealing with Flora was delegation, batted away their squabbling school-aged children, settled themselves on the grass on picnic blankets, unpacking a never-ending supply of juice boxes and chocolate biscuits. The children swarmed off, heading towards the climbing frame, already giddy with sugar.

She looked up, sensing Ned was on his way back. He raised a hand in greeting, smiling at her through a sea of people who were milling around the gazebo, reading the display of printed information about the church roof renovation fund.

At least if she was going to be stuck on raffle duty all afternoon, it was with Ned for company. It struck her in a second of guilt that she ought to be daydreaming about last night's date with George – which had been quite lovely – and not waiting eagerly for Ned to come back so they could spend the afternoon giggling over Flora's antics, and playing guess-the-mean-girls whilst spying on the gangs of PTA mothers. He'd become a brilliant ally, and he really made her laugh.

The huge barbecue was getting under way, plumes of smoke curling up into the air, filling the garden with delicious smells. Polly was sitting by the side of the table, nose in the air, appreciating the scent of sausages. Daisy could feel her stomach rumbling, but she was stuck behind the table – at least until Ned got back.

She peered through the crowds, trying to see where he'd got to, and saw him standing, one arm casually against a wall, leaning down, his wide mouth curved in a smile, chatting to a tanned, blonde – with those expensive honey-caramel streaks that you only got on the slopes, or from regular trips with Mummy and Daddy to their place in the South of France – and incredibly beautiful girl. Daisy felt a stab of something unfamiliar in her side.

The girl flicked her hair over her shoulder with a casual movement. It tumbled smoothly down her back. Whatever Ned had said was obviously incredibly amusing, because she roared with laughter, showing perfect white teeth. As she spoke, she lifted a wrist covered in friendship bracelets, twirling a strand of hair.

She was *actually* twirling a strand of hair, thought Daisy, who'd previously thought that was something people didn't actually do when flirting, except in cheesy made-for-TV movies. Unbelievable. She took the final handful of tickets and shoved them into the jar, deliberately keeping her eyes away from the spot where Ned and the girl were standing. She felt weirdly dizzy. Maybe she was just hungry. That was it – her blood sugar was low, and her mind was playing tricks. She gave herself a shake. Last night she'd had a fabulous date with the gorgeous, handsome, charming George. She needed to pull herself together and take a leaf out of Thomas's book – start being a bit more Zen about stuff. Ned was her mate. It was no business of hers who he flirted with.

Chapter Fifteen

Daisy was still frowning to herself when a shadow fell across the table. Momentarily dazzled by the sunlight, she squinted up at the two shapes in front of her.

'There you are!'

It was Jo, a plate of food in one hand and her daughter beside her. Daisy stood up, kissing her. Ned and the mysterious, super-glamorous girl would have to wait.

Fourteen-year-old Martha, rarely spotted outside of her bedroom and even more rarely outside in civilization, had clearly been at the hair dye again. The tip of one ear, her parting, and her hair were all a deep, vibrant red. Her eyes were obscured completely by a long fringe. While her mother stood looking cool and pretty in the sunshine, wearing a summery vest, a long twist of bright beads, and a short flower-print skirt, Martha was dressed from head to toe in layers of black. Her hands were buried deep in the pockets of a fluffy mohair cardigan, feet encased in shiny purple Doc Martens.

'Hi, you two,' said Daisy, her voice slightly too bright. 'Everything all right?

Jo cocked her head, looking at Daisy with a curious expression. 'Martha, sweetheart, do me a favour?' She pulled her purse out of her bag, withdrawing a ten-pound note. 'Pop over and get Daisy a burger with everything on it, will you?'

'Can I get a Coke?' Martha, taking the money, sensed her mother's focus was elsewhere.

'Go on, then,' said Jo, rolling her eyes. She knew when she'd been sussed out.

Daisy sat back down at the table.

'You okay?' Jo frowned at her again.

'Yes, yes, absolutely lovely,' said Daisy, trying to sound normal. 'Anyway,' she lowered her voice to a whisper, 'what's happening about our trip to South-beach next weekend? Is Martha *seriously* going to stay with Elaine and Leo?'

Jo looked across towards the queue for burgers. Martha, who'd now pulled a black woollen beanie hat over her hair despite the increasing heat, raised her eyebrows and pulled a face, indicating the wait was longer than expected. Jo took the opportunity to fill Daisy in.

'Weirdly, she's completely happy. I think discovering that Elaine's got a huge television in her den with Netflix on tap, and a guest bedroom with a huge jacuzzi bath, was enough to sway her. She seems to be quite into the idea.'

Jo's phone bleeped a message and she looked down, frowning.

'It's Elaine – says she can't make it, something's come up.'

Elaine had been looking forward to the afternoon. Hopefully it wasn't anything major.

'And how are *you* feeling about the weekend?' Daisy searched Jo's face.

Jo scrunched up her nose, shaking her head. 'Honestly? I have no idea. Sick with nerves, then excited, then terrified – but it's not like I'm turning up to a book festival with Martha in tow.' She paused for a second before continuing, with a wry smile.

'Congratulations, Mr Fox, on your literary prize – oh, and here's your surprise daughter . . .'

Daisy pulled a face. It was an incredibly brave thing Jo was doing, after all these years. The trip to Southbeach was going to be a difficult one – but selfishly, she couldn't help thinking that doing something to help Jo out would have the side-effect of getting her own mind off the sudden traffic-jam of things that were going on here in Steeple St John. She reached out, squeezing Jo's arm. 'I'll hold your hand, don't worry.'

'Thanks.' Jo's smile was warm with relief.

'Hello, you two, what're you whispering about? Am I missing village scandal?'

She'd forgotten Ned for a moment. Here he was, sandy blond hair hanging in his eyes as usual, perched on the edge of the table, two pints of cider in his hands.

'Hi, Jo.' He gave her a smile of welcome, handing a drink across the table to Daisy, who busied herself with straightening up the raffle sign, still feeling a bit weird about her reaction to the gorgeous blonde.

'Here, you have this pint, Jo. I'll nip back in and grab myself another.'

Jo took the drink gratefully, and they watched as he swung off the table and loped back towards the bar.

'He's such a sweetie, isn't he? Martha's going to be pleased he's here. She developed a bit of a crush on him when we had to take Ethel to the vet's. He told Martha she was the most intelligent-looking cat he'd ever met.'

Ethel, Martha's black and white cat, had two un-even splashes of black between her eyes, which looked from certain angles like a question mark. Martha ('don't ask me why,' said Jo, shaking her head in laughter and despair) was convinced she was the rein-carnation of Sherlock Holmes, and had set up a web-site dedicated to photographs of the unsuspecting creature.

Daisy couldn't help laughing – at Ned, with his effortless ability to put people at their ease, and at lovely, awkward, teenage Martha. She was now shuffling towards them, trying to balance two cans of Coke and a burger whilst pushing up the slipping beanie hat which was tipping forward, blinding her.

'I said ONE Coke,' said Jo, reprovingly.

'I know, Mummy dearest, but I thought seeing as you love me sooo much . . .' Martha plonked Daisy's burger down on the table. The top of the bun had slipped off, the onions slopping sideways onto the polystyrene plate. It looked utterly delicious, nonetheless. Daisy piled it all back together, scooping up the last of the onions with a finger. She took a huge bite, groaning with bliss. There was nothing so delicious as a charred, smokey-tasting burger with all the toppings. She swiped her chin with the back of her hand, not quite fast enough to stop a splodge of oniony juice from landing on her top and leaving an oily stain.

'What's going on here?' Ned returned, another drink in hand. He slipped into the chair beside Daisy, folding his hands in an official manner. 'Flora's on the rampage,' he explained. 'Right, you two girls: we've got a raffle to get under way. Fancy helping us out by taking a couple of books of tickets out and selling them? Reckon everyone's had at least one drink by now, so they shouldn't mind putting their hands in the pockets.'

Jo picked up a book, and Ned passed her a pen from the box Flora had given them. 'Don't go disappearing off with that biro, mind. I'll have Flora baying for blood. That's Parish Council property . . . Martha?' He flipped open another book of tickets. 'How's that gorgeous pussycat of yours doing? Fancy seeing if you can sell some of these for me?'

Blushing furiously, not catching his eye, Martha took the tickets and a pen. She ducked away, nodding mutely.

'That's impressive work.' Daisy turned to him, taking a sip of her cider. 'Getting Martha to do anything at the moment's a bit of a miraculous feat.'

'Ah,' said Ned, giving her a wise look, 'it's my irresistible charms, y'see.'

'That'll be it,' agreed Daisy, her tone completely neutral.

By the end of the afternoon Ned and Daisy had sold every single raffle ticket, leaving a delighted Flora speechless. The barbecue was grilling the last of the sausages, and they'd packed away the last few unclaimed prizes – a dusty bottle of port which looked like it had done the rounds of more than a few charity raffles, some slightly deflated Body Shop bath pearls ('Didn't even realize you could still buy them,' Jo had laughed. 'I don't think you can,' Daisy had replied, bundling them back into the cardboard box Flora had provided) and a box of violet creams.

'Well, you two, I can't thank you enough for your help today.' Flora bustled across, taking the box from Daisy. 'I'll pop this back in my car just now. You two deserve a drink.'

Ned beamed with relief. 'Oh, thanks, Flora.' He stood there, expectantly, an expression of confusion crossing his face as she sailed off in the direction of her little Fiesta.

'You thought she was going to buy us one, didn't you?' Daisy looked at his dismayed expression with amusement.

'Well, I did think, after we'd spent all day on the raffle stall, maybe she'd . . .'

'All for the good of the village, my dear,' fluted Daisy, in a passable impression of Flora's well-modulated tones. 'Come on, I'll get you a beer.'

The pub itself was deliciously quiet after the heat and busyness of the fundraiser. In silent agreement, they took their drinks and collapsed on one of the huge, squashy leather sofas, putting their feet up on the low table in front of them. Polly, who'd mooched around the whole afternoon hoovering up stray sausages and was clearly now stuffed to bursting, sagged down at their feet with an undignified and not very canine-sounding groan.

'We deserve a bloody medal.'

'You're telling me. And I'm on duty tomorrow at six.' Ned smothered a jaw-splitting yawn. He stretched his arms out high above his head, bringing them down to rest on the back of the sofa, along the line of Daisy's shoulders. She stiffened slightly and he pulled his arm away in the same instant, muttering an apology.

Daisy took a long, slow sip of her beer, closing her eyes and taking a deep breath. It had been a long day – a long few days, with so much going on that it was no wonder her head was all over the place.

She opened her eyes to see, sashaying across the wooden floor of the pub with eyes fixed firmly on her target, the bronzed blonde goddess of earlier. *She* didn't have burger juice sploshed down the front of her spotless white vest top, Daisy noticed.

'*There* you are, sweetie.'

Perching gracefully on the arm of the leather sofa, she tucked her long legs neatly to one side, her bronzed, perfectly dimple-free thighs sickeningly toned in a pair of tiny, cut-off denim shorts.

'Daisy, this is Fenella. Fen, this is Daisy.'

Fenella held out a well-mannered hand, flashing Daisy a smile which didn't quite reach her eyes.

'How do you do, Daisy? Very interesting to meet you at last.' Somehow these words didn't quite match up to the tone Daisy was sensing behind them. 'I seem to have heard an *awful* lot about you.'

Daisy wasn't quite sure what the appropriate response to that should be. She smiled vaguely, shaking Fenella's hand. She was absolutely Ned's type – not that Ned had mentioned having a type, but she had the glossy, expensive look that went with the county set. She'd have been at home hanging out with William and Kate, all dogs and horses and weekends in the country, darling.

'Lovely to meet you, too.' Daisy stood up, deciding to take the coward's way out and make a run for it, cheap flip-flops, stained top and all. Scooping up her beer, she gave a brief, apologetic smile. 'I'm awfully sorry, but I must go to the loo. Been on the raffle stall all day. I'm sure you understand.'

And with that, she whisked out of the pub, noticing as she did that Ned's forehead had scrunched up in that way it did when he was a bit confused about something, and that Fenella's face had 'Oh good, she's leaving' etched across it in large capital letters. The fact that she'd left for the loo taking a pint of Farrow and Farmer's finest ale with her, not to mention a reluctant golden retriever who was trailing along even more slowly than usual, was a minor detail she hoped they'd overlook.

Thank God there was an empty table round the side of the gazebo. Shoving a teetering pile of used paper plates to one side, she flopped down on the wooden chair with a sigh of relief. Polly gave her a look of disapproval which said she was absolutely not moving again today, thank you very much.

'S'all right, girl. I'm not planning on going anywhere for some time. My legs are killing me.'

'That's the first sign of madness, y'know,' said Jo's voice, behind her. 'And it's my job to know that stuff.'

'I thought you went home ages ago.' Daisy budged up on the wooden bench, making room.

'I did. When I got back to the house I realized I'd left my cardigan up here, so I dropped Martha off and took a walk back up. It's such a gorgeous day, I thought while I was here I'd see if you were still around and grab a drink. We didn't get much of a chance to talk, earlier.'

'That'd be lovely.'

Jo headed inside to find herself a drink. Daisy leaned her head in her hands, closing her eyes for a moment, taking a breath.

'Who's that with Ned?'

Jo had returned, bringing a round of drinks and a couple of packets of crisps into the bargain. She popped them open, offering Daisy the bag.

'No thanks, I'm still stuffed full of barbecue stuff.' Daisy shook her head. 'I dunno who she is exactly – she's super-posh, though.'

Jo gave a vague nod of acknowledgement. She'd no real interest in who Ned was passing time with in the pub – and nor do I, Daisy reminded herself. She pulled out her phone for the first time in hours, wondering if George had sent a message.

There was one from him (*Thanks for last night – let's do it again sometime soon,* with a kiss, proving that she still had it – or a bit of it, anyway) and there were two missed calls and a long, rambling text from her mother, explaining that they *knew* Daisy was going to be just *fine,* that she could always move in with Miranda, and ending cheerily with the news that the estate agent would be round to measure up tomorrow after lunch.

Daisy smothered a groan. That just added insult to injury, as well as reminding her about her imminent homelessness, which she'd managed to put to one side for ages today.

'So – I didn't want to risk talking about this today when Martha was around – but here's the plan for next weekend.' Jo was whispering, despite there being virtually nobody left in the beer garden except for a handful of stragglers, and the Parish Council volunteers who'd been roped into clearing up.

'Go on . . .' Daisy took another mouthful of beer.

'I've managed to get a cancellation at a B&B on the seafront at Southbeach – God knows how, when the place is apparently booked up months in advance. I'm taking it as a sign from the gods.' She shrugged with an open-handed gesture. 'So if we drive up on Saturday morning first thing – that's your first thing, I mean, not my idea of it – we'll get there in plenty of time. We can grab a drink, have a wander, and then I can just pop in to watch him doing his performance bit and then I'll just go and say hello.'

These words came tumbling out at about twice the speed of Jo's normal speech.

Daisy gave Jo a level stare. 'You're just going to "pop in and say hello"?'

Jo looked down into the depths of her glass. 'Yes, well, that's the theory. One foot in front of the other, I'm always saying to my clients. Now it's time for me to walk the walk – literally.'

Even if Tom did want to renew their friendship, it

was a completely different world when there was a fourteen-year-old child in the equation.

'So has Martha never asked about her dad?'

'It's come up occasionally over the years. I told her he was someone I knew once, but that we'd lost touch before I knew I was pregnant and I decided not to involve him because I thought we'd be fine on our own.'

Daisy pictured Martha's pale, pointed face. She was funny and sweet, with a sharp sense of humour: a real credit to her mother. She'd grown up knowing no other parent than Jo, and soon – if this all came off – there could be someone else in her life. She deserved to have that option, no matter how hard it might be in the short term.

'You're doing the right thing, y'know.' Daisy put her hand over Jo's, giving it a reassuring squeeze.

Jo shook her head thoughtfully. She traced a line in the condensation that ran down her glass, the faint line which sat between her eyebrows deepening with concern. 'I hope so, Daisy. I really do.'

Their thoughtful silence was broken by a spluttering cough from beneath the table, followed by the unmistakable sound of Polly throwing up, narrowly missing Daisy's shoes.

'*Ugh* – sorry, Jo,' said Daisy, scooting out of her chair. She bent down to check on the dog. Polly looked up at Daisy, and wagged her tail faintly. She made no attempt to get up.

'Come on, Poll.' Daisy urged her, stroking her ears gently.

'I'll nip in and see if Ned's still in the bar.' Jo dropped a hand onto Daisy's shoulder before heading inside.

'What's going on here, then?' Ned's tone was reassuring as he knelt down on the grass next to Daisy. He reached under the table, placing an expert hand on Polly's flank, counting her breaths.

'Sounds fine. I'd say she's eaten one too many burgers, that's all, haven't you, girl?'

She nudged his hand, hoping for more attention. 'Hang on, my darling, let me just have a look –'

He moved around the table, getting down on hands and knees to examine the vomit.

'Ugh, Ned – that's disgusting.'

'All part of the job, Daise.' He sat back on his heels. 'Looks like Madam P here might have sneaked in a stray bar of chocolate alongside the eighteen sausages. Sorry to be graphic.' He gave a shrug of apology, smiling.

'You spend eight years in vet school and come out with a degree in puke analysis?' Daisy shook her head.

'It's just another service I provide. Free of charge, seeing it's you.'

He reached under the table, giving Polly another gentle pat.

'Chocolate is poisonous to dogs. And golden

retrievers are notorious scavengers. The number of kids roaming around today while Polly was pottering around, I wouldn't be surprised if she'd helped herself to a stray Dairy Milk or two.'

Poor Polly. Daisy ruffled the hair under her ears, just where she loved to be tickled.

'So she's going to be okay?'

'From the size of her, and the fact she threw it straight back up, I'd say yes.' Ned stood and stretched, hands in the small of his back. 'Keep an eye on her, and give the surgery a ring in the morning. If she seems off colour at all, bring her in – but that quantity in a dog her size shouldn't do much more than make her feel a bit off her game.'

Daisy exhaled: a long, not-realizing-she'd-been-holding-her-breath sigh.

'Thanks, Ned.'

Their eyes met for a second.

'For you, my darling,' he said, half teasing, 'any-thing.'

'Come on, Ned, we're going to be late.'

Fenella's cool voice broke the moment. Ned and Daisy looked up at the same time to see her standing there, arms folded. Ned scrambled up, his long limbs unfolding.

'Give me a shout if you've got any worries, okay?' Green eyes searched Daisy's face for a moment.

She nodded, and they were gone.

*

With Polly settled on her bed, much brighter and looking comfortable, Daisy took a last wander round the garden of Orchard Villa before bed. The moon was hanging low in a lilac and pink streaked midsummer sky. With one thing and another, she'd neglected the garden a bit over the last few days. She'd had a chat with George earlier by text, arranging a drink in a pub in a nearby village next Monday when he got back from an unexpected trip to Dublin.

She thought back to their evening here in the garden. It had been lovely – not earth-shattering, but nice. He was handsome, a good cook, possibly not quite as solvent as her sister's rules might decree . . . but he was quite nice. And while he mightn't set the world on fire, her body certainly reacted to his – she gave a shiver, remembering the sensation of that first real kiss. If life had taught her anything by now, it was that there was no such thing as The One. She'd made enough mistakes following her heart to know that. She shuddered, remembering how much she'd believed herself in love with Jamie.

She stood thinking, barefoot, on the dew-soaked grass for a few moments, before exhaustion overtook her and she headed inside.

As she was heading up to bed with a magazine and a huge, cream-topped hot chocolate, a knock at the front door made her jump. Who the hell could be turning up at this time? Cautious, she put the chain on the door before opening it and peeking through the gap.

'It's just me.' Shivering in shirtsleeves, his stethoscope round his neck, Ned was standing on the doorstep. 'I was just passing by and I thought I'd check Polly was okay.'

She slid back the chain, welcoming him inside.

'Passing by?' She looked down the street, mocksearching for signs of where he might be going.

He rolled his eyes. 'Don't even ask. I got called in to give a hand with an emergency. Thank God I didn't have anything else to drink earlier. Anyway, when I finished I thought I'd just nip by on my way home and check the old girl was feeling better.' He crossed through into the kitchen to Polly, quickly checking her pulse and breathing.

'What a clever girl you are.' Polly grinned up at him, beating her tail in acknowledgement of the compliment. 'She's fine.'

'Thanks, Ned. I really appreciate it.' Goodness knows how much a private visit from a vet cost these days. He was so sweet, taking the time to call in and check on Polly on his way home.

'S'nothing, honestly.' He fiddled with his collar, standing awkwardly in the middle of the kitchen.

'D'you want a drink?' Daisy searched the cupboards, trying to remember if she had anything to offer. 'I've got half a bottle of wine or some flat tonic, or—'

He shook his head. 'Don't worry. I just wanted to check in on her.'

'Thanks, Ned. I owe you one.'

'You do. Next time I need some emergency gardening done, I'm going to be right on that phone.' With that, he gave her a teasing smile, and headed for the door.

'See you later, Daisy.'

Chapter Sixteen

Daisy was just getting ready to head to town on a shopping mission, having realized she had nothing to wear to a literary festival (what on earth *do* people wear to a literary festival, she'd wondered, visualizing lots of arty types floating around with shawls and note-pads) when her phone started buzzing in her bag. She ignored it the first time, deciding whatever it was could wait. It rang again as she pulled the door of Orchard Villa closed behind her. Some instinct told her to double-check. She fished it out of her bag just as it began ringing again.

Jo, flashed the screen.

'Daisy.' The normally unruffled Jo sounded breath-less. 'Thank God you haven't left. I need you to do me a favour. Can you get up to Brockville School?'

Daisy shoved the phone between ear and shoulder, fishing around in her bag to find the car keys. *Got them.*

'Brockville? Why – what's going on?'

'It's Elaine. Something's happened to Leo. I'd

nipped in to borrow a bag for the weekend, and she got a call from the secretary saying she'd better get up there ASAP. It must be serious – she's left *me* in charge of a load of cakes she's got in the oven.'

Daisy fished in her bag, pulling out the keys. Poor Elaine was having the week from hell, and she didn't even know it. 'I'll be there in five minutes.'

Putting her foot down, she nipped down the narrow lane that led down to Brockville School. The huge metal gates were wide open, Elaine's car parked at an unusually cavalier angle across two parking spaces. Daisy jumped out of the car, scanning the neatly painted signs that directed visitors to the school.

'Art block . . . reception . . . Headmaster's Office,' she read aloud, turning down the path towards the oak front door and pressing the entry buzzer.

'Brockville School Reception?' The voice on the intercom was unruffled.

'I'm a friend of Mrs Thornton-Green. I got a call?'

'Oh, gosh. Yes, you'd better come in.'

Poor Elaine. Daisy felt a mixture of emotions as the receptionist led her through the oak-panelled corridor. Even if Leo *was* an adulterous shit – what if he'd had a heart attack or something? Maybe this would be the wake-up call he needed.

The receptionist opened the door to an anteroom lined with green leather chairs. 'Just a moment.' She gave a discreet knock before opening a door with a brass plaque reading *Headmaster's Office*.

'Mrs Thornton-Green, there's someone here? Says you called?'

'Just one moment. Will you excuse me a second?' Daisy heard Elaine apologizing before she stepped out into the anteroom.

'Elaine – are you – is everything okay?'

'I'll leave you to it,' said the receptionist, taking one final look around the door into Leo's office. Daisy couldn't help thinking that was a bit ghoulish of her, given that Leo was quite possibly lying flat out being treated by paramedics – or worse.

'Everything is not,' said Elaine, firmly, not making much sense to Daisy. 'Did Jo call you?'

'Yeah. She said she had to stay and look after some cakes. I was just on my way, and –'

'Bugger the buggering cakes,' said Elaine, with unexpected force. Daisy, who couldn't remember ever having heard her friend swear, felt her eyes widening. Elaine's back was poker-straight, her face a patrician mask.

'Honestly, I've had quite enough of this.'

Daisy raised a hand to her mouth in amazement as Elaine pushed the door open. Inside, cornered behind a green leather chair, stood Leo. Seeing Daisy, he tried to arrange his face into its habitual expression of urbane welcome, but with one flicker of a glance at his furious wife, his features slid back into grey-tinged terror. Elaine pushed the door closed, revealing two suited men, arms folded, surveying their prey from the opposite corner of the room.

One of the men nodded politely to acknowledge her entry, well mannered even in awkward circumstances. Daisy shrank into the wall, trying to blend in with the wallpaper.

'If you can just give me a moment, I can explain,' piped up Leo from behind his chair. He gave Daisy a hopeful look, searching for an ally. She glared back at him, remembering the phone call.

'No.' Elaine, and both of the other men, snapped in unison. He piped down again.

'I'm very sorry about this, Daisy.' Elaine's cut-glass tones were even sharper than usual, one eyebrow ever so slightly raised, her face set in a slightly arch expression which had been worn, Daisy suspected, by many a grimly enduring woman in her lineage. Elaine really was quite unbelievably posh.

The two men looked at one another, then back at Elaine, who was inspecting her nails, somehow conveying the impression that this was nothing more than a minor inconvenience in her daily routine. She was *good*.

'Apparently my husband,' Elaine cast a glance at Leo which was so withering that he shrank visibly, 'has been using his considerable charm and influence on some of the mothers here at Brockville.' She paused, her nostrils flaring slightly in distaste. 'Mr Morrison and Mr Hapgood have been kind enough to get in touch and share their concerns.'

The two husbands looked at each other again. They'd clearly shared intelligence – that must've been an awkward conversation after dads' five-a-side football, thought Daisy – and had formed an uncomfortable, slightly embarrassing alliance before heading to the school office without thinking it through. Knowing Steeple St John, this would be round the village in record time, digested over lunch in the Grey Mare, and red-hot gossip at the school gates by 3 p.m.

Leo shrank a tiny bit more behind his chair. He looked like a small boy who'd been caught with a pocketful of sweets on the way out of the corner shop.

'I'm really *very* sorry to put you in this position, Mrs Thornton-Green.' One of the husbands turned to Elaine, pulling at his shirt collar in discomfort. *He* was apologizing, thought Daisy. This whole situation is so ridiculously British, it's not quite real.

'Yes.' The other irate husband turned to Elaine, his mouth a thin line. 'It's most distressing for everyone.'

'Not at all.' Elaine raised both hands, dismissing them. 'I think it's clear that the person here who owes the apology here is my –'

She stopped herself, Daisy noted. Leo remained half-crouched in position behind the chair, completely still.

'Is Mr Thornton-Green.'

The two husbands nodded, lulled into a sense of calm by Elaine's assurance. She probably reminded them of Mummy, thought Daisy, smothering a smile

252

behind her hand. God, it was like being caught up in an episode of *Downton Abbey*.

Sensing a change in the atmosphere, Leo began sidling out from behind the chair.

'What can I say?' He spoke quickly and smoothly. 'I am, of course, extremely apologetic. I will, naturally, be handing my resignation to the governors with immediate effect.'

Elaine's face remained completely impassive as everyone in the room turned to her, recognizing that she held the balance of power.

'Unfortunately,' she began, her voice crisp and controlled but dripping with ice, 'Mr Thornton-Green has a rather skewed concept of parent–teacher relations.'

'You're not bloody joking,' said one of the husbands.

'Even more unfortunately, this is not the first time – and for that I must take some of the blame.'

Daisy recoiled. Elaine *knew*?

'When he took up the post here at Brockville, it was following a successful period as head of an exclusive prep school in Dubai. A period which came to a rather sudden end after my husband was found in bed with the wife of a prominent businessman.'

Daisy's eyes widened. All this time, she'd been trying to find a way to tactfully raise her suspicions that Leo was a slimy git – and Elaine already knew what he was capable of. She felt a bit sick at the thought. She'd stormed off the very same day she'd discovered Jamie's infidelity. How on earth could Elaine have carried on living with Leo, knowing what he'd done? The whole perfect lifestyle thing, which had always made her a bit uneasy – it was built on a crumbling foundation of lies and deceit. Why on *earth* would Elaine stay?

'I accepted my husband's apology, and we moved back to the UK. Luckily for us, we were able to pull some strings, and we ended up here in Steeple St John.'

'Not exactly lucky for us,' said Husband Number Two, shaking his head angrily. Daisy noticed his hands were still balled into fists. She watched as Leo followed her gaze and shrank back slightly in discomfort.

'Well, I'm sorry, Leo,' Elaine used his name for the first time, but it was with such icy contempt that it sounded like an insult, 'but I'm not hiding behind your lies this time. You're on your own.'

'I'd get out of here pretty sharpish if I were you, mate,' said Husband Number One, his well-modulated accent slipping for the first time. His eyebrows flashed upwards for a brief moment, a gesture which gave the subtlest hint of violence – enough that Leo shot out from behind the chair, not even stopping to grab his leather briefcase, which sat open on the desk, and hurtled out of the room.

Daisy, Elaine and the two husbands stood in silence, listening to the rapid-fire clattering of Leo's leather-soled shoes along the corridor. There was a rumble as the heavy wooden doors swung open, and then silence.

'Right. Well, I'm sure you both have things to be getting on with,' said Elaine, briskly.

'I'm sure you're as keen as we are,' said the previously menacing husband, his accent now tuned back to neutral Home Counties, 'to keep this under wraps. Can I rely on Brockville to do everything it can to minimize the – disruption?'

The other husband adjusted his tie, clearing his throat awkwardly. 'Yes, yes, indeed – that would really be most helpful. My wife and I have agreed to put this unfortunate – incident – behind us, and . . .'

Elaine cut in, sharply. 'I'm terribly sorry.' You don't sound it, thought Daisy. 'As the soon-to-be-ex-wife of the soon-to-be-ex-head, I'm afraid I have no influence over Brockville whatsoever. You'll have to take it up with the Board of Governors.'

She picked up her Mulberry handbag from the chair and hooked it over her shoulder before continuing crisply, 'I suggest you start with the school secretary. She's been standing outside the door listening to the whole conversation. Should make it nice and straightforward.'

With that, she turned on her heel and strode out of the school, with a speechless Daisy scuttling along in her wake.

*

255

'Brockville School was established in 1910 . . .' Daisy was reading from one of the newly printed stack of promotional leaflets stacked on the bar in the Grey Mare, Leo's satisfied face beaming out from the back page. 'Distinguished alumni include former Cabinet Ministers, leaders of trade and industry, and several well-respected journalists.'

'Who hopefully won't be sniffing around looking for a bit of scandal,' said Jo, with feeling. She slid a gin and tonic across the pub table to Daisy. They'd returned to the Old Rectory, Daisy's beaten-up Vauxhall beetling along behind Elaine's glossy Audi. Elaine, her ice-cool veneer still impenetrable, had made it evident that she was absolutely fine, thanks, and yes, perhaps she'd give them a call later, and of course, yes, if there was anything they could do, she'd be in touch. And with that, just as Leo's car crunched into the drive, she had politely but very firmly shunted them out of the house. Leo had remained in the driver's seat, sunglasses on, face immobile.

The pub had been a no-brainer. Jo and Daisy had set off in that direction without a moment's discussion. Slightly relieved to be making their escape, they'd crunched down the path and out onto the street, both silent, neither looking the other in the eye until they were safely out of earshot.

'Bloody *hell*,' Daisy had exclaimed.

*

And so the week rushed by: Daisy packing her things for a weekend away, Thomas promising to look after Polly and make sure she got a nightly stroll round the park as he wandered down to say goodnight to his beloved Violet. Daisy tried texting Elaine, asking if she fancied dinner at the pub, but she left a breezy voicemail in return saying no, thanks, and that she was 'fine'. Jo tried, too, calling round one afternoon between clients, but Elaine gently shooed her away, claiming she had a conference call. Comparing notes on the phone, they both agreed that whatever was going on, Elaine was determined not to let her guard down for a second.

As the weekend approached, Jo became increasingly quiet as the reality of facing up to her past drew closer. Daisy dealt with a visit from the estate agent, first to measure up and take details, and then – sick-making reality – to take photographs of Orchard Villa and the gardens. She spent the week cleaning, tidying and making the gardens look as beautiful as possible. Hopefully someone would fall in love with them enough to carry on the work she and Thomas had begun. It was out of Daisy's hands, really, so all she could do was bury her head in the potting soil and cross her fingers that some of Thomas's Zen philosophy about things changing for the better would actually come good.

Chapter Seventeen

Jo picked Daisy up at six on Saturday morning with a scowling, yawning Martha slumped in the back seat. Despite the early hour, Daisy noticed she'd still managed to trowel on at least three layers of eyeliner. She glowered out of the window, muttering darkly at her mother.

'I don't know why you couldn't have just dropped me round at Elaine's house last night. I could have had an extra night in that lush spare bed, and I wouldn't have had to be up in the middle of the bloody night.'

'Don't swear, darling.' Jo indicated right, turning the car into Cavendish Lane. 'Elaine's got enough on her plate at the moment without any extra stress.'

Martha raised a single, sardonic eyebrow. She'd recently learned this skill and it was proving very useful. Jo, who'd told Daisy the other day that her daughter was pushing her to the edge of sanity, gritted her teeth.

'Oh yeah. *Mister* Thornton-Green and his extracurricular activities.' Martha gave a one-sided smile.

'Martha,' hissed Jo. 'If you *dare* upset Elaine this weekend, I will personally make sure you never access wifi under my roof again.'

Daisy hid a smile. Martha without wifi would shrivel and die. It was her lifeblood.

'As if,' Martha tutted. 'I actually like Elaine – even if she is a bit up her own arse.'

Jo inhaled, the long, slow, deep breath of a mother with a teenager. Her nostrils flared, but she didn't rise to the bait. Having seen the way Elaine had dealt with the wronged husbands earlier that week, Daisy suspected she'd be more than capable of handling one sarky fourteen-year-old. Especially as she, too, was in charge of the wifi connection.

Martha hopped out, opening the gate to the driveway of the Old Rectory. The car crunched to a halt, parking in the space behind Elaine's car which had previously been reserved for Leo's Audi estate.

Elaine opened the door, already dressed despite the early hour. A waft of something delicious hit Daisy's nostrils. Surely she'd not been baking at half past six in the morning? And she was fully made up, too, hair blow-dried neatly into its customary bouncy waves, a subtly patterned dove-grey top over cropped, narrow-legged trousers. Daisy, who'd been up for an hour making herself look respectable, looked down at her already creased skirt with dismay.

'Martha, darling, come in. I had a feeling you might

fancy a few hours more in bed, so if you pop upstairs – don't worry about the bags, I'll bring them up in a moment – I've turned the bed down for you.'

Shooting her mother an eloquent look, Martha hurtled upstairs two at a time, mobile phone in hand. She would get her lie-in after all.

'Bye, sweetheart,' called Jo fruitlessly, as she disappeared out of sight. 'Love you.'

'Yep,' called Martha's distant voice as she disappeared into the bedroom, the door thudding shut.

'King Lear was right, y'know.' Jo shook her head, laughing despite herself. 'That's probably the last you'll see of her until I get back.'

'Oh, don't worry, I'm sure I can tempt her down with something. I've got salted caramel fudge cooling in the kitchen, and I've just put a batch of white chocolate and cranberry cookies in the oven.' It was the first time they'd set eyes on Elaine since the incident at Brockville, and she seemed determined to maintain her veneer of calm.

'You going to be okay?' Jo put a hand on Elaine's arm.

'Me?' Elaine smiled brightly. 'Absolutely fine. Don't worry about me. Now, you two have a safe trip. Text me when you get there, okay? And Jo?' Elaine pulled her into an embrace, hugging her tightly for a moment. When she stepped back, Daisy watched as Elaine took an almost imperceptible breath, composing herself, thrown by the intimacy. 'You're doing a good thing. No matter how terrifying it might seem.'

Jo's smile was faint. Nerves were hitting now, as they moved closer and closer to the inevitable. 'I know.'

'I'll look after her, don't worry.' Elaine held the door open, motioning them out with her arm. 'Go. Drive safely.'

Main Street was deserted as they made their way out of the village, driving past the pub, up past the lane that led to Orchard Villa, and through the trees towards the dual carriageway that led them north. Forestry Commission signs flashed by as they passed the huge woodland on their right before cresting the hill and heading down, down, out of the safety of Steeple St John for their long drive to the seaside.

They sat for a while in silence, both lost in thought, not even putting on the radio. Daisy stared out of the window at the rolling countryside. She watched patchwork cows spilling back out of milking parlours and into the fields, realizing again just how early it was. The M25 was quiet for once, their only companions the huge, rumbling lorries headed for Felixstowe, their metal cargo crates painted brightly with every European language.

'So,' Daisy began cautiously. 'Tom?'

Jo shook her head. 'I haven't a clue. I have no idea how this is going to go – what I'm supposed to say. Christ, he might not even *remember* me.'

'I doubt that, somehow.' Daisy looked sideways at

Jo. She had both hands on the steering wheel, focusing intently on the road ahead. Her brows were lowered in concentration.

'He will remember me. I know that.' She gave a half-nod. 'Trouble is, it's all the stuff that comes afterwards.'

'I'm sorry, Jo. I don't want to drag this all up.'

'I'm the one that's dragging *you* up here to hold my hand.' Jo flashed Daisy a quick, grateful smile before returning her focus to the long, straight road ahead. 'Thing is, there's never a good time to do something like this. I have to keep talking myself through the worst-case scenarios. It helps.'

'So what are they?' Daisy turned in her seat, interested.

'Say he doesn't recognize me – okay, that's awkward, but a bit of prompting and he will. Say he recognizes me and tells me to fuck off—'

Daisy laughed. 'Come on, it's been what – fifteen years? If he did that, he's a bit of an arse.'

'Yeah, but he's still the arse who donated half his genes to make my daughter, so I kind of owe it to him to let him know.'

'Even if he *does* turn out to be a dickhead?' Daisy unwrapped a sweet, offering Jo the packet. She shook her head.

'Even if. I can't blame anyone else for this – I let it go on far too long, and now I need to repair the damage. Doesn't matter how terrifying it is.' Jo gave a wry half-smile. 'And Martha wouldn't be the first person to have a dickhead for a father, unfortunately. I'd be missing half my clients, if that was the case.'

'But you're not . . .' Daisy winced, treading carefully, 'planning on turning up with a photo and saying "surprise!", are you?'

She and Elaine had talked about it over coffee, deciding that there was no way the measured, thoughtful Jo would do anything like that – but still, better to ask, just in case by some miracle Jo was planning to spring the news on Tom like some unhinged Jeremy Kyle show guest . . .

'No.' Jo's expression said it all. 'Definitely not.'

'Didn't think so.' Daisy laughed. 'Just, y'know, thought I'd better check.'

Jo shot her a sideways look, eyebrows sky-high.

They drove on, up through the Essex countryside, spotting pretty pink-washed houses in the distance, the ancient, evocative village names written large on road signs. Jo drove one-handed, dropping back into silence, distractedly chewing on the thumbnail of her free hand. Daisy's stomach was churning with sympathetic nerves by the time they pulled off the busy A-road and started winding their way towards the seaside.

It was impossible not to feel that familiar childish surge of excitement as they crested a hill and the quality of light changed, with a sensation of the land shelving away. With another turn in the road, they could see flashes of the sea between tightly gathered terraces. Daisy wound down her window, delighting in the salt smell of the air. A gull whirled overhead, its voice dipping and falling in the wind. She was thrown back in time to a hundred happy days by the seaside as a child, the sweet vanilla scent of candyfloss and the sharp taste of vinegar on her tongue. Penny arcades flashed brightly, a kaleidoscope of colour and noise against a flat, blue-grey sea.

'This is it.' Jo eased the car to a halt outside their B&B, slotting it carefully into her designated spot between two much larger cars. Daisy, legs stiff from the journey, slid out through a narrow gap between door and white-painted wall. The road was lined with parked cars, stretching towards the centre of town in neat single file.

Southbeach Literary Festival had grown over the last few years into a weekend-long event which flooded the little seaside town with some of the biggest names in the literary world. Reading online yesterday, Daisy had seen an article on 'The Handsome New Stars of the Literary Scene' with Tom Fox ('gorgeously brooding Manc poet') featured at no. 8. She hadn't shared it with Jo.

With a sharp intake of breath, Jo slammed the boot closed. 'Right. Let's do this.'

The carpet in the hall of the B&B was a hideous giraffe-skin design. The walls, hung with flocked, swirling wallpaper, were hung with the spoils of a lifetime of trips abroad. Brightly coloured Spanish tiles jostled alongside silk hangings of the Buddha, serene in the lotus position, next to intricately painted, detailed Greek icons in ornate wooden frames.

'This is lovely,' said Daisy, politely. The owner didn't acknowledge her remark, not looking up from the screen of his computer where he sat, barricaded, behind a reception desk plastered with printed signs which had been Sellotaped in place.

Guests should note that NO music
should be played in the bedrooms after 9 p.m.

Would guests KINDLY remember that the bathrooms
are for the use of rooms 3, 5 AND 7, and that a toilet
brush HAS been provided.

Daisy grimaced at that one. If Jo hadn't been so pale and stressed, she'd have nudged her, making her giggle. But her friend stood, unseeing, fingers drumming anxiously on the desktop. Poor Jo. Normally so calm and measured, she seemed to have actually shrunk in size as the enormity of what she was about to do became a reality. Daisy reached across, giving her a reassuring rub on the arm. Jo looked up at her with a tiny, grateful smile.

'You're in the smallest room, I'm afraid,' said the owner, finally. He still didn't raise his eyes from the screen. 'Still, you're lucky to have got in at all. If you hadn't phoned the second I'd had a cancellation, you'd have had no luck. Can't get a room this weekend for love nor money.' He handed over one single room key, dangling from a six-inch-long strip of plastic.

'Thanks.' Daisy shot a look at Jo as she took the key. 'Do you – there's two of us staying, I'm not sure we'll be coming and going at the same time . . .'

'One room, one key.' The tone was final. He sat back on his chair, sizing them up. 'Don't forget to take note of the rules. There's a full list in the bedroom. Hot water's on tap, but we recommend guests don't take longer than ten minutes each in the bathroom.' He gave Daisy a warning stare.

'Oh, um, right. Thanks.' Daisy stepped back, landing on Jo's toe.

'Oh. My. God.'

They stood in the doorway of their room, gazing in horror. Two tiny beds, dressed in slippery, diamond-stitched turquoise polyester, were crammed into what would under any other circumstances have been a pretty poky single bedroom.

'I tell you what, Jo,' said Daisy, easing herself gingerly onto the bed closest to the wall. She moved a huge, overstuffed bolster pillow out of the way to peer through the window. The gorgeous seaside view she'd been visualizing on the journey was, in fact, the side wall of the building next door. 'You can bring the camera crews out now, if you like. This is a set-up, right?'

Jo squeezed herself into the wafer-thin gap between the beds and sat down. 'I forgot to tell *You've Been Framed* we were coming.' She started laughing. 'I hope this isn't an omen. Oh God, it's an omen, isn't it?'

'Positive thinking, counsellor-lady. It's going to be fine. And if it isn't fine, at least we've had a luxury spa break in beautiful Southbeach.'

With the room too small for both of them to move about in, and realizing that Jo needed some time to get herself ready for the evening and to gather her thoughts, Daisy left her behind in the B&B and headed out to explore Southbeach for a couple of hours.

The little seaside town had been overtaken by the literary world. Cafe tables spilled out across the pavement, with arty-looking types gesticulating over espressos and cake. Daisy squeezed into a tiny space with a wobbly table, and picked up a menu. The cafe was on a narrow lane which led down to the seafront. In the distance she could see colourful beach huts running parallel to the shore, with children dashing around on the sand in front of them.

'A latte and a big slice of coffee and walnut, please.' She smiled up at the woman taking her order, handing back the menu helpfully.

The waitress nodded briefly. She looked exhausted, eyes shadowed, strands of hair hanging loose from what had once been a neat bun.

This weekend, the arts section of Daisy's paper had informed her, was one of the busiest in the year-long calendar of events that had made Southbeach a success. Where other English seaside resorts had become boarded-up ghost towns, Southbeach was now busy all year round, art shops and expensive seafood restaurants thriving despite the never-ending recession.

Drinking coffee, she leafed through the festival programme that lay on the table – most events were sold out, including, Daisy noticed, a session on poetry by Tom Fox, which took place at 4 p.m. She felt a surge of nerves on Jo's behalf. The session was followed by a joint reading – she recognized some of the other names from yesterday's newspaper article – and then the presentation of the awards, including the Phoenix Poetry Award, followed by a celebration dinner.

And at some point, in amongst all that, Jo was going to seek out her long-lost lover, her ex-friend, the unknowing father of her child, and find the courage to say hello.

By the time she'd eaten her cake and finished the last of her coffee a couple of women, arms full of books, were hovering hopefully near her table. Taking the hint, she stood up. They swooped in, faster than the seagulls which circled overhead, and had the menu in their hands before Daisy had even edged her way out and down onto the lane that led towards the seafront.

'Ready?'

Daisy looked up. She'd washed and changed in her regulation ten minutes, and was waiting in the giraffe-patterned hall when Jo came downstairs, having had a last-minute wobble about what to wear.

'D'you think this is okay?' Jo stood awkwardly, holding herself for inspection.

She was wearing a knee-length dress in peacock blue, which brought out the colour of her eyes. Her pale blonde hair hung loosely around her shoulders. She'd finished the outfit with a pair of strappy gold Roman sandals.

'Perfect.' Daisy gave her a reassuring smile. 'You look absolutely gorgeous. Very together.'

'Not too dressed up?'

Daisy, who'd wandered the streets, people-watching, for a couple of sunny hours, shook her head. 'Nope, just right.'

'Okay.' Jo pulled a face. 'Let's go.'

'And I said to Jamie, it's an absolute *disgrace* these reality TV stars are getting six-figure book deals when people like Melissa have been dropped . . .'

Daisy raised her eyebrows at Jo. They were crammed shoulder-to-shoulder in the White Sands pub, drinks in hand, trying hard not to eavesdrop. Vaguely familiar faces were everywhere, a camera crew in one corner filming vox pop interviews with –

'Isn't that Melvyn Bragg?'

Daisy tried not to stare too obviously. 'God, yes, I think it is.'

'Shit, shit –' Jo pulled her back towards the bar through a sea of people, apologizing wildly.

'What is it?' said Daisy, who'd almost sloshed her gin and tonic down the back of a small woman who was clearly Very Important, as she'd been surrounded the whole time by a group of admirers who'd hung on her every word. Daisy edged in closer to the wall so she could hear her friend over the increasingly loud roar of conversation and laughter.

'It's him. Over there. Being interviewed.' Jo took a huge mouthful of her drink. 'I saw him, but I don't think he saw me – I moved pretty quickly.'

Daisy stood on tiptoe, forgetting to be discreet this time, and peered across the crowd. Sitting on a battered red Chesterfield sofa, arm stretched casually along the back, dark curls flopping over one eye, was Tom Fox. He looked across at her. Their eyes met briefly, and he pulled a *help me* face.

'Bloody hell.' She ducked back out of view.

She wasn't going to point out to Jo that Martha's father was the kind of scruffy, arty-looking gorgeous that made both women and men swoon. She took another, more surreptitious look. He was laughing as a production assistant clipped a microphone to his lapel, and then leaning forward to chat to the interviewer.

'It's fine.' She gave Jo a reassuring smile. 'You look gorgeous.'

'I'm not here on the pull, Daisy,' said Jo, grimly.

'No, no. Of course not. But it doesn't hurt, does it?' Daisy reached across, pulling a tiny loose thread which had tangled itself in Jo's gemstone pendant.

Jo didn't answer, hiding her face behind her glass. In an hour and a half Tom's poetry reading would be over, and then she'd have to bite the bullet and confront him.

The bar emptied out slightly as the clock reached the hour, and people scattered to the myriad venues around the little town where authors, publishers and poets were giving talks.

'There's a couple of seats there by the window, look –' Daisy headed for them, having learned to move fast. Within seconds she'd made it and was sitting down.

'Daisy,' Jo perched on the arm of the chair, her pale face crumpled with anxiety, 'I think I might go for a bit of a walk by the sea first, try and calm myself.'

'Good idea.' Jo needed space to think and gather her thoughts. 'I'll wait here – guard these seats with my life. Why don't you leave me the key for the B&B, just in case?'

'I'll text you and let you know what's happening, okay?'

'There's no rush. I'll be here, waiting.'

She blew Jo a kiss, watching as she slipped through the front door of the little pub and headed down to the sea, making her way between the beach huts and disappearing out of sight.

You okay, stranger? How's the seaside?

Daisy pulled her phone out from her bag, seeing Miranda's text.
She typed a quick reply.

Gorgeous. Feeling a bit sick on Jo's behalf. X

She'd told Miranda the whole saga on the phone the other night, knowing her sister was discreet enough for it to go no further, but keen to get another perspective on the situation. As much as they'd fought as teenagers, they'd always turned to each other for support and advice.

She's doing the right thing. Looking forward to seeing you soon. Miss you xx

Daisy curled up on the chair. She'd popped into the bookshop earlier and found a signed copy of Monty Don's latest book. With a drink beside her, worries about the future left miles away in Steeple St John, and the sight of the waves crashing gently outside, she sat back. There was nothing she could do now but wait.

Chapter Eighteen

Lost in Monty Don's descriptions of France, a glass of Norfolk cider in hand, Daisy didn't notice Jo until she was almost at the table.

She looked up expectantly.

'Can we go?' Jo was even paler than usual, her smooth blonde curtain of hair now wind-tangled and messy. She glanced towards the door.

'Of course.' Daisy put her drink down on the table, shoved her book back into her bag, and stood up. 'Where are we going?'

It wasn't until they were halfway to the B&B that Jo answered. Daisy had marched beside her in silent solidarity, realizing she needed to give her friend time to process whatever had happened.

'Oh God, Daisy, I am *so* sorry.'

She began to cry. Daisy stopped, spinning round in the street, and reached out, hugging Jo tightly. A crowd of festival-goers wove their way around them as they stood in the street, Jo's shoulders heaving with sobs.

'Sorry,' Jo repeated. She stepped back, wiping her eyes.

'You've nothing to apologize for.' Daisy rooted around in her bag for a tissue. She found a crumpled, dusty one lurking in the front pocket and handed it to Jo, who blew her nose loudly.

'I just – I couldn't do it.' Jo looked at her through eyes smudged with mascara. 'There was a question and answer session, and a girl asked him a question about poetry. She must've been about fifteen and he was so lovely to her, and I just . . .' She stopped for a moment, scrunching her eyes tightly shut for a moment, as if to block out the image. 'I just realized how vulnerable Martha is, and what a huge thing I'm doing. What if I screw it up?'

Daisy shook her head. 'I don't think you will, Jo, honestly.'

'Maybe not.' Jo looked up again, gratefully. 'But I need to have my head together, and right now I'm all over the place.' She indicated the mascara streaks and the soggy tissue.

She had a point. Daisy pulled out a fresh tissue from her bag, handing it over silently.

'You can't protect Martha – or Tom – from this forever, though.'

'No,' Jo conceded. 'But I can help cushion the blow a bit, and I've got to be the adult in all this. And it just hit me whilst I was sitting there that confronting Tom in a place like this wasn't exactly the most sensible way of behaving.'

'Fair enough.' Jo had a good point. There was no way of knowing how Tom might respond, let alone how Martha was going to react. 'If you want to get out of here, that's fine.' Daisy gave Jo's arm another squeeze. 'I mean, I know we've got a luxury room booked . . .'

Jo managed a damp smile at this.

'I'd really appreciate that. Seriously, if I never see another bloody writer, it'll be too soon.'

They gathered their things from the polyester prison, handing over the key to the B&B owner, who continued to maintain an air of complete disinterest. Signing the payment sheet, they headed out to the car, loading up the boot. Jo climbed into the driver's seat, and Daisy was just sidling along to manoeuvre her way in when she realized her bag was lighter than it should be.

'Shit – I've left my new book sitting in reception.'

She side-stepped back out past the car and down the little path that led to the front door. As she walked into the hall, she couldn't see her book. Bugger. She'd definitely left it sitting on top of the reception desk. She scanned the hall, leaning over the desk. There was their booking slip, with Jo's name and details – but no sign of her book.

She caught sight of a reflection in the mirror behind the desk. In the wall behind her was a tiny alcove, filled with books – including, she realized, spinning around, her brand new signed copy! Bloody hell, they'd snaffled it – and Mr Charm, the owner, was probably going to put up a fight if she tried to get it back.

'I'm sure I can find you a sewing kit,' came the familiar voice of the B&B owner, who had clearly been rationing his charm. He sounded positively eager to please.

Realizing she had a split second, she reached across, whipping the book off the shelf and hiding it behind her back, just as he rounded the corner of the staircase and came into view, followed two steps later by –

'I wouldn't normally bother, but I think if I've got a prize to collect, I'd better look half-decent,' said Tom Fox, in his deep Manchester accent. 'Oh – hello,' he said to Daisy, raising a hand automatically in greeting. He cocked his head with a frown before continuing, his tone cautious.

'This is going to sound a bit odd, but –'

But before he could continue, Daisy, who realized afterwards that she'd yet again engaged her favourite run-away mode when presented with an unexpected situation, shot backwards out of the front door with an apologetic 'Hi – sorry, must – just – bye!'

She ran to the car and squashed herself into the front seat. 'He's in there. Tom. In the grim B&B. He's there.'

Jo shook her head, putting the car into reverse and driving out of the parking space with unexpected speed. She didn't speak again until they'd made their way up through the narrow streets and out onto the road that led towards the dual carriageway.

'I went into the hall where the poetry reading was taking place,' Jo began slowly, letting it all out.

'The woman on the door said the tickets were completely sold out, but she told me I could slip into one of the press seats down the front. The lights were down, and I thought I could just sneak in without him noticing. But then he saw me.'

Like Jo, Daisy carried on staring at the road ahead, not wanting to disturb her friend's train of thought. 'Go on.'

'And then I think he caught my eye. Or I caught his.'

'Nooo. I didn't realize that bit.' Daisy put a hand to her mouth.

'I just – God. It's been fifteen years. And he doesn't look any different. And I still – I just – he –'

'It's not just telling him about Martha, is it?'

Jo shook her head.

'It all came back. The way I felt. The whole unspoken thing we had for years. And the reality hit me – what if he's a complete shit? We were best friends and we lost touch, and I expected to just turn up at his big moment and say "Hi, how're things?" as if the last fifteen years hadn't happened.'

Jo was silent for a moment as they pulled onto the dual carriageway, making her way through the steady stream of Saturday-night traffic, people-carriers loaded full of children heading home from the seaside. Talking of children, thought Daisy . . .

'So what *are* you going to do about Martha?'

'I know I need to tell him.' Jo paused for a minute before continuing.

'But I realized as soon as I walked in there and saw him up close, I need to get my head clear first. I need to stop worrying about what I did in the past, and start moving forward.'

They arrived in Steeple St John late that evening, driving towards the setting sun in contemplative silence. Neither chatted much. Jo, understandably, had a lot on her mind. Daisy, as they headed back to real life, had the grim prospect of three house viewings the following day, all of which she'd expected to avoid. The worry of what, exactly, she was supposed to do with her life once the house was sold was back, niggling at her. She updated Elaine – checking first with Jo that she didn't mind – on the whole saga, a long series of texts which took ages and left her feeling distinctly travel-sick.

And there'd been a text from George, telling her he was back from his trip to Dublin, asking if she'd meet him for a drink in the pub on Monday night. With no idea what the future held, Daisy had decided that at the very least, she could have some fun. She'd texted back an enthusiastic reply.

'You sure you don't want to head back to your place and get some sleep?'

They pulled up outside Elaine's house, Daisy preparing to climb out of the car and open the arched metal gates that led into the drive.

'Honestly, no. I don't mind if Martha decides to stay over – but I just want to see her, and give her a hug, and – well, you know.' Jo shrugged.

'Course I do,' said Daisy. She shut the car door, clanking open the gates.

Elaine opened the door before they'd even reached for the bell.

'I've said to Martha there was a change of plan.' She gestured inside. 'She doesn't seem particularly concerned.'

Jo raised her eyebrows. 'That's not a surprise.'

Elaine pulled the door back, welcoming them in. There was, as ever, a warm fug of something delicious coming from the kitchen.

'We made more cookies,' said Elaine, following Daisy's gaze. 'You two must be hungry.'

Daisy, who'd sailed on Jo's wave of nerves, anticipation, and then the crashing aftermath of the evening, felt her stomach groan in agreement. She hadn't eaten anything since the cake in the cafe that afternoon.

'I am *ravenous*, now you mention it.'

'Jo?' Elaine put a hand on her arm.

Jo frowned for a second, as if she'd only just remembered food was something she did. 'I could eat a horse. Or a gigantic pizza. Possibly both.'

The laughter broke the tension, and Elaine waved them into the kitchen. Sitting on the normally spotless countertop, smudges of flour on her face, her hair tied up in a ponytail – which made her look much younger – was Martha.

Jo rushed over, folding her into a hug which she accepted, pulling a surprised face over her mother's shoulder, which made both Elaine and Daisy giggle.

The worktops were spread with baking ingredients, a dusting of flour covering the shiny marble surface. Cookies lay cooling on a metal rack.

'Help yourself,' said Elaine, heading for the fridge. She pulled out a couple of bottles of beer, popping open the lids and handing them to Daisy and Jo.

'I'm just going to nip next door and see if that Nirvana thing's on yet. You're still going to watch it with me, though?' Martha hopped down, turning to Elaine, her face suddenly vulnerable.

'Course I am.' Elaine turned to Jo. 'You don't mind if Martha's up late, do you?'

Jo, eyes widening, shook her head. 'Not at all.'

'Two seconds,' said Elaine, as she followed Martha out of the room.

'Have we entered the Twilight Zone?'

'It's the only conclusion I can reach. Either that,'

said Jo, biting into another cookie with a groan of satisfaction, 'or Martha's spiked the cookies with something from one of her grungey mates from town.'

Elaine padded back into the room. She was dressed not in her usual crisply ironed, perfectly matching attire, but a pair of soft cotton pyjamas, a strappy vest top – and flip-flops. *Flip-flops*. Daisy, who'd never seen Elaine in any footwear that didn't cost well into three figures from Russell & Bromley, emitted a tiny gasp.

'Sorry, girls.' Elaine untied her ponytail (Daisy, taking it in for the first time, felt her eyes widening further), letting her hair fall down over her shoulders. She shook it out loosely so it fell in waves, still damp. 'Martha's happily installed in front of the TV. So . . .'

'So.' Jo bit into a third cookie, taking a swig of beer. 'That wasn't exactly my finest hour.' She sighed.

'Well, we live and learn,' said Elaine, with the wise expression of one who'd recently discovered the meaning of the phrase. 'What are you going to do now?'

'What I probably should have done in the first place.' Jo inspected the cookie, twirling it around in her hand before nibbling at a chocolate chunk. 'I'm going to get in touch the way normal people these days do it. Facebook, or I'll join Twitter, or I'll email him through his agent or something. The more I think about it, the more I realize I'd have looked like a stalker if I'd just appeared out of the blue.'

'Well,' Daisy cocked her head, her lips pursed,

thinking, 'it was a literary festival. You could've just been there anyway.'

'Oh.' Jo laughed. 'I'd forgotten that bit.'

'Anyone for another?' Elaine pulled three more beers out of the fridge.

In the end, they all stayed the night. By two in the morning, Jo, exhausted from the drive and tipped over the edge by Elaine's rum-spiked hot chocolate, had clambered up to the welcoming comfort of one of the beautifully appointed spare bedrooms, Daisy following behind carrying her overnight bag.

'What a night.' Daisy flopped back down on the sofa, where a determined Martha was trying her hardest to stay awake.

'How come you and Mum came back?' Martha, hours after their return, had finally twigged something was up.

'Oh, just—'

'Daisy had to get back,' Elaine cut in, smoothly. 'She's got an unexpected viewing on the house in the morning.'

Martha nodded vaguely. 'Right.'

Daisy headed back to Orchard Villa early the next morning, leaving a scribbled note for the others on the kitchen table. Even after a late night, she always found it hard to sleep in on a strange bed, and everything was turning over and over in her head.

She was in the front garden weaving loose strands

of clematis into the trellis when she heard the familiar squeak of the gate opening.

'Daisy Price?'

Standing on the path was a shiny-faced young man in a very pinstriped suit. He tucked the tablet he was holding under one arm, holding out his hand for Daisy to shake. She brushed her hand on her shorts, aware she was probably covered in greenfly and dust. It was a Sunday morning, and he looked like he was selling something. Her first thought was how best to get rid of him.

He pulled out a business card.

'Mike Redforth.' He really was *excessively* chirpy for this time of the morning. He nodded at the card, which Daisy, still not quite awake, was holding in mid-air.

'Redforth and Lewis?'

She looked more closely at his business card, realizing they were an estate agency.

'Oh. Um, we've already got an estate agent.' Daisy stepped forward to indicate the sign which stood amongst the flowers in the front garden.

'Yes, of course, yes.' Mike Redforth inched slightly further towards the house. Daisy, feeling very much out-suited, clenched her fist around the secateurs she was holding. She could always chop pieces off him if he started making her uncomfortable.

'You're house-sitting for Mr and Mrs Price, that's right, yes?' He looked at the house sign in an exaggerated manner, as if to make the point that yes, he was in the right place.

'Yes, they're my parents.'

'Great. Great.' He stepped another few inches forward, almost bouncing on the balls of his feet in his eagerness to get inside. 'Right then. Well, they've instructed me – well, us – Redforth and Lewis – that's us. I don't normally work on a Sunday, but I had an inspection on a site on the other side of the village. Thought I'd just pop by on the off chance – your parents said you'd more than likely be home.'

Did they indeed, thought Daisy, gritting her teeth.

'May I?'

And with that, she found herself letting him into the house, where he took a cursory look around downstairs before asking if he could step outside into the garden.

'That's some great development opportunity you've got out there.'

Daisy stepped back, frowning. What the hell was he on about?

'Look, I'm terribly sorry' (*lie*, thought Daisy, who was channelling her inner Elaine, her voice several tones sharper and posher than normal), 'but there seems to be a bit of a mix-up. The house is for sale. And the garden and the orchard come along with it as part of the package.'

'Oh yes, of course, yes,' he said, not making himself

any clearer. 'Now if you wouldn't mind, I'd like to take a few measurements of the property?'

'As I say, not my thing, these old places.'

They were standing in the bathroom. Outside, visible from the little window which peeped through the eaves, rainclouds were gathering. The room, which in the right light was atmospheric and beautiful – the claw-footed bath sitting magisterially in the middle, the exposed wooden beams highlighted by the whitewashed walls – now looked dark and depressing.

'Oh?' She wasn't quite sure what the appropriate response was, but she could feel herself becoming sharper and pricklier with every room they visited. He'd rhapsodized all the way round Orchard Villa about his love of easy-maintenance, smart new builds.

'Nope. Still, you never know. You may well get some romantic with more money than sense come in from London and fall for it.'

Daisy had by now balled her hands so tightly that she could feel her nails cutting into her palms.

'I think it's beautiful.'

'Like I say,' said Mike Redforth, with an ingratiating wink. 'Takes all sorts.'

'Tosser.' Closing the door behind him, possibly just a fraction too late, Daisy spat the word with feeling.

Chapter Nineteen

'They've changed estate agents, then?'

Letting himself in through the back gate of the garden, Thomas was, as had become their weekly routine, armed with cherry buns from the bakery. He nodded to the second sign which now stood on the opposite side of the rose arch.

Daisy, who had been on her knees cutting back the geraniums to encourage a second late summer flush of flowers, stood up with a groan.

'Don't ask. I've given up trying to understand my parents.' She stood up, stretching. 'My back! I've been at it all this morning. Ooh, buns – lovely.'

Thomas pulled out one of the wooden chairs, motioning for Daisy to sit down. She flopped into it gratefully. She'd been working hard on the garden all morning, taking notes and photographs as she went along. Elaine, delighted to discover Daisy's writing was bringing in a new crop of gardening-related followers, had encouraged her to write some more articles about summer in an English cottage garden. After that, still furious about yesterday's oily estate agent visit, she'd worked harder than usual, determined to distract herself. He'd called again that morning, saying he'd had some interest already and asking if she'd be in later that afternoon if they wanted to 'swing by'. Remembering his smarmy tones on the answerphone, she grimaced. Orchard Villa might be destined to have new owners, but Daisy – and Thomas – were hopeful that they'd be gardeners, people who'd really appreciate the history and the beauty of the place. Yesterday afternoon she'd made herself scarce while three different sets of people tramped around, investigating.

She sat back for a moment. The weather was unsettled again – the morning had started off beautifully clear, the low sunlight stretching across the garden, casting a golden glow on the flowers and foliage. As she'd set to work, the sky had begun to fill with ominous violet clouds that clung to the hills beyond, biding their time. Just now, though, the sun was shining, the heat warming her face. She closed her eyes, listening to the bees hovering around the thyme which grew between the cracks of the stones.

'So what's happening, my dear?' Thomas looked at Daisy, keen for an explanation.

She sighed. 'I don't even want to think about it. Apparently this lot are commercial property specialists.'

Thomas looked out across the garden to the orchard. His eyes closed briefly, and he too gave a sigh. 'I'm getting too old for this, Daisy. I don't think

I can sit by and watch them take this place apart.'

She felt a wrench of guilt in her stomach. Logic told her she couldn't be responsible for her parents, who weren't gardeners and who had no ties in Steeple St John; but she'd fallen in love with the village, the characters she'd got to know on the allotments, the Parish Council meetings where Ned would whisper asides which left her crying with laughter . . .

'What will you do when this place sells?' Thomas turned away from the garden.

'I spoke to Miranda again the other day. She's offered me the sofa-bed in her place for as long as I'd like. There's a gardening project in North London, and they're hiring right now. With the work I've done on Elaine's website, I've probably got a good chance of getting an interview.' The prospect made her feel sick with sadness. She'd promised Miranda she'd meet her in town sometime soon, but getting on that Marylebone train felt like an admission of defeat. She wasn't ready to do it just yet.

'Things might work out yet, my love.'

'Let's hope so.' Daisy didn't sound any more convincing than Thomas did.

They were just preparing to get to work on the vegetables when Daisy felt the buzz of her phone in her pocket. She pulled it out.

Still okay for that drink tonight? G x

*

'Daisy!' Jo's voice was yelling through the letterbox at the same time as the bell was ringing.

'Hang on, I'm coming,' she called, turning off the taps. She'd only just made it upstairs to get ready for her night out, and Jo's visit wasn't expected – but she wasn't given to yelling through doors, either, so something must be up.

Filthy and covered in scratches from an afternoon balanced on a ladder, thinning out the early apples to ensure a good crop, she and Thomas had retreated as the rain had started. Thomas had headed off in the direction of the Grey Mare, declaring that he'd rather see the evening in over a pint and a game of dominoes with his Legion friends than end up 'sat at home staring at a television quiz for old folks'. Daisy had laughed at the idea, watching him as he headed up the hill towards the pub at a surprising pace. He was a lovely friend, despite their age difference. She'd headed upstairs then, planning a good long soak for an hour, ready for an evening in the pub with George.

She opened the door. Jo, apparently oblivious to the now torrential rain, was standing there in a pale blue checked shirt and a pair of leggings. Her hair hung around her face in limp strands, each one with a little river of water pouring from it.

'My God, Jo.' Daisy stepped back, making space for her friend. 'Come in before you freeze to death.'

'It's fine,' said Jo, eyes wide.

'It's pissing down with rain. You're soaking wet. It's

not fine.' Daisy pulled her by the arm into the hall and closed the door. Jo stood there, her eyes still saucer-shaped.

Daisy leaned back against the dresser, assessing her normally calm friend's demeanour.

'Okay. You're freaking me out a bit now.'

'Tom.'

'What about him?'

'He's going to be in London.'

Daisy cocked her head, looking at Jo, confused. Polly, who'd decided to investigate the commotion in the hall, sat herself down on the stone floor with a heaving sigh.

'Yes. Before he heads back to Amsterdam.'

'Have you taken up Twitter-stalking, Jo?' Daisy couldn't imagine it.

'God, no. I got a call this lunchtime. "Hi, Jo."' She did a passable impression of a Manchester accent. '"How's tricks? Fancy a coffee in town?"'

'Bloody hell,' said Daisy. 'How? Why? D'you want a drink?'

'No time.' Jo looked at her watch. 'He's catching the 5.48 to Marylebone. He'll be there in an hour and a half.'

'Why are you here, soaking wet, telling me this?' Jo had clearly lost her mind.

'I tried texting, but you didn't reply. I've left Martha running a bath and she's staying with Elaine again –' She paused for breath.

'This is insane.' Daisy reached forward and gave Jo a hug. 'But how did he . . . ?'

'Find me? You won't believe this.' She shook her head. 'You know I thought he'd seen me at the reading? Well, turns out he'd seen us in the bar. When I disappeared in the interval, he headed out to look for me before he went back for the prize-giving.'

'And I saw him in the B&B,' said Daisy, frowning.

'Yep, and when you shot out the door (his words, not mine), he was about to ask you if you had my number.'

Daisy winced. 'Sorry about that.'

'Don't be. I wasn't exactly in the best state of mind.'

'So he thought he'd get your number from the B&B owner, get in touch and see if he could trace me. When he was handed a printout with my details, he decided it was a sign.'

Daisy shook her head again. 'Bloody hell.'

'I *know*.'

'So what did he say?'

'He wondered if, after fifteen years of not speaking, maybe it'd be nice to be friends.'

'Wow.'

Jo's face darkened. She pushed her wet hair back from her face, a shower of drops splashing across the wall. 'But it's not as straightforward as a coffee with an old friend, is it?'

She exhaled slowly. There was a rumble of thunder and the rain pelted down, even harder, battering the windows.

'What would you tell someone else if they were in this position?' Daisy, who didn't have a clue how to counsel a counsellor, took a stab in the dark.

Jo twisted her mouth sideways in thought. 'I s'pose . . . I'd say it's one step at a time.'

'Sounds like pretty good advice to me.'

Daisy looked up at the big clock above the dresser. It was half past five already. Jo had better get a move on, or she'd be heading into London with soaking hair and wet clothes.

'Your bath's going to be overflowing. Martha's probably got distracted sending photos of her cat to school friends.'

'Right. You're right.' Leaning across, Jo gave Daisy a kiss.

Armed with the dregs of a bottle of white which she decided she most definitely deserved after an entire day in the garden, Daisy was climbing the stairs when the doorbell buzzed once again. It had to be Jo. She'd probably left her phone on the sofa, or something. Heavy-legged, desperate for the bath, she turned on the stairs.

'Another two minutes and I'd have been under-water,' she said, laughing, brandishing the glass as she opened the door.

'Evening, Miss Price.' Mike Redforth looked up from the screen of his phone, his long waxed jacket glistening in the rain. He looked like a damp ferret, his little eyes peering at her from under pale brows. 'Not too late, am I?'

Daisy felt her shoulders sagging with dismay. She remembered his comment about 'swinging by'. Was he *never* off-duty? She looked pointedly at the clock.

'Well, it's not – I'm not quite –' She held onto the side of the door for reinforcement, trying to formulate an excuse.

'Only take two ticks. Got to take a couple of measurements I missed yesterday, if you don't –' and with that, the estate agent had somehow made his way into the house, and was heading for the back garden.

'I need to take a couple of details about the garden for a client. They're very interested – in fact, he was planning on popping by this afternoon, as I said – couldn't make it, though, think he got caught up on the golf course.'

Wish I could have a relaxing sporting afternoon – or even a blooming bath – without gits like you turning up and waving your measuring sticks around. Chance would be a fine thing, thought Daisy, resenting every bath-stealing second of polite conversation she was making.

'Can I just pop out?' Without waiting to be asked, he opened the kitchen door and headed out onto the patio. Daisy, coatless, wasn't leaving him out there in her beloved garden alone. He'd probably trample on the lettuce, or murder the redcurrants.

'Of course,' she said through gritted teeth, slipping

on her muddy wellington boots. 'I'll be there in one second.'

'There's no need for you to come out in this rain.'

By the time she'd made it out, he'd already made his way towards the orchard at the back of the garden. He turned, clicking the laser measuring device in his hand.

'All done. Just needed to confirm the measurements – my laser was on the blink the other day.' He slipped it back into his pocket, hunching his shoulders against the rain, which was hurtling down now. The delphiniums were being beaten sideways, Daisy noticed. They'd need to be staked up if this weather was going to carry on.

'I'll be in touch. I'm not a gardener myself. Can't see the appeal of spending all day messing around with plants. If it was up to me –' he paused mid-sentence, treading carefully on the flagstone steps, which were rain-slicked and not designed for his shiny brown leather shoes – 'I'd have my garden completely paved over. The wife likes doing her hanging baskets.'

With a sigh of relief, Daisy closed the kitchen door, leading him back through to the hall. She gave a non-committal noise of agreement.

'Takes all sorts, don't it?'

'Yes. Yes, definitely. Thanks so much for coming.' She opened the front door, and decanted him back onto the rainy street.

Chapter Twenty

Daisy pushed her way through the door into the Grey Mare, her jeans sodden. The rain had come at her sideways, meaning that whilst her hair had stayed dry under the umbrella, the rest of her was dripping wet.

'Look at the state of you.' George was sitting by an unseasonal fire. He stood up with a gentle laugh, taking her umbrella. He leaned in, kissing her on the cheek.

'Sit down here.' He pulled the chair closer to the fire. 'James behind the bar said tonight felt like an autumn evening, not mid-July. He was right to light a fire, was he not?'

Daisy sank gratefully into the tall, button-backed leather armchair. She could feel the warmth of the fire counteracting the dampness, which was soaking through to her knees.

'You stay there. I'll get you a hot toddy to warm you up, and then we'll talk.' George dropped a hand on the crown of her head and strode off to the bar.

The pub was almost empty tonight – a couple of

Thomas's domino-playing friends sat in a corner, cardigans buttoned over their shirts, sipping their pints in companionable silence. Through the glass divider, Daisy could make out a couple sharing dinner in the little restaurant area. The pub had a couple of rooms, which were regularly booked up by visitors to the village – often Americans, who loved the whole quaint English village thing, and who'd be seen, maps in hand, setting off to climb the hills that stretched out into the countryside beyond. True to form, as Daisy watched, the woman unfolded a huge Ordnance Survey map, shaking it flat. Her husband laughed at her, taking a side to help her out, and they put their heads together, laughing and chatting as they planned their expedition.

Outside was dark with rain. She wrapped her arms around herself, feeling the fire warming her bones.

'Drink this.'

George returned with two tall glasses full of steaming amber liquid. Inside each was a slice of lemon, studded with cloves.

'My ma swears by these. If we had colds as kids, she'd give us a little hot toddy to get rid of the germs.'

'My mother would be horrified.' Daisy, wrapping her fingers around the glass, smiled at the thought. 'She's your typical knit your own yoghurt type – we weren't even allowed sweets when we were growing up. If we got a carob bar, it was a treat.'

'What on earth is carob?' George's eyebrows shot up.

'Basically, chocolate with all the fun taken out. I wouldn't recommend trying it.'

'I love a good piece of chocolate. Back home we make a chocolate torte in the restaurant which is so rich, and smooth, and . . . Actually, Daisy, it's Dublin I wanted to talk to you about. I'm going to have to head back for a few more weeks – my cousin's needing a break. She's been running the show single-handed for months now.'

He fiddled with the beermat on the table, not catching her eye, before looking up at her again, his eyes dark.

'It's a big responsibility I've got back there. There are a lot of people back there relying on me to dig these restaurants out of the hole they're in.' He rubbed a hand over his eyes, closing them. 'Sometimes . . . I have to make decisions that're hard.'

She leaned forward, putting a hand on his knee.

'I'm sure you'll do the right thing.'

If he was going home to sack all his staff, reflected Daisy, that mightn't be the most helpful response.

'I hope so.' George's face was bleak, and he buried it in his glass for a moment. When he raised his head again, he took a deep breath. Daisy watched him visibly shake himself back into the present moment.

'Anyway, how about I get the menu and we get

something to eat. I don't know about you, but I'm starving.'

Nodding, Daisy took a larger gulp of her toddy than she intended to. She felt the fumes whirling up her nose, and her eyes filling with water. Well – it wasn't like he was disappearing back to Ireland for good, just for a couple of weeks. But everything was unravelling at once. Orchard Villa was up for sale, the house contents would have to be put into storage, and . . .

When she'd been living in Winchester, she'd felt the beginnings of roots forming there. If Jamie and Sylvia hadn't done the dirty on her, it's possible they'd have gravitated back there after working in France for a couple of years. But the reality was, she didn't have anywhere to call home.

'Daisy?'

George's words shook her from her thoughts. He handed her a menu.

'Sorry.' She took a final draught of the toddy. She was warm inside and out now. 'Just thinking about today. It's been a long one.'

'Let's get something to eat. You can tell me all about it.'

'I'd like that.' She smiled up at him. She remembered Thomas saying calmly in the garden that she mustn't worry about the future, but concentrate on the time being. She took a deep breath. There wasn't much point in getting stressed when so much of it was out of her hands. She was in a nice pub, with a good-looking man with a lovely Dublin accent, and while the rain beat down outside she had a log fire to sit by. And that, Daisy decided, was enough for now.

She had a very nice night. They sat chatting over drinks and enjoyed a delicious dinner which George insisted on paying for, despite her protestations. He seemed a bit distracted, but with stuff going on back in Dublin, Daisy decided, that wasn't surprising. And with her new approach of not worrying about the future (which, Daisy found herself thinking at one point as she stood in the loos soaping her hands absent mindedly, could veer quite easily into a state of denial about everything), she didn't have to think about anything at all except whether it would have stopped raining by the time they left the pub.

And it had. They wandered down Main Street together, the pavements black and slick, the moon hanging overhead in a clearing sky.

'Do you want to come in?' Daisy stood under the rose arch at the gateway of Orchard Villa.

George shook his head, apologetically. 'I – no, Daisy, I'd better not. I've a flight first thing.' He pronounced it 'ting'. 'I'm sorry.' He looked, for a moment, as if he wanted to tell her something, a fleeting expression crossing his face, but a moment later it was gone.

Kissing her goodnight, he turned, heading up the lane towards his Aunt Charlotte's cottage. Daisy turned her key in the latch, letting herself in to find Polly waiting with an expression which clearly stated that she'd prefer to be asleep, thank you very much. Daisy leaned over, giving her a pat, gazing out for a moment at the moonlit garden, then headed upstairs alone.

Daisy had spent the morning tidying up Elaine's garden after yesterday's stormy weather. Wanting to get on, she'd turned down the offer of coffee and cake mid-morning, saying she'd rather wait until lunch, when Jo had promised to drop by between clients.

As usual, Elaine had spread the table in the orangery with her usual beautiful lunchtime selection, throwing the huge doors wide open. There was a rainbow salad scattered with tiny flowers, two huge home-made quiches, fresh from the oven – one dotted with tomatoes and scattered with chives, the other full of roasted vegetables. And there were tiny flatbreads, too, brushed with herb-scented melted butter.

'Jo says just to start without her. She's on her way.'

Elaine passed her a polka-dotted Emma Bridgewater plate. 'So, how was your date last night with the gorgeous George?'

Daisy, who was more concerned with how Elaine was doing, noticed that while her perfect manicure remained in place, the cuticles around the nails were raw and frayed. Elaine was giving the impression of coping, because that's what she did best.

'It was lovely.' She helped herself to a slice of quiche, not taking her eyes off Elaine, who was pushing a few pieces of lettuce and a tiny piece of bread around her plate.

Daisy decided it was best to just come out with it, even if it did go against every one of Elaine's perfectly British stiff-upper-lip sensibilities.

'What's happening about Leo?'

Elaine's shoulders stiffened. 'I don't really—'

Daisy cut in before she had a chance to finish. 'I know you don't want to talk about it. But we're here. You've got friends, Elaine. You're not alone.'

Something in the words hit hard. Elaine pushed her plate away, turning to Daisy. Her hands were shaking. She held her eyes wide in an attempt to stay in control, nostrils flaring.

'That's where you're wrong.'

Daisy took Elaine's trembling hand, cupping it between hers. She looked down at the bitten cuticles and back up into Elaine's beautiful face, rigid with tension. She watched as one uncontrollable tear spilled out, making its way silently down her cheek. It landed on her shirt, soaking into the expensively cut fabric. It was joined by another. And one more. And then the flood came. With that, Daisy reached forward, putting her arms around Elaine's tiny frame, holding her gently, murmuring into her hair.

'You're not alone, you've got us. I promise. Promise.'

Elaine's shoulders heaved as she sobbed, collapsing into Daisy as if she'd had her strings cut.

'I'm so sorry,' she said eventually, pulling herself upright. Daisy passed her one of the napkins and she blew her nose.

'You've nothing to be sorry for. What he did – you lived with it for all that time, knowing what he'd done.'

'Knowing he was doing it *again*,' interrupted Elaine, putting the napkin down on her lap, rubbing at her eyes.

'You knew?' Daisy thought back to the moment she'd overheard him talking on the phone in the garden.

'I had my suspicions. I've become an old hand at watching for the signs.' Elaine's face darkened again. 'An extra meeting here and there. He'd be early to work, late home. There'd be a conference in London and I'd get a message saying he'd decided to stay over so he could woo potential new parents for the school. The phone was always on, never far from his side . . .' She shook her head, remembering.

'But you stayed?' Jo, who'd let herself in, the door open on the latch, was standing in the arched doorway of the orangery. She gave Elaine a gentle smile before crossing the room and sitting down by her side.

'I didn't have any choice.' Elaine's mouth was set in a sad, straight line. 'Well, I thought I didn't. I lost both my parents when I was young. When my grandparents died, I lost the only family I had left. Gained all this,' she waved vaguely in the air, indicating the Old Rectory. 'But that was all I had. And I've never found it exactly easy to make friends.'

Daisy felt her heart aching for Elaine – brittle, lonely, clinging on desperately to the only thing she felt she had. And the more desperate she became, the harder she'd found it to make friends.

'There's always a choice.' Jo squeezed her knee gently. 'Just sometimes we're so close we can't see it.'

'And I'm not alone.' Elaine tried the words out, quietly.

'No,' said Daisy and Jo simultaneously. They shared a smile. 'You're not alone.'

'I'm lucky to have you girls.' Elaine turned to each of them, giving both a kiss on the cheek. 'Y'know, I'm beginning to think I might just make it after all.' There was a faint quaver to her voice, but it was accompanied by a brave, genuine smile.

Daisy picked up her cup, taking a sideways look at her two friends, both already changed so much since they'd met in spring. Thomas was right. Life just kept on carrying you along, whether you liked it or not.

They finished lunch, and Daisy made a pot of coffee, noticing as she did so that there were still signs of Martha's visit. A pile of CDs stood on the dresser alongside a tiny mountain of hairbands and grips, her perpetual calling cards. Other than that, though, the place was its usual neat self. As she waited for the kettle to boil, her eyes were drawn to the calendar hanging by the kitchen window.

The words 'Divorce Lawyer: 12.30' were written in Elaine's small, precise lettering beside Thursday's date. Daisy moved away, sensing she'd invaded her friend's privacy. A tiny part of her cheered, though. Elaine wasn't going back this time.

'So.' Elaine curled her fingers around her coffee mug, sitting back against the huge cushions of the sofa. 'I don't mean to be intrusive, but . . .'

Daisy leaned towards her, a conspiratorial smile on her face, knowing what was coming next.

'Jo. We've been utterly discreet. Neither of us have chased you with text messages.'

Daisy shook her head, virtuously, before taking up the thread. 'But we can't help noticing you're looking . . . happier than we might have hoped, considering.'

In the moment before Jo spoke, a pink flush rose on her pale cheeks, lighting up her face. Her eyes were dancing brightly.

'Well, I . . .' She paused, as if checking Elaine was up to hearing something good on a day when she'd been through the wringer. Elaine nodded, eyebrows raised expectantly, and Jo continued, 'I needed a bit of time to process it all. It was – big. Bigger than I expected.'

Daisy, wide-eyed, choked on her coffee, laughing at the accidental innuendo like a fourteen-year-old. Elaine, catching on, started to laugh too, which set Jo off. It was a few minutes before anyone could speak.

'We're *supposed* to be functioning adults.' Elaine shook her head, still giggling.

'And we've had a hell of a lot to deal with this last while. Seriously – if you didn't laugh about this stuff, you'd go insane. Take it from me. I'm a professional, remember?' Jo pulled a distinctly un-professional face.

She explained then how they'd met in a cosy little bar in London, where they'd had an awkward five-minute conversation about work, life, and the weather, before Tom had made her laugh, and they'd fallen back in time to fifteen years ago where they'd talked and talked about their lives, where they'd been, the people they'd met . . .

'And . . .' Elaine cocked her head sideways in thought as Jo paused. 'You didn't mention you had a daughter?'

Jo shook her head, then nodded, confusingly.

'I did. Just in passing, to begin with, because – how do you bring *that* up in conversation?'

'But then he asked to see a photograph. And then he asked how old she was.'

Daisy looked at Jo, her eyes widening in horror. It wouldn't exactly take a mathematical genius to work out the timings . . .

'Yes. He took about five minutes before he started trying to work out if I'd been with anyone else during finals.'

Elaine recoiled slightly, her still-sensitive radar activated. 'That sounds a bit – controlling?'

Jo shook her head again. 'We were at a tiny little campus university. Everyone knew everyone else's business. Believe me, if I'd slept with anyone, the jungle drums would have been activated by the time he'd rolled out of bed.'

'Bit like village life, then?' said Daisy, thinking of the gossip she'd heard that morning in the Post Office queue. Everyone was talking about Leo's indiscretions, and it seemed pretty clear that Steeple St John was firmly on Team Elaine.

'Then he started asking if I was on good terms with Martha's dad,' said Jo. The flush had gone from her cheeks again, and she spoke slowly and carefully, plucking absently at the trim on the cushion she'd picked up and hugged, without thinking. 'And I – well, we were friends for a long time. We spent every day together. And I'm a shit liar. He picked up the photograph from the table and stared at it for a minute, and then he just came out with the big question, before I had a chance to find the words.'

Daisy's 'wow' in response was an exhalation of long-held breath. Elaine put an arm around Jo's shoulder, returning the hug she'd so gratefully received earlier.

Jo leaned in, thankfully, for a moment. 'He wants to get to know her.'

'I don't understand.' Daisy had thought about this for long hours whilst gardening. She loved her dad dearly – and while Jo was a brilliant mum, Martha had spent fourteen years not knowing her father. She blurted out the words, realizing as she did that they weren't exactly tactful. 'Wasn't he furious?'

Jo, surprisingly, was unruffled by this, agreeing with Daisy. 'I expected that. But – no. He was upset – shocked. Really quiet for a whole pint of Guinness.' Jo bit her lip, remembering. 'But then he was sad for me having to go through the last fifteen years alone. He did admit he'd have been hopeless if I'd turned up when we were still in our twenties, mind you –' she smiled as she spoke. 'But he seemed quite accepting. He's been studying Buddhism – always was a bit of a hippy, even back then.'

Daisy shot a look at Elaine over Jo's shoulder.

'He said, in the end, that it must be the right time for Martha to be in his life, and that he hoped she'd feel the same way.'

Elaine raised her eyebrows in return before speaking, thoughtfully. 'Well, if that's not a sign from the universe, I don't know what is.'

Daisy looked down, realizing she'd crossed her fingers without thinking. It was a pretty big thing they were wishing for. Jo and Tom were going to need every last bit of luck.

Chapter Twenty-one

'Miss Price . . . er, Daisy. Hello?'

Daisy felt her shoulders sag. Was every day going to be interrupted by Mike Redforth 'just popping by', or 'making a quick call'? She'd just settled into the greenhouse. The little portable radio was on low for company – tuned to Radio 4 – and it was muttering away happily in the background, while the garden beyond filled with the late-afternoon sounds of bees and birdsong. Polly was stretched out in the shade, luxuriating, her water bowl close by.

A couple of hours of potting and pottering, and Daisy would feel that today hadn't been totally wasted garden-wise. So when her phone rang, she kicked herself that she hadn't left it plugged in to the charger in the kitchen. Now she felt obliged to answer.

'Hi.' She couldn't even bring herself to sound enthusiastic. She'd recognized Mike Redforth's office number straight away. Could he not just bugger off for a few days and stop being so bloody efficient?

'Got a quick question for you.'

Of course you have, thought Daisy, pursing her lips crossly.

'Just following up on those garden measurements. Bloke interested in the house earlier. Wondered if he could pop in on his way back from work – about half-five?'

Daisy frowned down at the phone. That gave her ninety minutes of peace and quiet. Tempting as it was, she conceded that her parents wouldn't thank her if someone was actually interested in buying Orchard Villa and she turned them away because she couldn't be arsed.

'Fine. That's fine. I'll see you then.'

'I'm out on a site, won't make it back on time, I'm afraid. Do you mind doing the viewing yourself? He's not going to take long.'

Daisy rolled her eyes. Now she was expected to do his job, as well?

'Fine,' she repeated, this time rather less graciously.

'Excellent stuff.' Mike Redforth had slipped into extra-charming gear. 'You're an absolute doll.' Daisy cringed. 'Bloke seems to know a bit about the place already. That's usually a good sign. Anyway, I'll be in touch tomorrow, one way or the other. Have a good one.'

Daisy looked down at the now-silent phone and sighed. She turned back to her tiny honesty plants and set to work, transplanting them carefully from their little seedling pots into ones where they'd have room to put out roots and establish themselves. Whoever it was that was turning up later would just have to take her – and the house, which wasn't exactly in spotless show-home condition – as they found her.

Having headed down to the kitchen to wash her compost-covered hands, Daisy looked up at the clock when the doorbell rang. It was only quarter past five – the potential purchasers weren't due for another quarter of an hour, and she was hoping she'd have time to do a quick tidy round before they arrived.

'Afternoon, Daisy, how're you doing?'

She stepped back in surprise, doing a double take for a second. It wasn't George, as she'd first thought, but his twin brother, Stephen, standing on the doorstep of Orchard Villa, bouncing slightly from foot to foot, dressed in a sharp, clearly expensive suit. She held the door, cheeks frozen in a polite smile of greeting. If he was checking up on her for George, knowing she was alone following his return to Dublin, his timing wasn't great.

'Just got off the train and thought I'd pop by on the way past.'

'Oh, that's very kind, Stephen, but—'

'I'll only be two ticks.'

'Come in.' Daisy, being polite, held the door open, indicating with a sweep of her arm that he should make his way to the kitchen.

'Is everything all right? George –' she halted for a moment, not sure what to say. 'He's okay, isn't he?'

She'd had a strangely stilted text from him early that morning to say that he'd arrived in Dublin, and that he hoped she was well and would take care of herself.

'He's grand. Sure the family'll be pleased to have him back.'

Daisy glanced towards the window, checking the front path. Nobody in sight.

'I'm not holding you back, am I? I'll not be long at all.' Stephen pulled out his phone, tapping it quickly. 'I'd be lost without this thing altogether.'

This was a bit odd. Perhaps George *had* asked his brother to pop in and make sure she was okay. It was quite sweet, really.

'Would you like a drink?'

'Oh, no, got to get back. Michelle's expecting me this evening to help with the kids' bedtime. If I can just have a quick scoot round the garden, I'm not worried about the house. Can we just nip out the back and I'll have a look?'

The realization was dawning on Daisy, slowly. 'I'm sorry, I hadn't put two and two together. *You're* here to see the house?'

'The garden, yes. And your lovely self, of course.' He gave a smile that reminded her of George.

'Come on, then, I'll show you round. I'm much more of a garden person than a house one, too. It's my favourite part of the house.'

Stephen followed her across the terrace and up the

little flagstone steps, edged with lavender bushes. If George's brother bought this place, maybe she could carry on gardening here. Maybe – just maybe, they'd be her first clients. She shook herself before she disappeared off on a flight of imagination.

Reaching the top of the orchard, she turned, knowing as she did that the view was spectacular. The gardens stretched out down towards the terrace, the old house sitting proudly, nestling in amongst the greenery.

'I've had a lot of help from Thomas, who lives in the village – he's been gardening this place since he was eighteen. So he knew what was missing, and helped me cut back the stuff that had become overgrown since my parents moved in – they weren't exactly big gardening fans – and if you have a look over here,' she motioned towards the vegetable garden, neatly edged with box hedging, which she'd been trimming just the other day, 'you can see that it's possible to be almost self-sufficient for fruit and veg in summer.'

'Grand, right enough.' Stephen nodded politely.

'I've been planting here using the three sisters method so you can see the beans, corn and squashes growing all together – it's a planting method used by the Iroquois – have you heard of it?'

'No, I'm not much of a vegetable gardener myself, to be truthful – Michelle likes her pots of those brightly coloured ones, can't remember what they're called. Striped ones.'

'Petunias?' Daisy bit back a grimace, silencing her inner gardening snob. Each to their own, and all that.

'And up here we've got eight fruit trees – two Bramley apples' – she ducked underneath the taller of the two, patting the trunk affectionately – 'and there's a russet, here's the pear, cherry . . . and this is my favourite, the mulberry.' She stopped beside the huge old tree, waiting for him to admire it.

Stephen put his hands up, taking an opportunity whilst Daisy paused for breath to get a word in edgeways.

'I'm not looking at the place for myself.'

Daisy felt a sneaking moment of relief. Her gorgeous herbaceous borders weren't going to be festooned with hideous petunias which looked like candy-striped Victorian bloomers, after all.

'Oh?'

'No.' Stephen looked, she realized, slightly uncomfortable. The smile was gone, replaced with a half-raised eyebrow and an apologetic expression. 'I'm interested in buying the place for the redevelopment potential. Didn't George mention it last night?'

Daisy stepped backwards in shock, uprooting a row of newly planted box cuttings in the process.

'This place is – what – almost an acre?' He continued talking, animated for the first time since he'd arrived. 'It's a ten-minute walk from a mainline station into London.'

She couldn't speak. He was still talking, but she

couldn't take in anything else he was saying. Snippets made their way into her ears. Words like 'three decent-sized executive homes', and 'side road access'. The scent of crushed grass filled her nostrils as the hum of a lawnmower from a garden beyond filled the air. She remembered reading somewhere that the smell so reminiscent of summer, sunshine and happiness was actually a plant distress call – the grass emitting a compound indicating it was under attack. Funny, she thought, how these things come back to you at the most inopportune moments.

'So, that's what I'm thinking. Of course there'd be planning permission to look into, and no doubt there'd be some objection from the older villagers, but—'

'You can't turn this garden into a housing estate.' Daisy's voice was flat.

Stephen laughed, his tone slightly edgy. 'Come on, Daisy. That's hardly what I'm talking about. I can see you've done a lot of work here, but there's loads of other gardens, aren't there?'

'Not like this one.' Daisy looked down towards the house. This place had stood here for years. These lawns had seen the feet of generations of children running up and down. She could hear the echoes of Victorian garden parties, and imagine the family sheltering here during the war. She pictured a young Thomas here, sleeves rolled up, waistcoat on, digging the garden whilst the lady of the house looked on, asking for his advice on what best to plant that summer.

'Well,' Stephen turned to make his way back towards the house, and a welcome escape, 'it'll take a bit of time to think about, I'm sure. But George seemed to think your parents were pretty keen to sell the place ASAP. We'd give them a good price, of course.'

We, thought Daisy, narrowing her eyes in fury. No wonder George had slunk off so quickly last night.

'I think you'll find they're not in *that* much of a rush.' The words were icily polite.

'Well, I'll give Mike a ring first thing.' He came back, seemingly confident. How *dare* he presume to know what her parents would think over her? She could feel a wave of fury building inside her chest, her ears thrumming with noise.

With an awkward half-wave, Stephen suggested he let himself out. Daisy nodded curtly, and let him go.

She watched from the kitchen window as he sped off in the convertible she recognized from her first date with George.

'Bastard, bastard, *bastard*,' she hissed under her breath, then yelled out loud, 'You absolute shit,' startling Polly, who barked at her in agreement. Picking up a mug, Daisy threw it across the kitchen in temper. It shattered against the metal door of the Aga, shards spinning across the stone flags of the kitchen floor.

What the hell was Stephen playing at? Worse still, she realized, George, that lying shit, had clearly been

315

fishing for information from the first time they'd met, realizing the money-making potential that lay in an acre of prime land close to the middle of the village, with access to the back garden via a little lane. She swung the kitchen door open and stormed out into the garden, where she collapsed in a chair and burst into tears. Her head was thumping.

Oblivious to the sunshine, not hearing the riotous birdsong that surrounded her, Daisy sat with her head in her hands for a long time. As hard as she tried, it was impossible not to imagine the trees of the orchard being ripped up by the roots, the carefully planted vegetable patch scooped up in the jaws of a digger, a crude wooden fence dividing the long garden into what Stephen had referred to as 'manageable chunks'. Every time she chased away one picture in her mind, another appeared. She could even visualize the houses – they'd be called something hideous like The Old Orchard, no doubt, with not a sign left of the beautiful old trees that had been wiped out in their creation.

She felt her phone buzzing in her pocket, but ignored it.

It buzzed again a few moments later. She stood up, deciding she needed a drink. Polly, who was wise enough to stay out of the way, was lurking in her bed. The floor crunched underfoot. Sighing, Daisy picked up the dustpan and brush and started clearing up the mess she'd made. That was the trouble with having a tantrum alone – there was nobody to pick up the pieces afterwards. Tipping the china shards into the bin, she turned to the fridge and looked inside. A lump of dried-up cheese, half a litre of milk, and a load of garden vegetables. Not even a bit of leftover wine or a tin of gin and tonic to be seen. She'd have to head up to the little supermarket for supplies.

As she started walking, she realized her phone was still buzzing insistently from her pocket. With a sigh, she pulled it out to check.

Miranda, flashed the display. Daisy answered, talking as she walked up the hill to the shop.

'I hope your day's been better than mine.'

'What's up? Your turnips in a tangle? Are your peas playing up?'

'What's up is –' Daisy paused for a second, still too angry to think straight. 'The bloody parents have dropped me in it with the estate agent from hell, it turns out that George is a lying snake in the grass, and—'

'Hang on. Rewind.'

Daisy heard splashing from Miranda's end.

'Rewind to where?' Daisy took a deep breath.

'Start with Gorgeous George.'

'Stop calling him that,' hissed Daisy. 'He's a complete bastard. They all are.'

'All men? All people?'

'Everyone. Seriously. The parents have sold me down the river with the slimiest estate agent going.

The doorbell goes this afternoon and it's George's brother standing there, virtually with a bulldozer parked on the pavement outside, plans in hand for building three houses in the back garden.' She ran her free hand through her hair.

'He can't do that, surely? You can't just wipe out the house – isn't there some kind of preservation thingy in place?'

Daisy flopped down on the bench in the market square. Unlike her sister, who spent most of her life chatting on London buses and as she marched from one business meeting to another, phone tucked under her ear, Daisy couldn't concentrate on shopping and talking at the same time. She crossed one leg over the other and sat back, listening to Miranda.

'He doesn't want to wipe out the house. He wants to come in via the lane at the back, hoick out half the garden and leave three bloody great red-brick monstrosities in its place.'

Daisy heard Miranda sigh. After a moment, her sister began again, choosing her words carefully.

'Look, Daise. I know you've spent the last few months working on that place.'

Daisy sat up, bristling. She had a suspicion she knew what was coming next.

'But the thing is . . . it's not like it's our childhood home. And you knew you were only house-sitting. You need to be a bit Zen about it, let it happen.'

Bloody hell, was *everyone* in on this Buddhism thing?

'*Let it happen*?' Daisy yelled down the phone. An old lady, walking past with her West Highland terrier on a tartan lead, looked at her disapprovingly. Daisy glared back at her.

'Calm down.' Miranda was adding more hot water to her bath now; Daisy could hear the taps running. The contrast between her luxurious relaxation and Daisy's state of fury was too much to bear.

'I don't want to bloody calm down! They can't just come in here, buy a house, and then sell it to the highest bidder when they decide they don't fancy it after all.'

'Um, Daisy.' Miranda's voice was deliberately calm now. 'What you're describing there is the British property market. That's exactly what they're going to do.'

'And what about Thomas? And the garden? And all the—'

'You need a drink,' said Miranda. 'And I don't mean to sound like Mum, but you sound knackered. Have you had a long day?'

Daisy thought back. It was less than twenty-four hours since she'd sat in the pub having dinner with George, kissing him goodbye as he slunk off back to Dublin.

Just enough time to get out of the way whilst Stephen dropped the bombshell, Daisy realized, with fury. He'd mentioned last night he had difficult decisions to make – well, this one hadn't been that hard for him, had it? He'd dropped her in the shit and jumped on a plane.

'Bastard,' Daisy hissed, once again.

'Daisy?' Miranda's voice startled her.

'He's a complete shit,' she snapped at her sister, furious.

'I don't think you can say that.' Miranda's voice was measured and calm in reply. 'Come on, everyone's got to make a living, haven't they?'

'Yeah, but ripping apart the garden I've just spent months renovating is not okay.'

Miranda gave an almost imperceptible tut, followed by a sigh.

'Look, seriously, if you like him, I don't think you can write him off on the basis that his brother's interested in buying Orchard Villa and sticking a couple of houses in the garden.'

'Yes, I can. And to be honest –' Daisy realized even as she spoke in temper that the words held the truth – 'he might be good-looking, but that's not enough for me.' She frowned for a second, recalling George's face, double-checking. 'Nope. Nothing.'

'Even if you weren't furious about the garden being turned into a housing estate?'

'Even if.' Daisy's tone was final.

Miranda had never understood Daisy's love of gardening – it wasn't surprising, really, that she couldn't quite appreciate why this cut so deeply. There was no point trying to force her to understand.

'Look, darling, I know you're feeling shitty. You've had a crappy day. The parents have gone native in Nepal, or wherever they are this week. But you've got a room waiting here for you as soon as you want it.'

'Thanks.' Daisy felt the sting of tears forming, and screwed up her eyes to chase them back.

'S'all right. That's what I'm here for.' Miranda's voice was gentle. 'Look, it's not like you've got a life in that place. The garden's been therapy, you're feeling better – well, you were, anyway –'

Despite herself, Daisy gave a little snort of laughter.

'And you've got that job prospect in Hackney. You did put in the application the other day, didn't you?'

Daisy nodded, numbly. 'Yep. Got an email from them yesterday.'

'I knew it,' said Miranda. 'You're a star.'

Chapter Twenty-two

'Ladies and gentlemen!' Flora's voice was loud and purposeful. She clapped her hands together as she spoke, emphasizing her point. The Parish Council meeting fell silent.

Daisy, feeling rather conspicuous, wobbled on a stool beside Flora. She pulled down the hem of her dress once again. She hadn't thought about the fact that she'd be propped up on a high chair with everyone peering up at her, and she was fairly certain that the front row had already caught a glimpse of too much thigh for this time of the morning. From the back of the room Ned, looking unusually smart for once, caught her eye, pulling a face that made her laugh. She'd have to ignore him or he'd give her the giggles as usual.

'Before we get down to business, I want to raise an extra item that isn't on the agenda.'

There was a scuffling of chairs, and a few people cleared their throats. Flora, who seemed to be embracing the drama, had paused for a moment to allow the significance of her statement to sink in. Daisy, still feeling sick with anger and misery about George's deception, tried to put those feelings to one side and concentrate on what was happening. It was easier to just put him out of her head. She still had her phone switched off; it sat in her handbag like an unexploded bomb, waiting.

'Now.' Flora's voice fluted across the room. 'As you may have heard, there has been a worrying development in this dreadful practice of *garden-grabbing*.' She pulled a face as she said the words, nostrils curling and lips pursed in disgust.

'Daisy here, who has already been kind enough to take a place on our allotment committee as a horticultural advisor, has informed Thomas and myself,' Flora inclined her head in a queenly manner towards Thomas, who was sitting three chairs along from Daisy, 'that there are indications that a developer is interested in buying Orchard Villa. Daisy, would you like to fill us in?'

'Oh, um –' Taken by surprise, Daisy sat up, clutching desperately at the edge of her dress and pressing her knees together. It was a bit like being back at school, where she'd found herself on the debating team – more because nobody else had volunteered, than out of any desperate desire to discuss meaningful events with the sixth form of St Augustine's School for Boys. Back then, she'd generally ended up eyeing up the most handsome member of the opposing team. Going to an all-girls school had had some major disadvantages. She forced herself to concentrate, looking out at the sea of villagers who were surveying her with interest.

'Yes. The estate agent has suggested that the potential buyer is very keen. Unfortunately my parents, who own the house, don't have the same attachment to the garden as I do.' She looked across at Thomas, who smiled at her encouragingly. 'And so I just wondered if there's anything we can do to stop it.'

'Bloody incomers.' A voice came from the back of the room, which managed to be both a mutter and somehow heard by everyone.

'David, that's neither helpful nor kind.' Flora's voice was reproving. Murmurs of agreement, and mildly disapproving tuts, could be heard travelling through the massed group of residents.

'There must be something we can do.' A young woman, jogging a pushchair with one hand and with a toddler standing on her knee, looked around the room anxiously. 'I live in one of the houses on the lane that backs onto Orchard Villa. If they start building there, my children aren't going to be safe to play outside.'

Somehow this opened the floodgates. People from all over the room started calling out, discussing the situation amongst themselves. Daisy, Flora and the other committee members looked on.

'Can't we object on the grounds that the stream might be disrupted? There'd be flooding.'

'Isn't Orchard Villa listed in any case?'

'Don't think so.' The man who'd spoken looked at Daisy for confirmation. She shook her head. 'But the garden's big enough that they can develop it without any problems anyway.'

'I thought they did away with garden-grabbing during the last election?'

Voices echoed around the room.

'Yeah, in theory, but there's always loopholes.'

'Bloody politicians. They're all in each other's pockets.'

'Those builders pay 'em off in any case. Promise to make a play-park for the kids and get round the rules.'

Flora stood up, hands poised, ready to clap the meeting back into order, when a clear, reedy voice piped up from the corner of the hall.

'Don't know what the problem is, m'self. Folks have got to live somewhere.'

Everyone turned in surprise.

'Geoffrey Bulmer.' Flora's tone was schoolmarm sharp. 'I'm surprised at you. You've lived in this village all your life.'

An old man, his back bent with years of work, gnarled fingers holding onto a wooden walking stick, looked back at her with rheumy blue eyes that were still sharp.

'I have that, Flora Douglas. But times change. If nothing was ever built, we'd all be living in mud huts.'

'Well, yes.' Flora shook her head, raising her eyes

heavenwards. 'Yes, of course. But that doesn't mean we need these monstrosities built right in the middle of Steeple St John.'

'You want them kept well out of the way?' Geoffrey stood up as he spoke, wheezing between sentences, leaning heavily on his stick. The room was silent. 'Out of sight, out of mind? All right on the outskirts of the village? Am I onto something, Flora?'

'Yes – no – oh, for goodness' sake, we are getting completely off the subject. Thomas?' Flora tutted loudly, turning to Thomas for support.

Thomas gave his dominoes partner a nod of acknowledgement before he spoke. He watched as Geoffrey, having had his say, made his way slowly down the gap in the massed chairs and headed towards the Grey Mare for a pint. Daisy suspected that Thomas was wishing he could head in the same direction.

'I don't know the ins and outs. There's a housing shortage, the papers tell us,' said Thomas. 'But it's not about politics for me. The point is, Orchard Villa has a garden I'm very fond of, which holds a lot of memories. And I'm not sure ripping up that particular garden to build a few expensive executive homes is going to help any of these young folk of the village find a place to live, is it?'

There was a murmur of agreement, people nodding as he continued. 'We're here because we're interested in preserving the best of Steeple St John – not preserving it in aspic, but we need to find a way to make this village a place where people can continue to live safely.' He looked at the young woman, who was now juggling both of her children on her lap. She smiled at him gratefully as he continued talking, his voice clear and carrying across the now silent hall.

'And it's about making sure the village carries on being somewhere with a heart.'

The room burst into spontaneous applause. Thomas, looking surprised, turned to Flora and said, 'Will that do?' She beamed back at him in response, reaching across and putting a hand on his arm. He inclined his head towards her, gratefully.

'Looks like you've got a future in politics, Thomas,' said Daisy, smiling across at him.

The room was now filled with a clamour of excitement and chatter. People were turning in their chairs to talk to each other, nodding with enthusiasm. Flora stood up, giving another clap of her hands to silence them.

'Right then, everyone. After Thomas's *splendid* speech, I think we're all in agreement that something has to be done about these plans. I suspect that if we all club together, there will be strength in numbers. Daisy, you've done a spot of writing for Mrs Thornton-Green's website, haven't you? Perhaps you could pen something for the local paper? Might get people talking.'

Daisy winced. How would her parents react if they

got wind of her attempts to sabotage their house sale? But they were thousands of miles away. If they could just put off George's brother, maybe a buyer would come along . . .

'Excellent stuff. Right, well – back to the agenda. I'd like to take a moment to mention a couple of details pertaining to the village fête. It's only a few weeks away now, and I'd like to remind you all that entries for the home crafts section are open until the day before, so you can get in your best jams and cakes . . .'

Daisy drifted off as Flora continued to detail the various classes open to all at the fête. She'd been earmarked as one of three judges for the produce competitions – which, Thomas informed her, was a tremendous honour. Never having attended a village fête, she wasn't quite sure how she'd judge one carrot as being better than another, but she hoped that the other two judges would carry her along.

'I'd like to thank Daisy for her contribution today,' said Flora, rousing her from her thoughts.

Daisy smiled out at the now restless audience, who had begun pulling bags onto shoulders, checking their phones, and starting to shuffle their way out of their seats. Flora's meetings tended to go on for ten minutes longer than scheduled.

'Well, that's enough for today. Thank you all *so* much for coming.' Flora gave the room a final little clap, beaming out at them delightedly. She'd have made a wonderful Lady of the Manor, presiding over everyone at the garden party. Daisy smiled at the thought. Seeing this, Flora gave her a queenly incline of the head.

'Penny for your thoughts, Daisy?'

She looked up, feeling Thomas putting his hand on her shoulder. Whilst she'd been daydreaming, and with Flora still holding forth, he'd managed to escape from his chair, clearly heading in the same direction as his friend Geoffrey – towards the pub for a swift afternoon pint and a read of the paper.

Flora twisted in her chair, pausing mid-flow, her face falling. 'Are you leaving us, Thomas? I was hoping to go over some of these figures I have here about the village fête—'

'So sorry, Flora. Got an appointment, I'm afraid.' Thomas gave Daisy the tiniest wink, almost invisibly, and inclined an eyebrow towards the pub. Ned was hovering by the door, pretending to read one of the posters, the ghost of a smile playing at the corners of his mouth. He looked sideways at Daisy.

'I think Daisy might need to get off, too.'

'Yes.' Daisy grabbed her chance, realizing that otherwise she'd be stuck in the empty hall for at least another half-hour, discussing the minutest details of plans for the fête. She scrambled down from the stool, stooping to grab her bag, and started making her way down from the little stage and towards the door.

'Never mind, I'll be in touch shortly. Now that

you're judging, Daisy, perhaps we could find a slot for you on the village fête committee, too.'

Daisy gave a panicked, wide-eyed look at Thomas, who had turned back to catch her eye.

'I'm sure Daisy has quite enough on her plate right now, Flora. We mustn't overstretch her and take advantage of her good nature.'

'Of course not.' Flora picked up her ever-present clipboard and pen. 'Daisy, thank you so much for your help. Much appreciated.'

'You're welcome.' Daisy gave Flora a relieved smile as she headed out into the afternoon.

'Thanks for that.' She burst out laughing as they hit the sunshine outside the hall.

'Nice dress,' said Ned, with an expression which suggested he'd witnessed her initial, undignified wobble.

She shot him a mock-frosty look.

'*You're* looking surprisingly respectable.' She pretended to inspect his outfit. He was dressed, as always, in a pair of slightly battered cords, but these ones looked like they'd been hung up neatly instead of being picked up from the floor and thrown on, and his short-sleeved shirt appeared to have been ironed.

'We try. Trying to make a bit of an effort.'

'Oh, yes?' said Thomas, looking at Daisy with amusement. 'Who's the lucky girl?'

Ned raised his eyebrows, shaking his head. 'I can't divulge my secrets, Thomas.'

The perfect Fenella, of course. Daisy found herself swallowing a tiny, bitter pill of something she couldn't quite put her finger on.

Thomas spoke, breaking through her thoughts. 'Flora would have you on the village committee for committee meetings about committees, if you let her. She doesn't mess about. Reminds me in a funny way of my Violet.' He shook his head, smiling fondly. 'Now off you go and get that article written, young lady. It might just make a difference. Unless you fancy joining me and Geoffrey for a quick one, before you get to work?'

Daisy hesitated for a second. A cool drink in the Grey Mare would be a lovely reward to herself for sitting through the meeting, but on the other hand . . .

'Are you walking up Main Street?' Flora's voice could be heard as she bustled out of the village hall, pulling the door closed behind her. 'I'll walk with you, if you like.' God, she was persistent.

'I'll take care of this,' said Thomas, under his breath, with a knowing expression.

'Um, no, sorry,' said Daisy, having had her mind made up. The idea of Flora deciding to join her for a quick gin and tonic and a 'little chat' about the fête was too much to bear. 'I've really got to get on. See you soon!'

Giving Thomas a grateful squeeze on the arm as she left, Daisy headed back to Orchard Villa. With the discussion still clear in her head, she might as well write something for the local paper. With any luck, it'd stall George's bloody brother long enough for the perfect buyer to swoop in and make an offer. Her parents needn't hear a word of any of this.

Chapter Twenty-three

FURTHER GARDENS THREAT FOR
STEEPLE RESIDENTS

Daisy saw the hand-written sign outside the news-agent's shop when she was only halfway up the hill to Main Street. She'd emailed a 300-word article to the editor, rhapsodizing about the beauty of the Orchard Villa garden and its century-old mulberry tree. He'd replied straight away, keen to get the piece into the Friday edition of the twice-weekly local paper. She'd expected a tiny mention on page six, alongside the usual news about the local football team and the plans for an extension of the railway line from Steeple St John to nearby Wellbury.

But no – she opened the door to the newsagent's shop. There was a huge headline emblazoned across the front of the *Argus*, with her name written clearly underneath. It was a strange feeling. Her parents, who'd been far more supportive years ago when she'd studied English literature, had dismissed her horticulture course as a fad – and yet here she was, writing and gardening having collided – and all to stop their house being sold for redevelopment. It was a pity, though, she thought, buying two copies of the paper, that she was hoping they'd never see it.

Daisy headed out of the shop, impatient to see how the article looked in print. She stopped and leaned against the window ledge of the little cake shop, scanning the paper. It seemed to make sense, and hadn't misquoted anyone from the meeting. There was a photo in the middle of the page, taken at the barbecue fundraiser. She was standing alongside Thomas, Flora, and a couple of other committee members. Ned was in the background, laughing. She'd been captioned as Flora Price, aged 68. She burst out laughing.

Daisy checked the time. The village estate agent had called to say that he had a potential buyer interested in Orchard Villa. Daisy had been up since five that morning cleaning the house until it sparkled, leaving flowers on the scrubbed oak table in the kitchen and each room looking show-home perfect. She was determined to make them fall in love with the place. She crossed her fingers again for luck. If someone would just make a decent offer, her parents would snap it up and the garden would be saved from destruction.

*

The throng of tourists, travellers, and day-trippers spilled out of the doors of Marylebone station and onto the sunny pavement. Daisy dodged a man trying to thrust a copy of the *Metro* into her hands, and skipped past the sweet-faced young couple standing by the stall full of religious pamphlets. She marched down Marylebone Road, heading for the High Street. She marvelled at the trees as she made her way along. Year round they stood, breathing in traffic fumes from a never-ending ribbon of buses, taxis and cars, ignored by the commuters who marched past with their heads down, intent on getting to and from work.

Miranda was waiting outside their favourite cafe, tapping rapidly on her iPad. Daisy was almost at the table before she looked up, face breaking into a huge smile.

'I didn't order anything besides coffee yet.' Her sister indicated the empty mug by her bag. 'Wasn't sure if we were doing lunch, or going straight to chocolate cake therapy.'

Daisy peered in the window, checking nothing had changed. She sighed happily. Yes, just as it had always been: inside there was a glass-fronted counter stacked high with delicious patisserie.

'Shall we just do cake?'

'I hoped you'd say that.' Miranda stood up, enfolding her sister in a huge hug.

They stayed outside in the sunshine. The High Street had always been a family favourite – as children they'd known that if they behaved while their parents shopped, a trip into town would end with a visit to Paddington Street Gardens round the corner, an ice cream, and a chance to burn off their energy, squealing as they ran through the trees, their parents sitting peacefully on a bench reading the paper.

Talking of which, thought Daisy, reaching into her bag . . .

'Bloody hell.' Miranda held the *Argus* at arm's length. 'Front-page news.'

Daisy pulled a face. 'Yeah, I wasn't quite expecting that. Thought I might just put a spanner in the works. Didn't expect major village scandal. It turns out my throwaway comment about the mulberry tree's got some village tree expert thinking.'

Miranda shook her head, picking up her coffee. She sat back, observing her sister thoughtfully.

'And your previously charming Irishman? What's he saying?'

Daisy pulled her phone out of her bag, tapping the screen until the appropriate page appeared. She handed it across to Miranda, wordlessly.

Just spoken to Stephen. Can you ring me when you get this?

'No kiss,' observed Miranda, arching an eyebrow. 'And have you?'

Daisy shook her head. 'Still concocting a reply in my head. Every time I try and write one, it's got so many rude words that autocorrect goes into melt-down. I'm still working on it.'

'Well, you need to put him out of his misery, Daise.'

'Patisserie selection?' The waitress appeared, two plates in her hands.

They paused for a moment of reverence as the cakes were set down in front of them.

'Okay, I'll give you this. You don't get cake like this in Steeple St John.' Daisy picked up a tiny, jewel-bright tartlet, piled high with glistening fruit. She inspected it from all angles, her mouth watering in anticipation, before popping it into her mouth.

'These are obscenely delicious.'

'Well,' said Miranda, cheerfully, 'you'll have this lot on tap when you move here. Y'know, big sis, in a weird sort of way I'm quite looking forward to having you and Polly staying at my place.'

Daisy looked sceptical. 'One of us is covered in mud most of the time, and the other one's increasingly incontinent.'

'Yeah, but we can get a job lot of Tena Lady. You'll be fine.' Miranda wrinkled her nose, teasing. 'And there's always pelvic floor exercises.'

'Ha ha.'

Sitting on the train back home to Steeple St John, Daisy realized there was a clue in that phrase that she hadn't even noticed before. When had she started talking about the village as *home*, and not just the place she was staying temporarily? Much as she'd loved her day in London with Miranda, it was with a sense of relief that she climbed off the train and onto the pretty, flower-decked Victorian platform. Walking down Main Street towards home (there it was again, she thought with a half-smile), she found her thoughts going over and over the conversation they'd had earlier. Miranda, strong-willed as ever, had made her mind up that Daisy was coming to stay with her in the tiny little ground-floor flat she rented in North London. But the idea of living there, with no garden – she could feel the claustrophobia now, just thinking about it. Add in Polly, who'd miss wandering round the park every evening, and . . . it just wasn't going to work. She sighed in defeat. There didn't seem to be any other option.

As she walked down the road towards Orchard Villa, her phone began ringing. She pulled it out of her bag, as always half-dreading a call from George. Since his text, though, there'd been nothing but silence. She needed to sort it out, though – and soon.

'Daisy Price? Meg Stewart here from *Midshire News*. We're doing a feature tomorrow lunchtime, ties in with your piece in the *Argus*. Any chance we could have a word?'

Daisy did a double take, checking there wasn't any sign of hidden cameras waiting to prank her. Nothing in sight.

'Of course.' The prospect of delaying the house sale

seemed even more pressing after her trip into town. She couldn't face living there, but right now she didn't have a choice. 'Yes, that's fine.'

'About nine-thirty? We'll be in the area filming. If we can just come round about half an hour before we're due to air, I'll shoot a live piece to camera – just ask you a few questions, get a bit of the garden on film.'

'On film? Here?' Daisy echoed, aware she sounded clueless.

'That's not a problem, is it? We can do it elsewhere, but I gather your garden is particularly lovely?'

'Of course. No problem at all.'

Daisy shook her head, amazed, and set off towards home, the phone in her hand.

She stopped by the little supermarket to pick up something for dinner. As she headed back, a beaten-up van almost identical to George's pulled up on the road opposite. She felt her heart thudding with apprehension. It was ridiculous to be behaving like this when she hadn't done anything wrong. Sod it. She clicked her phone awake, scrolling down to find his text, hitting reply.

We don't have anything to talk about. You KNEW how much the garden means to me. It was only ever building potential to you.

Almost immediately a reply flashed back.

Daisy I'm sorry. When Stephen sent me round the Open Gardens to scout out some potential places, I'd no idea the trouble it was going to cause.

She boggled at the screen. His bloody brother had sent him round the village to suss out which ones were ripe for development? What an absolute *shit.*

I don't suppose you did.

Daisy jabbed at the phone screen with a furious finger.

Well, if you're ever in Dublin and fancy a drink to make up for it, just give me a shout.

Give him a – Daisy snorted with amazement.

Fun odd, you absolute arsenal

Bloody autocorrect.

She deleted it, and decided not to dignify his comment with a response.

'Ooh, this is exciting,' said Elaine, remote control in hand.

They sat waiting for the regional news programme to begin. Daisy had half-wanted to record it on her parents' satellite box to show them, but realized they mightn't be too impressed with their daughter's five minutes of fame if they knew its context. She'd compromised on saving it on Elaine's television, and they were sitting perched on the edge of the sofa, waiting impatiently.

' . . . And with environmental issues at the heart of the recent campaign across the county, we've been taking a look this week at some of the arguments.'

'That's her, it's her – it's on,' Daisy gasped, leaning forward.

'I was *there*, remember,' said Elaine, nodding as she laughed. She'd insisted on expertly applying a layer of make-up to Daisy's face that morning before the camera crew arrived, leaving her feeling she was in a thick mask, her eyes heavy with shadow. 'It won't show up on camera, I promise. You'll look like you're dead without it.' Daisy, her face immobile, not daring to blink too hard, had bitten back a sarcastic response.

Elaine, too, leaned towards the television expectantly. The reporter was standing talking to camera in a shot which had been filmed in the park, down by the stream where she walked Polly every evening. Daisy recognized Dave, her brass-playing friend from the allotment, who walked very slowly – rather more slowly than she'd ever seen him before – behind the reporter as she spoke. Just before he disappeared out of the picture he turned, giving an almost imperceptible wink to the camera. Daisy snorted back a giggle.

And there was the garden of Orchard Villa. The

camera had swept round, taking in the lush borders that she and Thomas had worked so hard to bring back to life; the rose trellis, heavy with flowers; the vegetable garden. It stopped at the orchard.

'Daisy Price, tenant of the property here in Steeple St John,' intoned the voiceover, inaccurately, 'has begun a single-handed campaign to save this beautiful garden from destruction.'

Daisy turned to Elaine with alarm. God, if her parents saw this she'd be disinherited, not just homeless. How on earth had life in this sleepy little village turned her into the sort of person who protested on local news?

'This mulberry tree is a century old,' her voice was saying *on television*. Did she always sound that squeaky and breathless?

The camera showed the gorgeous old mulberry tree, its branches laden with fruit.

'And now back to the studio,' said the voice.

Was that it? One mouse-voiced line? She looked at Elaine, who had paused the television and was pressing the rewind button. 'You look gorgeous, darling,' she said, freezing the screen on a close-up of Daisy, hand raised to her face, pushing a strand of hair back from her eyes.

She had to admit that Elaine's trowelful of make-up didn't show on screen. She looked fresh-faced, pink-cheeked and healthy. The perfect gardener. The only trouble was, she was about to be left with no garden. The mulberry tree might be a century old, but Daisy's online research suggested there was nothing to stop Stephen from buying the house anyway – and an application for a tree preservation order would be on pretty shaky ground. Hours of reading had left her none the wiser, and the man she'd spoken to at the local council office had been vague. Her only hope was the tree expert who'd piped up after the newspaper article; but so far he'd come up with nothing.

If she was honest with herself, Daisy thought as she trudged home, things looked pretty bleak. Thomas seemed to have accepted that the garden might well be destroyed. Maybe it was time for her to give up fighting and do the same.

Despondent, she got home, taking a book to the back of the garden where she lay in the dappled shade of the condemned orchard, feeling sympathy with the trees. She picked up her phone, hearing the ping of an email arriving.

Hi Daisy. Thank you for your application for the post of Assistant Gardening Head here at the Periwinkle Project based in Hackney. We'd like to invite you for an interview on Wednesday, 15 August . . .

Daisy dropped the phone onto the grass. If that was another one of those signs from the universe everyone kept banging on about, she wasn't listening.

*

She was still feeling flat late that evening. Turning off the television, she hauled herself off the sofa. The night sky was still streaked with red, and a crescent moon was glowing over the tops of the hills beyond Steeple St John. A stroll might clear her head. Polly would be glad of the chance to have a wander round by night, taking in the scents of the evening. Daisy picked up the dog lead and slipped on an old fleece left over from her horticulture college days, and together they headed out into the village.

St John's Church looked beautiful in the pale evening light as Daisy and Polly made their way along the river path. Despite darkness falling, Daisy felt quite safe walking through Steeple St John with the old dog by her side. She stopped for a second to zip up her fleece against the chill before they manoeuvred their way through the wooden kissing gate and headed along the narrow path down the side of the cricket pitch and back through town. They wove between the houses, Daisy peeking in through windows lit brightly but with curtains still not drawn, watching the people of the village as they pottered around, getting ready for another day. A man stood by the window in boxer shorts, ironing a shirt. Through the window of the cottage next door Daisy could see a couple play-fighting, throwing bubbles from the washing-up bowl at each other. Peering out of her bedroom window, chin in hand, a little girl had sneaked behind her bedroom curtains after bedtime and was watching the world go by. Daisy gave her a smile and she waved back, delighted that a grown-up was complicit in her trickery.

They passed through the car park of the Grey Mare, where the beer garden still held the last stragglers, nursing their final drink of the evening. Over in the corner Daisy recognized a familiar outline in the dusk: Ned, chin in hand, leaning into the conversation, sat opposite Fenella. Her thick blonde hair was knotted up casually in a loose bun, long tendrils highlighted by the string of fairy lights that hung in a swathe behind their table. She threw her head back, laughing, a hand reaching out to touch Ned on his upper arm. Daisy stepped sideways into the shadows, hugging the fence to avoid being spotted as she made her way through the stone carriage arch. Shoulders sagging, her mood now even lower than before, she headed down the hill towards Orchard Villa.

'Evening, stranger.'

The voice came out of the shadows. Daisy, who was fiddling in her pocket searching for her keys, jumped in shock. She turned around, the hairs on the back of her neck prickling in sudden fear.

A familiar shape stepped out from beside the honeysuckle which arched over the doorway. Daisy stepped back in surprise, dropping her keys. He bent down, picking them up. For a second, she thought he wasn't going to give them back.

'You going to invite me in?' He passed the keys to her, stepping from foot to foot. 'It's freezing out here, Daise.'

She hesitated for a second, then turned the key in the latch with a sigh of resignation.

'Come on, then.'

Thank God she'd picked up a bottle of red when she popped to the supermarket earlier. Hands shaking, Daisy unscrewed the lid. She poured two glasses, and turned around. Jamie was sitting at the kitchen table, chin resting on his hand, looking at her with that confident, lazy half-smile she'd once loved so much.

'Here.' She slid the glass across the table, sitting down opposite him.

'Cheers.' He reached across, clinking his glass against hers, and raised it to his lips. His dark eyes didn't stray from hers for one second.

'So – you're not in France?'

Jamie laughed, dismissively. 'God, no. We lasted about a month – two, maybe? I've been working in London – landscape design on a new development.'

Daisy took a mouthful of wine, and closed her eyes. She let it sit on her tongue, tasting the raspberry sharpness and the tannin, blotting out the outside world for a moment. A memory flickered alive – she and Jamie on a fortnight in France. They'd spent every night sitting together in the evening sun, sampling bottle after bottle of cheap red wine. And now here they were, facing each other once again.

'And –' she took a second to get the name out. 'Sylvia?'

'She stayed on in France.'

So they weren't together any more. Daisy hid her face in the wine glass, looking down at the table.

'I happened to turn on the TV at lunchtime today – and there you were. I realized—'

'Don't, Jamie.' Daisy put both hands up in protest. She couldn't bear to hear whatever he had to say. Pushing her chair back so suddenly that the wooden legs screeched on the floor, she stood up.

At the same time, Jamie stood up, glass in hand. As she took a step towards the door he reached out, grabbing her wrist. He pulled her gently towards him, putting down his drink at the same time.

'You looked beautiful on screen.' His voice was lower now. He reached across, taking her glass from her hand. With a practised motion he set it to one side, taking her hand. 'I recognized your mum and dad's place straight away. Daise, I knew I had to come – knew you'd be here.'

He took a strand of Daisy's hair, curling it around his finger thoughtfully. Daisy had seen all these moves before. And yet, as if in a dream, she felt herself take a step towards him.

'You looked so sad – I recognized that look in your eyes.' He reached for her hand and took it in his. 'Thing is, Daise, I know you. I could tell something was up.'

347

'It's nothing. It's just –'

'Come on, honey.' Taking the wine again, he passed her the glass.

She took a gulp so big that her eyes watered, and she coughed. Jamie's hand slid onto her waist. It felt familiar, and safe. She was so tired, and he felt like home – or the closest she was going to get.

'What you need is a hot bath, and bed.'

It was so tempting. She was exhausted. And here was a familiar face, ready to swoop in and rescue her. It was such a lovely thought. Even if he was a lying, duplicitous, two-timing –

She stepped backwards suddenly.

'No.'

'Come on, Daisy. You're knackered,' he gave a self-confident grin, 'I'm gorgeous . . .'

She shook her head violently, the fog clearing completely. Arrogant *shit* – he hadn't changed one bit. But she had, thankfully.

'Piss off, Jamie. You're pathetic. I don't know what the *hell* you're doing here, but –' she looked up at the kitchen clock – 'there's a train back into London in fifteen minutes. I suggest you take yourself back there and find some other mug.'

He raised his eyebrows in surprise.

'Got a bit of attitude in my absence, have we?' He reached out, fingering the collar of the old hoodie she was still wearing. 'Come on, Daise, you were tempted for a moment. The old Daisy wouldn't have sent me packing.'

'The *old* Daisy didn't realize you were in bed with my best friend all the way through our last year of college.'

Fired up with temper, horrified that for one second she'd even let the idea of him cross her mind, she wrenched the kitchen door open and stormed out into the hall.

'I don't care what reason you had for coming here, Jamie. I suspect you were at a loose end, and knowing you as I do, you probably thought you'd head through here and get a guaranteed pity shag.'

Jamie laughed at her, contemptuously.

Fired up, Daisy continued. 'You know what? I've worked my backside off on this garden and it's about to be destroyed. I've got enough on my plate. I don't need an arsehole like you turning up to take advantage.'

He shrugged. 'Your loss, Daise.'

'I don't think so.'

Bastard, bastard, bastard, thought Daisy, once again. God, they were *all* shits. She closed the door and double-locked it, sliding the big old metal bolt across the latch just to be sure. With a groan of disbelief, she took her wine glass and headed upstairs to bed.

Chapter Twenty-four

Daisy lay in bed the next morning, propped up against a mountain of pillows. She was texting Miranda with updates about the night before. Her sister, ostensibly in a sales development meeting and bored out of her mind, was chasing her for details.

> I always thought Jamie was a dickhead. So what's happening now?

Daisy tapped out her reply:

> Well, I've got no boyfriend, no house to speak of, I've spent months working on a garden that's about to be trashed — but apart from that, everything's going great.

She sat back against the pillows with a sigh. She couldn't even face getting out of bed. Last night's wine glass had fallen over somehow, a trickle of red oozing across the floor. Her arms and legs were aching, and her head felt like someone had put it in a vice. She was completely exhausted, physically and mentally, but Elaine and Jo were expecting her for lunch at the pub. She couldn't really turn up with mad hair, in a pair of ancient pyjamas. Heavy-legged, she pulled back the covers.

Scowling at her appearance, Daisy checked her hair in the hall mirror as she prepared to go out for lunch. A shower hadn't improved her mood, she was still bone-tired, and she felt utterly deflated. And now the phone was ringing.

'Mum.'

'No,' said her dad, laughter in his voice. 'It's the other one. You're like the Scarlet Pimpernel these days – never thought we'd find it easier to get hold of your sister for a chat. Have you been busy?'

'Hardly,' muttered Daisy, realizing she sounded like Martha on a bad morning.

'Just calling with an update. We've been in touch with Mike from the estate agency, and he tells us that there's an Irish chap who seems pretty keen on the house?'

Daisy rolled her eyes at her reflection. Her parents insisted on giving her regular updates on what was happening with the house sale, not realizing that she was the one fielding the repeated agency calls and making herself scarce for viewings.

'As I've pointed out, he's not keen on the *house*, Dad, he's keen on the potential to make a quick buck by ripping the garden apart. I don't understand why you're in such a rush – why can't you sell the house to someone who'll appreciate it?'

'Oh, darling,' her dad began, consolingly, 'I know you're a bit put out, but we must move with the times . . .'

Daisy let out an exasperated huff of air. 'There's moving with the times, and there's destroying a perfectly good garden for the sake of it. He could buy a patch of land on the outskirts of the village and build houses there. Why on earth does he have to do it in *my* garden?'

'*Your* garden, darling?'

The distance couldn't disguise the amusement in her father's voice.

'You know what I mean. I'm not just going to lie back and take this, you know.' She could hear her mum insistently muttering in the background, trying to get her oar in. There was a scuffling.

'Darling.' Her mum's voice had the particular soothing tone she reserved for moments when Daisy or her sister had fallen over. 'You sound like you need an early night. You've had a bit of a time of it, haven't you? I wonder if it's been a bit much for you, looking after that place when you've been dealing with everything else. I could skin that Jamie alive if I ever saw him.'

Just as well you weren't here last night, thought Daisy.

'I'm fine, Mum. I'm just a bit –' Pissed off, she thought. 'I don't see why you bothered getting me here to invest all this time in the garden, if you didn't care what happened to it. And to be honest I can't see why you're in such a rush to sell the place. I'm not planning on staying forever, if that's what you're worried about.'

Daisy caught another glimpse of herself in the mirror. Her hair was dull, violet shadows under her eyes. Throwing herself into the renovation of Orchard Villa's garden had taken its toll.

'Darling, you've worked *so* hard, and of course we appreciate it.'

'It's not just a garden, Mum, you know. It actually *matters*.'

There was a long silence, during which Daisy wondered whether her mother was actually thinking about what her daughter had said for once, instead of just hearing what she wanted to hear.

'Daisy, darling, I know you're disappointed,' her mother began, cautiously.

Apparently not, thought Daisy, with an inaudible groan.

Elaine was standing chatting to the barmaid of the Grey Mare, her hair in loose waves, pinned back on one side with a silver clip. Every time I see her, thought Daisy, she looks five years younger. Elaine caught her eye in the mirror behind the bar, giving her a wide smile. She was in a simple white T-shirt today, slim legs in a pair of pretty dark blue cropped jeans and – bright red Converse sneakers. She turned to Daisy, kissing her on the cheek.

'Like the shoes,' said Daisy, surprised.

'I'm embracing my teenage self.' Elaine set their two cups of coffee down on the table, before lifting a foot and waggling it in demonstration. 'Martha told me I should get them. We got the train into town and went to Camden Market the other day.'

'With Jo?'

'Nope.' Elaine shook her head, laughing. 'Just us two. Well, as far as Martha's concerned, Jo was heading on the train to town *for a meeting*.' She raised her eyebrows meaningfully. 'So Martha and I tagged along, and headed off for an adventure. And we had one. Look.'

Elaine pulled her T-shirt up, revealing a toned stomach. A tiny jewelled silver ring sat neatly in her navel. Bloody hell, Elaine was going for the full divorce meltdown.

Daisy's eyes and mouth formed circles of shock. 'You got pierced?'

'I wanted to when I was a teenager. My poor grandparents would've gone mad. And funnily enough, Leo never struck me as the type who'd appreciate a bit of rebellion.'

'So.' Daisy looked across at Elaine. She was glowing, her eyes sparkling with her newfound freedom.

She looked like a younger, fresher version of herself. 'If Leo was such a stick in the mud . . .'

'. . . why was I married to him?' Elaine traced a pattern in the foam of her latte. 'I was bounced from boarding school to my grandparents' house. My parents died when I was very young. All I ever wanted was the perfect family life, nice house, husband, two point four children—'

Daisy frowned. 'But you didn't?'

'Oh, Leo kept saying next year, next year. There was always some reason why we were going to wait before we started trying.'

No wonder Elaine had thrown everything into making the perfect life.

'And then you went to Dubai.'

'Yeah, and then we left pretty damn quickly. If Leo's affair had come out, he'd have been in serious trouble. They don't mess around over there.' Elaine looked up, a shrewd expression on her face. 'I think, if I'm honest with myself, I knew it wasn't going to last. I stopped pushing the children thing after Dubai.'

'I don't mean to sound heartless – but thank goodness you did.' Daisy shook her head, looking out of the pub window at the cars passing down Main Street.

'You're telling me. At least this way he's out of my hair permanently. If we'd had children, I'd have had to deal with him visiting every weekend.'

Their eyes met, an expression of mutual horror on their faces.

'Hi, you two. What's up?'

Jo slipped in to join them at the table by the window.

'Well, Elaine's embraced her inner teenager and started hanging out at Camden Market. And we've just been discussing her lucky escape from Leo. I'm about to be homeless. Anything you want to confess?' Daisy leaned across, giving Jo a kiss followed by a searching look.

Jo shook her head. 'Nope.'

'You're not heading to Thailand for a three-month silent meditation with Tom – nothing like that?'

At the mention of his name, Daisy noticed, Jo's cheeks flushed faintly, the palest colouring against her creamy white skin.

Jo smiled to herself. 'No, definitely no meditation retreats. He's staying with a friend in London for a couple of months, though. We had a long lunch the other day, talking about Martha and how best to introduce them.'

Daisy smiled, too. It was clear to her, even if Jo wasn't admitting it to herself yet, that some day there might be more than just friendship there.

'What we're trying to work out – and in fact, we'd really appreciate your thoughts . . .'

Daisy noted the 'we' with quiet approval. She gazed vacantly through the glass into the restaurant section of the pub. A vaguely familiar-looking young couple tried to wedge a child each into wooden high chairs. One was spread-eagled in an obstinate star-shape, arms and legs rigid. It took both of them a lot of manoeuvring to slot the child in place. The father stood up, red-faced, wiping his brow. With a resigned expression, they turned to a third child who was screaming with fury, a howling scarlet ball of temper. Things could be worse, thought Daisy.

Jo carried on. 'Do you think we should tell Martha, then introduce them? Or let her get to know him, and *then* let her know?'

Daisy looked blankly back at her. Both suggestions carried a huge weight of worry. She was so tired that her brain couldn't even come up with a preference. She wrinkled her forehead in thought.

'I think you might be surprised,' said Elaine, coming to the rescue after a moment. 'I think Martha's pretty sharp. Your main concern is going to be making it clear that Tom's not going to come in and start throwing his weight around.'

'It's not really his style.' Jo smiled.

Daisy, who'd encountered him briefly on the stairs in the B&B, remembered a tall, gentle, laid-back sort.

The woman from behind the bar popped over to the table. 'You forgot these, ladies.' She handed a sheaf of menus to Elaine, motioning to the hand-lettered blackboard beside the fireplace where Daisy had sat sharing a drink with George. 'Specials on the board. Oh, soup's off, sorry.'

She whisked away, gathering used glasses from the nearby table with an efficient clatter.

'You're quiet.' Elaine passed Daisy a menu as she spoke. 'What's happening with the house? Any news on the protest stuff?'

She looked across Daisy's shoulder, giving a friendly wave and a smile.

Unthinking, Daisy turned, following her gaze. A group of women were heading out in the direction of the beer garden. One turned back, calling across to Elaine.

'Tomorrow at eight, don't forget.'

'I won't.'

Daisy gave her a quizzical look over her menu.

'PTA mums from Brockville,' explained Elaine, pulling a slightly self-conscious face. 'They clubbed together, brought me a huge bunch of flowers and a voucher for a spa day at the place near the woods. And they've invited me to their book club tomorrow night.'

'That's so lovely, Elaine.' Jo's voice was full of warmth.

'Not *all* the mums,' said Elaine, steepling her fingers and balancing her chin on the top, thoughtfully. 'I suspect the ones who were caught in bed with my husband probably didn't chip in . . .'

Daisy grimaced, but Elaine started laughing.

'Sorry. I should say ex-husband, anyway – or he will be, soon enough. I'm going for a quick divorce.

And if he even *thinks* about going for half the house – well, I'll get your lovely vet friend to castrate him.'

Daisy felt a twist of discomfort. She didn't want to think about Ned, or their so far failed mission to save the garden. All in all, she was running out of time, and a new life in London was starting to look like an inescapable part of her future.

'And the funniest thing happened the other day, too.' Elaine, fizzing with happiness, was happy to fill in the spaces, not noticing Daisy was quieter than usual. 'I was chatting to the lovely man at the market stall . . .'

'Oh, yes,' said Jo, with a knowing expression.

'Hush, you,' said Elaine, smiling. 'Anyway, a couple of women standing in the queue came up and tapped me on the arm. I thought they were about to complain I was holding them up, but they wanted to let me know they'd heard about Leo and that they were completely on my side. Isn't that sweet?'

'It's lovely,' agreed Daisy. She must be a horrible person. All this amazing stuff was happening to her friends, yet all she felt was a weird sense of detachment. It was as if someone had cut her loose from village life. She was floating away, very slowly but inexorably, like a child's helium balloon after a trip to the funfair.

Chapter Twenty-five

'Miss Price. Sorry to trouble you again.'

'Daisy.' She gritted her teeth and lied through them. 'Not at all. It's no trouble.'

A couple of weeks had passed. The negotiations for the sale of Orchard Villa seemed to be an unstoppable juggernaut. They'd reached a dead end with their investigations about tree preservation orders, and with a chequebook big enough to circumvent any protests (and, Daisy suspected, to buy his way out of any minor inconveniences), Stephen O'Hara and his brother looked certain to be the new owners of the house and land.

Daisy had been subjected to a constant barrage of phone calls from Mike Redforth. There was a never-ending stream of queries regarding paperwork and plans, and Daisy had found herself acting as unwilling go-between to a group of surveyors, ground analysts, planning specialists, and goodness knew what else.

'Just give me a second.' Daisy stepped over a pile of empty cardboard boxes in the hall. She'd decided last night that it was time to face facts, and she'd started sorting through her things – when she'd left Winchester she'd been in such a rush, furious and humiliated, that she'd just thrown everything in, not caring whether she needed it or not. Faced now with a spell living in Miranda's tiny, minimalist flat, she'd decided it was probably a good idea to get rid of some of the clutter – and it turned out there was a lot more of it than she'd thought. Shoving through the door, which was partly blocked by a heap of black bin bags, she made her way into the kitchen with an exhalation of relief.

'Everything okay?' There was a note of concern in the estate agent's voice.

'Fine.' She sat down at the kitchen table. 'Just getting organized.'

'You're still pressing ahead with plans to leave the property, then?'

'I am, yes.'

'I've had a chat with your parents this morning. There's been a – progression.'

She frowned at the phone. Since the last conversation with her parents, she'd been avoiding their calls, feeling utterly pissed off that they appeared to have no consideration for the effort she – and Thomas – had put into the garden. And now she had Mike bloody Redforth on the phone, talking in riddles.

He continued briskly, 'I've got a new surveyor wanting to come out today – are you about?'

'I'm at the village fête this afternoon – I'm not around. Can you give him your key?'

'Yes, yes, of course. But I'd like to have a quick word with you if you've got a second – in person, preferably.'

She rolled her eyes. Another quick chat with Mike Redforth would see the morning gone before she knew it, and she had so much to do.

'I'm a bit busy at the moment—'

As if on cue, the home phone rang.

'You see?' Daisy scanned the screen to see if she recognized the number. Withheld. Whoever it was could leave a message, but she wasn't going to tell Mike Redforth that when it was the perfect opportunity to escape. 'I'm really sorry – I've got to take this call. Can we speak later, perhaps?'

Not giving him a chance to reply, she hung up. The home phone rang out, and whoever it was didn't leave a message, to her relief.

She tapped at the table with a pen that she'd left lying there the night before, when she was making yet another list.

Letting Polly out into the garden to stretch her legs, Daisy stood by the door looking out at the garden. It stood on the verge of change. Leaves were beginning to curl, their edges fading. In a few weeks the slow, inevitable move towards the harvest, and autumn, would begin.

Maybe Thomas *was* right. Gardens were meant to

grow and change – and if that meant being chopped into pieces and shared out amongst new houses, maybe she just needed to grit her teeth and accept it. With a sigh of resignation, she closed the door, watching as Polly flopped down on her comfortable bed.

The sweeping park beyond the stream that led down to the church was dotted with white tents. The ever-present fabric bunting flapped from lamp post to lamp post. Having decided that Polly would not thank her for a day of being buffeted around and squished lovingly by overenthusiastic small children, sticky with candy floss and ice cream, Daisy had left her snoozing in the kitchen of Orchard Villa. She'd set off, glad of the sunshine, towards her fate in Flora's Village Fête Administration Tent.

'If we can just pop this on you here . . .' Flora reached across to Daisy's shirt, fastening on a huge electric-blue rosette with JUDGE stamped in the circle in huge, gold letters. 'And if you could just sign in, here.' She handed Daisy her clipboard, indicating where a signature was required with a brisk tap of one neatly manicured finger. With that, she marched out of the tent, leaving Daisy standing confused.

'Is that me done?' She felt like a parcel, destination unknown. She'd been efficiently processed and was ready to go.

'I'm not sure blue's my colour.'

Daisy spun round. Ned ducked as he made his way

into the tent, a pair of sunglasses balancing atop the scruffy thatch of hair, green eyes bright with laughter. He was holding his own rosette in one hand, the ribbons fluttering in the breeze. Daisy felt a now-familiar jolt in her stomach as he caught her eye.

'*Hello*, stranger.' He gave her a huge smile, loping across the tent and embracing her in an unexpected, awkward hug. Pressed into his chest for a brief moment, Daisy felt the warmth of his skin through his shirt, a clean, woody scent of aftershave in her nostrils. She stepped back, her heart thumping disobediently.

'Do me a favour, Daisy.' He looked down at her with a soulful gaze.

She felt a catch in her breath.

'Can you pin this on my shirt?'

'Let me do that,' said Flora, reappearing suddenly. She did it, and patted Ned's chest briskly. 'All sorted. Susan, I'm leaving you in charge here.'

A grey-haired woman was sitting at a wobbly plastic table, folding raffle tickets in half and popping them into a huge glass jar.

'Ned, you wait there,' Flora went on. 'Someone will be along to take you to the animal tent in a second.'

Daisy caught Ned's eye for a brief moment. His face indicated mock-terror.

'Come on, then, Daisy. Let's get you over to the produce tent!'

Thomas, looking smart in a pale checked shirt, a tie

and a tweed coat, stood up from the folding chair he was sitting on as Flora and Daisy approached.

'I'm afraid our usual head judge, Major Gressing-ham-Smith from the Manor House, has been indisposed recently, and Thomas has very kindly agreed to step into the breach,' said Flora.

Thomas's face remained almost completely impassive, but a tiny twinkle in his eye and the smallest hint of a raised eyebrow made Daisy smother a giggle.

'I just want to run over the details of the judging before we—'

'No need.' Thomas laid a reassuring hand on Flora's arm, steering her gently towards the front of the gazebo as he did so. Daisy was impressed.

'Well, I do need to make sure that the stalls are organized for the W.I. cake sale, I suppose . . .'

'We have everything under control, Daisy, don't we?'

Daisy nodded, trying not to laugh.

A little girl of about ten ran into the tent just as Flora was leaving. 'Grandma, Susan says to tell you that she doesn't think she's got enough lottery tickets.'

Daisy and Thomas sat down to have a quick cup of tea from his ever-present flask.

'They take this very seriously, y'know,' Thomas explained, sipping tea from his plastic mug. 'There are folks up at the allotments who work all year for this.'

Daisy thought of the allotments, and the hours she'd spent there chatting to the gardeners. She'd been viewed with suspicion at first, but as she grew to know the cast of regulars who spent their spare time working up there, they'd begun to welcome her with sweet tea from their flasks or hand her armfuls of produce. She felt the knot of sadness in her stomach again. Standing up, she brushed down her pale blue cropped trousers and straightened her shirt. No point dwelling on it.

They laughed for the whole hour they spent choosing their favourites. Daisy was amused by Thomas's tales of night-time subterfuge at the allotments: gigantic leeks grown in seaside sand and fertilized with secret concoctions, and vigilant veg-growers on night watch, convinced their carrots would be nobbled before the competition.

'But the prize is a rosette and a five-pound gift voucher for the garden centre!'

Thomas nodded. 'I know. It's a mysterious world, isn't it?'

Looking down at the plates of almost identical, completely perfect carrots they'd had to judge, Daisy had to agree.

'Anyway, my dear, that's your part over – we've marked the winners, and the prizes will be given out at the end of the day. All you have to do now is enjoy some of those lovely cakes on the W.I. stall.' Thomas pointed out the delicious-looking display that was now being finished off with pretty jam jars full of sweet peas and strings of crocheted bunting draped around the edges of the tables.

'I wonder how Ned's getting on?' Daisy looked across the field. In the distance she could just make out his tall shape beside a clipboard-wielding Flora, heading for the tent where an assortment of pet rabbits and guinea pigs were waiting to be judged in the Best Pet competition.

'That lad's done well this year.'

'I know,' agreed Daisy. 'Mind you, he's got the bosses from hell, if you ask me – he's never off duty.'

Thomas looked at her, laughing, his blue eyes bright. 'He's only got himself to answer to, my dear.'

The realization dawned slowly. 'So he's not . . .'

Thomas shook his head. 'No, Daisy.' He gave a chortle of laughter. 'Ned took over the practice a few months before you arrived in the village. He doesn't shout about it, he told me, because people tend to think he's too young to be in charge.'

Daisy frowned, thinking back – she'd never asked directly, and he'd never offered the information. No wonder he always looked so exhausted, and never took a day off. She looked across, watching as he ducked his head and disappeared through the entrance of the tent, Flora bustling behind him.

'I had no idea. I just assumed –'

Thomas nodded, sagely. 'You, and most of the others here in the village, I think. Probably better that way.'

It was hard to imagine scatterbrained, chaotic Ned in charge of the whole surgery. And the other vets she'd seen him chatting to in the pub, or heading off on call – *he* was the ogre boss she'd imagined. She stood silently for a moment, taking it in.

'Right, my love, I'm going to pop up and see if Flora needs a hand with anything.'

Daisy looked at her old friend, thoughtfully. She'd caught him looking across the park towards the grave-yard where his beloved wife lay, and felt a sudden wave of sadness for him. She felt her chin wobble for a second. She'd been so good the last couple of weeks about just getting on with stuff, and not letting herself wallow any more – but she was going to miss Thomas horribly, not to mention life in Steeple St John. Look-ing across the park, she could see Ned striding towards them. His rosette had come adrift and was hanging, lopsided, on his shirt.

'Thomas . . . I'm sorry we couldn't save the garden,' she began, her voice thick with emotion.

'Not now.' He looked at her kindly. 'No sadness today, my dear. Violet loved the village fête. I prom-ised myself after she died that I'd enjoy it twice each year – once for myself, and once for her. You can help me out with that. Stiff upper lip, old girl.'

Daisy gave him a brave smile and nodded. 'Stiff upper lip.'

'I'm going to leave you young ones to it.' Thomas patted her on the shoulder, and set off across the field.

'Let's get a drink.'

Daisy and Ned headed down towards the stall

where huge kegs of cider stood, the bitter-sweet scent of apples filling the air. Ned bought two plastic glasses full, and they strolled across to sit under the tree by the stream in companionable silence.

'Nobody else from the practice here today?' said Daisy, trying to sound nonchalant.

Ned sat back against the tree trunk, crossing one long leg over the other.

He reached up and took her cider cup so she could sit down. 'No, just me again . . . we're taking on a new graduate in October. Reckon I could hand over village dogsbody duties to him – won't be much fun going to Parish Council meetings without you there.' He looked at her fleetingly, before taking a long drink.

'No Fenella today?' She tried the name out, carefully, being sure to sound casual.

'Fenella? God, no.' Ned shook his head, laughing. 'She was only a locum vet. She's off to Venezuela for three months on some aid project.'

Daisy looked at him sideways. Ned had his eyes closed now, head back against the huge tree, three-day stubble marking his jawline. He looked exhausted – as usual.

A couple of early leaves floated down from the branches, landing by their feet.

'I thought she'd just – you –' She faltered for a second, trying to choose her words. Ned's eyes snapped open and he turned to face her, looking at her steadily.

'Fenella and me?' He raised his eyebrows for a brief second. 'Yeah.' He pulled a face, awkwardly. 'She – well, she did indicate that she might . . .'

Daisy's heart was thumping unevenly.

He shook his head. 'I told her no.'

Another leaf spun through the air. Ned caught it in one hand, looking at her with triumph. 'You get a lucky day for every falling leaf you catch, y'know.'

There was a long moment of silence, broken by the unmistakable cry of Flora in full voice.

'Daisy! Ned!' She was beetling towards them at speed, one arm flapping in the air. 'Ned – there you are. You're needed to judge Best in Show.'

'Perfect timing,' groaned Ned, climbing up from the grass. He reached down, pulling Daisy up, his hand warm and strong in hers. It stayed there for the shortest moment before Daisy stepped backwards, breaking the spell.

'Come along too, Daisy, if you like,' called Flora, cheerfully.

'I'll be there in a second,' said Daisy to Ned. 'I just want to grab the girls and say hello, quickly.'

'Official judge!' Elaine fingered the rosette on Daisy's lapel. 'Very posh. Should we curtsy, or just bow?'

Thomas beamed with delight as Elaine kissed him hello. 'You're looking very nice, my dear.'

'You old flirt.' She laughed in delight. She did look well: tanned and happy, hair tied back from her face in a soft knot, loose waves framing her face in complete contrast to her perfect blow-dries.

'Are you two judges off duty now?'

Thomas looked at Daisy with a smile. 'Yes, she's free to go. I'm going to stay here and keep an eye on the judging certificates, give Flora a hand – it wouldn't be the first time someone's tried to switch the first and second prizes around.'

'Is there a lot of competition for – ' Jo reached forward, picking up the certificate closest to hand – 'best trio of cucumbers?'

Raising his eyebrows with a smile, Thomas said, 'I'm sure Daisy will tell you all about it. Meanwhile, I'm going to have a seat down here.' He held up a hip flask. 'You young ones get off and have some fun.'

'There's a Waltzer over there – come on, Daisy, let's give it a go.' Elaine pointed beyond the tents, to where a few travelling funfair rides had set up.

'I haven't even had anything to eat yet.'

'Best time to go then!'

Daisy, grabbed by the elbow, found herself being dragged across the field by Elaine. It was getting busy now that Flora had officially declared the fête open with a megaphone. ('Not convinced she needs that,' Ned had muttered to Daisy in an undertone, making her laugh and causing Flora to fix them with a disapproving glare.)

Daisy spotted Flora now, standing by the W.I. cake stalls, still clutching the megaphone in one hand. She looked quite happy. The fields were flooding with people, the cars parking in rows along the narrow lane beyond the church. Children were hurtling down the huge inflatable slide. Daisy spotted Martha and a group of her girlfriends laughing as they headed away from the face-painting stall, twice the size of the rest of the artist's customers, their cheeks emblazoned with flowers. Martha gave her a tiny, cool-teenager wave of acknowledgement. Daisy grinned back.

They sat inside the Waltzer car, waiting for the ride to fill up, swinging gently from side to side.

'How's your week been?' Elaine turned to Daisy, clearly bursting with a secret of some sort. What she meant was 'ask me what I've been up to'. Daisy gave her a knowing look.

'Mine? Oh, you know, packing, and – come on, spill! What have you done?'

Elaine gave her a surprisingly impish grin, her clear voice low and confiding. 'You won't believe me if I tell you . . .'

The car whirled round suddenly as the ride creaked into life.

'Last car – come on, give it a go!' The operator called to a group of teenagers who were standing by, trying to make up their minds. Laughing, they jumped up the steps and clambered into the remaining car. The youth collecting the change spun Daisy and Elaine round with a grin and a wink before hopping nimbly across to collect their money.

'Oof.' Daisy wondered belatedly whether a pint of home-made cider was the best warm-up to being whirled round like a maniac on the Waltzer.

'Go on, spill the beans.'

'Y'know Mark, the lovely chap from the market stall?'

Daisy looked at Elaine, her eyebrows shooting upwards. The 'lovely chap' in whom Elaine had protested, slightly too vigorously, that she had *no* interest whatsoever?

'Well – he asked me out for a drink.'

The machine clanked slightly as the motor whirred into life. Daisy had a second to look at her friend with amazement before they were off, the world a kaleidoscope of colour and blaring house music, louder than Flora's megaphone could ever dream of being. Daisy felt herself laughing and laughing as they whirled round and round, clinging onto the metal bar, thrown from side to side against each other.

They slowed for a second, the car swinging drunkenly back and forth. Elaine brushed a handful of hair from her face, her eyes bright.

'And did you say yes?'

They whirled round and around again, the reply whipped from Elaine's mouth by the wind. As the fairground ride slowed again, Daisy wiped tears of laughter from her eyes.

Elaine, blonde hair tangled by the wind, turned to

her again. 'Say yes?' She snorted with laughter. 'I only kicked him out of bed an hour ago.'

Daisy's eyes widened with amazement. Before she could speak, they were whirled round yet again, faster and faster this time, the young lad in charge of the ride straddling the wooden platform behind them, spinning their car round and round until Daisy's head was spinning and they were shrieking with laughter, hardly able to catch their breath.

It was late in the afternoon by the time Daisy and Thomas – along with Ned, the judges in the floral section, and the W.I. expert who'd chosen the best jam and cake – had handed out the last rosette, shaken the last hand, and made polite chit-chat with the winners. There'd been a minimum of disruption this year ('unlike that summer a few years back', Flora had said under her breath to Thomas with an unreadable expression), with most winners and runners-up appearing quite content. As soon as Flora was out of earshot and the last contestants had made their way out of the tent, Daisy turned to Thomas, intrigued. Ned had been pinned down by one of the other judges and was being quizzed on her cat's eating habits. Nodding attentively, he caught Daisy's eye over the judge's head for a split second. She'd try and rescue him if he was still stuck in five minutes.

'So what's the great mystery?'

'Well, we like our routine here in Steeple St John, as you know.'

Daisy nodded.

'As long as old Rod gets best in show for his plum tomatoes, and Bert from the allotments knows he'll get a ribbon for his cucumbers, everyone's happy. Don't matter if they beat each other, as long as they've each got a certificate to take home for the sitting-room wall. The only year we'd fireworks was when a new judge came along, same year as a load of new entrants. That put the cat among the pigeons. I reckon the fuss was enough to put them off, 'cause they didn't enter the next year. Thing is, my dear,' concluded Thomas, 'times change. We have to change with them.'

'Even if that means –' Daisy paused, not ready to say it aloud.

'Even if it means that gardens like Orchard Villa's get dug over and turned into new homes, yes.' Thomas finished the sentence for her. 'I've said it to you before, Daisy – I've seen a lot of change in this village over the last eighty-odd years, and there'll be a lot more change to come.'

'But you've worked on it for years.'

'I have. And I've worked on plenty more, and seen them paved over, or turned into play areas for kids. It's taken me a while to come to terms with it, but when you're my age, all that doesn't matter quite as much as it did.'

He waved his arm in the direction of the W.I. tent.

A couple of the women Daisy recognized as mothers from Leo's school were running the stall, floral aprons tied around their waists. 'Without you young ones, the heart of this place'll be gone. I've thought about it, and I've sat down by Violet's grave and had a chat.'

Daisy smiled at him.

'I've loved spending time with you young ones, this last few months. You two –' he gestured towards Ned, who was now nodding with increasing desperation, his eyes wild – 'you're such a lovely pair.'

Daisy looked at him, feeling her brows knitting together in confusion. 'We're not actually –'

'Mmm,' said Thomas, enigmatically. 'He's a very nice young man.'

Daisy, feeling edgy, turned to Thomas before he said anything more.

'I'd better get going. The girls are already back at Elaine's house, waiting.'

'That sounds nice.' The deep lines around Thomas's eyes crinkled as he smiled.

'You should come.'

'Don't go worrying about me, my dear.' He'd seen the concern on her face, and reassured her. 'I've got a bit of clearing up to do here – no doubt Flora will keep me on my toes – and then I'm going to nip back to the Grey Mare for a pint. I think I deserve it.'

Impulsively, Daisy leaned across and kissed him on the cheek. He might be eighty-four, but his friendship was one of her favourite things about living in Steeple

St John. She realized she was going to miss him horribly.

'Thank you, Thomas.'

'Oh, shush.' He looked pleased, batting her away with a chuckle. 'Go and have fun with youngsters your own age, and leave us old folks to tidy up.'

She popped back to the house to check on Polly, before heading up to Elaine's. The answerphone was flashing. Whoever it was could wait until later. Daisy's feet were killing her, and she couldn't wait to collapse with one of Elaine's mojitos in the last of the sunshine. The village was still festooned with bunting, but the crowds from the fête were heading home now, groups of sunburnt families with tired children snoozing in pushchairs, younger couples laughing and joking and heading towards the pub to carry on the drinking they'd started at the cider stall. A red balloon drifted up into the sky.

She pulled out her phone to text Ned. Maybe if he wasn't busy, he might come round later and join them for a drink. There was a message from her mother.

Darling can you please, PLEASE call estate agent. Urgent.

Daisy checked the time – quarter past five. She wasn't going to get him off her back until she did – at least if she rang now, he wouldn't turn up on the doorstep with a measuring tape at half-eight tomorrow morning . . .

'Redforth and Lewis – Mike Redforth?'

'Mr Redforth, it's Daisy Price.'

'Miss Price. The elusive Miss Price.' He sounded highly amused. 'You've been a difficult one to track down.'

Daisy pushed her hair out of her face as she walked up the hill towards Cavendish Lane. She didn't want to ask, but –

'I've got some good news for you. Better for your parents, I suppose, but I think we could agree it's a very satisfactory ending all round.'

Get on with it, thought Daisy.

'We've had an offer on the house, from a Mr and Mrs Grey.'

Daisy stopped dead in the street. A couple who'd been walking closely behind her tutted in irritation as they shifted to avoid a collision. She took a step sideways, leaning against the window of the craft gallery. Her legs were feeling peculiar.

'But – what about Stephen O'Hara? The redevelopment?'

'The Greys have topped the figure the O'Haras were willing to pay for the property. We've had some other offers, as you know, but nothing that came close to the figure the developers were willing to pay.'

'But how – where?'

'They saw the house when they came through with

their children to the Open Gardens, apparently. Very nice couple, three small children. He's something in the city, so you can imagine . . .' Mike Redforth's voice trailed off, suggestive of vast fortunes and untold wealth. 'They love the house *and* the gardens, you'll be happy to hear.'

She was only half-listening as Mike Redforth rattled on about timescales and indications, completion dates and exchanges. The other half of her mind was trying to recall the legalities of house purchasing in the UK, which hadn't been one of her specialist subjects until recently.

'But isn't this completely illegal?' Daisy had a sudden recollection of newspaper articles about the horrors of gazumping.

'Unethical, yes, if the original offer was still in place. But when I spoke to Mr O'Hara this morning, he said they weren't sure they were going to proceed. Too much opposition locally, he said.'

Daisy's legs went on strike. She slid down the wall, sitting on the pavement, knees tucked up to her chest, the phone to her ear.

The fight – the fight she'd started, then given up on, thinking it was hopeless – in the end, they'd won.

'I did try and ring you earlier to let you know. But as we know, you're allergic to phone calls.'

Daisy closed her eyes, seeing the flashing digits of the answering machine in her mind.

'I thought you'd be pleased.' He sounded slightly injured.

'Oh God.' Daisy opened her eyes again, looking down Main Street, imagining the garden of Orchard Villa filled with children's noise and laughter, just as Thomas had described it. 'I am. I really am.'

'Oh,' said Mike Redforth, laughing now, just as Daisy opened her mouth to say goodbye, 'and they're looking for a gardener. You don't happen to know anyone, do you?'

Elaine's house was silent when Daisy got to the front door. Peering through the window, she could make out some shapes at the far end of the garden. She rang the doorbell again, hoping someone might hear her before giving up and banging on the side gate, which swung open.

'Hello, gorgeous.' Elaine was wearing a pair of blue flip-flops, barbecue tongs in one hand. She'd changed into a pair of surprisingly brief denim shorts, showing off toned, slim legs which had previously been hidden beneath slightly starchy headmaster's-wife cigarette pants. A blue-striped apron was tied around her waist. She looked amazing. She leaned across to give Daisy a kiss.

'Sorry I'm late.'

'No problem. Grab a drink.'

A wide metal bucket stood on the patio, filled with ice cubes and stuffed full of bottles of beer and white wine. The barbecue was smoking hot, neat rows of sausages already beginning to spit. Elaine stood turning them, bottle of beer in hand. It was a million miles from their first night here, where they'd sat awkwardly on the chairs in the orangery making stilted conversation.

'Where's Jo?'

'Ah,' said Elaine, with a conspiratorial smile. She pointed discreetly to the far end of the garden, where their friend stood, her pale hair glowing in the lowering sunlight, deep in conversation with . . .

'Oh my God.' Daisy turned to Elaine. 'Is that – *Tom*?'

'Martha's gone for a sleepover with friends in the next village. He rang when we were leaving the fête to ask if Jo fancied getting together.'

Daisy peered up the garden. Jo and Tom were leaning against the low wall, chatting animatedly. She watched as his arm described an arc before they both bent over, collapsed in laughter.

'D'you think there might be a happy ending there?' Daisy turned back to Elaine, picking up a plate which she held out helpfully as her friend stacked the cooked sausages in a heap (again, thought Daisy – the old Elaine would have had them in perfect rows, camera out, photographing everything as evidence of her domestic goddess status).

'I think there might well be.' Elaine peeled off the lid from a packet of burgers.

Daisy looked at her, eyebrows shooting upwards. 'You *bought* burgers?'

'I was going to make them this morning but I was otherwise engaged. So shoot me,' said Elaine with a cheeky grin, clinking her bottle against Daisy's.

'I don't think the Martha stuff's going to be plain sailing,' she continued, 'but y'know, Martha's a lovely girl. They'll work it out, the three of them.'

Daisy was still holding onto her own news, waiting for the right moment.

Elaine took a quick glance at her phone, checking the time. 'Daisy, would you do me a favour, my lovely, and grab the salads from the fridge? I've only done a couple.'

Daisy gave her a look.

'Two salads does *not* a control freak make, thank you,' said Elaine, before she could be called out on her latent Martha Stewart tendencies.

'Only when we've got you eating microwave meals for one in front of the *Coronation Street* omnibus,' Daisy said, darkly, 'will the assimilation be complete.'

She ducked, laughing, as Elaine threw an olive at her head as she turned for the kitchen.

'Get that, will you?' Elaine shouted through the window of the kitchen as the doorbell chimed. Standing there was a beaming Thomas, a slightly awkward-looking Flora on his arm.

Daisy stood there, not moving.

'Are you going to let us in, my dear, or are we having a party on the front step?'

'You said you were going to the pub!' Daisy looked

at Thomas, realizing as she did so that she sounded far ruder than she meant to. Flora smiled at her affectionately.

'Ah, you don't want to go listening to old folk like us, Daisy. We get a bit forgetful.' His eyes sparkled.

'There you are,' said Elaine, giving him a kiss. Jo and Tom had made their way down the garden.

'Tom, this is Daisy,' Jo, her face suffused with happiness, turned to her new old friend.

'We've met,' said both Daisy and Tom, laughing, remembering their encounter in the hall of the hideous B&B.

'If you could call it that,' said Tom, his Manchester accent still strong despite years spent living and travelling abroad. 'I've heard all about it.' He turned to Jo, nodding. They looked so comfortable together, and he was so laid-back and relaxed, that it didn't feel awkward having someone new there at all.

'Right, everything's ready. Help yourselves – and grab another drink if you need one.' Elaine waved a hand in the direction of the huge ice bucket. 'Thomas, what would you like?'

'I'll have a beer, please, my dear.'

They'd finished their main course, everyone so full that they were sitting back, stuffed, when Daisy found the moment to speak.

'I spoke to the estate agent earlier.'

Jo and Elaine groaned in sympathy. They'd been

subjected to the delights of Mike Redforth's attentions on numerous occasions, and knew he'd been driving Daisy bonkers.

She shook her head. 'No, this time it wasn't bad news. It's amazing, in fact.'

Elaine leaned forward in anticipation.

'The O'Haras pulled out of the sale.' There was a cheer, led by Thomas, who gave Daisy's hand an affectionate squeeze. Flora beamed at her.

'But that's not all. Apparently a couple from London fell in love with the place during Open Gardens weekend. And not only are they buying it for a price that's made my parents ecstatic – they just happen to be looking for a gardener.'

Jo jumped up, rushing over to Daisy, putting her arms around her. Elaine was a split second behind her. Daisy, lost under a sea of kisses, tried to make herself heard. The girls stepped back, giving her space.

'Thing is, I'm going to need somewhere to live – my parents have offered to give me some money to help me out and find a place, if I want to stay here in Steeple St John . . .'

'*If* you want to stay,' said Jo, laughing. 'You've not been secretly looking forward to London life all the time you've been moaning about it, have you?'

Daisy smiled. Much as she loved her sister, she'd got the impression, when she rang quickly as she made her way along Cavendish Lane, that Miranda was even more relieved not to be adding two extra residents to her little flat.

'Not that I don't adore you, Daise,' Miranda had added, laughing.

'Likewise,' Daisy had replied. Having spoken briefly to her delighted parents, she couldn't quite believe that they had offered to put 'a little something' in the bank for both their daughters, just to make sure they had something to fall back on.

'I've decided,' explained Daisy – it hadn't taken much thinking, because it was what she'd been dreaming of all along, and somehow, amazingly, it was coming true – 'that I'm going to use some of the money to set myself up with my own gardening business. Get a decent van that doesn't conk out on hills like my ancient car. I just need to start advertising for clients.'

'Well, you've already got two,' said Elaine. 'Orchard Villa, and – if you'll have me, I'd be honoured.'

It was Daisy's turn to hug Elaine in return. 'I'd love to.'

'And –' Elaine began, carefully, 'I don't want you to make any decisions right now – think about it. But I'm living in this place, and it's miles too big for one person. If you're looking for a flatmate . . .'

Daisy looked up at the beautiful stone of the Old Rectory, glowing in the late summer sun.

'I'd love to.'

There was a gentle knock at the side gate. Daisy,

who'd spent the last hour painfully aware there was one person she wished was there to witness the celebration, felt her stomach flip with nervous anticipation.

'D'you want to get that?' asked Elaine, busying herself with the plates. 'Thomas, why don't you stay where you are for a moment? I'll go and get the pudding from the kitchen.'

Jo and Tom looked up briefly from their conversation as Daisy slipped along the terrace, opening the gate to reveal Ned, his sleeves pushed up untidily, sandy hair flopping over one eye. He pushed it back, giving her a brief smile.

'Daisy, hi.'

'Are you coming in? We're just about to have pudding if you'd like – or a beer? Come and have a beer.' Daisy was talking far too quickly, her heart thumping in her ears so loudly she felt sure he could hear.

Ned straightened his shoulders, looking at her intently. 'Can't stay for a beer, I'm on call at ten, but I just wanted to –'

He frowned for a second, as if doubting himself, before shaking his head.

'Daisy, I know you're moving to London. And I know I'm hopelessly disorganized and half the time I'm covered in straw and the other half I'm late, but the thing is . . .' He reached out then, taking her hand in his. 'The thing is – I know you're going to be in London, but it's only a train ride away. And I'd like it very much if you'd come out with me sometime. Please.'

Daisy looked into his eyes, feeling the same uneven thump of her heart that she'd tried to ignore earlier that afternoon at the fête.

'I'd love to.'

Ned's face was one huge smile. 'That's brilliant. Amazing. Have a great evening. I'll give you a call later –'

He had dropped her hand and was stepping backwards as he said this, bumbling and gorgeous and disorganized . . . Daisy followed, a few steps apart from him, laughing. She hadn't noticed that her friends were gathering on the path behind her.

'Ned.'

He turned, one hand on the gate. A lock of hair, which Daisy longed to push back into place, fell down again over his eyes.

'Daisy?'

'There's just one thing. I'm not moving to London. I'm staying right here.'

And at that, Ned let go of the gate, covering the space between them in three long strides. Impetuously he pulled Daisy close, so that she could feel his heart thumping through the fabric of his shirt. She reached up, pushing the disobedient strands of hair out of his eyes, and they kissed in the garden, surrounded by the flowers she'd tended, and the friendships she'd made along the way.

It had been a long road, but she'd made it home.

The End

387

Acknowledgements

This book has several threads of real life woven through it. I met a lovely old man in a hospital waiting room one day, and he told me all about his life. I knew I wanted to write him into a story, and so the character of Thomas was born.

Secondly, although my heart will always be in the Highlands of Scotland, I've lived in England for a long time now and, until recently, always in little villages. Whilst I love living by the seaside, I do miss the gossip and intrigue of village life, my lovely allotment, and being roped in to help out on the stalls at the village fête. So this book is for all my friends in Wendover and Gawcott – and no, I didn't base any of the characters on you lot, I promise.

The same goes for all my friends in the blogging world. I promise Elaine is a figment of my imagination – apart from her name, which I borrowed from one of my Twitter friends, Elaine Alguire of Louisiana. (Thank you!)

To everyone on Twitter who makes me laugh and

cheers me on, and to the gang on my Facebook page who're always happy to chat when I'm in procrastination mode – thanks, all of you. It's lovely to have you all living in my computer, and even nicer still when we get to meet up in real life.

Enormous thanks, and a large gin and tonic, to Amanda Preston: agent, friend, sanity saver. I couldn't have done it without you.

To Caroline Hogg, for being the best combination of editor and cheering squad any writer could want, and to Natasha Harding for always being so lovely – thank you both.

Huge thanks to my friend Jacq Mitchell, BVSc MRCVS, for advising me on the effects of chocolate on greedy dogs.

To my sister Zoe and my niece, Mae – thank you for providing me with a Scottish escape this summer, just when I was beginning to wonder if I'd be writing forever. (Does this make up for taping over your Madonna video?)

To the children: Verity, Rosie, Archie, Jude, Charlie and Rory – yes, I'm *really* finished now, and *yes*, we can watch *Doctor Who* and have hot chocolate.

To Ross, who juggled six children, the house, the school runs, and everything else whilst providing me with love, coffee, and chocolate – thank you, darling.

Last of all, this book is dedicated to the memory of our beloved Pollydog.

My Favourite Gardens

Writing about gardens has been bliss for me. Before I started writing full time, I wrote a gardening blog, and used to spend long hours tending to the garden and the allotment, taking photographs and writing about what I was up to.

Now I'm living in town and no longer have 100 feet of lawn to mow, I find I have a lot more time for exploring my favourite gardens. I thought I'd share them here so that you can go and discover them too. Most of them come with a tea room attached, which is always a plus in my book.

Back home in Scotland, I have a huge affection for the gardens of **Mount Stuart House** on the Isle of Bute. I lived in a cottage there when first married and it was the inspiration for my first novel, *Sealed with a Kiss*. The gardens there cover an amazing 300 acres. You can explore everything from a beautifully kept kitchen garden to the wilds of the woods that lead down to the rocky shoreline, and then there's the exotic Wee Garden, full of plants from all over the world – a bit of a misnomer, as it's five acres in size. Take a pair of sensible boots and allow yourself a whole day to explore, or better still, stay in one of their self-catering cottages. You might even find yourself in my old house!

Hidcote Manor Garden in the Cotswolds is another of my favourites. It was designed by Major Lawrence Johnston in the early twentieth century and it's set out as a series of garden rooms, which start off very formal and neat and become wilder as they stretch away from the gorgeous manor house. You can wander down grass paths, surrounded by huge herbaceous borders, and discover the gorgeously old-fashioned bathing pool. There's a beautifully kept vegetable plot there, too, which I had in mind when writing about Elaine's garden. And of course, as it is a National Trust property, there is cake – and lots of it.

When we were living in Buckinghamshire we spent many weekends letting the children run wild in the grounds of **Waddesdon Manor** – country retreat of the Rothschilds, built a century ago in the style of a French chateau. In contrast to the looser style of Hidcote, all of the gardens at Waddesdon are more formal – in particular the precisely planted parterre at the front of the house, which is immaculate all year round. My absolute favourite place is the rose garden, which was created in 2000 and is home to over 600 roses. The smell is heavenly – and it's not far to walk to the cafe, where you can grab a drink and sit looking out over the amazing view of Aylesbury Vale, or take a walk around the grounds and through the woodland.

Closer to home, I've fallen in love with the gardens of **Rufford Old Hall**: fourteen acres of beautifully maintained woodland, manicured lawns and my favourite herbaceous borders, which are a rainbow of colour in early summer. You can sit by the canal and watch the boats slowly chug past, and their lemon drizzle cake is to die for. Once you've had your fill of the gardens (which are beautiful all year round) you can take a tour of the sixteenth-century Tudor house, where the huge Great Hall is reputed to have played host to a young Shakespeare.

And don't forget to take a trip to **Paddington Street Gardens** in London (where Daisy and Miranda played as children). If you're in town, it's the perfect place to go – just round the corner from Marylebone High Street, it's a breath of fresh, green air in the middle of the capital. Grab some lunch, hire a stripy deck chair and sit back. It's one of my favourite people-watching spots. Have fun!

Sealed With A Kiss

By Rachael Lucas

Being dumped by the world's most boring boyfriend wasn't exactly on Kate's To Do list, but at least it's a wake-up call. Jobless and now homeless and boyfriend-less too, she needs a new start. Or just anything to avoid moving back in with her mother.

And taking a job as a Girl Friday on a remote Scottish island is definitely something new. Auchenmor is the perfect place to escape to: friendly locals, gorgeous scenery – and an even more gorgeous bagpipe player called Finn. Her new boss Roddy (the Laird, no less) might be as chatty as one of Auchenmor's native seals, but Kate can see there's a softer side beneath his prickly demeanour.

When Roddy's demanding ex suddenly reappears, she'll do anything to keep Kate and her boss apart. Just what is Fiona up to? Island life has no room for secrets . . .

This funny, big-hearted novel is the perfect read for fans of Carole Matthews and Trisha Ashley.

'Wonderful escapism with a gloriously romantic setting'
Katie Fforde

'A wonderfully feel-good read'   Julia Williams

extracts reading groups
competitions books new
discounts extracts extracts
competitions discounts events
books new extracts reading groups
reading groups events books
events books discounts
extracts new titles reading groups
interviews events new
books events extracts extracts books
discounts events
new books events interviews new
events new books extracts
discounts extracts discounts
www.panmacmillan.com
extracts events reading groups
competitions books extracts new books